IRISHWOMEN

SPIRITED FRIEND

A Novel by S B Farrell

Terri

Lots of Love

S B Farrell

xx

FIRST PUBLISHED IN GREAT BRITAIN IN 2025 BY LIBRATUM BOOKS.

Copyright © 2025 S B Farrell

IBAN Number 9798284523254

This story in entirely fictitious. Places and street names mentioned in Dublin and Sweden exist, but the characters are imagined.

All rights reserved. No part of this book may be reproduced without permission from the publisher or be circulated in any other form.

Libratumbooks.com

ABOUT THE AUTHOR

Suzanne Farrell, originally from Dublin writes atmospheric stories rooted in the Irish culture she grew up with.

Her passion for noir, crime and murder mysteries infused with humour and heart shines through her work.

Known for weaving the Irish accent into her conversations and characters alike, she brings a distinct voice to her storytelling.

Suzanne moved to the UK in 1992 and is the proud mother of three grown-up sons.

FOR ME DA

We'll never forget ye.

IRISH WOMEN

TABLE OF CONTENTS

A Dublin Nightclub Twenty Years Ago
Prologue
1
2
3
4
5
6
7
8
9
10
11
12
13
A Dublin Nightclub Twenty Years Ago
14
15
16
17

18
19
20
21
22
23
24
25
26
27
28
29
30
31
32
33
34
35
36
37
38
39
40
41
42
43

44
45
46
47
48
49
50
51
52
53
54
55
56
57
Epilogue 1
Epilogue 2

A DUBLIN NIGHTCLUB - TWENTY YEARS AGO

Aisling, Gillian and Sinead - all seventeen, stepped out of the luxurious black car feeling like superstars. It was Friday night - they'd been invited to a private party in Dublin's best nightclub, and to add to the excitement, a car had been sent to pick them up.

'We'll definitely meet someone famous tonight,' said Sinead, leaning on Gillian's arm while trying to balance in her sky-high heels.

'Justin Timberlake is playing at the RDS - imagine if he's here,' said Gillian, excitedly hugging her best friend. 'How did we get so lucky?' she asked.

Aisling, clip-clopping behind them in another pair of ridiculously high heels - her feet already killing her, called.

'It's nothing to do with luck – we're just fecking gorgeous.'

The three girls giggled as they climbed the stairs - delighted to swagger past the long line of scantily dressed girls *without invites*, waiting in the freezing cold to enter the nightclub below. They were VIPs, and they felt smug about it.

'Right girls - let's have the best night of our lives,' said Aisling, high-fiving her best friend and her cousin, before taking a breath, pushing open the double doors and walking into the famous member's bar of Lily's nightclub.

Red leather sofas, black walls with ornate mirrors, and French-style lamps were scattered around the room, giving the impression of being in a boudoir. On the wall behind a red velvet bar, hundreds of bottles of champagne were displayed on brightly lit mirrored shelves.

'Oh my God, it's incredible,' whispered Gillian, looking around in awe. 'I've never seen anything like it.'

'It's just like they described in the magazines,' said Sinead, her eyes alight.

Aisling wasn't as easily impressed.

'Where is everyone?' she asked, feeling

suspicious.

She glanced at her watch – nine thirty - were they early? Erik, who'd invited them, was there with three other men, but there was no one else - not even the bar staff.

'More people come later,' said Erik, in heavily accented English, obviously noticing Aisling's look of concern, but it was too late - her Spidey senses were on high alert.

When they'd met him a week earlier at The Oval – a bar known for serving underage drinkers, Erik had said this was a celebrity party and everyone who was anyone would be there.

'I'm not staying here - there's something not right,' Aisling whispered to Sinead and Gillian, but they ignored her, their eyes lighting up when the cork of a champagne bottle popped - champagne this was exactly how they expected the night to go.

'Champagne! Ash,' said Gillian excitedly, 'and Erik said more people are coming later - we're just early.'

Gillian looked older than seventeen in orange hot pants that highlighted her long fishnet-clad legs. Her sheer orange top left nothing to the imagination, and her cropped blond hair was trendy and sexy. She'd been scouted a few weeks earlier and had her first photo shoot on Monday. Sinead was wearing a black figure-hugging body suit that accentuated her tiny waist, enormous tits and huge arse. Her thick black hair was swept into a high ponytail, making her look like a bad-ass Barbie. Aisling was more reserved in a sparkly black dress, her blonde curls bouncing from the perm she'd had at Christmas.

'Fucks sake,' mumbled Aisling, then added, 'just one drink Gill, and we're going.'

Gillian nodded - her eyes wide as Erik passed out tall glasses filled to the brim with bubbly champagne.

'Welcome to Lily's,' he said with a slight bow.

Gillian closed her eyes, savouring her first-ever taste of the golden liquid. Sinead sighed as she drank, but Aisling said no. *This fucker is up to something*, she thought.

'Just have one - it's the good stuff,' said Erik, holding the glass in front of Aisling's face.

'I'm grand - I don't want any,' she replied, but when he insisted in a way that gave her no choice, Aisling took the glass and drank tiny sips, letting the champagne roll down her chin and onto her dress. He didn't notice in the dark room. 'Fuck off, creep,' she muttered.

'Please, come – my friends would very much like to meet you,' said Erik, leading them across the bar.

His friends sat at a table, laden with champagne bottles, and although handsome, they were a lot older than Aisling had expected. The men kissed them on both cheeks and while Sinead and Gillian lapped up the attention, Aisling couldn't rid herself of the suspicion that something was wrong.

'Where are the bar staff?' she asked.

The men looked at each other, but Erik answered.

'This is a private party – when the other guests arrive, some bar staff will come from the club downstairs – don't worry – you ladies are just a bit early,' he said.

Aisling was worried as she sat down, and sometime later, when a tray of cocaine was passed around, her heart stopped. Cocaine? Who the fuck were these people? She shook her head, relieved not to be pressured this time but shocked when her cousin and friend happily snorted a line.

'What the fuck are yous two doing? We need to get out of here,' she whispered, frantically.

Was she the only one who knew something was very wrong?

'Fucks sake, Ash - it's grand. Just enjoy yourself for once, will ye,' said Gillian, tipsy on champagne.

'The men are really nice, Ash,' said Sinead, sipping her third - or was it her fourth glass.

As far as Aisling was concerned, the men were weird. Erik and Sven were stocky with blond hair and blue eyes. They were dressed in jeans and T-shirts and looked like twins. The one called Robert, looked scary, with a scar running down one side of his face, and then there was Lars with intense grey eyes - he was the best looking of them all.

As the evening progressed, no other guests or bar staff arrived. Erik opened bottle after bottle of champagne, and Aisling's anxiety soared through the roof - Sinead, drunk by now, was sitting on Lars's lap, giggling at whatever he whispered in her ear. Gillian was dancing provocatively and completely out of control. Aisling, who'd been secretly tipping her drinks to the floor, suspecting them spiked, grew more nervous by the second. When Gillian, usually shy - climbed onto Erik's lap and let him undress her as she laughed and kissed him, Aisling knew the drinks had been tampered with. Erik opened his jeans and shoved his massive dick inside Gillian - riding her in front of them all, like a sex show in Amsterdam. Aisling was horrified and jumped up to save her friend, but Robert caught her arm.

'Just a bit of fun,' he said in a thick Swedish accent that sounded like a threat.

Aisling slowly sat back down with a thumping heart - *what the fuck was going on?* She was in a nightmare. When Lars carried Sinead to a table and spread her out like a sacrificial offering, Aisling thought her heart would burst through her chest with fear. Sinead's bodysuit hit the floor, her knickers were yanked down to her ankles, and Lars's hands dove between her legs. *Jesus fucking Christ.* Sandwiched between Robert and Sven,

Aisling frantically tried to plan their escape. Over the loud music, she called out that they needed to go, but the men ignored her - more interested in the sex shows and the cocaine. Trembling with fear, Aisling looked towards the exit – maybe she could make a run for it and get the bouncers downstairs to help them. Just as she was about to move, the door opened - five women walked in, and she felt dizzy with relief.

'Oh, thank God,' she murmured, almost jumping in delight.

Immediately clocking the newcomers, Lars pulled away from Sinead and whistled at Erik, who threw Gillian to the floor, discarding her like a piece of dirt. The loud music suddenly stopped, and the silence was deafening. Five women, older than Aisling and her friends by a few years, watched the scene in horror until one of them, a beautiful redhead whom Aisling assumed was Lars's girlfriend, slapped him in the face.

'How could you do this,' she screamed.

He tried to talk himself out of it until she slapped him again and all hell broke out when he punched her and sent her flying across the room. Her friends tried to attack him, tables were knocked over, champagne bottles smashed, and Gillian and Sinead finally snapped out of their trance. Aisling grabbed their coats - they were leaving, but before they reached the stairs, Erik, Sven, and Robert ushered them into a small office - leaving Lars alone with the women.

The carpet was dirty, there were no windows, and the room stank of cigarettes. A large desk sat empty in the corner, and on the wall behind it, a neon light with the word BAR crackled as it flickered on and off. Dance music from the nightclub below sounded further away than it was, the dull beat vibrating on the sticky floor beneath them.

'What are you doing? We need to go,' said Aisling, pulling at Erik's arm.

'You can go soon, sweetheart – we just need you to wait a minute,' he said, distractedly.

He was arguing with Sven and Robert in Swedish, the language sounding rapid and strange to her ears.

'We need to go now,' Aisling tried again and pushed past Erik, who was blocking the door. 'What's going on?' she asked, but he ignored her.

Gillian and Sinead had sobered up and were huddled together like frightened mice. Their faces were stained with tears and mascara - their clothes dishevelled from being hurriedly put back on.

'Why are we in here, Ash?' whispered Sinead, 'we need to go home.'

'It's alright, we're going in a minute,' said Aisling, trying to reassure her but feeling very scared.

Gillian was pale and nervously biting her lip. Having never had sex before, Aisling knew she was devastated by her earlier madness.

'What the fuck happened in there, Ash?' she asked, her voice tinged with panic.

'I think they drugged ye - I didn't drink the champagne,' whispered Aisling.

The men continued arguing, while Aisling shook like a leaf. What had they gotten into, and how had their big night out gone so wrong?

'We need to go,' Aisling called again, but she was ignored.

When Erik moved closer to the other

men - their voices raised in anger, Sinead made a dash for the door. She pulled it open and was almost through until Robert kicked it shut and smashed it into her face. Blood erupted from her nose and a scream of terror from her mouth.

'Oh my God, are you alright?' asked Aisling, rushing to her side. 'What the fuck did you do that for?' she screamed at Robert.

'I want to go home,' sobbed Sinead as blood poured down her face.

'Shhh, it's alright - we're going now,' said Aisling, leading Sinead toward the door. She was done with this shit. 'Come on, Gill,' she called over her shoulder.

The men were silent, and Aisling felt hopeful. They just needed to get out of there and home to the flats where they'd be safe - everything would be okay. Reaching for the door handle, her stomach dropped when she found it locked.

'Can you let us out, please?' asked Aisling, turning to the men.

Sinead and Gillian began to sob harder.

'They can't keep us here - I'm calling the guards,' cried Sinead.

Pulling out of Aisling's grip, she ran towards the desk and reached for the phone - Aisling hadn't noticed it and felt hopeful again. *Yes, call the guards - they'd get them out of here*, but before Sinead dialled one number, Robert was beside her, this time with a gun pointed to her head.

'Put the phone down and shut the fuck up,' he said in a tone that indicated how bored he was of her antics.

The receiver fell from Sinead's hand, and with terror in her eyes, she turned to Aisling and Gillian - silently pleading for help as Robert's gun pressed against her head. Aisling was speechless – what was going on? Before she could work it out, several things happened in rapid succession:

First, something splashed across her face. She thought a drink had been thrown until Gillian screamed, and Sinead fell to the floor. With a coppery taste in her mouth and a sense of dread, Aisling looked down at her new dress sprinkled with red. Her gaze moved to the floor, and her cousin - eyes open and a pool of blood forming around her head - she was dead.

Next, Erik roared and cursed at Robert

while pulling another gun from the back pocket of his jeans.

'You fucking arsehole,' he screamed, as he aimed his gun at Gillian and shot her in the head as well.

Gillian fell to the floor with a thump, her blond hair a red mess. Then, the men turned to Aisling with resigned expressions, as Sven slowly raised his gun. In slow motion, Aisling's life flashed before her eyes. She thought of her mam and wanted to tell her how much she loved her - her driving lesson the next day - the date she had with Liam Cunningham on Tuesday night and Gill's photoshoot on Monday – they'd all been so excited about it.

'Please...' she sobbed, '... I'm only seventeen.'

The last thing Aisling ever saw was a stranger shrugging his shoulders.

'Sorry,' said Sven, as he pulled the trigger.

PROLOGUE

The floor beneath me was cold and damp, the light hurt my eyes, and my brain felt fuzzy. Where was I? Quickly scanning the room, I was relieved to be alone and not sure why. Then, overcome with a strong urge to get the hell out of there, I stood up, ready to run, but as soon as my feet touched the floor, a sudden onset of nausea stopped me in my tracks. My body convulsed - ten times, twenty - I was vomiting air with a ferocity I'd never experienced before. When it eventually stopped, I wiped my mouth with the sleeve of my jacket and noticed how different everything felt.

'Oh shit – please, don't let this be what I think it is,' I whispered as a sense of dread wound around my body like a wild bramble tightening its grip.

I slowly turned my head and at first, my mind couldn't process the scene behind me. A large pool of blood, crimson and thick spread across the white tiled floor. A body slumped against the wall, skin white as snow, glazed eyes staring at nothing, and a large knife wedged into its neck - it was me, and I was unmistakably dead. Stumbling backwards, I glanced down at myself wearing identical clothes, slightly transparent and without all the blood - what was going on?

A clock on the kitchen wall said ten past three. Four hours had passed since I arrived back at the apartment. I shook my head, desperate for a memory after that, but none came. If I was dead, who had killed me, and more to the point, why was I still here? Where was the white light and the chorus of angels I'd been promised, or even the fires of hell I'd been threatened with by the strict catholic nuns at school? Terrified, confused and trying to keep the panic at bay, a loud knock on the front door frightened the life out of me – oh wait!

'Jesus, what next?' I asked.

'Hello. It's the guards - is there anyone home?' a man's voice called.

I didn't move my...well, it wasn't my body, that was on the kitchen floor. I didn't move my silhouette and waited. Another knock, louder this time - when no one answered, he called again.

'Right, we're coming in.'

The door handle rattled - I held my breath until I realised, I no longer had one, then laughed, even though none of this was funny. Two men walked through the door and immediately clocked the scene in the kitchen - an open-plan apartment, modern and white - the bloodbath was hard to miss.

'Oh, Jesus Christ - call an ambulance,' called the first guard, holding his hand to his mouth as if to be sick.

I didn't blame him - it was pretty gruesome. The other guard bent down for a closer look.

'It's a bit late for an ambulance, Des - sure, we need the coroner,' he said, taking a phone from his pocket and dialling a number. What he said next surprised me. 'We found her, and it's not good - you'll need to send forensics.'

They were looking for me? Before I had time to think about it, the apartment was filled with members of An Garda Siochana, or, as they were more commonly known in

Ireland, the Guards, the police, or the pigs, depending on where you lived. Some were inspecting my body, others taking pictures and looking for fingerprints - that sort of thing. One of them seemed particularly distressed - was she crying? Moving closer for a better look, I couldn't believe it was my old school friend, Audrey O'Brien, or Sergeant O'Brien, as indicated by the badge around her neck. We hadn't seen each other for twenty years, but she obviously recognised me, even though my face resembled a purple turnip.

'Can someone tell me where the fuck is the coroner?' called a tall, serious-looking chap in an awful brown suit - *that colour really did nothing for him.* Audrey stood beside him, both of them staring at my body.

'I knew her,' she said, sadly.

'What?' your man asked, but before Audrey could explain, a commotion at the front door caught his attention as the coroner arrived.

'Out - the lot of ye. Fuck's sake, there's too many people in here,' he said in a strong Cork accent.

The room cleared, except for Audrey and

Mr Brown Suit.

'Eamon,' he said by way of introduction, and with no messing around, he opened a large metal case, put on a pair of latex gloves and after a bit of poking and prodding, declared me dead for at least three to four hours. 'I think it's safe to say she didn't die of natural causes,' he added, nodding at the knife.

'Ye don't say,' muttered Audrey.

Eventually, I was moved onto a trolley and without all the blood, I got a good look at myself - it was bad, alright.

'And she got a good hiding before that knife went into her neck,' said Eamon, pointing to my bruised and battered face. 'The poor woman fought for her life,' he sighed.

I stared at my body, wondering what had happened to me - who had killed me and why? Having tried to get Audrey's attention earlier, I realised no one in the room could see or hear me.

'Audrey, it's me, Laura. Can you hear me, I'm still here?' I yelled, waving my hands in front of her face and jumping around like a lunatic - she didn't bat an eyelid.

A few hours later, the guards left, and I

floated around the apartment, wondering if I could ever leave it. What if this was hell? What if I was trapped here for eternity? Panic began to rise until suddenly, and without any effort on my part, I was transported to a different kitchen. This time, Orla Reed sat eating a fish pie at a large farmhouse table. Okay, now this was weird. First Audrey O'Brien in Dublin and now Orla Reed in...I looked out the window - was I in the Cotswolds? Two friends I hadn't seen in twenty years on the same day as my murder – what was going on? At her feet, a large white dog raised its head and looked in my direction before sniffing the air, licking its lips and snuggling back into Orla's slippers. Could dogs sense spirits, ghosts, whatever I was? I didn't know, but I sat next to Orla, waving my hand in front of her face, just in case - no reaction.

'Why am I here, Orla?' I whispered to my old friend, but she didn't answer.

After dinner, she wandered into a gorgeous sitting room, and I followed. She lit the fire and settled in front of the TV, and so did I while telling myself there had to be a reason for me being here because this definitely wasn't the *rest in peace*, promised by Fr. Pat during all those years, spent bored out of my mind in mass.

1 ~ ORLA

Orla Reed was focused, driven, and efficient in her work. She didn't have time for distractions - beating deadlines was her thing, and she prided herself on it, but today, her mind was busy thinking about an old friend, and she wasn't happy. *Why can't I get that bloody woman out of my head?* What had Laura Quinn done with her life? Was Laura Quinn still in Dublin? Did Laura Quinn have all the babies she'd dreamed about?

When they were young, Laura had been the star of the gang. The beautiful one - the one the boys fancied - the one with all the potential and the one they all wanted to be. Orla - considered an underachiever by the nuns at St Brigid's Convent had hidden in Laura's shadow. Laura had beauty and brains, and Orla was sure she'd done great things with her life. *I'll ask me ma tomorrow,* she thought - if anyone knew what happened to Laura, it would be Orla's mam, Patsy, for not much got past the eagle eye of Patsy Reed, and if she didn't know, she'd find out.

Feeling slightly better, Orla pushed the thoughts away and concentrated on her yoga. Too much wine at the village fair the day before was playing havoc with her flow. As president of the village council, Marjorie Norris had insisted Orla - the guest of honour, should have a wine glass that remained perpetually full. Orla suspected Marjorie's motive was to keep the local, semi-famous author available for chats with the villagers or to get her pissed – whatever it was, she'd succeeded in both.

Orla looked around the crowded yoga studio, its floor hidden beneath a blanket of brightly coloured mats and yogis sweating out the day or, in Orla's case, their hangover. The vaulted ceiling, low lighting and heat gave the impression of being underground and reminded Orla of a tube station in London - some might find it claustrophobic, but Orla loved it. Smiling, she stretched, breathed, and downward-dogged the wine out of her system.

Laura: 'Ohhhh. This was nice, even without a body

to stretch.'

Catching sight of her reflection in the wall of mirrors, Orla sighed – not bad for forty-five she supposed. Her body was strong and agile - lack of sleep made her eyes tired, but a recent trip to Barbados gave her a winter tan, *something at least.* People often thought Orla was Spanish or Italian with her dark hair and eyes.

'You're the black Irish,' her Nana Nellie used to say and tell old stories *Orla now knew to be fairy tales* of sailors, shipwrecked on Ireland's coastline during the Spanish Armada. As a teenager, Orla would daydream about her great, great, and so on grandmother seducing the captain of a great Galleon and falling madly in love.

'Make your way into our final pose,' said Lori and at the thought of Savasana, Orla lay down in bliss.

Hot yoga was Orla's happy place - somewhere to quieten her overactive mind and relieve her stress. The heat felt amazing on her body, especially when the weather outside was arctic. Heavy white clouds had hovered over the village for most of the week, and the air had an icy feel to it - snow was definitely on the way. While lying in the darkened room, Orla reflected on her unproductive day, frustrated that not one word of her new book, *The Unanswered Call*, had appeared in her mind - just memories of Laura Quinn and her life twenty years ago.

Her meeting with Dorothy the next day would be interesting. Dorothy was Orla's no-nonsense agent, and she was expecting tremendous progress on Orla's seventh book. Mackenzie and Hope had represented Orla for five brilliant years and were based in London. Dorothy Mackenzie and her life partner, June Hope, were two strong-minded lesbians who only represented women and made no apologies about it.

'Do I need to be a lesbian for you to accept me as a client?' Orla had asked at their first meeting,

'No, as long as you have a vagina - that will do,' Dorothy answered without hesitation and they fell around the place laughing - that had been the beginning of a beautiful friendship.

Dorothy, a chain-smoking sixty-year-old who could slice you in half with a look, loved to argue - *she'd say she loved to debate* about Orla's books and ideas, but she was a diamond and responsible for six of Orla's books being published, all successful murder mysteries. She had high hopes for number seven, and so had Orla - it just hadn't materialised in her mind, but as she lay in Savasana, she decided tomorrow would be better. She'd be inspired, motivated and focused - her distracting thoughts would vanish, and the words would pour out of her, but for now…relax.

She's so talented. I love her books.'

After class and a quick chai latte, Orla navigated her way through the dark country lanes of Gloucestershire. Even after two years of making the same journey twice a week, the narrow, winding roads still made her nervous. Her thoughts drifted to Laura again, old memories of how gorgeous she'd been and their nights out together. Laura had loved concerts and had a knack for blagging her way backstage. Usually so enamoured with her beauty, the bouncers let her pass - every single time. Her best success was a Guns and Roses afterparty where, if Orla remembered correctly, Laura had snogged Slash, and Orla let one of the band members feel her tits. She laughed out loud - God, that was a memory, but he was cute, and she was as wild as a weed back then.

'You were more than wild, Orla.'

Another attribute of Laura's was her sense of fairness - she despised injustice. A protest march for anything saw her on the frontline, and on the odd occasion Orla joined her, Laura would drag her there as well.

'I loved those marches - the fun we had.'

'What's the fucking point in being here if we're not leading the pack,' Laura would say with such vigour that you had no choice but to follow her.

Sighing, Orla had forgotten about those days - she missed those girls - why didn't they speak anymore?

'Because I fell in love with a madman and wouldn't listen to any of you.'

She knew perfectly well why and immediately pushed it from her mind. Her phone rang, interrupting her nostalgia, and Max's voice filled her car. He was her eldest son studying at Leeds University and usually rang once a week. His younger brother Connor was travelling around Southeast Asia and didn't. Con checked in once a month to let Orla know he was alive, ask for money, and disappear off the radar again.

'You won't believe this, ma,' said Max, without a greeting.

'Hello to you too,' said Orla, smiling at his Irish accent.

Even though they grew up in England, Orla's sons had spent their summers, Christmases, and Easter holidays in Ireland. Both had pronounced Dublin accents, and Orla was secretly thrilled.

'What?' said Max, confused before adding, 'Oh - heya ma - guess what?'

He told Orla all about being asked to

speak at the university's annual dinner and how stressed he felt about it.

'Sure, that's brilliant news - what's the problem?' asked Orla.

'Are you for real? I'm not you, ma. Public speaking is the problem.'

'You'll be grand. What's the subject?'

Even though Max didn't enjoy speaking, as a public speaker herself, Orla knew how talented her son was on stage. *Learned from the best*, she thought shamelessly.

'The challenges young entrepreneurs face in the current economic climate - can you come?' he asked.

'Of course - wouldn't miss it for the world - send me the date,' she asked, and he promised to email.

'Anyway. I'll see you next weekend - I need your help writing it.'

'Of course,' said Orla. 'Happy to help.'

They chatted about other things, and Orla told him about the old friend on her mind.

'It's strange, but I've been thinking about her all day,' she said.

'Maybe you should ring her - she's obviously on your mind for a reason,' suggested Max.

Orla doubted that - she didn't even know where Laura lived these days and hadn't seen her in a very long time. As always, they moved on to Max's love life.

'So, do we have a girlfriend this week, or is it a no-girlfriend week?'

As the mother of two handsome boys, Orla couldn't keep track of their relationships. Over the years, too many girls had snuck to the bathroom in the middle of the night.

'I'm too busy for girls,' said Max, sounding serious, but Orla knew that could change in a millisecond, so she didn't bother commenting.

Their call finished as Orla pulled onto her driveway. When she opened her front door, her gorgeous German Shepherd, Ray, nearly knocked her off her feet. Wagging his tail and going crazy, he acted as if she'd been gone for a month instead of two hours, but she forgave his neediness, because he was gorgeous, and she adored him.

So did I. "Hi Ray, baby, come to Auntie Laura." Ray could definitely sense me – now if only I could get his mammy to do the same.'

'Calm down, boy. I'm here,' said Orla, rubbing his ears before letting him into the garden.

In the kitchen, she poured a large glass of white wine to balance the yoga. Yin and yang or the hair of the dog? Both - she decided while popping a fish curry in the microwave. She looked around her fabulous new kitchen and sighed. Light grey presses, a black stone floor and a beamed, gable ceiling gave the impression of being in a small barn. On the back wall, a magnificent black AGA thrilled her. Orla had dreamed of owning an AGA for years, but hadn't worked out how to cook on it, so it was micro meals for now. Irish tweed curtains adorned glass doors that looked out to the valley below, and an old farmhouse table ran the length of the room – it was the perfect country kitchen, and she loved it.

'My dream kitchen – I loved it.'

The people in the village knew her as the Irish writer in Nook Cottage. When she first moved in, crowds of curious villagers had knocked on her door, some with homemade casseroles - something Orla thought only happened in American films. Eventually, the gossip mill settled down, and the community welcomed her with open arms. Now, life in the sleepy village in The Cotswolds was marvellous. She had friendly neighbours, gorgeous views and enough space to think and write.

Two years earlier, Orla's lying, cheating scumbag of an ex had been behind the decision to move to the country. James was going to commute to London for work, while Orla wrote books inspired by the beautiful scenery surrounding her. They'd been so excited until six weeks before signing the contract when James left. No explanation, no apology - he just packed his stuff and walked out of their London flat without so much as a fuck you, Orla. A text message a few days later said, *'I can't do this - I'm sorry.'* After the initial shock, Orla nearly cancelled the sale until an awkward phone call from his PA changed her mind. Jacinta revealed James's affair with a girl from the office, half his age, and Orla was mortified.

'I'm sorry if this is overstepping, but I thought you had the right to know. He transferred to the Glasgow office, and she went with him,' said Jacinta.

Orla nearly died - talk about a kick in the teeth.

'Don't apologise, lovely. I'm glad you told me.'

The sense of betrayal was excruciating until anger kicked in, and even though it was a huge financial stretch, she bought the house on her own, *fuck you, James.*

'Asshole! Better off without him, luv.'

The ding of the microwave pulled Orla from her thoughts. Starving, she quickly dished up her curry and ate at her new farmhouse table. Afterwards, with more wine, she wandered into the lounge with its inglenook fireplace, an original feature and the reason Orla fell in love with the cottage. Lighting the wood burner, she snuggled on the comfiest sofa she could find, more Irish tweed - she was obsessed and watched a film with Ray. When she heard a loud knock on the front door, a smile formed on her lips – she'd been hoping he'd pop around. Neil was standing outside with a bottle of wine and something wrapped in gold paper.

'Ohh, he's nice.'

'A little something from America,' he said, waving the small square package in the air.

Leaning in for a kiss, Orla inhaled his familiar scent and led him into the lounge. Ray growled before realising who it was, then wagged his tail for a minute or two and settled in front of the fire.

'How was the trip?' asked Orla, returning from the kitchen with another wine glass.

'Boring, but necessary,' said Neil, holding the glass as Orla poured. 'I'm sick and fucking tired of working with idiots and cleaning up their mess,' he continued.

'The New Yorkers again?' asked Orla, knowing he had a long history of stress with that division of his business.

'Yeah, but I don't want to talk about it – what's happening around here?' he asked.

'Well,' said Orla, wetting her lips with more wine, 'the village fair was a scandal – all sorts of drunken shenanigans.'

They laughed at the idea of the ladies from The WI being drunk and disorderly, and after more wine and a shared shower, they fell into bed. What followed was some had the best sex Orla had ever had. Neil really was a champion in bed and knew how to press all her buttons. Sated and happy, Orla drifted off to sleep wrapped in her lover's arms until the shrill of her phone woke her.

'What the fuck?' muffled Neil, who'd been out cold and jumped at the sound.

An Irish number flashed on Orla's screen, and her first thought went to her mother, famous for losing phones – this might be another new one. Rolling her eyes, Orla almost rejected the call until she realised her mam wouldn't call this late at night.

'Someone's dead,' said Orla while fiddling with the lamp in the dark, 'only explanation for such a late call,' she added. Switching on the light, she blew out a breath and answered. 'Mam, is that you? What's wrong?'

When a voice Orla hadn't heard in

twenty years answered, she was speechless.

Laura
I didn't know why I was with Orla if I couldn't even communicate with her. I tried to push over her glass of wine when she was eating dinner, but nothing happened. Just when I was beginning to think it was all a waste of time, I heard who was on the other end of the line, and I nearly died... again.

2 ~ LAURA

Six Months Before
My Murder

I didn't know that in a mere six months, I'd be violently murdered, and everyone in Dublin would be talking about it. The question - 'Who murdered Laura Karlsson?' would become headline news - not only in my hometown but in the whole of Ireland. At forty-five, I was finally famous, *something I'd been desperate for when I was young* - because I was dead.

At the time, my life had reached a turning point. You could say the straw had finally broken the camel's back, and I was having the biggest wake-up call of my life. An epiphany that demanded I get away from my husband, and I get away from him now. Until then, my marriage had limped along - I knew what kind of man Lars was, I'd always known, but I told myself he wasn't the worst. The reality was I had no choice – I was my husband's prisoner, and there was nothing I could do about it.

Early in our marriage, after the initial charm – romance - kindness and love wore off, my husband's darkness reared its ugly head. If I did something to piss him off and that might be to talk to the waiter or look at someone in a way he didn't like, or say something he disagreed with, or tell him I didn't want sex - he'd kick me, punch my stomach, or push me to the floor and somehow that became normal. Lars would sometimes squeeze my arms or legs so hard that purple hand-print bruises stained my white skin, and I didn't even notice them. I endured his viciousness in bed - tying me up and biting my nipples so hard that they bled by using numbing cream before sex. For years, I accepted his violence until it upped a notch, and suddenly, I was afraid for my life. My self-respect that was buried somewhere deep in my subconscious mind began to surface, and I gained a terrifying clarity – leave or die. When Lars returned from a business trip one evening in June, the bough finally broke.

He'd been in America for ten days and rang to say he wouldn't be back until Saturday. I couldn't believe my luck - two more days of freedom, it was like winning the lottery. When Lars travelled for work, I'd play the pretend game and act as if my life was normal. I'd go to work without listening to his smart remarks. *Spending a lot of time at the hospital - what draws my wife there, I wonder*. Eat my dinner on my lap in front of the TV, without Lars insisting we sit at the table. As if I didn't know his comment – *I'm dressing for dinner* was my cue to do the same. And swim in the lake every night - my favourite thing to do, without him joining me and ruining it.

In celebration of my prolonged freedom, I decided to cook a meal while enjoying a glass of wine and a few Madonna songs, *forever an eighties girl*. Hilda had cleaned the house, and it was spotless. Sighing, I looked around my chalet-style home - almost entirely built of glass. Wooden beams ran the length and breadth of it - a large kitchen led to an even larger dining room with an open fireplace and a table that sat fourteen people. On the far side of the room, a sunken lounge with comfy cream sofas, faced a wall of glass that looked out to the lake below and at the back of the house, a long hallway led to Lars's office, three large bedrooms and a huge garage. It was gorgeous, and I loved it – just a shame I had to share it with psycho Sid, as I liked to call him in my head.

After my phone call from Lars earlier that day, I immediately rang Astrid to meet for lunch the next afternoon. It had been so long since we'd been out together - a nice restaurant, a few glasses of wine and some girlie chat was just what I needed, and I'd have reason to wear my new dress - a classic Chanel bought two weeks earlier in Stockholm when Lars forced me to attend one of his mind-numbing business lunches - *a shopping trip softened the blow.*

'Yay, I'll book the table for 2pm,' said Astrid, who'd been on holiday with her family all week and needed some me-time.

'How about noon?' I asked. 'That gives me more time to spend with you.'

Even though Lars was travelling, I still had to follow the rules. As far as he was concerned, I worked till six and was home by seven. Security cameras monitored my movements, and I was being extra careful as he was being particularly vile of late. Astrid knew the drill, agreed to a noon lunch and we said goodbye. I smiled and sang while dishing up my dinner - baked salmon with mashed potatoes, my mouth watered until I looked up and saw Lars leaning against the kitchen door, quietly watching me.

'Jesus,' I yelped, almost dropping the pan of food.

He was home, and I wanted to drop to my knees and scream. The phone call was a ruse - a test to catch me out. Ladies and gentlemen - my husband, the psychopath who loves to play sick mind games.

'Smiling and dancing, Laura. Who's that for? One of the nice doctors at work?' he snarled.

The viciousness in his voice terrified me - his jealousy was off the charts since I started working at the hospital, with constant accusations flying out of his dirty mouth. Lars hated me doing anything that didn't involve him. He was jealous, insecure, and needed complete control of my life, and I hated him.

'No, love,' I said, calmly, with a warm, fake smile. 'I was talking to my sister and nephews earlier - you know that always makes me happy.'

Lars thought I was broken about not having kids with him, *dickhead*. The mention of my nephews made him cringe, and I liked twisting the knife. I didn't have much control over my life, but I knew how to survive this fucker. Early in my marriage, *I'll tell you about that later*, when my terrible mistake became clear, having kids with Lars was not an option. Any chance of escaping him wouldn't exist if they were involved, and I worried about passing on his psycho-mutated genes, so I took measures to guarantee it never happened. He watched me for a minute or two - *God, I was so over his mood swings,* then asked if there was enough food for him, and I sighed with relief - that meant he'd let it go.

'Of course, you're just in time - grab a plate. Do you want a glass of wine?' I asked with another fake smile plastered to my face – I was so fucking good at this.

Over dinner, I asked about his trip - he

gave me a diamond bracelet, the usual crap and when we finished eating, he disappeared into his office and stayed there for most of the night. When he came to bed and woke me for sex, I wanted to die. His hands roughly pinched my nipples as his mouth slathered my neck. *Yeah, Lars, that's really doing it for me.* When he forced himself inside me, I cried out in pain, and when he kissed me, I wanted to puke. Having learned the hard way what happened if I rejected my husband, or tried to fake an orgasm, I forced myself to get into it - found my sweet spot - closed my eyes and thought about one of the nice doctors I'd been accused of thinking about. Afterwards, I lay beside him in the dark, hating him and loathing myself.

The next day, his mood was foul, and my anxiety was through the roof. I didn't have lunch with Astrid or go to work. Another rule – I could work when he wasn't home - *fucking arsehole*. Thankfully, because of his rapid rise through the ranks of the Swedish government, Lars was travelling more and spending more time in Stockholm – the two reasons I hadn't thrown myself off the jetty at the bottom of the garden with weights chained to my feet.

Most weeks, he left early on Monday and returned late on Friday and those days in between kept me sane. I loved the solitude of my house, my little boat that I took out when Lars wasn't around - my work at the hospital - my walks in the surrounding woods and, in the warmer months - my night swims. It was my peace.

He didn't hit me every weekend, but the attacks were becoming more frequent because my mask was slipping and my hatred for him was becoming harder to hide. One wrong word, and he'd belt me - I was a nervous wreck. After a beating, he'd want sex - a sick fucker who got off on my pain while whispering in my ear how much he loved me - I'd feel like I was being raped. Working at the hospital was my lifeline. Hanging out with the kids, reading to them or just being there gave my shitty life meaning, and I clung to it. Even though Lars hated it, having a wife who did charity work was good for his political profile, so he hadn't forced me to quit.

'Don't commit to too many hours,' he'd say every single weekend, or 'my work takes priority over yours.' *I know, Lars - you've told me enough fucking times.*

He had complete control, and although my life was privileged, I paid the price by living with Satan himself. I often thought about my old Irish friends, wishing I'd listened to them years before. They knew who Lars was after that awful night in Dublin, but I was a fool, blinded by romance and, if I was honest - by money. The months following the first glimpse of Lars Karlsson's real personality were the most magical of my life. He pursued and romanced me like a maniac. Flowers every other day, shopping trips to Paris, Rome, Stockholm, and New York. I was in complete awe of him and honestly thought I'd imagined the punch in the face and the attack on my friends. He convinced me it was all taken in the wrong context - that they were never in danger, and like a nodding dog, I believed him.

He never raised a hand to me in those months *that started when we moved to Sweden -* but his violent nature was apparent. Of course, I convinced myself it was all my imagination, and my friends were furious. I lied to them and chose him, but I honestly thought we'd get over it. Never in a fecking million years did I think

I'd never see them again.

Just after five, Lars wandered into the kitchen wearing shorts and a linen shirt – his work obviously finished because he always wore a suit, even at home. I tried not to jump - *flighty as a baby foal* and watched him select a bottle of wine from the fridge. He opened it without looking at me and poured himself a glass - drank a couple of large gulps and savoured the wine for a minute or two, still not looking at me. Then he refilled his glass and took it outside to sit by the pool and enjoy the evening sun. *Prick.*

'What's for dinner?' he asked before walking through the doors.

'Steak and salad,' I said, smiling like a Stepford wife.

It was his favourite, and I was trying to cheer him up to protect myself.

'You might have told me before I opened the white,' he replied, raising the glass of wine in his hand, and I thought *fuck, he's spoiling for a fight.*

'Sure, you can have a glass of the white now – dinner won't be ready for a couple of hours,' I said, trying to calm my nerves and smiling even brighter.

He mumbled something as he left, and my face ached from the forced smiling. With a sense of foreboding, I poured myself some wine - popped a couple of codeine - two ibuprofens and washed them down with a large gulp. *Just to be on the safe side.*

It happened ten minutes after dinner, it was the worst one yet - the turning point in my life.

3 ~ ORLA

'Eh, hello - is this Orla Reed?'

Orla immediately recognised the voice but couldn't believe her ears.

'Audrey O'Brien,' she said in utter astonishment.

'Why was Audrey ringing Orla?'

Audrey laughed.

'Howya missus, I got your number from your ma - I hope you don't mind,' she said.

Orla didn't mind at all, but she was shocked and confused for two reasons. First, she hadn't spoken to Audrey in twenty years, and second, she'd been thinking about Laura Quinn all day. Two friends from the same gang on the same day – why?

'I don't mind. I'm just surprised to hear from ye - especially at midnight on a Monday night. What's wrong?' asked Orla.

Audrey and Laura were part of a gang of girls Orla grew up with in Dublin. Best friends from their first day of school, they spent every minute together. As teenagers, they went to the same dance classes, determined to be the next girl band or at least backing dancers for someone famous. When they left school, the band was forgotten, and every weekend was spent discoing around Dublin's best nightclubs. Even when scattered to different universities around Ireland, they came home Friday night to go into town. When they were officially grown up – *in their twenties* - the gatherings became less frequent, but without fail, they met for lunch in Dublin on the last Friday of the month. One particular Friday, their lunch turned into an epic session that ended in a nightclub, and what happened there was so traumatic that they never had lunch together again.

'Sorry it's so late, luv. Jesus, I didn't realise the time – the days are blending together. I wanted to tell you what happened in Dublin today,' said Audrey.

Orla thought that was odd but didn't say so.

'Is Audrey telling Orla about me? Is that why I'm here?'

'I'm not sure if you know, but I'm with the guards these days,' Audrey continued.

Orla didn't know and wondered why Audrey was telling her. She hadn't spoken to the woman in twenty years - was she ringing to tell her she'd joined the police?

'Actually, I'm a detective,' said Audrey, with a hint of pride. 'Anyway, I spoke to the old gang tonight because I wanted you to hear it from me.'

Okay, this was getting weird, and just as Orla was about to say so, Audrey finally got to the point.

'Well, as I said, there was an incident in Dublin today.' Audrey didn't sugar-coat it as she broke the news. 'Laura Quinn was beaten to a pulp and stabbed to death,' she said to a stunned Orla.

'I was beaten to a pulp and stabbed to death - hearing that felt weird.'

Orla couldn't take it in. Did she just say Laura was dead? As in the Laura, she'd been thinking about all day?

'Jesus Christ,' whispered Orla.

'Her body was found in a rented flat in Grand Canal, and I'm part of the team investigating her murder,' said Audrey.

'Jesus Christ,' she whispered again, unable to process it. She glanced at Neil, sitting up in bed, with a look of concern. 'Told ye,' she mouthed before asking Audrey for more details.

'She was stabbed in the neck with a kitchen knife,' said Audrey, then added, 'and badly beaten before that.'

'Why couldn't I remember who did it?'

Oh my God, poor Laura, but why had Orla been thinking about her on the day of her murder? Freaking out, she told Audrey.

'From the minute I opened my eyes this morning - she's been on my mind,' said Orla.

'That's mad. Do ye think about her a lot - have ye seen her over the years?' asked Audrey.

'Never,' said Orla, then realising that wasn't quite right, added, 'well now and then perhaps, and I haven't seen Laura in over twenty years.'

'Orla can sense me - she just doesn't know it yet.'

They both agreed it was strange, and when Audrey asked if Orla was psychic, Orla might have laughed if the circumstances hadn't been so tragic. She considered herself spiritual – as in, she did yoga twice a week, meditated when she remembered, and sometimes read her friend's tarot cards, but only for a laugh and only when white wine was involved. She answered Audrey with a firm no.

'Orla was a bit psychic, and I was new to the job. It wasn't going to be easy.'

'Chief Superintendent Burke is in the thick of it because it's a high-profile case,' said Audrey, explaining how he'd spoken to Laura's parents that afternoon.

'My poor mam and dad – this would devastate

them.'

'Oh God, how did they take it?' asked Orla, remembering how protective they were of Laura.

'Awful. Mrs Quinn was in bits, and she said something I can't get off my mind,' said Audrey.

'What?' asked Orla, her curiosity ignited.

'What did mam say?'

'She said she was afraid this might happen one day,' said Audrey.

'Why would she say that, and why is it high-profile?' asked Orla, more intrigued than ever. 'Was Laura famous?' Surely, if she was, Orla would know. Without waiting for an answer, Orla continued with her questions. 'And who killed her? Do you have any idea?' It seemed incomprehensible to Orla that anyone would kill Laura Quinn.

'Laura's not famous - her husband is - well, sort of,' said Audrey.

'Her husband? Who did she marry?' asked Orla, her thoughts immediately going to

Laura's boyfriend from years before and the nightclub incident that ended their friendship. 'Please tell me it wasn't that Swedish prick - what was his name?'

'Ye, it was – she'd been living in Sweden for the past twenty years,' said Audrey.

'Guilty as charged.'

'You are fucking joking – Laura married that psycho?' asked Orla, gobsmacked.

'Yeah – arrived in Dublin yesterday morning and murdered today,' said Audrey.

'Oh my God, that's awful, poor Laura, but why in the name of God did she marry him?' asked Orla again.

'You know what she was like about him back then,' said Audrey.

'Obsessed.'

'Jesus, how could I forget? You don't think that's what Mrs Quinn meant, do you? That he did something to her?' asked Orla, the thought popping into her head and out of her mouth.

'As bad as Lars is, he wouldn't have killed me.'

'He didn't - he was at a conference in Belgium all weekend,' said Audrey, sounding convinced, but Orla wasn't so sure.

The thought of Laura living with that monster for twenty years was horrific. From day one, he had *arsehole* written all over him. Ex-Swedish army, he surrounded himself with the same kind of assholes. Orla's opinion of him back then was that he could easily kill Laura, and she used to worry he would. After the nightclub incident, they pleaded with Laura to leave him, but she ignored them, and their friendship fell apart. Orla assumed that car-crash relationship would run its course or that Laura would finally get some sense, but obviously, she didn't.

'What happens now?' asked Orla, wondering if she should get involved.

As a crime writer, Orla had an eye for small details sometimes overlooked in murder cases. It was why her books were so successful, and she'd been thinking about Laura all day. Orla believed in signposts, and that was a neon one!

'Lars, that's his name, by the way, is flying into Dublin in the morning,' said Audrey, and Orla remembered – Lars, the lunatic as they'd referred to him back then. 'He was frantic on the phone, demanded we find her killer and wants every man on the job.'

'God, Audrey, I can't believe she married that animal, fucks sake,' said Orla.

'Neither can I - years wasted on him.'

'Me either,' said Audrey.

They spoke for a few more minutes, and when they said goodbye, Orla turned to Neil and relayed the story while opening her laptop and searching through different Irish news channels, horrified to see Laura's face plastered all over them. Having been a Miss Ireland finalist years before, the headlines read. *'Beauty Queen Murdered in Dublin'* or *'Former Miss Ireland Finalist Found Dead.'*

'I stared at the photos of me in The Belgard that night - was I ever that carefree?'

Orla didn't read them - she couldn't stomach it.

'Go back to sleep. I'm going downstairs to try and make sense of this,' said Orla.

'You sure you're, okay?' asked Neil.

'Yeah, I'm grand,' said Orla, 'but I won't sleep - you stay here.'

Leaving him in bed, Orla went downstairs with Ray. She turned on the AGA, made some tea, and sat at the kitchen table, watching the rain lash against the glass doors. A salt lamp in the corner gave the room a warm glow, and as she drank hot camomile tea, she replayed Audrey's conversation in her head, remembering that awful night when Laura wanted to surprise Lars. Should they have tried harder to get her away from him? Had he hurt her throughout their marriage? Had he killed her? Orla couldn't help feeling the answer to all of the above was a big fat yes.

Laura
I refused to believe Lars killed me. Batter me, absolutely - but kill me? He was too obsessed. Orla needed to find out what happened, or I'd be stuck

between life and death for God knows how long. Concentrating hard - I tried to move the teaspoon in her cup, but it didn't work. Ray growled in my direction a couple of times. 'Oh hush, I'm mammy's friend,' I said, patting his head.

4 ~ LAURA

We looked like a normal couple - married for twenty years and having dinner together. Drinking wine and checking our phones, I even tried to sound enthusiastic when I asked about his job, but it didn't interest me - nothing about my husband did. He was a miserable fucker, and every second spent in his company was agony. Sometimes, I'd try to remember when we'd been happy. When I didn't have to force a smile or feel dread when he walked into a room. When had I last laughed out loud, or felt horny, or excited, or safe? I'd been walking on eggshells for twenty years, pandering to Lars's every need while forgetting about my own. I lived in constant survival mode, and I was tired.

'Any news on the election? Are you excited about the new role?' I asked, cringing at the insincerity in my voice.

In the past, I never asked about his job

because I knew it was illegal. The pallets of cash I'd seen in the garage over the years – the offshore accounts in his name and the men he kept close were criminals. Still, somehow, he'd become a government minister and was well respected. I couldn't begin to imagine how that had happened.

Lars leaned back in his chair, rolled a glass of French Bordeaux between his long, elegant fingers, and silently examined me. He thought this intimidated me - and I had to fight not to roll my eyes. *Grow the fuck up*, I wanted to scream.

'Why are you pretending to be interested in my job, Laura? What do you care if I'm excited about my new position? he asked calmly but accusingly.

Fucks sake, I stopped moving the food around my plate in the pretence of eating, looked at him and smiled. In my head, I said, *of course, I care*, but the words that came out of my mouth were quite different. Much later, when I lay in bed, bruised and battered and thinking about it - the only conclusion I came to for saying what I was about to say - was the drugs I took before dinner - mixed with hardly any food - a glass of white wine and two rather large glasses of red.

'Actually, I couldn't give a flying fuck about any of it. I'm just keeping up the pretence so you'll keep your filthy hands off me.'

He turned with the wine glass, paused at his mouth, and my knife and fork clattered against my plate - *Jesus fucking Christ, did I just say that out loud?* The murderous look on his face said I did, and my insides turned to liquid.

'What did you say to me?' he asked, his voice low and vicious.

Shocked, I simply stared, then desperate to save myself, I tried to backpedal.

'I'm only joking, love,' I said, half laughing, but it was too late.

The crystal glass hit the wall behind my head and shattered into a million pieces. Tiny shards of glass dug into the back of my neck, but before I could say, ouch - my chair was kicked from under me, and I fell to the floor. Lars was on top of me in a second with his hand around my neck.

'What did you say to me?' he demanded again. I wanted to scream - *you heard me loud and clear dickhead*, but I'd already pushed him too far. He was going to kick the shit out of me for this, so I stayed silent. 'You fucking bitch - who the fuck do you think you're talking to?' he spat with his face inches from mine - I wanted to vomit.

'Please let me go, love - I didn't mean it, and you're hurting me,' I said, trying to reason with him.

I called him love to keep him happy, even though it stuck in my throat. Most of the time, it pacified him, but he was too far gone. His hand tightened around my neck, and I was seconds away from a panic attack. I kicked my legs and tried to buck him off, but he was too strong.

'You need to remember something, cunt - your life is mine. Everything you have is because of me, and everything you do is because I allow it. Do you fucking understand that?'

Oh, I understood it, alright - he was in charge of everything. I tried to nod, but his other hand clamped around my neck, and I couldn't move. Overcome with terror, I frantically kicked my legs.

'Lars,' I gasped, but his hands kept

tightening.

My lungs were on fire - my eyes pleading with him, but he squeezed harder. The fucker was going to kill me, and there was nothing I could do about it. Suddenly - and I don't know how or why it happened, but a sense of calm descended upon me, and I resigned myself to death. Surely being dead was better than this shit. I closed my eyes, stopped resisting him and lay on the floor like Sleeping fucking Beauty. Fuck him, he could strangle me to death, I didn't care anymore.

When he realised I was no longer fighting, his grip loosened. My eyes flew open, and for a second, we stared at each other, my eyes defiant - *do it, you prick,* his confused. Then, in a rage, he grabbed my hair and slammed my head into the floor. Luckily, or unluckily, depending on how you look at it - a thick rug saved my skull from being cracked on the stone floor, but he wasn't done yet. He stood up and kicked my stomach so many times that I threw up, red wine spraying all over the rug. When I stopped puking, he yanked me to my feet and flung me against the dining table. The agony of my ribs cracking forced a cry from my lips, and even though I hated giving in to him - I begged him to stop. He ignored me and pushed my head against the table while fiddling with his zip.

'Please, Lars, not like this,' I begged, but he ignored me, ripped my knickers down, and with one hard push, slammed his cock inside me.

He didn't think of it as rape – I was his possession to do with as he pleased and my resistance aroused him - so I denied him that and lay still – *fuck you, Lars.* His breath quickened as he leaned over me, pumping in and out while pressing my head against the table. He came with a groan and nuzzled into my neck for a few seconds of intimacy before snapping back to psycho mode.

'You make me do this every fucking time,' he snarled while zipping himself up.

I didn't move – I didn't even look at him. I just lay face down on the table, dying of shame and hating myself for choosing this life. My knickers were around my ankles, Lars's cum leaked out of me, and my own vomit tangled through my hair. The pain of my cracked rib was excruciating, and I wheezed as

I breathed - *what had I done to deserve this?* Lars watched for a minute, uncomfortable with my submissiveness – he preferred me to fight back, to shout and scream which I had done in the past, but I was broken. After a few minutes, he snatched a bottle of red wine from the table and for a second, I thought he might smash it over my head - still not sure if I cared.

'Clean up this mess before you go to bed,' he sneered, and he was gone.

5 ~ ORLA

The morning after Orla's shocking phone call from Audrey, she woke up on her hard kitchen bench, whose soft cushions had somehow scattered to the floor, feeling as stiff as a board. Bleary-eyed, but thankful for the AGA's heat radiating through the room, she drank her badly needed coffee.

'I miss coffee.'

Ray, like an electric blanket, was fast asleep at her feet, his fur keeping her warm - his snores making her smile. Outside, the freezing rain still lashed against the windows, but no snow, even though everyone expected it and every drop of milk and slice of bread had been gone when Orla went grocery shopping the day before - talk about panic buying. The BBC weatherman had warned to *prepare for a blizzard*, and it seemed everyone had.

'I hope it snows – my favourite thing about living in Sweden.'

Neil wandered into the kitchen looking sexy in his boxer shorts - his dark hair was messy, and yesterday's clothes were in his hand.

'You really should leave a few things here,' said Orla, nibbling on homemade Sourdough toast with Irish butter and strawberry jam. 'Want coffee?' she asked.

'No, I need to go home, shower, and get to work. I'm flying to Frankfurt tomorrow, back on Friday,' said Neil, as he pulled on his jeans. 'See you over the weekend?' he asked, leaning down for a kiss and pinching some of Orla's toast.

When he left, Orla's thoughts drifted to Laura and her other three best friends. Suddenly, the years of separation seemed pointless. She recalled Niamh's vibrant personality that drew people to her and how she could be friends with strangers within minutes of meeting them. Maggie had always been more standoffish and had seemed indifferent to fun. At the time, it was annoying, but now Orla realised it was just part of her personality. They'd laugh and say Audrey was responsible for bringing culture to their lives. There wasn't an art expo or a museum in Ireland she hadn't visited, usually forcing them to go with her. Orla had been the nerdy writer of the group and always on the lookout for a story, and their fashion queen, Laura, could wear a black plastic sack and still look like a supermodel. She'd had a talent for making cheap look expensive, which was handy because, back then, cheap was all they could afford. Sighing, Orla picked up her phone and rang Audrey.

'Did you know Laura was missing, or did someone stumble across her body?' she asked.

'Good morning to you too,' said Audrey.

'Sorry, Audrey, that's been on my mind all night - I didn't sleep a wink. I just can't believe Laura Quinn is dead,' said Orla.

'I know, me either. Her mam reported her missing. Laura stayed with them on Sunday night, went into town to see a solicitor on Monday, and never returned.'

'Why was Laura seeing a solicitor?' asked Orla.

'If I'd gone straight back to my mams, this wouldn't have happened.'

'We don't know yet, but when she didn't show up for lunch or answer her phone, Mrs Quinn panicked and called the guards. It would usually take more than that to investigate a missing person, but Mrs Quinn was hysterical and begged for someone to check the apartment. She knew the building but not the door number, and we couldn't find it because Laura booked it using a different name.'

'My heart was broken for my mam.'

'Whose name?' asked Orla, riveted.
'A Swedish name, Astrid something. When we eventually found the right apartment, Laura had been dead for hours.'

It suddenly occurred to Orla that she was having a conversation with an old friend about another old friend who'd been murdered, and she hadn't spoken to either of them in twenty years – it was surreal.

'Why did Mrs Quinn panic at Laura not answering her phone? Even though she was right, is that not a bit overboard?' asked Orla. 'Did she think Laura was in danger?'

'Apparently, Laura always answered her phone, and when I asked Mrs Quinn why she panicked, she looked at her husband, then, she shut down and seemed nervous - they both did,' said Audrey and Orla's ears pricked up at this information.

'So did mine.'

'Why were they nervous?' she asked, but Audrey didn't know. 'What about the other girls? How did they react?'

Orla didn't want to think about poor Mr & Mrs Quinn - it was too distressing.

Niamh cried and dropped the phone. I could hear her sobbing until her husband picked it up and said she'd call me back - she still hasn't,' said Audrey.

'Ah, Poor Niamh. God love her.'

Orla wasn't surprised - Niamh had always been the emotional friend and would cry at the drop of a hat.

'What about Maggie?'

'I'm a bit pissed off at her if I'm honest,' said Audrey.

'Why, what happened?' asked Orla.

'She went quiet, then said if Laura had stayed with Lars, it was something we expected to hear one day and hung up,' said Audrey.

'No way,' said Orla, laughing.

Talk about getting straight to the point. Maggie had always been more practical/less emotional, but still, that was a bit harsh.

'I'm coming to Dublin. Can you meet for a coffee on Thursday?' asked Orla, feeling a sudden urge to be there.

'Yay. I knew Orla would help me – I had to get her to hear me.'

The funeral wouldn't take place until the investigation was over, but Orla wanted to get involved. She didn't mention that to Audrey in case she thought she was interfering in Garda business.

'Yep, and Orla, I'm glad you're coming,' said Audrey.

It felt like the right thing to do.

'Let's try and meet the others, too,' suggested Orla, thinking it was probably time for a reunion.

Audrey thought that was a great idea and promised to organise it. When they hung up, Orla got dressed, walked her dog, and began arranging her trip. Ray could stay with her neighbour, who adored him. Orla would stay with her parents in Dublin - she just needed a flight and to ring Dorothy, who, as always, got straight to the point.

'Tell me you're motivated and inspired, and I'll be getting something solid this week,' said Dorothy, but before she could muster another word, Orla blurted out what had happened in Dublin.

'Good God, that's dreadful, I'm so sorry, Orla,' said Dorothy.

It sounded weird saying Laura was dead.

'I'm heading to Dublin tomorrow. I need to be there while the investigation is ongoing,' explained Orla, and Dorothy agreed.

'Of course, but please bring your laptop in case you have free time,' she said.

Orla smiled - as if she'd ever go anywhere without it.

When they hung up, she rang Max, emailed Connor and texted Neil. The boys didn't know Laura but were shocked to hear the news, and Neil thought it was a good idea to go. Opening her laptop to book a flight, Orla glanced out the window at her gorgeous new black Mercedes. A Christmas present to herself - it could do with a good spin, and she'd need a car in Dublin - she decided to drive.

'Woohoo!! Road trip.'

The rest of the day was spent writing, and when Orla climbed into bed that night, she set her alarm for five the following morning and was asleep in minutes.

Laura
I stayed in the kitchen reading Orla's latest novel – gripped. I was delighted to go to Dublin - we had loads to do. Lars and Erik needed to be stopped,

and maybe being there would jog my memory as to who murdered me. I remembered walking into the apartment after meeting with Marcus - everything after that was blank. Was my killer waiting for me, or had he followed me?

6 ~ LAURA

Ten minutes after Lars left the dining room, I lay on the exquisite oak table - specially made for that room - like a statue amongst the smashed plates, spilt wine, and scattered food unable to move and wondering how my life had become this.

Eventually, I stood up and almost fainted from the pain. My stomach and ribs were on fire - my hair was sticky with vomit - the coppery taste in my mouth sickened me, and Lars's cum on the inside of my legs made me want to die. When I heard laughing from the direction of his office, I felt sick with shame. Erik had been in the house during the attack, had heard everything, and had done nothing. In all the years of beatings, he'd never once helped me, *fucking animal*, and I didn't know who I despised more.

While cleaning, I came to a decision. This had been the most violent attack to date

- Lars had never strangled me before - I saw the madness in his eyes. He'd crossed a line, and I had to get away from him. Fighting back the tears and nausea, I washed wine and vomit off the floor and walls, put unbroken dishes in the dishwasher, and rolled up the stained rug to go in the bin. *Do not cry - do not cry*. When the room was spotless, I crawled into a hot bath, desperate to wash the filth of Lars off my body. I bandaged the cuts on my neck from the flying glass and eventually fell into bed and sobbed myself to sleep. Dark and chaotic dreams tormented me - I was chasing someone - I didn't know who it was, but I had to reach them. When I woke up with a start, I felt bereft, then relieved to see the bed empty beside me - Lars was still in his office, probably pissed by now. I slowly inched my pain-ridden body out of bed and limped to the kitchen for more codeine, thankful for the stone floor with no creaks. On my way back, I stopped outside Lars's office, held my breath and put my ear to the door. I could hear their conversation clearly and was about to limp back to bed until Erik mentioned my name.

'Being that young, they were worth lots

of money, but you were right - it was too risky when Laura and those cunts showed up - definitely the right thing to get rid of them,' he said.

'You knew my motto back then,' said Lars, 'not even the slightest risk. The second Laura turned up - it was a no. Those girls were far too volatile, although why you chose to kill them in my fucking office, I'll never know,' said Lars, laughing as if it was the funniest story he'd ever told.

'The plan was to take them to the yard, but one of them went fucking mad, and that crazy bastard Robert shot her in the head, forcing us to do the same to the other two,' said Erik, laughing as well.

Although fluent in Swedish, it took a minute for me to translate in my head and realise they were talking about the night Lars first hit me and the young girls already in the nightclub when we arrived.

'Shame – I enjoyed that kitten and would have liked more of her,' said Lars.

'Laura turning up saved our asses,' said Erik as I stood frozen and wanting to puke at my husband's comment. 'Those girls were being delivered to Nikoli the next day, and the cops were watching.'

Who the fuck was Nikoli?

'Fuck, I forgot about that,' said Lars.

'He spent years in prison in Dublin, then Belarus. Those stupid fucks missed his connection to us - man, you don't get much luckier than that,' said Erik, both of them laughing again.

I stood rooted to the spot, trying to process what Erik had just said. They'd been sex trafficking those girls but murdered them instead? My mind was spinning. Did it happen while we were still in the club? Terrified, I began to sneak away until Lars spoke again.

'Remind me where you buried them,' he said, and when Erik revealed where the bodies were, I gasped. 'Did you hear something?' asked Erik.

A chair squeaked - I dashed down the hall in terror, every step excruciating and quietly closed my bedroom door. I lay down and used the box breathing technique - another survival trick I'd taught myself over the years, to slow my heart rate. When Lars came into the room a few minutes later, he leaned over the bed, but it looked like I was out cold. When he left, I lay in the darkness, processing what I'd heard and trying to remember the details of that night so many years ago. The devastation of seeing Lars all over that kitten as he'd referred to her. Did Erik say they'd shot them, or did I imagine that? How could it be possible? Who were they?

Lars didn't come to bed that night, and I finally fell into a pitiful sleep - still exhausted, when I woke the following morning. The rest of the weekend was quiet. One guarantee I had after a beating was that Lars treated me like I was made of priceless glass. He apologised - begged for forgiveness - promised it would never happen again and blamed his good old PTSD. Same old, same old. I smiled and pretended it was okay, anything for him to leave me alone - *whatever dickhead*. On Monday morning, he left for Stockholm in the early hours, and I fell apart. Only then could I process what had happened.

Astrid came over - we went straight to the jetty and took my boat out. I couldn't talk in the house because of the security cameras. Lars said they were for my safety, but they were to spy on me. When we reached the middle of the lake, I showed her the bruising around my stomach and the red welt around my neck - she was horrified.

'You have to leave him, Laura - the man will kill you one of these days,' said Astrid.

'I don't think he'd kill me - Lars is obsessed with me, but he's never strangled me before. You're right - I have to find a way out,' I said, then finished the story about the sex trafficking and murder.

'My goodness - what will you do?' asked Astrid, even more shocked.

'I don't know. Should I tell the guards in Dublin where the bodies are? I asked. 'Imagine what their families are going through? I can't bear it.'

Astrid blew out a long breath.

'You need to be very careful, Laura. You just told me your husband is a murderer,' said Astrid, then added. 'There are many questions in my mind. How would you tell these guards in Dublin? Would they believe a random stranger? What happens to you when Lars finds out? Do you have proof he did this? What if these guards blame you?'

'I don't know the answer to any of it, but

MS S B FARRELL

you're right about one thing, I have to get away from Lars.

7 ~ ORLA

At noon the next day, Orla drove into the packed ferry terminal at Holyhead and waited to board the Dublin Swift. The cold weather made the journey long and harsh - the rough crossing made her seasick, and she was exhausted when her car finally splashed through Dublin's cold, wet streets. Home - no matter where she went, Dublin was home. Pulling into the driveway of her parent's house, her mam was waiting at the front door with tears in her eyes.

'I just can't believe Laura is dead - she was so young,' she said, wiping her eyes with a tissue before hugging her daughter.

'Hey, Mrs Reed.'

'I don't think any of us can, ma - and to be taken in such a violent way,' said Orla.

'It's shocking,' said Patsy, leading Orla

into the house.

Orla's dad was waiting in the kitchen, and the kettle was already on.

'Heya da,' said Orla, hugging her dad.

'Howya, love. How was it?' he asked, referring to a ferry crossing in wild Irish weather.

'Horrible,' said Orla, laughing.

'Thank God ye got here in one piece,' he said.

Orla's mam made the tea because tea was the answer to everything in Ireland. At seventy-nine, Patsy Reed was a powerhouse - sharp-minded and in excellent health. She handed a steaming mug to Orla and, for the first time in twenty years, asked why Orla had fallen out with her friends all those years before. Orla promised to tell the whole story but said she needed to speak to Audrey before opening that can of worms.

'Besides, I haven't seen you in ages – what's happening around here?' asked Orla, knowing her mam was a fountain of information when it came to the neighbours.

Patsy huffed and shared a few scraps of general gossip before moving on to the big stuff.

'Ah here. That's enough for me,' said Joe, taking his tea and paper into the lounge.

'Well,' said Patsy, sipping her tea to get the juices flowing, 'that one across the road had another baby, and I don't think he's happy about it.' Her raised eyebrows asked, *can you believe that?* Orla wondered if she was supposed to know who *that one* was and who wasn't happy about it? Noticing Orla's blank look, Patsy elaborated. 'Irene McGinty, you know her. Four babies, all under six, and her husband is a drip. He's giving out about another mouth to feed,' she said.

'Ah ma – I'm sure he's not – it's his child,' said Orla, trying not to laugh.

'He is,' said Patsy, 'You should have seen the face on him that day after she told him.'

'Slapped arse?' asked Orla.

'Worse,' said Patsy and they laughed. Then, lowering her voice to make her gossiping sound more respectable, she announced the next big headline. 'Remember Mary Lynch?' Orla nodded - her old Irish dancing teacher - how could she forget Mary. 'Well, she fecking fell down the road last week and nearly went under a bus. Day drinking at her age, and she's a grandmother,' said Patsy with a disapproving tone that indicated how scandalous day drinking was considered.

'You stop that gossiping,' called Joe from the other room.

Orla laughed while thinking about the many boozy lunches she enjoyed with her friends - glad to be in a different country and away from the gossip mill, poor Mary.

'You mind your business, Joe Reed,' called Patsy, then turned to Orla to finish the story. 'Anyway, Aggie Burke saved her life - pulled her off the road and carried her home. She hasn't shown her face since, and it's no wonder.'

'God, I missed living in Ireland.'

Orla laughed - it was good to be home. She spent the rest of the afternoon catching up on more *shocking news*, drinking mugs of tea and eating ham sandwiches. When she finally escaped her mam's clutches, Orla went to her room and rang Neil.

'Can ye talk?' asked Orla when Neil

answered.

'Yeah, how was the trip?' he asked.

'A bit rough,' said Orla, 'but I'm glad I came. Laura's murder is all over the place. RTE news is running the story, and she's on the front page of every newspaper.'

'Jesus – have they got any suspects?' asked Neil.

'I don't know – the papers are saying it might be a break-in gone wrong,' said Orla. 'I'll get more information when I see Audrey tomorrow, then I'm going to pop by Laura's parent's house,' she added.

'Yikes – that'll be tough,' said Neil.

'I know – I dread it, but I have to speak to them,' said Orla.

They spoke for a bit longer, and after a long shower, Orla decided it was probably time to buy her own place in Dublin. She loved staying in her old house but could afford her own apartment now. Thinking it might be a nice project for her mam, she went downstairs to find her watching Coronation Street with her dad.

'What about those new apartments on St Stephen's Green? They're gorgeous - they were on the telly last week,' said Patsy, then turned to Joe. 'What was that program called? The one with those new apartments in town?'

'I haven't a clue,' said Joe, irritated.

Orla's dad had zero interest in such matters.

'Don't worry, ma, I'll Google it. Maybe we'll view one while I'm here,' said Orla, liking the idea of living on The Green, her favourite part of Dublin.

Laura
This was more like it. Although being back in Dublin felt strange, I was happy – maybe we'd get somewhere now. I was dying to know what Lars was up to in Sweden and tried to imagine myself in his office several times, but it didn't work. Apprentice ghost, it was annoying. When I wandered from Orla on the ferry, I realised I could only move a certain distance from her - it seemed we were locked together.

8 ~ LAURA

Three Months Before
My Murder

The last day of my life was hurtling towards me, and I was oblivious. In three months, I'd be dead - my life ripped from me in the most devastating way, and I wasn't ready to go. I wanted to live - to be free of Lars and have the life I'd dreamed about for twenty years.

Since deciding to leave him, my days had turned into a frenzy of collecting evidence to use against my husband. After the last beating, it took two weeks for my body to recover. My immune system was compromised - I caught the flu and couldn't get out of bed for almost ten days. Lars was mortified by how close he'd come to killing me, and the house was overflowing with fresh flowers. He apologised daily and promised to die rather than hurt me again, and in the three months since it happened, he'd lived up to his word, but I knew it wouldn't last.

When I was well again, the girls in Dublin became my obsession. I used Astrid's laptop during breaks at work to conduct my research – devastated to discover who they were. I wanted to contact the guards in Dublin, but Astrid words stopped me - would they believe me, and how would I go about it? They'd want to know who I was and how I learned about the bodies. I couldn't give them my phone number, or Lars would find out.

'What about an anonymous tip,' asked Astrid one morning over coffee in the hospital canteen.

'Then Lars and Erik get away with it, and this might be my only way out, Ast,' I said. 'I need more information about the girls and use it at the right time.'

As the days went on, I was desperate to share everything with my super sleuth sister Louise - *she'd know exactly what to do,* but I didn't want to give my family hope. Over the years, they'd begged me to leave Lars, but when it didn't happen, they gave up. One Friday in

September, Lars went to America again, and my heart soared. I rarely got excited when he travelled in Europe - he could fly home at the drop of a hat, but America was the whole Atlantic Ocean away. With the information about the girls documented, phase two of my plan could take shape - a divorce lawyer in Dublin. Using Astrid's laptop again, I found Marcus Ryan, who specialised in domestic abuse, and I knew he was the one. I set up a fake email address and explained my situation. *Escape from my violent, powerful and dangerous husband.* I told him about the beatings and asked if he'd fit me in at short notice.

'Yeah, if you get to Dublin, I'll fit you in - that's no problem, but do you have any proof of the abuse? I only ask because you won't get far in court if it's your word against his. Without solid evidence, these things tend to go nowhere,' said Marcus in his email response.

Suddenly, I had a phase three to consider - how did I prove Lars abused me? He was meticulous, only leaving marks where others couldn't see them. Everyone in Sweden thought Lars Karlsson - member of parliament, was a model husband, a respected businessman and generous philanthropist. Erik and Sven knew the truth, but those two would die rather than expose him. How did I get proof of his abuse, and how did I get to Dublin without him? Something that hadn't happened in twenty years.

'Record him,' said Astrid one afternoon while out in my boat, which I'd thoroughly checked for listening devices - determined to have some privacy.

'How? He checks my phone and can see what websites I access - I can't do anything except shop and listen to books on that thing,' I pointed to my phone on the bench.

'Get another phone,' she said, and I stared.

'And do what?' I asked.

'Hide it and record him beating you,' said Astrid.

The thought terrified me, but she was right. What better way to get proof than to catch him in the act?

'If I give you cash, will you get one for me?' I asked, and she nodded.

The next afternoon, Astrid arrived at work with my new phone. We discussed where to hide it and decided on the bedroom. Historically, that was where most of his attacks occurred. My old friend Orla was an author, and her books were my prized possessions, displayed proudly on a bookcase in my bedroom. I placed the phone behind them, left a small gap for the camera to peep through, and did a test run to ensure it captured the room - it did, and I was all set.

'When he's home, press record and leave it,' said Astrid and I nodded as fear whizzed around my body.

As expected, Lars's run of being nice soon ran its course. Two beatings occurred in the bedroom, the first when he returned from America and was pissed off about something that happened there and took it out on me. The next, a month later, when I told him to fuck off under my breath. I hadn't meant to – it was another slip of the tongue, and he went fucking mad. Although the latest beatings weren't as violent as the night in the dining room, the depravity of his attacks increased. In one of them, instead of raping me like he usually did, he pissed on me instead, and my humiliation was complete.

One afternoon, while Lars was at work, I decided to check the recordings. If his face was visible, that would do. I couldn't cope with the stress of trying to record any more beatings. Retrieving the phone from behind the books, I snuck into the garage and hid in my car, the only place besides my boat where I had any privacy. I watched both videos, and the level of violence took my breath away. Was I really that woman being pulled around by the hair and kicked in the stomach? Tears poured down my cheeks, and I wanted to scream at the bastard to leave her alone.

When Erik walked into the garage, I jumped and almost threw myself to the floor until I remembered the blackened glass in my Range Rover. Quickly pressing pause, I stayed still as I watched him. *What was that fucker doing here?* He only came when Lars was home, and I hadn't heard his car because I was using earphones. Talking on the phone, he didn't notice me and stomped towards a wall of shelves, reaching for a hammer hanging there - *what, he was a maintenance man now?* However, instead of taking it in his hand, he pressed it like a handle, and one of the shelves slid sideways to reveal a hidden door. *What the fuck?* On a small keypad, he keyed in a six-digit code that I quickly noted - the door opened, and he disappeared behind it. My instinct was to run, but fear stopped me. We'd lived in this house for fifteen years, and I didn't know about that door. Had it always been there? Rooted to my seat, I was glad I stayed when, five minutes later, Erik reappeared carrying what looked like a box file. He closed the door, locked it with the same code - the shelf slid back into place, and he left the garage without a glance in my direction. When I heard his sports car roar to life and drive off, I went straight to my bedroom to process what I'd just seen - *there was a secret room in my house.*

Later, when Lars came home, I played the *vulnerability card* against Erik.

'He needs to tell me when he's coming to the house - I heard someone in the garage today and thought we were being robbed.' Sprinkling a few tears into the mix, I added. 'I mean, I don't mind him being here,' *I hated him being here*, 'I just need to know when he's coming.'

I had to know if Erik would unexpectedly turn up again because I had to know what was in that room. What the fuck was my husband up to? Lars said he'd talk to him, and a text message from Erik later that night apologised and said there'd be no more unannounced visits. *Bet that stuck in your throat, dickhead.* I didn't tell Astrid or Hilda - *my other confidant*, about the room, I wanted to know what I was dealing with first, and when Lars went to Germany a week later, I got my chance.

Shaking like a leaf, I tiptoed across the garage. That - Lars's office and the bedrooms were the only rooms without *security cameras*. I'd always wondered why his precious cars seemed unprotected - obviously because of this. With clammy palms and a churning stomach, I pulled the hammer and just like it had with Erik, the shelf slid sideways. My trembling fingers keyed in the six-digit code, the lock clicked, and the door opened to reveal a staircase. Oh, my fucking God, I was positive Lars, Erik and Sven would rush at me, any minute now - like a swat team and shoot me on the spot. My hands shook so badly that I couldn't to find a light switch, so used the flashlight on my phone to sneak down the stairs. What would I find? Checking behind me a hundred times, to make sure no one was following me, I slowly pushed open the door at the bottom of the stairs with my heart was in my mouth. There was wall of security screens showing the rooms in my house, the garden and the jetty. In front of the screens, on a large desk, sat a computer and two more screens.

'What the fuck,' I whispered and couldn't work out if I was relieved or disappointed.

All this secrecy for a security room? Hidden doors and codes for this? I looked around – there had to be more to it, but there wasn't – it was just a plain old security room. What had I expected - a dungeon? I laughed at my own dramatics, but nothing would have surprised me with my husband.

'Get a grip, Laura,' I whispered, thinking I was getting caught up in hunting for evidence against Lars.

I turned to leave until movement on one of the screens caught my eye. I almost bolted, thinking someone was in the house, until I realised that room wasn't in this house. I crept towards the screen for a closer look, my brain trying hard to figure out what I saw. A woman – no, a young girl - sitting on a bed in a room with no furniture, who, to my absolute horror, was naked and chained to the wall.

9 ~ ORLA

Bewley's Café on Grafton Street was a trip down memory lane for Orla. She breathed in the familiar air and smiled at the old-world style still prominent, except now mixed with modern coffee machines and paper napkins. The afternoons spent here, drinking coffee and writing articles at university, had been the best of her life. Noticing her favourite table in the window was free, Orla sat down, surprised at how nervous she felt. *What did one say to an ex-best friend after twenty years?*

On top of that, her mind was bombarded by *what-ifs*. *What-if...* they'd forced Laura to leave Lars? *What-if...* they'd told her parents about their suspicions? *What-if...* they'd gone to the guards that night? When a familiar voice from behind pulled her from her thoughts, Orla smiled.

'Would ye look at what the fecking cat's dragged in. As I live and breathe, it's Orla Reed.'

Orla turned to see Audrey looking exactly as she had twenty years earlier. The same short blond hair and bright blue eyes that twinkled with mischief. Audrey, the smallest of their group at five feet one, looked like a pixie but had the heart and personality of a giant.

'Have you got a fecking time machine?' asked Orla, amazed to see Audrey wearing the same black jeans and Doc Martins as always. An oversized silver puffer coat made her look wrapped in a duvet.

'I wish,' said Audrey, pulling Orla into a hug. 'I can't believe you're here. You look brilliant, and... I've read all your books,' she said, letting her go and shaking the rain from her hair. Unwrapping herself from her coat, she continued, 'you were always a clever bitch - I fucking knew you'd be famous.'

'Hardly famous,' said Orla, laughing at her honesty. 'And I was never clever. Underachiever - easily led - could pay more attention in class - you saw the school report.'

'You were far too clever for those nuns to teach you anything,' said Audrey, then added, 'and you were far too interested in what other people were doing - a writer seems obvious now.'

Orla laughed again - it was true - other people's stories had always intrigued her.

'I was hugging Audrey - I missed her so much.'

After reacquainting themselves, Orla and Audrey ordered coffee with toasted tea cakes and got down to the business of Laura. Orla was desperate for more information, so Audrey filled in the blanks.

'She rented an apartment under the name Astrid Nilsson. Her suitcase and some of her clothes were there, but her handbag, phone, wallet and passport are all missing. Her mam said she was wearing jewellery – that's gone as well. Two cups of coffee in the kitchen, one smashed on the floor - one on the island - untouched. Laura's blood was all over the place, and there were no fingerprints except hers.'

'I had flashbacks of what happened but couldn't work them out.'

'Fucking hell, I can't get my head around it. What about Lars? Have you spoken to him?'

asked Orla.

Audrey rolled her eyes and explained how devastated he'd been on the phone.

'Then he rocks up yesterday - kicks up a shit storm and locks himself in the office with Burke for most of the afternoon. He insisted Burke put every man on the job, then fucked off back to Sweden and said he'd answer any questions from there.'

'Still a prick then?' asked Orla, and Audrey nodded.

'When we asked why Laura was in Dublin, staying in an apartment using a false name, he said he had no idea and thought she was visiting her sick mother in the hospital. There's no record of Mrs Quinn being in the hospital, so Laura lied to him.'

The cogs were turning in Orla's mind - why would Laura lie about something as simple as her mam being in hospital? There had to be more to it.

'What's his story these days? Did you say he was famous?' asked Orla, recalling their conversation from Monday night.

'Not exactly famous, but he works for the Swedish government,' said Audrey.

'What, a politician?' asked Orla, astonished when Audrey nodded.

That thug was a politician. After the violence they'd witnessed, Orla was surprised he hadn't ended up in jail, never mind parliament.

'Laura lived some life in Sweden - mixing with the stars. There are pictures of her and Lars in all the society rags, even posing with the royal family,' said Audrey.

'I hated every second of it.'

'What about kids?' asked Orla, and when Audrey said Laura never had any, she almost wept.

'There was no way I was having kids with psycho Swede.'

Of the five of them, Laura had dreamed of becoming a mother the most. In Orla's opinion, twenty years ago, Lars was a psychopath, and she didn't believe he changed. The violence came too naturally to him. He was obsessed with Laura back then, wouldn't let her out of his sight, and Laura was so captivated by him that she thought his behaviour was cute. Had it stayed that way throughout their marriage?

'Yes.'

Had he continued to abuse her?

'Yes.'

Why the fuck did she marry him?

'I temporarily lost my mind.'

She put these questions to Audrey, feeling as guilty as sin. Audrey had no answers but recognised the look on Orla's face.
'Don't go there. We don't know if Lars had anything to do with this. Laura might have been happy for the past twenty years,' she said.

'Guffaw.'

Orla doubted it.
'Should we have tried harder to get her

away from him?' she asked.

'We did try, we begged and pleaded - we even threatened her. You know that's what broke us in the end,' said Audrey.

Orla couldn't help thinking of Laura at the mercy of Lars for twenty years. What happened to make her come to Dublin? Why use a false name? What did she tell her solicitor, and how did she end up dead?

Laura
I could answer the first three questions, but I still didn't know how I ended up dead. Flashbacks of a coffee cup being smashed replayed in my mind, and I could see blood on a white shirt.
What was the point of being here if I couldn't get through to Orla? My plan was in tatters - no one would find the girl's bodies or discover what Lars and Erik were doing to innocent girls in Sweden. I sighed - being dead sucked ass.

10 ~ LAURA

For a few minutes, I stared at the image on the screen, unable to comprehend it. The girl looked terrified, curled in a ball on a small single bed, her shoulders shaking - she was crying. My gaze moved to a different screen - another room with two girls on a double bed, both chained, both naked and huddled together - my stomach dropped. Two other rooms had the same chains on the walls but were empty. One had a bed in the centre of the room, the other, a large metal crate - what was that for? Feeling overwhelmed and nauseous, I backed out of the room, carefully locked the door and ensured the shelf swung back into place. I left the garage with my mind reeling - *Lars and Erik were still trafficking girls.* My mind cast back a few months when I heard Erik say something about a shipment to Nikoli. Jesus Christ, had they been doing this for twenty years? How many girls had they kidnapped -

raped - sold? I want to consider the last option - murdered?

On the phone with my sister later that night, I was desperate to confide in her, but as usual, the conversation went something like this. *How's the kids, anything going on, how's mam and dad, how's work, what are you up to the weekend* - I wanted to scream, but I couldn't risk being overheard. My phone was bugged - Erik, the tech specialist, had ensured that. The cameras and listening devices in the house were his work as well. Years before, I'd worked out Lars listened to my conversations when, after a drunken beating, he let slip that he knew everything - *even your plans for a girlie weekend to Dublin* - he'd mimicked my voice before telling me it would be a cold day in hell before that happened. My blood ran cold - Astrid and I had spoken on the phone the day before and planned the trip. Lars didn't remember the next morning, but I did and had been on my guard ever since.

Anyway, I needed more information, and I needed to get to Dublin - meet Marcus - tell my sister everything - then we could take my bastard of a husband to the ground and save those poor girls from working as prossies in fucking Belarus or wherever they were headed. At work the next day, I toyed with the idea of telling Astrid, but the risk was too great. If anything happened to her, I couldn't live with myself. When Lars came home and said we were leaving for a holiday in Italy the next day, I nodded and smiled but wanted to scream.

'I better get packed then,' I said, then added, 'want me to pack for you.'

I knew the answer, but like the obedient wifey, I asked anyway.

'No, Olga came to the apartment earlier and packed what I needed. My bag is already in the car,' he said.

I just bet she did, *right after your morning fuck*. I smiled again and left the room.

Although beautiful, the two nights in Naples - *official government work* - and three in Capri were the last thing I needed. Thankfully, during the day, Lars busied himself while I lay by the pool reading. Dinners with politicians and their wives offered a temporary respite in the evenings. Still, for five days, I thought about three girls - chained to a wall in rooms somewhere in Sweden.

When we arrived home from Italy, Lars went straight to Stockholm, and I went to the secret room to find all the rooms empty and the girls gone. My gaze moved to the large Apple desktop computer. I shook the mouse - no password required - I began scrolling. Maybe I could find the location of the rooms and call the police anonymously. Scanning the screen and ignoring the usual apps, my eyes stopped at a Laura folder, and I clicked it open. My email accounts - phone records - doctor's appointments - Amazon deliveries - everything I did, available for Lars, Erik, and I suspected Sven to see. *Bastards.*

The folder below was called *Pengar Och Makt.* Erik's favourite drinking toast meant money and power. I'd heard him say it many times over the years and always thought him an asshole. Clicking it open, a list of files appeared before my eyes, each with a video clip attached and a name and date beneath it. I scrolled down the page, recognising some names while feeling confused. Clicking play one of the video clips from three years earlier - I watched two men spit-roast a young girl while kissing each other. A more recent clip showed a girl being sodomised - her arms chained to the ceiling and a bondage gag in her mouth – she didn't look like she was enjoying it. When the camera zoomed in on the man's face – I recognised him. It was Hans. We'd had dinner with him and his beautiful wife in Italy. Elaena had recently given birth to their third child – she wasn't the girl being fucked in the video.

Feeling sick, I closed the file and scrolled further down the page, shocked to see so many familiar names - government officials – police – celebrities - even a member of the royal family. The room began to spin as the pieces flew together. Lars's rapid ascension to a position of power in the Swedish government - how the police never helped me in the early days when I ran. My relief at making it to the police station only to be driven straight back to my waiting husband. They were all snared in Lars's trap - he was blackmailing them, and even though none of it was funny, I laughed out loud.

'You disgusting, evil, clever bastard,' I whispered as I closed down the files and quickly left the room.

During my lunch break the following day, I found an electrical shop in town and bought a USB stick – a novelty one.

11 ~ ORLA

Orla and Audrey wandered down Grafton Street - friends again after twenty years – it felt nice. Audrey promised to organise a reunion with Niamh and Maggie the following week. Orla suggested a pub, thinking wine would definitely be on the cards. She took the bus back to her mam's house and immediately googled Lars Karlsson, shocked to discover he was Sweden's Minister for Foreign Affairs and a highly respected businessman. How the fuck did that animal become a minister?

'Blackmail.'

There were photos of him attending government functions and fabulous galas with Laura on his arm, looking like a model. An authentic Irish beauty with red hair, pale skin, and green eyes, she gave those Swedish girls a run for their money.

'Aw, thanks, chick, I'm blushing.'

In full research mode, Orla tried to find information about Laura and was surprised to find nothing - she didn't even have a social media account. Apart from her murder, everything was related to or associated with Lars. *Just as he'd want it.*

'You got it, sister.'

Thirsty for more, Orla rang Laura's parents - there were questions only they could answer. Mr Quinn was surprised but happy to hear from her and agreed to a visit.

'Do you want me to come with you?' asked Patsy when Orla hung up.

'I'll go on my own this time, mam - I'm not sure what state they're in,' she said.

'Send my condolences to them – that poor family,' said Patsy.

When Mr Quinn opened his front door an hour later, he hugged Orla tightly.

'It's been far too long,' he said.

Orla passed on her mam's condolences, and she was sorry for their loss. They cried – the two of them broken by their daughter's death.

'I wrapped myself around them.'

'Will you have a tea?' asked Mr Quinn, pulling himself together.

'Ah no, I'm grand, thanks,' said Orla, then added, 'unless you're making one.'

She'd love one.

'Ah, sure, I'm always making one in this house,' he said, shuffling off to the kitchen in his slippers as Orla turned to his wife.

'I can't believe this has happened and keep asking myself why we went all these years without seeing each other – my heart is in pieces.'

'You girls tried to talk sense to her back then, but she was mad about Lars and wouldn't listen,' said Mrs Quinn.

'It's true, I was obsessed with him.'

Mr Quinn returned with the tea, and as

she drank, Orla wondered if they thought Lars was involved in Laura's murder or if she was the only one who'd jumped to that conclusion. Trying to gauge their thoughts, she asked if Laura was happy in her marriage and if she liked living in Sweden. Laura had always been such a home-bird - the idea of her living abroad seemed ridiculous. When they looked at each other nervously, Orla knew something was wrong.

'We begged her not to move to that godforsaken place, but she wouldn't listen. She was as obsessed with Lars as he was with her,' said Mrs Quinn.

'Ah, ma, I couldn't help it. We were all under his spell for a while.'

'Have you spoken to him since it happened?' asked Orla.

Mrs Quinn shook her head as tears gently rolled down her face.

'Jesus, no. We saw him at the station on Tuesday morning. I can't remember what he said if I'm honest. He rang here on Sunday - Laura told him I was in the hospital, and he wanted to wish me well, but that was a lie. He was checking on her – terribly suspicious he was, although I don't know what on God's earth, he thought she was doing.'

'Insecure prick.'

'Why did Laura tell him you were in the hospital if you weren't?' asked Orla.

'He didn't like her travelling. Actually, he didn't like her doing anything, but because he was at a conference somewhere,' she turned to her husband, 'where was it, Mick?'

'Brussels,' said Mick and Orla at the same time.

'Ah yeah, that's it. Well, anyway, Laura knew he'd be busy. Even Lars, bad as he is, wouldn't stop her from seeing her sick mother.'

Mr Quinn handed his wife a tissue to dry her eyes, and Orla felt awful for questioning them. Just as she was about to stop, Mrs Quinn said Laura was going to change everything.

'What do you mean, change everything?' asked Orla, looking from one to the other.

'She was getting away from him, had evidence to help her come home,' said Mrs

Quinn, dabbing at her tears with the hankie. 'Not much good to her now.'

'Evidence of what?' asked Orla, desperate to know, but Mr Quinn told his wife to shush.

Sensing his fear, Orla quickly tried to reassure him.

'I wish I'd told them, but I thought I was protecting them, and I didn't know I was about to die.'

'Please don't worry,' said Orla, 'whatever you say won't be repeated outside this room and even though the guards are investigating the case, I'd like to look into it as well.'

'Orla would get to the bottom of this.'

Then, Mr Quinn broke down, and the sight of it nearly finished Orla off. Closing his eyes tightly as if to stop the tears, he described the hell of watching his beautiful daughter ruined by that man.

'Ah, da stop. I can't handle this.'

'He's evil - it's behind the eyes, and the

terrifying part is how charming he is,' said Mr Quinn in a scratchy voice, full of emotion.

Orla remembered just how charming Lars was. She'd been so envious of Laura when she first met him - he seemed to have it all. Handsome, rich and charming. Then his true nature was revealed, and a small part of her felt relieved - she'd been right, the whole package didn't exist.

'Even though we hated visiting Sweden and staying in that house, we did it because Laura wouldn't have survived without us being there twice a year,' he continued.

What house? Where in Sweden?

'He was right, I wouldn't have.'

Orla's mind was full of questions, but she let him talk.

'I should have put a stop to it,' he cried, visibly shaking as he took another tissue from the pocket of his cardigan, 'I should have helped her, and now it's too late - my poor lass.' Big fat tears escaped from the corner of his eyes and rolled down his crumpled face to rest in his white beard. 'Did he kill her in the end?'

he asked, looking directly at Orla with heart-breaking misery in his eyes. 'Or was it someone else?' he whispered, defeated.

Orla didn't know, but she was determined to find out. Mrs Quinn held her husband's hand and took over, explaining how the guards thought it might be random, a robbery gone wrong - a case of Laura being in the wrong place at the wrong time, but Orla found that hard to believe.

'What evidence did she have?' asked Orla, trying not to sound pushy but needing to know.

'Something to help her escape him, that's all we know,' said Mrs Quinn.

'Why not just leave him? Why need evidence to do that?' asked Orla.

'Ha! If only.'

The look on both their faces confirmed her suspicion - the prick hadn't changed, which meant Laura's life was probably hell. They finished their tea in silence, and later, when Orla was leaving - the phone rang. Mr Quinn said he wasn't answering.

'You're the only person who knew Laura to ring today - mostly, it's the people from the papers, and we don't want to talk to them.'

Orla took the old-fashioned dial phone off the hook and asked if they were okay with that - they were.

'Do you want to come to mam's house for a few days and lay low?' she asked, thinking a break from the media attention might help them, and knowing her mother would be glad to help.

'No, thank you, love. Louise is on her way from Kildare with the boys, and my sisters are coming over this afternoon,' said Mrs Quinn, opening the door for her.

'Right, so, well, mind yourself,' said Orla, hugging the old woman.

Walking back to her car, Orla thought about Laura's older sister Louise and realised she'd forgotten all about her. Laura and Lou were close growing up, best friends as well as sisters. Lou had begged Laura to leave Lars, but she didn't listen to her either. Orla hoped they managed to stay close over the years, but she had a feeling Laura didn't stay close to anyone except Lars.

Laura

My poor mam and dad. I hated that they had to lose me, but I'd see them soon. Time worked differently where I was, and I was proof that it wasn't all over when you died. Instead of death being the end, it was the beginning of something - I didn't know what yet – but I knew it was going to be alright.

12 ~ LAURA

One Month Before
My Murder

In five months, I'd found out three kids were murdered in Dublin twenty years earlier, and my husband sex trafficked girls and secretly recorded important people in compromising positions. I assumed the men raping and sodomising the girls hadn't agreed to be recorded, so the only explanation I could reach was blackmail. Desperate to escape Lars, my evidence pile was growing, and even though I lived in a constant state of anxiety, terrified Lars or Erik would find out what I was doing, I was proud of myself.

Two domestic abuse recordings showed Lars subjecting me to brutal beatings. Marcus Ryan was primed to help me at a moment's notice. The information about the girl's bodies was documented and hidden. One hundred and seventy-two disgusting videos of young girls being brutalised and forced into sex by so-called, respectable, influential and often married men were downloaded onto my USB lipstick. I still hadn't found the locations of the rooms even though I went to the secret room as often as I could, disgusted to sometimes see more girls chained to the wall and searched the computer with a fine-tooth comb - the information simply wasn't there.

'What is next?' asked Hilda while we walked in the woods one afternoon.

I had no choice but to tell her everything - she needed to be my eyes while I downloaded the files. She stayed on high alert in the kitchen, watching the road in case Lars decided to come home early, or Erik turned up unannounced.

'I need to find the rooms and a way to get to Dublin. God, Hilda - what if I'd gone to the police in Sweden with my videos of Lars's abuse? Or the location of the girl's bodies? Or even told them about the room? There are senior police officers in those files, old men abusing those girls – Lars would have immediately known what I was up to. I can't think about what would've happened then.'

'It's so bad, and I'm proud of you, but please be careful,' said Hilda.

'I will,' I said, squeezing her hand.

Hilda kept watch the next day while I snuck into Lars's office to check his computer. Shaking with nerves, I pressed the return button on his keyboard, terrified an alarm would go off, a gate would slam, and I'd be trapped there, but nothing quite so dramatic happened. I didn't get past his password and left bitterly disappointed, but entirely by chance, an opportunity presented itself a week later. Having been ordered to Stockholm for drinks with the cabinet ministers and their wives at parliament, I was to arrive at Lars's office at four - *not a minute later*, so, deciding not to risk the traffic, I left early and went shopping in Stockholm.

Wandering around the shops, I reflected on how excited I'd been when I'd first moved to Sweden. Busy planning my wedding, I didn't have time for a job, and Lars took care of me. The first major red flag happened a week before flying to Dublin to marry, but I ignored it. Lars had organised drinks with some friends, and I, eager to please, be popular and fit in - happily chatted with everyone while laughing like a hyena and drinking far too much. When Lars dragged me into the toilet, I thought he was playing around or wanted a quick shag, and I was up for it, but his hand squeezed my arm so tight that I winced.

'If you ignore me for one more fucking minute, I will not be held responsible,' he spat.

'What's wrong?' I asked, shocked.

'Just stay by my fucking side and stop fucking flirting with everyone in the room,' he snarled as my cheeks reddened - had I been flirting?

When we got home, he slept in the spare room, ignored me for two days, and I nearly lost my mind. On day three, he asked if I was sorry, and I nodded - anything to get him to talk to me again. The second red flag occurred on our wedding day - I was talking to too many people - ignoring him - being overfriendly. My arms were bare in my dress, so he squeezed the top of my legs so hard that black fingerprint bruises appeared. Once again, I was flabbergasted. What had I done to piss him off?

He was an angel on honeymoon, so I convinced myself I'd imagined it, but soon after returning to Sweden, the monster reared its head for the first time.

'Hi babe,' I said when he arrived home early one afternoon. I was in the kitchen answering an email on my laptop. 'You won't believe this, but I got a job - a job,' I squealed, 'in Chanel – and I don't need to speak Swedish.'

I was so excited and had been dying to tell him all day, but the temperature in the room immediately plummeted.

'You didn't tell me you were looking for a job,' he said, his voice ice cold.

'Eh,' I answered, not sure what he meant. 'I didn't think you'd be interested - I know how busy you are, but now that the wedding is over, I thought it was time to support myself.'

'Tell them no. You're not working there.'

'But' I started until he grabbed my laptop from the counter and threw it in the bin.

'No wife of mine is working in a shop,' he said calmly and walked out of the room, leaving me gawking at him.

I retrieved my laptop from the bin and followed him into the lounge. He couldn't tell me what to do. I had to put a stop to this right now because our marriage wasn't going to work this way.

'Lars, you're being ridiculous. It's a part-time job and you know I love fashion. I don't need Swedish because of their international clientele, and it'll be fun.'

'You're not doing it,' he said, flicking through TV channels.

'Actually, I am, and there's nothing you can do to stop me,' I replied as I sat beside him and opened my laptop to write a big fat yes in my email response. 'You can't keep bossing me,' I began until my laptop was ripped from my hands, thrown to the tiled floor, and Lars grabbed my hair.

'Listen to me - I said you weren't getting that job, and I fucking meant it,' he sneered, his face inches from mine.

'What are you on about? It's just a part-time job.' I countered, utterly confused.

What happened next was so devastating that even thinking about it twenty years later made me cringe. It wasn't the most violent beating, but it was the first one - the hardest one and the fear I felt was all-consuming.

When I tried to get out of his clutches, Lars punched me in the stomach and threw me to the floor. I was so shocked that I just lay beside my broken laptop and stared at him. Then he kicked my ribs and cracked them, the pain unbearable, and I lay on the floor, sobbing. Without a word, he scooped up my useless laptop, put my phone in his pocket and left the apartment, locking the door behind him. He came back the following day with a bag of food, and I begged him to stop - to talk to me, but he ignored me and left again. I didn't see him for four days and couldn't leave the penthouse. The receptionist in the building ignored my calls, there was no external phone line, it was snowing outside, the streets were deserted, and I didn't know what to do. When Lars finally returned, he cried in my arms and begged forgiveness. I was so confused, broken and terrified that I just held him as he sobbed. A week later, he arranged for me to meet his friend at an art gallery - the shop work was forgotten, and my charity career began.

While deep in thought, I realised I'd arrived at Lars's office early. Even though I hated the idea of seeing Olga, I took the lift to his floor.

'Lars is in a meeting - he won't be finished for at least half an hour,' she said when I arrived in the outer office of Lars's parliament suite.

'That's fine, I have some private calls to make - I'll wait in his office,' I said, suddenly brimming with excitement. 'Don't disturb me,' I added, just in case the bitch got any ideas. 'Shit, shit, shit,' I closed the door and practically ran behind Lars's desk, thrilled when no password was needed for his laptop. Googling Solitaire, I opened the card game after seeing someone on CSI Miami do it a week earlier. I thought it was a great idea at the time, but I never imagined using it a week later. With the card game open, I clicked on different files to find anything non-government related. Ten minutes passed, then twenty - he'd be back any second. I was a nervous wreck and about to give up, admit defeat and run for my life until I noticed something quite unusual. Could it be hidden in plain sight? A small flower app sat amongst the many folders and files. When I looked closely, I realised it was a Lily – the name of the nightclub where it all began, surely not.

I clicked it open, scanned through the pages, and there they were. Properties in Copenhagen, Malmo, Belarus, Riga, and Stockholm - this had to be where they kept the girls. Retrieving my lipstick-disguised USB from my bag, and with my heart in my mouth, I downloaded the file. When I heard Lars outside talking to Olga, I thought it was game over.

'Come on,' I begged as the download completed and was back in my bag - just as the door opened, and Lars walked in. His eyes narrowed as he quickly strode towards his desk while I calmly clicked away. When he snatched his laptop off the desk, he saw the card game in play.

'Sorry, I'm a bit addicted to that lately,' I said, laughing and shaking my head.

Lars looked at my face, trying to determine if I was lying, but I was way ahead of him and didn't bat an eyelid. *Come at me, dickhead.* I smiled sweetly.

'I think we're a bit late – you ready?' I asked, walking out from behind his desk.

13 ~ ORLA

A thousand questions were on Orla's mind as she left Laura's parent's house. *What was Laura doing? Why the lies? Evidence of what? What happened in the apartment? Who was the solicitor? Who killed her? Why had she been killed?*

When she arrived home, she made some tea and finally told her mother what had happened on that awful night so many years before.

'Jesus, tonight, that's a terrible story - why didn't you call the fecking guards?' asked Patsy, astonished.

'So many reasons, ma. We were terrified - young - they threatened us with guns - Laura asked us not to say anything - begged us to forget the whole thing,' said Orla.

Imagine thinking you could forget about something like that? It spread like cancer - trauma buried deep that grew roots and affected them in ways they could never have imagined. No wonder their friendship imploded. Orla didn't mention the change in Laura within weeks of meeting Lars. To begin with, Laura was excited and feeling the effects of being in love. Her friends were thrilled and jealous – he was rich and handsome and spoiled Laura rotten, but she seemed different somehow, and they couldn't put their finger on it. If anyone mentioned it, Laura would immediately brush it off.

'I'm grand, we're grand, he's an angel, and I can't believe how lucky I am,' she'd say so convincingly that they began questioning it themselves.

'I actually thought he was my soul mate - the love of my life.'

Then the nightclub happened - the real Lars Karlsson was revealed, and the penny dropped. They hadn't imagined it, but Laura still denied it. Orla, Niamh, and Audrey had been traumatised by what happened that night - Maggie was annihilated by it, but Laura seemed unfazed. She broke up with Lars, but only because Orla and the others shamed her into doing so. Then, she became preoccupied and unavailable, and they were worried sick about her. One afternoon, the four of them, led by Orla, turned up unannounced at Laura's flat, confronted her and discovered the truth - the breakup had been a farce, and she'd been back with Lars for months.

'After everything he did?' Maggie had asked incredulously.

'He has PTSD, that's why he did it, and he said the others just panicked - they didn't mean to scare you,' said Laura.

'And you believe that?' asked Niamh, raging.

'He didn't know it was me. I triggered something when I slapped him. Anyway, I love him. I'm sorry, girls, but I can't help it, and he feels the same way,' said Laura and at that moment, Orla knew she was lost to them.

Laura refused to see anything other than the prince she believed Lars to be, and very soon, their friendship began to fall apart. Whenever they made plans, Laura would cancel at the last minute.

'I had to - Lars hated those girls because I loved them.'

For the rest of them, it became too hard. They'd meet and talk nonstop about Laura, or they'd meet and try not to talk about Laura. The conversations became strained, and rightly or wrongly, they wanted to distance themselves from it. At the time, they didn't realise they were distancing themselves from each other, but that's what happened.

'Even so, you should have called the guards,' said Patsy disapprovingly.

'Ah, ma, will you stop the lights. Not in a fecking million years did we think she'd end up married to him,' said Orla, annoyed because her mam was right - they should have called the guards.

'They wouldn't have helped, and I'd still have married him.'

'Do you think he murdered her?' asked Patsy.

Orla explained how Lars was in Brussels

at the time of Laura's death, but she couldn't help thinking he was involved.

'How could he be in two places at the same time?' she asked.

'I don't know,' said Patsy, then added. 'And you haven't spoken to any of the girls since then?'

'Not one. Audrey O Brien ringing on Monday night was the first time I've spoken to any of them in twenty years,' said Orla.

Patsy thought that was the stupidest thing she'd ever heard, but Orla didn't rise to it. Her mam had a way of pressing her buttons - Orla was sure their close relationship was because they lived in different countries. She brushed it off and suggested they go out for dinner.

'You go with your mammy and your sister - I'll stay here,' said Joe in response to an invitation.

'Are you sure da? You don't fancy a nice bowl of pasta and a glass of wine?' asked Orla with a knowing smile.

'I do not - I wouldn't eat that stuff. There's leftover stew - that'll do me.'

Orla laughed as she called a taxi, ringing

her sister on the way. Breda was two years older and didn't know Orla was home until she got the call. Not needing to be asked twice, she was waiting at the front gate when the taxi pulled up.

'Do I get to see my nephew and niece?' called Orla from the back seat of the taxi, but Breda waved her off.

'See them tomorrow - I need a glass of wine,' she said.

'Ohhh, so do I. A glass of wine would be lovely right now.'

Over dinner, Orla filled her in on what happened to Laura.

'Jesus, tonight. It makes you think, doesn't it? How quickly your life can be snatched from you,' said Breda.

Orla nodded. It certainly did. Poor Laura.

'Tell her what you told me this afternoon,' said Patsy and Orla threw a, *for God's sake*, look at her mam.

It wasn't that she didn't want to tell Breda - she just couldn't be bothered to dredge through the whole sorry tale - again.

'Tell me,' Breda insisted, and knowing there was no way out of it, Orla gave her the short version while throwing daggers at her mam for opening her mouth.

'My God, you went through that in a Dublin nightclub?' asked Breda, dipping chunks of bread into balsamic vinegar and popping them into her mouth. 'God, this is gorgeous,' she waved at the basket before continuing. 'It sounds like something out of a film. Why didn't you call the guards?' she asked, echoing their mam's question and causing Orla to roll her eyes at Patsy's smug face. Once again, Orla explained why they didn't. 'That's incredible - I always wondered what happened to you five. You were thick as thieves, and then you stopped seeing each other altogether. You moved to London, and God knows what happened to the rest,' she said, finishing the bread and moving on to the olives.

'Well, we know Laura ended up in Sweden, married to a psycho and is now dead,' said Orla sadly. 'And Audrey O'Brien is now Sergeant O'Brien.'

'What?' shrieked Breda. 'Audrey O'Brien

is a guard - no fecking way.'

She screamed, laughing, and when Orla thought about it, she realised it was funny. Audrey was the last person you'd expect to join An Garda Siochana. She'd been such a rebel in their youth - very anti-establishment. Orla didn't know what happened to her other two friends - she'd find out on Monday.

They drank more wine than they should have on a school night and ate delicious food, and as the evening wore on, Orla's thoughts drifted to Laura. She was tempted to ring Audrey for an update but decided to wait until Maggie and Niamh were there. When the waiter placed the bill on the table, Orla's phone beeped.

'A text from James,' she said astonished.

She hadn't heard a whisper from James in two years. He lived in Scotland with his girlfriend - that was all she knew about him.

'What the fuck does he want?' asked Breda, her voice laced with anger.

Orla turned her phone to show the short text message: *Can we talk? James X*

No, hello. No, how are you? It might be funny if it wasn't so typical of him. In hindsight and with some deep self-reflection, Orla realised their whole relationship had been about what James needed.

'Don't answer that fucker,' instructed Breda, swigging back the last of her wine.

Breda still hadn't forgiven him for what he put Orla through, but Orla had forgiven him, more for her sake than his. She couldn't handle the negative energy of a broken heart, and anyway, Neil was proving to be a million times better, not only in the sack but in every aspect of their relationship – she was definitely falling in love again. Typing '*no*' into her phone, she pressed send and smiled at her mother and sister.

'Such a wise owl.'

'Are you sure you're over that one?' asked Patsy, then added, 'never liked him.'

'The lies were hard to take, I suppose. He was so excited about buying the house while secretly shagging someone in the office - the neck of him. Anyway, I've put it behind me now and moved on. Honestly, it was one of the best lessons of my life. Forced me to let go and stop trying to control everything,' said Orla, and when Breda demanded an explanation, Orla promised one, but not tonight - that story was for another time.

'Right so,' said Patsy, looking thoughtful before asking, 'so, when will we meet Neil?'

'When I find out who murdered Laura, I'll invite him over to Dublin for a weekend,' said Orla.

'Great – can't wait to meet him,' said Breda.

Laura
There was something to be said for listening to your instinct. I knew Lars was bad news when I met him. No one liked him, and I mean no one - my friends, my family, my work colleagues. At the time, I wondered how they could all be so wrong. How stupid it seems when you're dead.

A DUBLIN NIGHTCLUB - TWENTY YEARS AGO

Orla's bank account had been running at zero for days, and she dreaded asking Maggie for another loan, but what was she to do? Audrey's email suggested an extended lunch - a session if you like and Orla had no choice.

'Don't be stupid, of course, I'll lend you,' said Maggie when Orla plucked up the courage to ring.

'I'll pay you back on Monday,' she promised, mortified.

The volley of emails had made Orla laugh. Audrey said the table was booked for 2pm. Maggie, who knew her friends well, suggested 4pm. Niamh said 2pm was late enough, and Orla suggested a compromise of 3pm. Laura didn't respond - as was the norm these days. Since meeting her new boyfriend, she'd been full of mystery and, quite frankly… acting odd. Her friends were happy for her, but also slightly concerned.

'It's just love sickness,' said Maggie when they'd last bitched about it.

'I don't know – something not quite right - I can't put my finger on it,' said Orla.

'Well, he's rich and gorgeous – I don't blame her for falling so hard,' said Niamh.

'I'm with Orla – something's off,' said Audrey.

As they sat down for lunch in The Saddle Room restaurant in the Shelbourne Hotel, Audrey wore her usual black jeans and black Dock Martins. Niamh, on a half day from work, wore office attire. Maggie, as always, looked immaculate in cream trousers and a navy blazer. Orla's ancient John Rocha brown cord dress - bought for a fiver in the posh Oxfam near Rathfarnham- had delighted Orla until Laura turned up - an hour late and looked like a supermodel. An ensemble of grey cashmere - her dress, coat and scarf were obviously new and definitely expensive. Long black leather boots with four-inch heels added insult to injury, but the Chanel handbag hanging on her shoulder was the limit for Niamh.

'Is that fucking real?' she asked, aghast.

Laura nodded, opening the bag so they could see the matching purse inside.

'Isn't it gorgeous,' she gushed.

Orla smiled, happy for their fashion queen, as did Maggie - Audrey couldn't care less, but Niamh was fuming.

'This is getting out of hand - how much money does Lars actually have?' she asked, not bothering to hide her jealousy.

Laura's shopping addiction was off the charts since meeting Lars. Fashion had always been her thing, but she'd been unable to afford couture until Lars came along. Now, he took her to Brown Thomas so often that they were convinced he owned shares in the company.

'Loads,' said Laura, her eyes lighting up. 'In fact, he wants to buy us lunch today,' she added, waving his credit card and ordering a bottle of champagne.

'Well. Okay, then,' said Niamh, slightly mollified.

'Yay,' said Orla, thinking she could reimburse Maggie.

'That's nice of him,' said Audrey, her tone sounding suspicious to everyone except Laura.

The champagne arrived, and lunch

started with an air of celebration. Maggie and Niamh had recently turned twenty-five. Orla was reaching that milestone the next day, and Laura and Audrey within a few weeks.

'Happy birthday to us,' said Laura, raising a glass.

After a long and rather boozy lunch, Laura insisted they see the latest spring collection she'd spent most of the morning trying on. Under protest, and because her boyfriend's credit card had funded their day so far, they dashed down Grafton Street in the rain, trouped to the first-floor designer department of Brown Thomas, and followed Laura as she pointed out designers like a pro. However, their enthusiasm soon waned as Lars wasn't picking up that bill.

'Let's go to the Westbury for a Mojito,' suggested Orla.

After the Westbury, Audrey suggested The Old Stand, where her favourite band were playing. After that, Laura insisted they gate-crash Lars's night out with the boys. When they got to the busy club, there was no standing in line like the common folk - no, sir, they'd moved up in the world and walked straight to the top of the queue. Lars ran security there, and although slightly possessive of Laura, with free lunches and free admission to nightclubs, they'd all decided he was handy to know. Walking straight past the ticket booth, the five women were halfway up the stairs to Lily's member's bar when a commotion behind them made them pause. Two burly-looking bouncers sprinted up the stairs after them.

'Sorry ladies, the member's bar is closed for a private party,' said one bouncer, guiding them back down.

'But you can use the main nightclub,' said the other.

'Fine by me,' said Audrey, shrugging her shoulders.

Orla did the same - no skin off her nose. Maggie and Niamh were already walking back down, but Laura looked at the men suspiciously, then ran up the stairs and through the double doors. Orla and the others followed with the bouncers hot on their heels. The scenes that greeted them were simply unbelievable and something Orla would never forget.

Scene one: Young girl spread across a

table – Lars naked from the waist with jeans open, grinding himself into girl – girl's knickers around her ankles – Lars's hands between her legs as, like a starving baby, he suckled her huge breasts.

Scene two: On a sofa behind Lars - Erik bouncing naked girl up and down on his colossal penis. Girl in impressive reverse cowgirl position – Erik's head thrown back and eyes closed – girl's eyes rolling in her head from pleasure or drugs – Orla suspected the latter.

Scene three: Terrified girl sitting between two men - champagne bottles open on table - tray of cocaine on table – men ignoring girl and watching sex shows - dance music blaring – rest of bar empty - as in completely empty.

'What the fuck,' Orla silently mouthed to Audrey.

When Lars came up for air and noticed the five women staring at him, he froze – except his eyes moved to the bouncers standing behind them.

'Someone's getting fired tonight,' Audrey mouthed back.

Lars whistled at Erik, who pushed the

girl off him. She fell to the floor and scurried around for her clothes while Erik pulled up his jeans and tucked his very aroused dick back inside. Slowly walking towards them, Orla looked at her friends, *ewe - vile.* He whispered to the bouncers, who left the room and closed the door, as the first alarm bell rang in Orla's head.

Laura's eyes were on Lars, but Orla's were on the girls – they were too young to be in a nightclub. She felt relieved when they put their coats on – they needed to leave. Orla turned to her friends and nodded towards the door to do the same thing, but Laura wouldn't move. She stared at Lars with devastation written all over her face. One word from him was all it took, '*Laura*' and she slapped him.

'How could you do this to me?' she cried.

Initially caught off guard, Lars stumbled back but quickly recovered and grabbed her arms.

'Relax, baby. It's not what you think,' he said, and Orla almost laughed - *yeah, right.*

When he tried to pull her into his arms, Laura jumped back.

'Don't fucking touch me,' she said, sounding broken.

Audrey led her towards the door, but just as they were through and free of the whole situation, Laura stomped back to Lars like the fiery redhead she was. Orla expected her to tell him to fuck off - that she never wanted to see him again - hoped he died in a car crash and rotted in hell - the usual stuff, but what she did next caused a catalyst of events that would change their lives forever. In magnificent Laura style, she walloped him across the face – this time, the slap would definitely leave a handprint. Lars didn't move - he just stared as if trying to work something out before turning away.

'I never want to see you a...,'

Laura didn't get the last word past her lips because as he turned back and, with the ferocity of a high-speed train, Lars punched her square in the face and launched her to the other side of the room. Pandemonium ensued as Audrey tried to get at Lars, but Erik caught her and threw her against a wall. When Niamh attempted to get a swipe, Erik punched her on the side of the head and knocked her to the floor. The young girls screamed - *why were they still here?* The other men jumped up and knocked over a table full of champagne. Maggie ran to Laura's side, but Orla stood still as if watching the scene in slow motion.

Then, as if waking from a trance, Lars shook his head, looked around and clocked Laura lying on the floor - unconscious. His face dropped as he shouted for everyone to shut the fuck up, and with the force of his roar, everyone shut the fuck up. Erik stood in front of Lars, his hands out in protection mode.

'Just calm the fuck down,' said Lars, quietly this time.

The young girls sobbed louder, and Lars whispered to Erik, who rounded them up and, with the other two men, took them from the room.

'Ouch, that fucking hurt,' said Niamh trying to sit up.

Audrey untangled herself from the tables. Lars went to Laura, who was starting to rouse, and Orla finally sprang into action and went behind the bar. She wrapped some ice in a couple of bar towels, handed one to Niamh and brought the other to Laura, who rubbed her jaw.

'What happened?' asked Laura, looking

from Lars to her friends in confusion.

'We need to call the guards,' said Maggie, taking her phone from her bag, but as soon as she flipped it open, Lars knocked it from her hand.

'No fucking guards,' he said.

Maggie froze, Niamh froze, and Audrey looked at Orla - shit.

'Put your phone away, Maggie - we're leaving. Laura needs to get to the hospital,' said Orla, acting braver than she felt.

A few minutes later, Erik returned with the other men and locked the door behind him. He said something to Lars in Swedish, and all four men walked to the other side of the room. Orla couldn't understand their language but recognised the universal term for, *fuck's sake*. Lars was furious - something was definitely wrong.

'We're leaving,' called Audrey, walking to the door, and rattling the handle.

Erik slowly walked towards her with Lars and the others behind him. In his hand and pointing towards the floor was a gun. Was it real? Orla could hardly believe her eyes as alarm bells rang like church bells in her head.

'Laura needs a hospital, Lars,' said Audrey with a shaky voice.

Niamh was okay, a little bruised and battered, but Laura, at the very least, had a concussion and possibly a fractured fucking jaw. Ignoring Audrey, Lars bent down and scooped Laura into his arms. Then, as if she was made of crystal, he gently placed her on one of the sofas.

'No one's going anywhere,' he said, then nodded at Erik, who, with a gleam in his eye, waved his gun in their faces.

'Phones,' he said, 'and over to that sofa - we'll take care of Laura.'

No one moved until the other two men produced guns. *They all had one - how cute.* Erik smirked as he pressed his against Orla's cheek.

'Don't think I won't use this, sweetheart - all I need is a reason,' he whispered.

With a churning stomach and shaking hands, Orla handed over her phone. The others did the same, and on trembling legs, they walked towards the sofa and sat down.

'Lars, what's going on?' asked Laura, groggy and confused.

'It's okay, baby, don't worry. I just can't

have the guards here tonight,' said Lars, tenderly pushing a piece of her hair behind her ear.

Orla, Niamh, and Audrey looked at each other bewildered. Did he really just do that? Maggie was hanging on by a thread, her eyes glued to the floor and her arms wrapped tightly around her body. Erik handed a chair to Lars, who placed it between both sofas and sat down. Four girls on one, and Laura on the other. Orla was reminded of a mafia film. Were these men actually going to kill them? Lars seemed to ponder the situation while Erik and his cronies stood behind - their guns displayed proudly.

'It's such a shame you came here tonight,' he finally said, and Orla felt sick.

What did that mean?

'I wanted to surprise you,' whispered Laura.

'Baby, you need to listen better. I said I was unavailable tonight and that the boys needed to let off some steam,' said Lars as if talking to an actual baby.

Orla always imagined the boys letting off steam might be a few pints while watching football, not a group orgy with cocaine and underage girls. Lars was silent again as if thinking about his next move, and Orla wanted to throw up - she'd never been so terrified. When Erik whispered in his ear, Orla made her move.

'Lars, Laura needs a hospital,' she said, 'she's concussed.'

'Shut the fuck up. I said we'd take care of Laura,' said Erik.

'Shhh, Erik,' said Lars, rubbing his face, then added. 'I have something else to deal with tonight, so you can go, but don't contact the guards, or there will be consequences.'

The threat in his eyes was crystal clear.

'Lars,' repeated Laura.

'You're going to the hospital now, baby - tell the doctor you fell over, okay?' he said, sounding as gentle as a lamb. When she nodded, Orla almost laughed. 'Your phones will be at Laura's flat tomorrow afternoon.'

'Give us back our phones. We won't call the guards, but we're not going to Laura's flat,' said Audrey, sounding authoritative, and she hadn't joined the guards yet.

'Then stay here all night,' said Lars, scooping Laura into his arms again and walking towards the back of the bar while whispering in her ear.

That was the last straw for Maggie, who curled into a ball and sobbed. With no other choice, they agreed to Lars's terms, and twenty minutes later, practically ran out of the club, into a taxi and straight to St James Hospital. They didn't call the guards.

14 ~ LAURA

One Week Before
My Murder

The week before my murder was probably the most frantic week of my life. Last Monday, Lars mentioned a conference in Brussels, and I knew it was my chance. I flew into action, making sure everything was ready, and waited until the day before he left to ring him at work. As his mobile rang, my nerves were in shreds, *now or never,* but Olga answered, and I rolled my eyes.

'Laura - how are you?' she asked and explained how Lars was in an important meeting and wasn't taking calls - her sweet tone laced with poison.

Olga thought regularly fucking my husband was part of her job and didn't realise I knew all about it. She was welcome to Lars, but her two-facedness bothered me. *Power-grabbing bitch.*

'I need to speak to Lars now,' I said, in no mood for her games.

The tone of my voice warned her not to fuck with me today. I heard her moving around, then mumbling, a door closing, and Lars was on the line.

'Laura - are you okay?' he asked, sounding alarmed.

Using every acting skill I could muster - I sobbed down the phone.

'My mam is sick, Lars - she's been rushed to hospital. It's her heart.' Sob. 'What if she dies?' Sob. 'Oh my God, Lars, what if she dies?' Sob, sob, sob.

It was a risk, but I knew he wouldn't check. As far as Lars was concerned, I would never lie to him.

'Calm down, Laura,' he said, then instructed me to explain the details.

'She's having an operation. Can I go, love? Please,' I begged - my dignity well and truly abandoned. 'I need to see her - I could go to the airport with you, get a flight to Dublin and be back on Tuesday morning.'

Silence. *The bastard.* I'd backed him into a corner, and he knew it.

'They're operating now?' he asked.

'Yeah – Louise just rang. Please, Lars,' I begged again, sobbing even louder this time.

How could he say no to me seeing my sick mam? He had a mother, and he was close to her. I held my breath.

'Get a flight for Sunday morning – your family are with her, and I'm not leaving until late Saturday,' he said.

Dickhead. I wanted to scream at the prick, at the unfairness of my life - he couldn't just say yes – he had to play his fucking power games, but I agreed - what choice did I have?

'Okay, I'll go straight to the hospital from the airport. Thank you, love,' I said, the words almost sticking in my throat.

He said he'd see me later, and when I hung up, Astrid high-fived me.

'He fell for it?' she asked, and I nodded.

We were hiding in one of the empty patient rooms, taking a well-needed break from an early shift. Having checked that no one was hovering outside, I quickly used Astrid's phone to ring Marcus Ryan and confirm our appointment on Monday morning. Marcus didn't know about my evidence to put my husband in prison and cause trouble for a lot of important people – I wanted to tell him in person. When he asked why I hadn't left Lars before, I told him I used to, and he got my point.

In the early days, when I worked out that Lars was never sorry - no matter how hard he cried - I started to run. I never got far – either Erik or the police would find me and bring me back. The price paid for my disobedience was catastrophic. As well as a beating, Lars would tell my family I was at a retreat in Switzerland for my mental health and lock me away for weeks. No phone, books, TV, nothing except the room I was in and three meals a day. He'd instruct me to phone my family once a week. A few minutes of - *Hey, I'm fine. I'm missing you all. I'll be in touch when I'm back in Sweden.* I stopped running after the fifth *trip to Switzerland.*

'Let's get back to work before anyone misses us,' said Astrid when I finished the call.

It was finally happening. I felt elated and nervous at the same time. Getting away from Lars was all that mattered now. Hopefully, the threat of ruining his career with my domestic abuse videos would be enough to convince him to let me go. Then I'd tell the guards where the girls were buried in Dublin and give them the USB stick to stop Lars and his gang from trafficking innocent girls in Sweden. Since discovering the location of the houses, I'd done some detective work on Google Earth and discovered all the properties from Lars's laptop were remote.

'I'm meeting Marcus on Monday morning,' I told Astrid as we walked down the corridor to the wards.

'You're so brave, Laura,' said Astrid.

I really wasn't - I felt scared every second of the day. Astrid didn't know about the trafficking - only about the conversation overheard and the videos recorded. To protect her, I'd kept the rest to myself. When I got home a few hours later, I checked the secret phone, which was safely hidden inside one of my boots - in their box – at the back of my closet. I'd been terrified Lars might send Erik to do a spot check. Over the years, Erik would randomly turn up and ransack everything I owned. On Lars's instruction, he'd go through my handbags and phone - flip open my books, etc. I don't know what Lars thought to find, and even though it had stopped in recent years, I felt as jittery as a bug. When Lars came home later that night, he was extra nice and suggested we go for dinner.

'Sure, just let me get dressed,' I said, as if I had any choice.

At the restaurant, people gravitated toward Lars. He pretended it bothered him, but he secretly loved the attention. Of course, Erik was in the background, never far from Lars. He was in love with him - I knew it, he knew it, and Lars knew it. I sometimes wondered if they'd had the odd shag over the years. I didn't think so, as Lars was too hetero, but with these two bastards - nothing would have surprised me.

'What did the doctors say about your mother?' asked Lars over dinner. 'Does she need to be moved to a private hospital? Let me know, and I'll take care of it,' he added - money no object.

'No, she's in good hands - I'm going straight there on Sunday morning - she's heavily sedated. Thank you for letting me go, love. It means the world to me,' I said, the lies rolling off my tongue.

How convincing I sounded - the prick actually thought he'd broken me, that I wouldn't dare disobey or lie to my master - *fucking asshole*. Maybe I'd take an acting class when I got away from him and be an actress in Ireland.

After dinner, we went home, where Lars made love to me, and I wanted to puke. I was used to being fucked by him - his gentleness was harder to stomach. The next day, *thank the lord*, he was preoccupied with the conference and spent most of the day on the phone in his office. I kept out of his way, quietly packing my case for Ireland. *Just go*, I begged on tenterhooks. I held my breath when he walked into the kitchen to say goodbye.

'Text me when you get to Dublin and give my regards to your mother. Erik will get you on Tuesday morning. I want you to stay in Stockholm for a few days next week,' he commanded, and I nodded, but he wasn't finished. 'And when you're next at the hospital, tell them you're no longer available. You can work notice, but my new job will mean more commitment from you, and I need you by my side.'

Always finding ways to punish me - I was devastated, but I quickly hid it, smiled, and nodded again. *Such an obedient wife.* So, he was getting the Deputy Prime Minister role - I wasn't surprised. No doubt, he'd blackmailed his way to the very top. His new position meant nothing to me - I wanted to be as far away from him and his political mates as possible. When he finally left, I went into my bedroom, retrieved the phone, slipped it into my suitcase, and got the last bits ready for my flight the next day. Astrid came to dinner - I met her at the door and jumped into her car for five minutes to discuss my overall plan.

'Just tell the solicitor everything - Lars has no influence in Ireland,' said Astrid when I told her I was afraid.

'What if he gets away with it? Erik wouldn't think twice about killing me, and he can make people disappear - that's why Lars keeps him so close,' I said.

'They murdered three girls, Laura. I don't think even Lars has the power to get away with something like that. You know where the bodies are, and the videos clearly show him beating you - this is good evidence.' said Astrid, trying to reassure me, but she didn't know the half of it.

The idea of taking on a gang of sex traffickers was terrifying. Lars and Erik had been doing this for a long time without being caught. Could little old Laura Quinn from Ireland really stop them? The thought made me nauseous.

At the airport the following day, I waited to board my flight and, fascinated, watched the people around me - all free and living their lives. Did they know my terrible secret? Did they know I was the victim of horrific abuse? Did they know my husband was a sadist, a sex trafficker and a murderer and that I was going to Ireland to save my life? It felt like they did.

15 ~ ORLA

After four days in Ireland, Orla missed her dog and rang her neighbour to check on him. Jan said Ray was having the time of his life running around with Hugo and Bertie - her teenage boys. Her dogs, Prince and King, were far too old to entertain Ray and his never-ending energy. Before they hung up, Jan mentioned a bouquet of flowers delivered to Orla's house.

'They're at your front door - I only noticed them this morning,' she said.

'Get them and put them on your table - they're likely to do with my books,' said Orla.

Ten minutes later, Jan sent a photo of a card that read. *Please can we talk? I miss you. James X.* Orla deleted the picture, *fuck off, James.*

'Good woman - he sounds like a prick.'

In full investigative mode, she had a

list of questions and was trying to figure out what Laura was doing. Why was she seeing a solicitor in Ireland when she lived in Sweden? The only word that came to mind was - divorce. Who was this solicitor? What did Laura tell him? Would he speak to Orla? Laura's parents were confident Lars abused Laura. As far as Orla was concerned, once an abuser – always an abuser. What evidence did Laura have against Lars? Why did she stay in an apartment? Picking up the phone, Orla rang Audrey for an update.

'I can't say too much - it's confidential,' said Audrey when Orla grilled her for information. 'But one thing is certain - there's something off about this. The theory at the station is that Laura was followed to her apartment and robbed. Her jewellery was gone, and according to Lars, it was very valuable, but the coffee cups keep sticking in my mind. Why two cups? To me, that suggests Laura made coffee for her killer.'

'I made coffee for my killer. Why can't I remember who it was?'

Orla agreed it sounded dodgy.

'Mrs Quinn said Laura had evidence to use against Lars that would help her come home. She wanted to leave him, Audrey - that much is clear. Did Lars say anything when you spoke to him?' asked Orla.

'Not a word - and what evidence?' asked Audrey.

'Mrs Quinn didn't know,' said Orla.

'Why didn't I just email everything to my sister? Was I being careful or paranoid? I didn't know anymore - years of living with Lars had blurred the lines.

'Why need evidence to leave him?' asked Audrey.

'My question exactly. Mr Quinn said Lars is basically an evil bastard who abused Laura and that Laura wouldn't have survived if they didn't visit her in Sweden twice a year,' said Orla.

'Fucking hell,' said Audrey, then, 'so, what was Laura doing in Dublin? Everyone's being super careful around here because of who Lars is, and they've no reason to suspect him.'

'No one has - Lars is very good at hiding who he truly is.'

'Have you spoken to Laura's solicitor?' asked Orla.

'Not yet - he's been away on business - back today. Dave and I have an appointment this afternoon,' said Audrey.

'I think he knows something - what's his name?" asked Orla.

'I can't tell you until we've spoken to him at least,' said Audrey.

They wrapped up their conversation and agreed to catch up the following day. Orla got back to writing and, an hour later, while fully engrossed, glanced up to see her mam walking into the kitchen, looking like she'd seen a ghost. Orla immediately jumped up.

'What's wrong?' she asked.

Patsy didn't answer. She just handed over the pile of envelopes in her hand and sat back down.

'Jesus, I need a cup of tea,' she said,

standing up again.

The four envelopes had The Shelbourne Hotel emblem printed on the left-hand corner, which was odd, but even more so was Orla's name, Audrey's, Niamh's, and Maggie's, care of Mrs Reed at this address.

'Turn them over,' said Patsy, filling the kettle, and when Orla saw what was written on the back of each envelope, she understood her mother's shock.

It simply said...*love from Laura.*

'My letters - I'd forgotten all about them.'

Orla stared at the letters, feeling utterly confused, then opened the one addressed to her and began to read.

Laura

Hopefully, Marcus would give Audrey some answers. He knew about the abuse, had seen the videos, and he'd tell them I asked about the sex trafficking. It was frustrating that I still couldn't communicate with Orla, but I was confident something would happen soon.

16 ~ LAURA

The Day Before My Murder

In twenty-four hours, I'd be dead, and I'd kick my own arse for not realising it was coming. Even while standing in the passport queue at Dublin airport, I had a feeling of being followed - had my darling husband sent someone to spy on me? *Stop being a mad paranoid bitch,* I reprimanded myself while slowly approaching the booth. I handed over my Irish passport with a shaking hand. *God, I was a wreck.*

'Good morning, Missus - been anywhere nice?' asked the border control officer, with bright red hair and freckles on his face and hands, the only part of him visible beneath his uniform.

'Sweden, I live there,' I said distractedly.

'Lovely, well, welcome home,' he said, returning my passport.

I managed a meek *thank you* before continuing to the arrival hall. A large sign with the gates of Guinness's Brewery was next to welcome me home and forced me to smile. I was home - my beloved Dublin. Sweden was beautiful, but it wasn't Ireland. It wasn't the familiar sights, the lousy weather, and my family. *One step at a time, you can do this.* I repeated my mantra in my head to stop myself from freaking out. Two days to leave my husband - save countless girls from a life of drugs and prostitution - find the bodies of three murdered girls - and hopefully have Lars thrown into prison for the rest of his life.

'Jesus, help me,' I whispered.

Glancing behind, I noticed a familiar-looking face - was that man on my flight? I quickened my pace and almost laughed when a small child ran from her mother's arms to greet him. *Jesus, the madness is taking over.* I tucked my hair into my black winter coat, pulled up my hood to protect me from the driving rain, and walked outside to join another queue - for a taxi this time. After the initial pleasantries that came with most Irish taximen, we drove to the apartment I rented in Grand Canal. However, when the car pulled up in front of the massive glass building, I stayed seated.

'Can you wait for a few minutes?' I asked. 'I'll pay extra.'

The taximan shrugged his shoulders.

'Grand,' he said, watching me through his rear-view mirror. 'Everything alright?'

'Yeah, I just need to make sure I wasn't followed,' I said, past caring and sure he was used to all sorts of weirdos.

I looked behind again, and the coast was clear. I paid the man and practically ran through the revolving doors. The key to my apartment was in a lock box in a vast, empty reception area. I got it and ran towards the lift as two men stepped in.

'Hold the lift,' I called.

The strangers smiled - I smiled back, then inhaled the divine smell of their takeaway coffee. As we ascended, the glass elevator revealed beautiful views of the city.

'Wow,' I said, amazed.

'Great view, isn't it,' said one of them, then asked if I was moving in.

Similar in age to me, he wore cute round glasses and had messy brown hair like an older version of Harry Potter or a gay version with pink cords, a bright yellow puffer jacket, and red Converse. I assumed the man beside him was his boyfriend - tall and slim with wavey blond hair tucked into a grey beanie - he wore a black leather jacket with blue jeans and looked like a biker.

'No, just visiting from Sweden for a couple of days. I've rented one of the apartments here,' I said, not used to people being so direct.

In Sweden, no one would dare ask about your business.

'Ohh, how lovely, I've heard Sweden is gorge. It's definitely on our *to-visit* list,' said Mr Pink Cords.

'Yeah, it's beautiful, but I prefer it here,' I said, somewhat bursting his bubble.

When we got to the sixth floor, I took a deep breath and slowly exited the lift - half expecting to see one of Lars's men waiting to bag me up and drag me home. I knew my husband might have been playing mind games in allowing me to come home, or he might have changed his mind and sent someone to fetch me. That's how powerless I was in my own life. The couple behind watched - I could sense waves of curiosity radiating towards me as I slowly walked down the long hall to my apartment. When they followed, I almost ran until it became apparent we were neighbours.

'Well, I'm Adam, and this is the hubby, Donal - you know where we are if you need a cup of sugar,' said Adam, opening the door opposite mine.

'Thanks, I'm Laura,' I said, quickly letting myself inside, shutting the door and sliding down it.

Jesus, Mary, and holy St Joseph - when had I become so fucking afraid of the world? After a few minutes and a good talking to, *get your shit together, Laura,* I wandered around the gorgeous apartment - as luxurious as any five-star hotel but with more privacy for the wife of a well-known politician. An open-plan lounge, diner and kitchen had floor-to-ceiling windows that looked out to the river Liffey below. Much to my delight, a hamper stacked with coffee, milk, fruit, Irish chocolates, and wine sat on the kitchen island. *Welcome Astrid Nilsson*, it said on a small card, and I smiled, thinking about Ast. My incognito for the weekend, and my wingman. I texted her to let her know I'd arrived, then quickly unpacked, showered and changed into jeans, Ugg boots, and a gorgeous Gucci sweater, baby pink with dark pink trim on the sleeve - it was fabulous. My husband might be a dangerous psychopath, but he was rich, and fashion was my passion. Lars's black Amex card had been my only friend for years, and I'd never felt guilty about spending his money - until recently. Discovering his source of income had left a bad taste in my mouth, and I'd been using my own money since.

Back in the kitchen, the lure of fresh coffee was too much to resist. I made a steaming mug, settled on the sofa by the window and drank while enjoying the views of Dublin and the Irish chocolates. When finished, the controlled and defeated version of me automatically washed the mug until it dawned on me - *he's not here.* I stopped mid-clean and dropped it in the sink, *fuck you, Lars.*

Half an hour later, while wandering through the streets of Dublin in the freezing rain, I felt like a tourist. The cold bit my face, but I didn't care - the deserted Sunday morning streets helped me relax, and I reflected on my life as I walked.

Twenty years of convincing myself that Lars wasn't the worst - that there was some good in him, only to discover exactly what kind of man he was - I felt like a fool. Crossing the road towards Grafton Street, I paused - Maggie's bookshop was around the corner. Should I have a quick look? Maggie most likely didn't work on Sunday mornings, especially cold, wet ones in January – I decided to have a peek. Stylish and classy, the shop was just like its owner and had Maggie stamped all over it. From a bus stop directly opposite, I pulled up my hood and watched, and when Maggie appeared in the window, I nearly died. She sat on a sofa with a cup of coffee in one hand and a book in the other. Twenty years and nothing had changed - except her hair was shorter, and I liked it. I wanted to run through the door, fall to my knees, and beg for forgiveness, but I couldn't. I had to fix things first and hopefully survive what I was about to do - then, I'd contact my friends.

An hour later, laden with shopping bags, mostly gifts for my mam and sister, I left

Brown Thomas *or the mothership as I referred to it* and made my way to The Shelbourne Hotel for lunch. Walking through the revolving doors into the newly refurbished bar with plush carpet, beautiful furniture, and fine art on panelled walls - I thought the girls would love this, then realised they probably saw it all the time. I was the one rarely in Dublin and, apart from my family, the one who'd lost everyone who mattered to me.

Over the years, glimpses of their lives had filtered through from my family. It was hard seeing them all free as birds and making their dreams come true. My life paled in comparison – it was glamorous and privileged, yes - but I was isolated, alone and broken in Sweden. A few tables from where I was drinking a glass of white wine, an old man sat quietly, drinking a pint of Guinness and writing a letter.

'Hello, beautiful lady,' he said, catching me staring, and I blushed.

'I was just thinking, you don't see too many people writing letters these days.'

I nodded to the piece of paper in his hand.

'And isn't it a great shame. I'm writing to my daughter in America. We also email, but I occasionally surprise her with an old-fashioned letter.'

'What a lovely thing to do - is she delighted to get them?' I asked.

'Thrilled,' he said.

Suddenly, an idea formed in my mind - I could write an old-fashioned letter to my friends, maybe break the ice, and pave the way for us to see each other again. I ordered a toasted sandwich from the bar, went to the hotel reception for some paper and envelopes, and sat down with a smile. I laughed when I realised they gave me four stamps - only in Ireland and raised my wine glass to the old man.

'You've inspired me. I'm going to write to some old friends,' I said.

He raised his pint in a cheers motion and returned to his letter while I thought about the girl's reactions to the Shelbourne Hotel-headed paper. How ironic, but hopefully, they got a kick out of it. As I drank my wine, I wondered what to say to my best friends I hadn't seen in twenty years because I fell in love with a lunatic. Sorry didn't cut it, so the truth seemed like the only option. I wasn't looking for sympathy - just for them to know the price paid for bad decisions and for us to be friends again - that meant everything to me.

A couple of hours passed, and another glass of wine was drunk. I finished the letters and wrote each of the girl's names - care of Mrs Reed, whom I knew still lived in the house I'd practically grown up in. Then, I popped them in the letter box outside the hotel as I left.

Walking through St Stephen's Green, the trees glistened in the rain - the park was empty of the usual crowds, and I felt a rare moment of peace. When the light began to fade, the travelling, stress and wine began to take their toll, and an early night seemed like a good idea.

My appointment with Marcus Ryan was early the next day, and I had questions to consider. What did I tell him? Did I just spew it all out? Would he help me? Could he help me? Someone had to tell me what to do because I didn't know where to start. My sister would know, and my plan was to ring her later using the apartment phone and then surprise my parents the next day.

Quickening my pace, I thought to quickly check my phone. I wasn't expecting to hear from Lars - he was locked away at a conference in Brussels, but I rooted around in my bag just in case. When I saw six missed calls and a text saying he'd be on the next plane to Dublin if I didn't answer his call in an hour, my heart stopped - that was twenty minutes ago.

17 ~ ORLA

Orla stared at the letters.

'How?'

She turned to her mam, who handed her a cup of tea and shook her shoulders.

'I don't know - sure, open it and see,' said Patsy.

Orla ripped open her letter and began to read.

Dear Orla,

Where to start? What to say? I don't know yet, but writing this letter feels like the right thing to do, so here goes. I'm sitting in the Shelbourne Hotel - it's Sunday afternoon, and I can't believe I'm here. I have a glass of wine and a toasted sandwich and am reminiscing about the old days. I love being in Dublin alone for the first time in years, but being in this hotel has made me realise how much I've missed you all. Actually, I don't need to be here to realise that. I've lived with it every day for the past twenty years.

Orla, I'm sorry for so many things, but mainly for choosing Lars over you. I completely ignored the red flags and convinced myself he was something he simply wasn't. I have no defence other than being madly in love. He hated that I loved you girls - hated anyone else having my attention and gradually began to ostracise me. I didn't know how far he'd go or how completely helpless I'd become until it was too late. He's been chipping away at my confidence for years, and I've become a shadow of my old self. Talk about rose-tinted glasses. Let's say I learned the hard way.

I passed the point of no return when I moved to Sweden. He promised the sun, moon, and stars and delivered on most of it, but the price was my soul. On the outside, my life is glamorous and privileged, but I yearn to come home. The violence you saw in Lily's continued throughout my marriage. In fact, it got worse - the first real beating happened a week after my honeymoon, and I was so shocked that I didn't even think of running. After that? Well, you might say he wore me down. When he wasn't beating me, he was declaring his undying love. He's very good at playing the role of a devoted husband, respectable businessman and politician, but beneath it all, he's the devil himself, and I'm terrified of him. I didn't dare have kids - it would have destroyed me, and I wasn't sure Lars could have shared me, even with them. I was also worried about how they'd turn out with psycho Swede as a dad. Even though it was the hardest thing I've ever done, I chose to be sterilised - he never knew and thought it was women's problems.

I'm never alone - there's always someone watching. Lars is still obsessed with me and needs to know where I am every minute of the day. I only have a phone because he regularly checks it, but with the help of my friend Astrid, I finally have something that will allow me to escape my prison and maybe put him into one. Tomorrow morning, I'm meeting my solicitor to show him video evidence of Lars beating me - hopefully, my ticket to freedom. I also have something that will be the nail in his coffin, but I'm scared because it's game over if he finds out what I'm up to. I've spent six months living in fear, walking on eggshells and covering my tracks. After the meeting, I'll surprise mam and dad, and spend the night there before returning to Sweden on Tuesday morning. If this works out, I hope to be living in Dublin very soon, and even though I know you live in England these days, I'd love to meet up. It feels like a lifetime since I saw you, but also five minutes ago. Know what I mean?

I can't give you any of my details (even after all these years, Lars still feels threatened by you girls), but mam is still in the same house, so could you respond there? I know you write books and I've read every one of them so many times. They are my prized possessions, and I feel so proud of you - always knew you were a brainy bitch.

Orla, please listen to me. I'd need you to have those books if anything ever happened to me. Please remember that. You'd need to get the books.

Take care of yourself, and I hope to see you soon.

Lots of love

Laura

Tears blurred Orla's eyes. Poor Laura, she just wanted to come home.

'That's all I ever wanted.'

Videos of Lars beating her - was that his motive for killing Laura? And what was the *nail in his coffin*? Also, why did Laura want Orla to have her books?

'Can I read it?' asked Patsy, her hand held out to take the letter.

Orla nodded and passed the letter to her mam while her mind reeled. What was the nail in the coffin? Where were the videos? Did Laura's solicitor have them? She rang Audrey, but it went to voicemail.

'It's like a letter from beyond the grave,' said Patsy when she finished reading. 'What sort of man torments his wife like that?' she asked.

'An evil bastard.'

Orla didn't know, but she was convinced Lars killed Laura and just needed to figure out how he was in two places at the same time.

'Lars didn't know about the videos or anything else. Why would he kill me?'

'Laura came to Dublin on Sunday morning,' said Orla, trying to establish a timeline. 'In her letter, she said she was seeing her parents after her meeting on Monday, but she spent Sunday night with them. Why?' Orla made a mental note to ask the Quinns. 'And why stay in an apartment in town in the first place? Why not just stay with her parents?' asked Orla

'I thought it would be safer for them until I offloaded the evidence.'

'She might have wanted a bit of peace and quiet. She said in the letter that she's never alone,' said Patsy, making an excellent point.

'That too.'

'Lars told the guards he thought Laura was staying with her parents, so Laura lied about that. Did he find the videos and get one of his dodgy contacts in Dublin to kill her?' asked Orla, thinking that sounded a bit farfetched.

'He didn't know about them, Orla. This was so frustrating - she needed to hear me.'

Patsy considered it and then responded again with more helpful insight.
'Why kill her? Surely, he'd just destroy

the videos,' she said.

What if Lars found out Laura was leaving him? Would he risk everything by killing her? To keep her - yes, but to kill her didn't make sense unless he found out about *the nail in his coffin*. Orla picked up the letter and read it aloud to her ma.

'If Lars knew, he wouldn't have let me come to Ireland.'

'Where is it?' she scanned, 'Ah, here. "*I also have something that might be the nail in his coffin. I'm so scared because it's game over if he finds out what I'm up to. I've spent six months living in fear, walking on eggshells and covering my tracks.*" What was she up to?' asked Orla.

'I tried to move a teaspoon on the table again, but nothing happened. Feeling pissed off, I screamed, and the light flickered.

'I don't know, but you need to find out,' said Patsy.

'I know,' said Orla, wondering how she'd do that.

'Shit, Did I imagine that? I tried screaming again, and the same thing happened. Orla and Mrs Reed didn't notice, but I did.'

On Saturday afternoon, Audrey rang, and Orla told her about the letters. They decided to wait until their lunch on Monday to discuss it. On Sunday morning, Orla walked to mass with her ma. The snow had started in England, but Ireland had escaped it so far - even though it was bitterly cold and lashing with rain.

'I like walking- it helps me gather my thoughts,' said Patsy as they huddled under a broken umbrella, trying to fight the driving rain.

By the time they reached the church, thunder was rolling overhead, and Orla wondered why her mam couldn't gather her thoughts in the car. Despite her anti-religious tendencies, she enjoyed the service. The choir singing old, familiar hymns sounded almost ethereal and afterwards, Orla lit a candle for Laura.

'Rest in peace, love,' she whispered,

promising to find Laura's killer.

Laura
I couldn't rest in peace until we sorted this out, but I felt better because I'd finally found a way to communicate with Orla. - I just had to get better at it. It felt weird to think of Lars killing me. The ferocity of his beatings in the past year told me it was possible, but would he go that far? And why would he? Even if Lars found out what I was up to, he'd likely just lock me up and beat me into submission again.

18 ~ LAURA

Frantically waving down a taxi, I gave the driver my parent's address as anxiety ripped through my body. When he tried to chat, my ability to speak almost deserted me.

'Are you on holiday, love?' he asked.

'Visiting family - I live in Sweden,' I managed after a few deep breaths.

He said that must be nice, and I almost laughed. Thankfully, his phone rang, and he spent the rest of the journey happily chatting to Loopy Lisa. When we pulled into Orchard Crescent, where my parents lived, nostalgia threatened to consume me. *Soon*, I thought, *just keep going*. Standing on the small porch outside my parent's front door, I took a deep breath and rang the bell. My dad was so shocked when he answered that he nearly fell over. Hugging him tight, I let relief flood through my body - then, my mam was standing beside him with a look of disbelief on her face.

'What in the name of God are ye doing here?' she asked.

With no time for the ins and outs, I gave her a quick outline of what was happening.

'He's ringing in a few minutes. You've been sick in the hospital, and I'm home visiting you. He'll want to talk to you - I just know it. Say you got home this afternoon, and you have a problem with your heart.'

My poor mam blessed herself and turned as white as a ghost, but she agreed to the plan, and precisely one hour after Lars's last text, my phone rang.

'Hi, love,' I said, sounding cheery while my stomach churned - there was too much at stake.

'You didn't answer my texts, Laura,' said Lars - I could tell he was barely holding it together.

'I didn't see them, love. My phone was in my bag, and we were at the hospital,' I said, then, trying to distract him from his rage, quickly added. 'Mam's home now - I'm caring for her for the rest of the day.'

He ordered me back to Sweden immediately.

'I can't come back now - we agreed Tuesday,' I countered.

'Surely your father can care for his sick wife,' he sneered, and I rolled her eyes. *Prick!*

'Dad's not well, and Lou has the kids - she can't help till Tuesday,' I explained.

A prolonged silence - I held my breath. Would he insist?

'Tuesday,' he relented, and I smiled. *Dickhead.*

I asked about the conference, but he was too angry to engage and said he needed to go. However, before he did, and just as I predicted, he asked to speak to my mam.

'Let me wish your mother well,' said Lars.

So - fucking - predictable. I passed the phone to mam, who did her part and played the role perfectly.

'Jesus, Mary, and holy St Joseph, I'm going to have a heart attack if you don't tell us what's happening.'

Mam had to sit down to recover from the shock.

'Dad, put the kettle on, will you?' I asked.

What I had to say would take time, and

we'd need tea. My dad headed into the kitchen while I hugged my mam – I missed her so much. Even though we talked constantly, and they visited Sweden, Lars was always in the background, and I was always on edge. When dad returned with a tray of tea and biscuits, we all sat down, and I calmly broke the news.

'I'm leaving him,' I said as terror flashed across their faces. They had every right to be scared - they knew exactly who Lars was and what I endured living with him, even though I tried to hide it from them.

'How can you?' whispered my dad.

I hated seeing him so helpless. All he ever wanted was to protect me, but he couldn't go up against Lars.

'I can't take it anymore, and I have something to use against him. Something I found out a few months ago. If this works, I'll be free of him. I'm seeing a solicitor in town tomorrow, and when I go back to Sweden, I'm packing up and coming home.'

By now, we were all crying - my parent's, tears of relief that I'd finally be home - mine, tears of guilt for putting them through so many years of this shit. Spending the evening at home with my family was just what I needed - the luxury apartment was forgotten as I relaxed in front of the fire in my parent's tiny living room. Lou was in Cork and wouldn't be back till later that night, but we spoke on the phone, and I gave her an outline of what I'd discovered in the past six months. As expected, she took charge.

'Don't tell Marcus too much - you never know with that fucker Lars. If he finds out, he might force Marcus to cough up. This is fucking huge, Laura, but we need to be very careful. Why the fuck didn't you tell me before now?' she asked, furious.

'I couldn't tell you - you know he listens to my calls, tracks everything I do – I couldn't risk being overheard, even at work, but I've got all the information stored - I'll give you the details when I see you tomorrow,' I said.

'Okay, I'll drop the boys to school and drive to mam's house. See you there after your meeting,' said Lou before hanging up.

When I gave my mam her bag of gifts, she complained as usual.

'You shouldn't be spending your money on me,' she said, and I laughed.

'Why not, mam? I like buying you things.'

I made her try on her new blouse while dad cooked a Sunday roast, and afterwards, we snuggled up with white wine and watched TV together. When I climbed into bed later that night, I prayed to God, something I hadn't done in years.

'Please make this happen for me,' I begged before falling asleep.

When I woke in my childhood bed to the delicious aroma of coffee and the heart-warming sound of my parents chatting in the kitchen, I smiled. The recent floods in Kildare were the topic of conversation, and it was music to my ears. After a quick shower, I put on some make-up and left my make-up bag on the dresser with the lipstick USB inside - it would be safer here.

'Ah, there you are,' said mam when I walked into the kitchen. 'Do you want a tea?'

'Coffee, please,' I said, then realising there might be an old jar of instant coffee at the back of the press since 1987, I changed my mind. 'Actually, I will have tea. Da, can you ring me a taxi?'

After two cups and a rasher sandwich that my mam insisted I eat, I said goodbye and promised to see them at lunchtime.

'Do you need me to pick up anything,' I asked when the taxi arrived.

'No, just get back here and mind yourself,' said mam.

The taxi took me to the apartment to change for my meeting with Marcus. When I passed Donal in the lobby, he wore a suit and looked very non-biker.

'Morning, Laura. How's it going? Enjoying your stay?' he asked in a friendly tone.

'Yeah, thanks, so far, so good,' I said, smiling.

Stepping into the lift, I wished for friends like him. Loneliness was a cloak I'd worn for so long that life without it seemed impossible. As I dressed, I half-packed my bag - my mam had insisted I stay there again that night.

'Why on earth you'd waste your money on that place, I'll never know,' she said.

'I wanted to surprise you, and anyway, I haven't stayed in this house in years,' I retorted.

'That's only because of him,' she flung back. 'This is always your home.'

The idea of another night at my parent's house warmed me, and the gorgeous apartment was abandoned. I thought about taking my case with me but decided to return after my meeting, make one more of those delicious coffees, pack properly, and grab a taxi home.

'Come on through, Laura,' called Marcus as I stood alone on the small landing of his office.

I walked into a large room where Marcus stood behind a messy desk and shook my hand. He was fair-haired and ruggedly handsome, and although I'd never met him in person, I instantly liked him. He didn't know who Lars was - *I'd kept it under wraps* - but a quick Google search fixed that.

'Shit,' he said while reading Lars's Wikipedia page.

When he asked for the evidence, I hesitated, thinking about what Lou said. What if Lars found out about Marcus and forced him to talk? The past six months of terror would be for nothing. Terrified and erring on caution, I promised to email the details.

'That's grand, Laura, but just so you know, everything you tell me is confidential. I'll only use the information if you want me to,' said Marcus, in a pronounced South Dublin accent that I found very attractive.

His messy office was endearing in its disarray. His tweed jacket and brown cords made him look like a university professor, and his honest face demanded trust. I retrieved my secret phone from the inside pocket of my handbag and showed him the videos of Lars beating me.

'Let's start with this,' I said.

As he watched Lars pissing on me, my cheeks reddened in shame. Marcus didn't comment, but the scowl on his face suggested murder on his mind. In the other video, Lars kicked my stomach and pulled me around by the hair – like a rag doll, and I was mortified, but once again, Marcus didn't comment. I showed him photos of the black bruising around my stomach and legs, and he was quiet for a few minutes before asking if I had anything else. I shook my head.

'See if you can get more, even if it's a

voice recording,' he said, showing me how to access the microphone. 'It's not as valuable as video evidence, but it's still admissible, and the more you have, the better.'

I nodded, then deciding to test the waters, asked about sex trafficking laws in Ireland. Marcus looked surprised.

'Why do you want to know about that?'

'I might have access to some information involving important people. What would someone do with that? Who would they talk to?' I asked.

'The guards, of course,' he said, but when I shook my head, he paused.

'Say some of them were involved?' I asked.

'Are you trying to tell me you know of guards involved in sex trafficking?'

'No, but maybe connected somehow,' I said, trying to play down what I knew.

'Well, not all of them would be – I know some good men in the guards, men you can trust, and I'd be happy to set up a meeting.' Marcus took my hand. 'Sorry if this is over-familiar, but I want you to know you can trust me.'

'I need to talk to my sister - maybe I won't feel so overwhelmed. We'll email you the details, then go from there,' I said, then after a minute added. 'To be honest, I'm not even sure if I can go back to Sweden.' I'd been thinking about it all morning. Why go back? Why not just stay here? It would make it harder for Lars to get to me if I was with my family. 'If I stay in Dublin for a while, will you meet myself and Lou later this week?'

Marcus said he'd be happy to fit us in. When the meeting was over, I paid in cash from my Irish bank account, another secret I'd kept from Lars and something I thought of as my escape money. As I walked toward the apartment, I felt optimistic for the first time in years. God, not go back to Sweden - there was a thought. Could I really do it? Could I start again? Forty-five without ever having a career, my options were limited, but with Lars in a different country or, better yet, prison - surely, I'd be entitled to some of his money - not the illegal stuff, just enough to buy a flat in Dublin, get a part-time job and live in peace. Now that it was within my grasp, I wanted it badly.

19 ~ ORLA

On Monday morning, Orla took the bus into town to meet the girls. The first to arrive at the Bailey on Duke Street, she ordered a gin and tonic to calm her nerves, then noticed a free table in the corner and grabbed it. In the pocket of her handbag sat Laura's letters, patiently waiting to be delivered to their rightful owners. Orla would hand them out after their reacquaintance. When her ex-best friends walked through the door together, she was rocked by many emotions - happiness - sadness - regret - and excitement. They all looked the same, just a little bit older. Niamh, petite like Audrey, had thick, curly brown hair that bounced when she walked. Her green eyes looked like saucers - the only change was the black-rimmed glasses that now framed them. Tall and slender, Maggie had an elegance that reminded Orla of someone you'd meet at a polo match - or somewhere posh. Her hair was cut into a sharp bob, and her hazel eyes were thoughtful - the kind that missed nothing.

'Oh, my God, I can't fecking believe it's you,' squealed Niamh, loud enough for people to turn in their seats. She ran into Orla's arms and hugged her. 'Orla Reed,' she said, holding her back as if her eyes couldn't believe it. Maggie and Audrey watched.

'Good to see you, Orla,' whispered Maggie when Niamh finally let her go.

Orla smiled, thinking that reserved elegance was still there.

'Raging, I'm not there.'

Audrey nodded and went to the bar for a round of drinks, and within ten minutes, it was as if no time had passed. They were back to normal, except Laura had been murdered, and normal would never exist again. Niamh's eyes welled up at the mention of her name, so Orla deliberately steered the conversation elsewhere and discovered they'd seen each other over the years.

'Only for things related to the school,' said Maggie, noticing Orla's look of disappointment.

'Tina Taylor's funeral, remember her?' asked Audrey.

How could Orla forget Tina Taylor - the school bully she'd spent most of her senior year hiding from in the third-floor toilets.

'What happened to her?' asked Orla, somewhat surprised at how sad she felt at the death of her nemesis.

'Killed herself - she'd been on drugs for years,' said Audrey.

'Poor Tina, I'll look her up when I get upstairs.'

Orla wasn't surprised and recalled seeing Tina too many times behind the bike sheds sniffing glue, and that was at fifteen - a tormented soul, bless her.

'Then there was a school reunion about two years ago. You, Laura, and Tina were the only ones not there,' said Niamh.

Orla remembered the email but didn't think twice about it, something she now regretted. Then again, James had just left, so an email from her old school might have slipped her attention. Over lunch, she discovered

Niamh lived in West Cork and ran a pub in beautiful Kinsale.

'Wow, how did you end up there?' asked Orla - it seemed so random.

'I know, me running a pub - you couldn't make it up. My husband is a chef, and we always wanted our own place. About eight years ago, a friend of his was selling his pub. He asked if we wanted it, and I immediately said yes. I sold the house, packed the kids, and moved to West Cork. We love it,' she said.

'How many kids do you have?' asked Orla, more than curious.

Niamh had always insisted she wasn't having any brats - when she said five girls, Orla nearly choked on her wine.

'The twins are seventeen, the next fifteen, then thirteen, and seven. Ray was desperate for a boy, but he finally accepted defeat after Maisie,' she said, half laughing.

Orla reminded her that once upon a time, Niamh Moore hated kids and was never having any.

'I know, but when the twins came along, we were thrown in the deep end, and then I just kept finding myself pregnant,' she said, laughing again.

Orla laughed, thinking how wonderfully chaotic her life sounded.

'Me too. How fun.'

Maggie's life was very different. She owned a bookshop not far from where they were having lunch.

'I stock your books, and I've read them all. Even though murder mystery is not my thing, I enjoyed them,' said Maggie and Orla knew that was a Maggie-style compliment.

She said she had two boys like Orla, but hers were younger, at seventeen and fifteen. She lived in Ballsbridge with her husband, and Orla thought that neighbourhood suited her.

'Very nice.'

'Artie travels quite a bit – he works in the classical music world. I tag along if he's performing anywhere nice,' she continued, and Orla thought how lovely.

Then she felt sad that their children hadn't met. They'd all grown up so close - it seemed a shame their kids didn't know each other. Audrey explained how she'd recently been promoted to sergeant, never married, had no kids, and was still with her partner, Nina, who they knew from back in the day.

'Did you two not want kids?' asked Orla, thinking about her gay friends with large families.

'We thought about it for a while, but it never seemed the right time,' said Audrey.

'What about Nina? What does she do now?' asked Niamh.

Nina had always been sensible, not one to fall out of pubs and nightclubs like the rest of them.

'She's a paediatrician at Beaumont Hospital,' announced Audrey proudly.

'Wow, go, Nina.'

Niamh then turned to Orla.

'What about you? You married Mark in the end?' she asked, referring to Orla's ex-husband from years before..

Orla was surprised Niamh remembered his name. She met Mark a year before their friendship fell apart. At the time, he was in Dublin on a temporary contract and was always going back to London. When that time came, they were living together - she was between jobs and wasn't talking to her friends anymore. When he asked her to go - she did. Soon after, they got married, and she had Max. Two years later, Connor came along, and their family was complete. They had about eight happy years before things started to deteriorate.

'Yeah, I married him, lived in London and had two kids. Max is at university now, and Connor is travelling. We divorced about ten years ago, but we're friends and have always shared the boys,' said Orla.

'When did you start writing the books?' asked Audrey.

'I was toying with the idea for years and finished the first book two years before getting a publishing deal. That was about five years ago, and I haven't stopped since.'

'Fair play to you - they're great,' said Niamh, 'I loved them all.'

'Thanks,' said Orla, feeling proud. 'I loved writing them.'

As the afternoon wore on, the conversation inevitably turned to Laura. Orla had so many questions for Audrey, but first, she took the letters from her bag and handed them out, explaining how they'd been delivered to her mam's house on Friday morning. Niamh gasped when she saw Laura's name on the back, and Maggie wore a stunned look. Audrey, who knew about the letter, immediately opened hers and began reading.

'I've already read mine, and I've got a couple of calls to make,' said Orla, leaving her friends to read.

'At least I got to say hello before I died.'

The outdoor area had heaters to protect Orla as she sat down and looked at her phone. Four missed calls from Dorothy - she rang her first.

'I know your friend has been murdered, and I'm so sorry, but I had to tell you - your latest book is number one in America, and the publisher wants you to do a book tour in March. Can you commit?' asked Dorothy.

Wow, this was like a dream come true.

'Oh my God, yes, I can commit - that's brilliant news,' said Orla, delighted.

'Well done, Orla. So bloody proud of you.'

They discussed it for a few minutes with the promise to talk soon, then Orla rang her mam, who was upset rereading Laura's letter that morning.

'Hello, is that you, Orla?' Patsy practically shouted down the line.

Orla laughed - old people trying to use technology was hilarious.

'Heya ma. I'm just ringing to make sure you're not still upset,' said Orla.

'Ah no, I'm grand now. I'm just having a steak and kidney pie in the pub with your dad,' she said, loud enough for the whole pub to know what she was having for lunch.

'Grand, so. Well, I was just checking - I'll see you later,' said Orla.

'Mind yourself - I'll see you when you're back. Have you got your key?' asked Patsy.

Orla said she had - they said goodbye, and she re-joined the girls.

Laura

It was a shame I had to be murdered for my friends to reunite, but I had a feeling these women were supposed to be involved, and Lars would never suspect them. I thanked God for the old man in the Shelbourne Hotel. Because of him, the girls at least had some insight into my life. They'd help find my murderer and hopefully the bodies of the girls. If I got lucky and contacted Orla, maybe they'd stop the trafficking as well.

20 ~ LAURA

My Murder

I wished I'd known I was about to be murdered. I would have run so far, so fast that even death itself wouldn't have caught me.

Eager to get home to discuss my escape plan with my sister, I didn't notice the apartment door wasn't double locked, so I went straight to the kitchen for a coffee. A habit picked up in Sweden - coffee was life. While waiting for it to brew, I daydreamed about a new life in Ireland, feeling - *dare I say it* - happy. My sister would help me, and everything would be alright. The relief of not being completely alone in my task had a dizzying effect on me, and in a rare moment of optimism, a song burst from my lips while I imagined all sorts of wonderful scenarios.

Lars in prison - me living in Ireland and coming and going as I pleased. A holiday to

Donegal - I'd always loved it there. Regular dinner dates with my best friends. Maybe a new man, someone who made me feel safe instead of afraid. An image of ruggedly handsome Marcus Ryan popped into my head that terrified and thrilled me. *Get a grip, Laura - a man is the last thing you need.* I laughed as I poured coffee into a mug until the hair on the back of my neck began to tingle. Someone was watching me. I whipped around, but there was no one there. I laughed again while shaking my head. The sooner I got away from Lars, the better for my paranoia. Turning back to my coffee, I sipped until the same feeling hit me again. This time, I closed my eyes – *please no* - I slowly turned to face the room and saw him standing near the island, watching me and looking as cool as a cat.

'No,' I gasped, feeling utterly destroyed. It was Lars.

My handbag in front of him was snatched up and rummaged through, but the phone with the videos was in the pocket of my trousers. *What was he doing here? How was he here?* Schooled at hiding my terror, I calmly asked why he followed me. He ignored me while flicking through my phone, checking my messages and calls.

'Want a coffee?' I asked, trying to keep things normal and knowing his addiction was as bad as my own.

He nodded while putting my passport and phone into his jacket pocket and praying he didn't notice - I furtively took the other phone out of my pocket as I turned to pour his coffee. Noticing a gap at the base of the coffee machine - the perfect hiding place, I pressed the voice record button while silently thanking Marcus for showing me where it was, then my trembling fingers pushed the phone into the gap - maybe I'd get beating number three recorded. I almost laughed at how dysfunctional that was - *nice one, Laura. Take a good beating so you can leave your husband.* Trying hard to stop my hands from shaking, I placed Lars's coffee on the counter before him as fear coiled in my stomach - my foreboding warning he'd hurt me for this.

'Why did you follow me, Lars?' I thought to at least get his name recorded, and feeling braver than usual, I asked if the Swedish Government would survive for a day without the famous Lars Karlsson.

He watched me closely, his grey eyes taking in everything, and I wondered if my boldness had worked - maybe he wasn't so tough after all. I felt slightly smug until he flew around the island, grabbed my hair and knocked my coffee to the floor. It smashed into a thousand pieces on the kitchen tiles, splashing black coffee all over my white trousers. *Dickhead.*

'What the fuck are you up to, Laura?' asked Lars, his eyes menacing. 'Why are you in this apartment? Who are you with, a lover?'

Oh, for fucks sake – I rolled my eyes until I realised his accusation was good news - it meant he didn't know what I was doing.

'I haven't got a lover, Lars,' I said as his hand twisted in my hair.

'Do you think I don't know every fucking move you make? You were in the Shelbourne Hotel for three hours yesterday - lunch with those bitches from years ago? You got to your mother's house ten minutes before my call, who, by the way, was never in the fucking hospital.'

My heart sank - he did have someone

following me, after all. My naivety was almost embarrassing as I realised Lars would never let me travel without knowing my every move.

'Please let go of my hair,' I asked, but he ignored me.

'You were in Wicklow Street this morning. I don't know why, but I'll find out,' he continued, referring to my meeting with Marcus, and I realised my clever sister was right - no one was immune to Lars's reach.

My plan began slipping through my fingers, but instead of feeling defeated, I felt calm as years of suppressed fear evaporated from my body. This bastard wasn't draining my power anymore. I wanted to scratch his eyes out and scream at the unfairness of his being there. Instead, I asked him again to let go of my hair, and he did. The uncertainty in his eyes turned to surprise when I took a deep breath and looked him straight in the eye.

'Why don't you just fuck off,' I said, then slowly and deliberately, I laid it out for him. 'This marriage is over – I'm done with you and your sick fucking games. I'm leaving you, and the person I met in Wicklow Street was my solicitor, who saw videos of you beating the shit out of me. How do you think it will look when the people of Sweden discover that high and mighty Lars Karlsson, Minister for Foreign Affairs, is nothing but a filthy wife beater?'

Lars was speechless, and I mentally patted myself on the back. He stared, but a tick on his jaw gave him away – I'd definitely struck a chord. *Woohoo, score, Laura!* My victory was short-lived, however, when his face turned to stone.

'Were you thinking of blackmailing me, Laura?' he asked, sounding deadly, and when I didn't answer and tried to stare him down, he laughed - a manic, terrifying laugh. 'You just can't help being a stupid fucking bitch,' he said.

'I also know what happened in that nightclub twenty years ago. I have proof, and I'll get the girls to make statements,' I said, wanting to wipe the smile off his face.

It worked - he went still. Was he worried? He looked worried but quickly recovered, saying I wouldn't prove shit.

'My lawyers will rip anyone to shreds if they try to attack my reputation.'

'Ha! You think I give a fuck about your reputation - I know what you did to those kids

- what you're still doing to kids in Sweden. How could you? You make me fucking sick.'

The look of shock on his face was almost comical.

'You don't know what the fuck you're talking about,' he sneered.

'Don't I?' I asked.

He was stuck for words - probably for the first time in his life until the usual verbal diarrhoea kicked in.

'I should never have married a dirty tramp like you,' he sneered.

I almost laughed - the script was the same every time, and I should have seen it coming, but his fist colliding with the side of my face and knocking me to the floor was completely unexpected. He'd only struck my face once - on that fateful night twenty years earlier. I lay in the spilt coffee and broken crockery, hating the man who'd terrorised me for half of my life. After a few minutes, holding onto the counter to steady myself, I stood up and washed the coffee from my hands. Through the microwave door, I noticed a bruise forming on my cheek. Then, turning, I studied my husband while drying my hands.

His beautiful navy suit, cashmere coat and fine leather gloves reeked of money. Big and bulky at six foot four - his dark wavy hair touched the collar of his white shirt, and his eyes, the colour of the North Sea, watched me. Stunning but rotten to the core - at that moment, I decided Sweden was no longer an option. The image of being curled up on the sofa watching a film with my parents the night before flashed before my eyes - I wanted to go home - I was tired of being lonely, afraid and sad all the time.

'Get your things - we're going home,' barked Lars and as I watched him, I had an epiphany.

My evidence was worthless - Lars was too powerful, and no matter what I did, Lars would never let me go - the bodies would probably never be found - the trafficking would continue, and I'd be forced to live with him for the rest of my life. I simply couldn't allow that to happen - there was no other option but for me to kill him. Placing the towel on the counter, I noticed a knife block beside the hob - *now or never.* I slid one of the larger knives out and turned to face him.

'Keep the fuck away from me, you piece of shit,' I said, with a slight wobble to my voice. 'I hate you - you make me sick, and I'm not going back with you. In fact, I'm never going to Sweden again.'

He watched, probably thinking I'd gone mad. Not once in twenty years had I stood up to him. He folded his arms as he watched me, then spoke as if I was a child.

'You are coming home, Laura and we'll talk about this there,' he said.

It pissed me off.

'Did you not hear what I just said? I'm not going back - for the record, Sweden was never my home - Dublin is my home.'

I realised a prison term in Ireland was more appealing than a gilded cage in Sweden, so before I could think about it too much, I ran at him with my knife pointed at his chest - ready for the kill.

'What the fuck,' he said, jumping back with a look of surprise. 'Put the fucking knife down, Laura,' he snarled, but it was too late – I'd officially lost the plot and was out of my mind - driven there by him. The knife nicked him, and a small pool of red appeared on his white shirt. He looked down in shock and realised I was serious. Egged on by my success, I lunged again, but this time, he was ready and grabbed my hand, violently shaking the knife, which clattered to the floor. Then, he backhanded me so hard that I hit the floor...again, this time cracking my head on the corner of the island. A river of blood sprayed out of a large gash as I lay on the floor and watched my husband unleash his monster within. Kneeling down, he grabbed the lapels of my jacket in one hand and used his other hand to annihilate my face.

'You fucking slut,' thump. 'I own you,' thump. 'I'm going to make sure you never forget that,' thump.

Through my rapidly swelling eyes, I noticed his were wild with rage. When he pulled me to my feet, threw me against the fridge door and pushed me against it using his body, I could feel his hard cock pressing into my bum, *sick bastard*. However, instead of raping me as usual, he twisted my arm so hard that it broke, and I almost passed out with the pain.

'You think you can attack me,' he seethed, his gloved hand muffling my screams.

I fell back and hung in his arms -

delirious and covered in blood. My face was pulverised, and my arm hung loosely - I prayed he was finished, that he'd had enough to feed the monster, but he was just warming up. With his hand to my throat, he turned me to face him, but my legs gave way, and I fell to the floor again, exhausted. Lars immediately straddled me and pressed his knee into my broken arm, causing me to momentarily pass out. When I came around, both of his hands were on my neck, and his enraged face was inches from mine.

'Stop, Lars,' I whispered - this had gone too far.

'Stop? Do you think you can threaten me with a fucking knife? You think I'd let you away with that?' he spit the words at me.

'I'm sorry, Lars, but please stop. I can't breathe,' I begged. In the past, I'd felt safe knowing he wouldn't kill me - he was obsessed and couldn't live without me, but now, I wasn't so sure. 'Stop Lars,' I tried again, but he wasn't hearing me.

Bucking beneath him, the agony of my broken arm took my breath away, but he squeezed my neck, and I couldn't breathe. Was he actually going to kill me? I thought of my sister. I hadn't given her enough information or told her where the USB stick was. I thought about my parents and how devastated they'd be if I died. I thought about my best friends and my dream of reuniting with them. That gave me strength - this had to stop, I wasn't dying today.

From the corner of my eye, I noticed the knife on the floor beside us, and with a strength given to me by God, I reached out, grabbed it and managed to get it beneath Lars's coat. With one last push of strength, I stabbed him between the ribs, causing him to snap out of his rage and fall back on his knees. His white shirt turned red as his blood flowed.

'What the fuck?' he sounded more shocked than I'd ever heard him while looking down at himself.

It gave me the precious seconds I needed to get off the floor. Like a woman possessed, I screamed as I pulled the knife out of him - not caring one bit if his blood erupted like a geyser and finished him off. Stumbling to my feet, I used the advantage of him being on his knees and held the knife over my head - *this fucker was going to die.* I aimed it at his chest and plunged - wanting to slice his black heart in half, but he was too fast. He grabbed my arm as he slowly stood up, and even though I tried to resist - for half a chance, I needed both arms and my broken one hung by my side - useless.

'You fucking bitch,' he whispered. 'Fucking bitch.' He sounded deranged - as if talking to someone else. 'Fucking cunt,' he said again while slowly twisting my arm.

Suddenly, the knife pointed towards me, and he was pushing.

'Lars, please stop, I'm sorry,' I said, trying to get the situation under control.

He muttered something as the knife inched forward, and I felt a pinch when it pierced the skin of my neck.

'Lars, stop please,' I cried, trying to stop him from pushing the knife forward and feeling weaker by the second. I couldn't die now, not after everything I'd gone through in the past six months - I had to save the girls. 'I don't want to die - please stop, Lars,' I begged, but he wasn't listening. 'Please, Lars,' I begged again, feeling completely panicked, but he was gone, lost in his own madness. The knife dug deeper into my neck. 'Please, Lars,' I screamed this time, desperate for him to snap him out of it and terrified of dying. He continued to ignore me, then as if in slow motion, the tiny amount of strength I had left deserted me - my arm fell, the knife plunged, and I felt a searing pain until I felt... nothing.

21 ~ ORLA

In the bar, Orla's friends were devastated by reading their letters. Laura knew about Maggie's shop – she knew Niamh lived in Kinsale and that Audrey was a guard. As she'd said in her letter to Orla, she hoped to escape from Lars and live in Dublin again.

'He's been killing her for years, and now she's dead,' said Niamh.

As far as Orla was concerned, Lars was her prime suspect.

'She was outside my shop on Sunday morning – said she saw me reading - watched from the bus stop across the road,' said Maggie quietly. 'Two buses went past before she left - why didn't she come in? Why didn't she ask for help?'

Orla didn't know, but she wished Laura had. She asked Audrey about any developments in the case, and Audrey shared what she could do.

'Lars was in Brussels at a political conference that ended on Monday. From there, he flew to Stockholm after checking out of his hotel late on Monday afternoon.

'I listened with bated breath.'

He spoke to Laura on Sunday at her mam's house, which Mrs Quinn confirmed, and he was supposed to pick her up from Stockholm Airport on Tuesday morning.'

'Well, Erik was - I remember that much.'

'Why didn't Lars fly to Dublin on Monday night? Surely that's what anyone would do if their wife had been murdered, and how long is the flight from Brussels to here?' asked Orla, wondering if he'd slipped into Dublin, killed Laura, and slipped out again like the snake he was.

'Lars knew I'd been murdered and flew to Sweden? That didn't sound right.'

'He was already at the airport when we

called on Monday, ready to board a flight to Stockholm. He said it was easier to fly from there the next day,' said Audrey.

'No, it wasn't - that didn't make sense.'

'How convenient for him and clever - giving himself time to think,' said Orla.

'Think about what?'

'The flight time from Brussels to Dublin is an hour and a half, and we already checked the airport security - he didn't arrive in Dublin until Tuesday morning,' said Audrey, reading Orla's mind.

'What about Laura's solicitor? Did you speak to him?' asked Orla.

'Yeah - he said Laura turned up and showed him the videos of Lars beating the shit out of her - videos she was to send him by email, but obviously she didn't,' said Audrey.

'Why not just give them to him?' asked Orla, wondering why Laura hesitated.

'Because I chickened out and wanted my sister to

help.'

'I don't know, but apparently, there was something else,' Audrey took a deep breath and lowered her voice. 'I could lose my job for what I'm about to tell you, but I think you deserve to know.' All four women leaned in. 'Laura asked Marcus about sex trafficking and said she had information regarding important people. She wanted to know who to contact, and when Marcus suggested the guards, Laura said that wasn't an option.'

'Fucking hell,' said Orla, astonished. 'You don't think that's what she meant by the nail in Lars's coffin she mentioned in her letter to me?'

'She didn't mention that in my letter,' said Niamh.

'I don't know,' said Audrey, 'but it sounds like Laura was onto something big. Why ask about sex trafficking, and what has it got to do with Lars? He's a government minister, for fuck's sake. Even more interesting is that Lars went to Marcus's office on Tuesday when he left the station.'

'How did Lars know about Marcus? "I don't know

why you were there, but I'll find out." Had Lars said that to me?'

'Ohh, that is interesting - what did he want?' asked Orla, guessing it wasn't a polite hello.

'He wanted to know why Laura was there - demanded Marcus hand over anything Laura might have given him, but Marcus told him nothing.

'Slander - sex-trafficking - domestic abuse videos,' said Maggie, who'd been quietly taking it all in. 'That all sounds like a motive for murder,' she added.

'How did Lars know about Marcus? Laura said in her letter that Lars didn't know what she was doing - a letter she wrote in Dublin the day before she died,' said Orla.

There was silence around the table as they all processed that nugget of information.

'Maybe Lars had Laura followed,' suggested Audrey.

'Or maybe he found out she was leaving him and paid someone to kill her,' suggested Niamh.

'Or maybe he somehow made his way to

Dublin and did it himself,' suggested Orla and when no one responded, she asked, 'am I the only one who thinks Lars is a killer? You all know what he was like back then - is it likely he changed?'

Maggie and Niamh thought Lars was the prime suspect, and Audrey agreed but explained the complication.

'After everything I'd been through, he killed me in the end? No – I wouldn't accept it.'

'The chief superintendent is personally involved because of Lars's position in government. He's pushing for a quick result. The pressure is unreal, and the investigation is leaning towards a robbery that resulted in death.'

'How can that be? Especially after what Marcus said?' asked Orla, stunned.

'It's all hearsay, Orla. There's no evidence - no videos to back up his statement. Laura's phone is gone, along with her bag and jewellery that we assume was taken by the killer. The blood on the knife is being analysed as we speak - but the only fingerprints on it were

Laura's, indicating she held the knife that killed her.'

'Why would Laura hold the knife that killed her?' asked Niamh with tears in her eyes, but Audrey ignored her and continued in her explanation.

'What the public don't know is that Laura was badly beaten. Her face was smashed to bits, and her arm was broken in two places. It was a savage attack, and I'm just not sure Lars, as bad as he is, could do that to his own wife.'

'Audrey's words made me uneasy because I was sure he could.'

Niamh practically sobbed at that information, echoing what they all felt.

'Maybe he snapped like he did all those years ago,' said Maggie.

'We all know Laura was terrified of Lars - she told us in these letters,' said Orla, pointing to the table where Laura's letters lay, 'she said he hadn't changed, and she wanted to leave him. Maybe she tried to blackmail him, he found out and killed her for it,'

'I get what you're saying,' said Audrey,

'but Lars being a lowlife, scumbag, wife-beater doesn't make him a murderer. His reputation is impeccable, a bit too impeccable if I'm honest, and there's no report about that night in Lily's nightclub on file. None of us reported it, and I'll regret that till I die.'

'I regretted it even after I was dead.'

'We spoke to the owner of the apartment who lives abroad. It's an automatic booking system with the key left in a box by reception - he'd never even met Laura.'

'And the neighbours saw nothing?' asked Orla.

'The couple across the hall spoke to her in the lift on Sunday morning. They said she seemed okay, chatty, and so on, and one of them saw her on Monday morning when he was leaving for work - he just said hello in passing. The apartment is on Grand Canal Dock - you know how busy it is - thousands of apartments - no one sees a thing.'

'When will she be buried,' asked Niamh, 'and will Lars get to decide where?'

The thought of Lars shipping Laura's

body back to Sweden was horrific. Laura would want to be buried in Dublin.

'Her body will be released next week, and Lars gets to decide. He's next of kin,' said Audrey.

'If he brings me back to Sweden, I'll turn in my grave before I'm in it.'

This was going from bad to worse. Orla was furious. She wanted to interview Marcus Ryan as soon as possible and was definitely visiting the Quinn's again. Who was Astrid Nilsson? Orla had a strong urge to speak to her. Audrey said it was Laura's incognito, but Laura referred to her as her friend. Deciding now wasn't the time, she turned to Niamh, who hadn't stopped crying since reading her letter and gently steered the conversations elsewhere.

'Where are you staying, Niamh? I assumed you're not going back to Cork tonight,' asked Orla.

'God, no,' said Niamh, wiping her tears, 'I'm staying in mam's house.'

'How is your mother these days?' asked

Orla.

'Grand, still the same, but getting on a bit now. It nearly killed her when I first moved to Cork, but she has a free travel pass, so she's always turning up - the kids love it. She works behind the bar and makes a fortune in tips,' said Niamh as they all laughed at the idea of little Marie Moore in her seventies, pulling pints and chatting up American tourists.

'Dad died of cancer about ten years ago,' continued Niamh, so blasé that, at first, Orla thought she was joking.

'Oh no, I'm so sorry, I didn't know,' said Orla.

'I'm sorry too,' said Maggie, squeezing her hand, and Audrey did the same.

'I'm sorry too.'

Niamh smiled sadly.

'It's grand. He was so sick at the end that it was a relief when he finally went. What about yours?' she asked Orla. 'All still good with them?'

Orla described how her folks were still alive and thriving. Maggie said the same about hers - they drove her crazy, but she could spread the burden with her five older siblings. Maggie had been born when her brothers and sisters were teenagers, so it was lonely at home. Orla always thought that was the reason for her seriousness and sensibleness. Back then, Maggie would always go home first or say she had enough to drink while the rest kept going until they passed out, usually in a gutter somewhere. Maggie also got straight to the point with everything, which made sense if you had to fight to be heard at home. When they looked at Audrey, she put her hands up in a *don't even go there* way, and they knew what that meant.

'Are you seriously telling me your ma still doesn't know you're gay? Surely, after all these years?' asked Orla, flabbergasted.

An only child whose father was never around, it was just Audrey and her ma growing up. Mrs O'Brien was old-fashioned - she didn't stop Audrey from living her life but quietly disapproved.

'We don't talk about it. She hopes I'll get better one day, meet a nice man, and give her a grandchild. She still calls Nina my friend even though she knows we sleep in the same bed,' said Audrey, rolling her eyes as the other laughed.

Orla looked at her three friends and felt grateful to have them back in her life. They didn't discuss why their friendship ended - there was no point anymore. They'd always been five best friends who knew everything about each other, and now they were four.

Laura
It was good to be with the girls – even if they didn't know I was there. The thought of Lars killing me was devastating, but Orla made some good points. I somehow knew that whoever killed me was waiting in the apartment – I just couldn't remember the rest of it, but I had a feeling it would come back to me. Communicating with Orla was my top priority – she had to hear me soon.

22 ~ LARS

Stockholm

When Lars Karlsson arrived at Stockholm International Airport, his rage was building. He'd just returned from Dublin, where he'd officially identified the body of his wife, and he wanted answers. As always, his faithful foot soldier, Erik, was waiting.

'Phone is clean,' said Erik, handing Laura's phone to Lars.

'How can it be? Where else would the videos be?' asked Lars.

' If they exist, they're not on this,' said Erik, then added, 'just the usual stuff - calls to her mother, a few photos, and some texts to you.'

'What the fuck?' roared Lars, sliding into the back seat of the waiting car that Sven was driving. 'Laura said she showed them to her lawyer. On what?' He handed the phone back to Erik, 'check it again,' barked Lars, feeling the need to pulverise someone.

During his interrogation in Dublin, Lars had to work hard to hide his anger. The Irish guards had fired question after question at him, and all he could do was think about his wife - his dead wife, and it didn't seem real. Remaining composed, Lars eventually convinced them he had nothing to do with Laura's murder – pulled his diplomatic immunity card, demanded they prioritise her case and insisted they find her killer. Then he kicked up a shit storm about how he'd been treated and left the station, saying he'd answer any further questions from Sweden. A quick visit to Mr Ryan's office proved uneventful.

'I can't discuss my client with you, Mr Karlsson,' the smart fucker said when Lars demanded he hand over any evidence Laura might have given him. 'She didn't give me anything - I wish she had,' said Marcus.

The disgust on his face hadn't bothered Lars, and the videos wouldn't have bothered him if Laura hadn't said what she said. *I know what you did to those kids. What you're still doing to kids in Sweden.* What did she mean?

'She doesn't know,' said Erik when Lars told him what happened.

Erik and Sven ran the largest export of girls in Northern Europe. Although owned by Lars, he wasn't involved in transporting the girls to Eastern Europe. The product was recruited and detained in several properties in Scandinavia. Friends, business associates, or whomever Lars deemed valuable were invited to enjoy the girls and live out their darkest fantasies. After a few weeks, the girls were shipped to Eastern Europe for a new life in the sex industry, and the men sent a small video clip for any future favours required.

'Why would she say it then?' asked Lars.

'I don't know, but you've always known every move Laura made - she didn't know,' said Erik.

'I didn't know about the lawyer or the fucking videos,' said Lars.

'She recorded a few videos and contacted a lawyer, but if she'd found out about the stable - she'd have called the cops. You know that, and we'd have been informed immediately. Anyway, I've pulled the plug on any new stock - we're laying low until Laura's investigation is wrapped up,' said Erik.

'The blood on the knife?' asked Lars.

'Sorted,' said Erik, with a smirk. 'The chief of forensics in Dublin enjoys *business trips* to Malmo - he was easily persuaded.'

Lars nodded, and as they sped along the motorway towards central Stockholm, he allowed his mind to recall what happened in Dublin. Killing Laura had been the last thing on his mind. He wanted to bring her home where she belonged until she went fucking crazy. Why had she spoken to him like that? What the fuck had gotten into her? Blackmailing him, then attacking him with a knife - his PTSD had been immediately triggered, and by the time he'd calmed down - she was dead. Dead - he still couldn't believe his angel was gone. *How do I live without her?*

Even though he should have gone home, Lars told Sven to drive to the office – he needed to work, anything to keep his mind off Laura. When he walked through the door, Olga nearly fell over with surprise.

'Lars, w-what are you doing here?' she stuttered, shocked to see him.

Lars walked into his office, slammed

the door, and spent most of the afternoon watching the snow falling outside his window. The view of Stockholm's old town looked(was) more beautiful than normal. The Strommen was still - as snowdrops disappeared beneath it. A view that usually soothed him - today, he felt out of control. He grieved his wife, and he was angry at her. *What had she been up to? How did she get one over on him?*

A light knock on the door pulled him from his gloom - Olga strutted in carrying a tray of coffee that she placed on his desk, bending over enough for him to see down her white silk blouse. Her skin-tight navy skirt, high heels and big tits slightly aroused him. If in a better mood, he might have bent her over his desk for a hard afternoon fuck, but when she spoke, the sympathy in her voice immediately deflated his growing cock.

'You okay,' she asked, putting her hand on his arm in a familiar way he didn't like.

'Don't,' his eyes said, and she immediately withdrew it.

'The prime minister is on the line. Will I put him through?' she asked, all business again.

Lars nodded, pissed off about playing the role of grieving husband when he wanted to hit someone - preferably Olga.

'Prime Minister,' said Lars, picking up the phone.

The Prime Minister offered his condolences at such shocking news and insisted Lars take time off to grieve.

'I'm better here, sir,' said Lars, trying to sound sad instead of angry.

'Lars, it's good to talk. How are you, and when did you get back to Sweden?'

'Today, I was in Dublin briefly to talk to the Irish police.'

He wasn't in the mood for this shit, and when the PM began firing questions, *had the police identified the perpetrator? What were they doing? How did this happen?* Lars wanted to hang up.

'The Irish guards are investigating the possibility of drug-related burglaries close to where Laura was staying, they suspect,' he paused, not sure how to say the following words, 'her death might be related to that.'

The PM said he'd personally see to it that Laura's killer was found, and Lars, thinking he needed that like a hole in the head, quickly interjected.

'Thank you, sir - but the Irish guards are doing all they can - I have complete faith in them,' he said, hoping the message was loud and clear - back the fuck off.

'I'm so very sorry, Lars, this is such a tragedy,' he continued as Lars rolled his eyes, keen to get off the phone.

'Thank you, sir - I'm spending the weekend at the lake house, but I'd rather keep working for now - it keeps my mind off everything.'

They talked for a few more minutes, and when they said goodbye, Lars told Olga to hold all further calls. He already had at least two hundred text messages, a stack of emails, and voice messages from friends and colleagues - all offering support - all annoying the fuck out of him. Just after six, he finally admitted defeat and went home.

'I'm in the office tomorrow till Friday - keep my appointments light,' he barked while walking past Olga's desk, 'and I'm unavailable this weekend.'

More pity, Lars didn't answer whatever

she called after him. He wanted to get home and go through Laura's things. What else had she been hiding? How did she have videos of him hurting her? Sneaky little bitch - he thought he'd beaten that boldness out of her. *Obviously fucking not, because she tried to stab me.* Laura knew better than anyone what had happened to him in the army and how he reacted when provoked. If she hadn't started this, she'd be alive - a bit bruised and battered but fucking alive.

At the penthouse, Lars took a shower and walked into Laura's huge walk-in closet, amazed by how full it was. He began pulling it apart and, two hours later, found nothing out of the ordinary. When Erik called to say the phone was definitely clean, he was furious.

'You sure?' asked Lars.

'Completely boss, there's nothing on it,' said Erik.

'Did she delete them or send them to someone?' asked Lars again.

'No email account on the phone - no sent or WhatsApp messages either,' said Erik.

'Okay, get rid of it, burn it, do whatever you need, just make sure that phone doesn't exist,'

Lars hung up and poured a large glass of whiskey - his mind trying to process the last few days. During a coffee break at the conference, Erik had said Laura was in Grafton Street, and Lars was confused - sure he'd made a mistake.

'She was going straight to the hospital - her mother is there,' he'd said.

Laura wouldn't dare lie to him, but he knew she had when Erik revealed the tracking data from her phone. Grand Canal Dock from Dublin Airport, which he now knew was the apartment she rented. Four hours near St Stephens Green - he instantly knew it was The Shelbourne Hotel. Laura never stopped going on about how much she missed having lunch there. He rang her immediately and nearly lost his mind when she didn't answer.

'Check the hospital and find out if Mona Quinn is a patient there,' he told Erik, then quickly texted Laura to say if she didn't answer her phone, he'd be on the next plane to Dublin, and he meant it.

When the last presentation finished, Erik said there was no record of Laura's mother in St James Hospital and that Laura was now in Kimmage. The little bitch had read his text and dashed to her mother's house. Then she lied and got her mother to do the same. He'd pretended not to know - his hands itching to bruise that beautiful white skin. She'd given him no choice - he had to go to Dublin and get her.

It had almost been too easy to get there. No one missed him at the conference, and Lars was standing outside Laura's apartment building by 11am the next morning. Her phone had pinpointed the location, and Erik didn't take long to find the apartment. Astrid Nilsson? He laughed - could she be any more obvious? A quick fiddle with the lock, and he was inside. When Laura walked in, the sight of her and the sound of her singing - something he hadn't heard in years, nearly knocked him off his feet. He knew he was responsible for her sadness, and even though she tried to hide it, he knew she despised him. He saw the disgust on her face when she looked at him. Laura didn't love him anymore, but Lars could never allow her to love anyone else.

23 ~ ORLA

The days following the reunion with her friends were a blur of emails, meetings, and writing for Orla. On Wednesday, she flew to the UK for an urgent meeting with Dorothy, who was horrified by the goings on in Ireland but not surprised to hear of Orla's involvement.

'You'll get to the truth - you can't help yourself,' said Dorothy, smiling.

Orla asked Dorothy to push the book tour to May at the earliest.

'I'll suggest June or July - then you can enjoy a few weeks in the summer. Your publishing company want to promote all your books, so it should be fine,' said Dorothy.

Orla liked that idea. Con would be back from travelling, and Max finished university for the summer. They could join her for a stint on tour and enjoy America together. After lunch, she took the train to the Cotswolds and was surprised to find Max was home. Orla was delighted to see him and Ray, who was back from the neighbours. After dinner in the village pub, they video-called Connor, and Orla felt calmer. It was good to talk to her sons - they grounded her. When she told them what was happening in Dublin - they were worried.

'Fucking hell - be careful, ma. The husband sounds like a prick,' said Con, Orla's easy-going nomad son and the worrier of the family.

'I plan on being very careful, but I have to find the truth,' said Orla.

'Well, just take it easy - you're not as young as you used to be,' said Con.

'Oi, cheeky sod,' said Orla, mock gasping, 'I might not be twenty-five anymore, but there's still some life left in me.'

They laughed and chatted about other things before saying goodbye. When Orla got into her own bed that night - she had a vivid dream about Laura. They were in Bewley's Café. Laura looked as gorgeous as ever and was trying to tell Orla something. Orla could sense it was important, but the background noise made it impossible to hear what she was saying. The next morning, while making her coffee, Orla remembered the dream and wrote down the details. Dreams sometimes meant something – could Laura be trying to tell her something? She laughed at her own dramatics and drank her coffee.

'Woohoo. "This dream means something, Orla," I called while inhaling the scent of coffee.'

The next day, Orla flew back to Dublin, determined to crack Laura's case. Now that her world was in order, she could dedicate her time to finding out what had happened in that apartment. The journalist in her was keen to see the bigger picture - her fascination with crime driving her. For years, Orla had studied the minds of criminals, interviewing them and reviewing their case files. She always wondered how they thought they'd get away with murder - it was why she started writing books.

'Orla will find the truth.'

In the taxi from Dublin airport, she rang Audrey to see how the investigation was progressing. It had been almost ten days since

Laura was murdered - maybe there'd been a breakthrough. Perhaps a witness who saw a tall, dark and ruggedly handsome man going into Laura's apartment. For everything Orla hated about Lars, *and there was a lot* she couldn't deny he was gorgeous. If his black soul matched his face, he'd be a horror show. Instead, he resembled a fallen angel, moody and pissed off but beautiful, charismatic, charming, and wealthy. Orla could understand why Laura had fallen madly in love with him. *Pity he was a psychopath,* she thought while waiting for Audrey to answer.

'I missed the psychopath bit until it was too late.'

'Hey, hang on, I just need to get away from my desk - too many people here,' said Audrey, moving around and closing a door.

Orla asked how it was going.

'It's not,' sighed Audrey. 'The apartment has no CCTV - the entrance is on a busy street with loads of people coming and going, and there's nothing to link Lars to it,' she said, then added, 'and...somehow, Laura's blood got contaminated. Initially, we were told there was two people's blood on the knife - I don't know what happened, but it's useless now.

'How does something like that happen?' asked Orla, shocked by the incompetence.

'It's more common than you think,' said Audrey.

Orla had a thought.

'Does your boss know Laura was your friend?' she asked, thinking surely Audrey would have shared what kind of man Lars was.

'Yeah, he knows. I'm lucky to be working with Dave Healy - the inspector leading the case. I told him about the nightclub and Laura's letters. Dave said it's suspicious, alright, but it doesn't prove Lars killed her, and if he got someone else to do it, there's not a trace of it.'

Orla thought the latter was more likely - his shadow, Erik, sprung to mind.

'We rechecked the apartment for fingerprints, and Dave asked me to ring Lars the other day. He listened on another line while I talked to him. I said I wanted to discuss the case further, but we just wanted to hear his reaction to a few developments.'

'What developments?' asked Orla, feeling slightly optimistic - maybe the fucker would slip up.

'They weren't really developments. I mentioned the assault in the nightclub and said we heard Laura wanted to leave him.

'What did he say?'

'He knew I was blowing smoke up his arse - cool as a fucking cucumber, he didn't flinch. He said it was a load of old rubbish - someone trying to ruin his reputation, and he was used to that.'

'Cool as a cucumber – I had a flashback - Lars watching me, but where?'

'Did he know who you were?' asked Orla, guessing he didn't.

'I don't think so. I said Sergeant O'Brien, and let's face it, he probably doesn't even remember my first name, never mind my last,' said Audrey and Orla agreed, but you never know with him. 'He still has that pit bull Erik working for him - doesn't go anywhere without him,' said Audrey, saving Orla the bother of asking about him.

'Did you check if he was in Dublin when Laura was murdered,' she asked and heard paper rustling.

'There's photos of him with Lars at the conference in Brussels,' said Audrey, and something about that troubled Orla, but she couldn't put her finger on it.

'What about the name Laura used to book the apartment? Ingrid, was it?' asked Orla. 'Laura mentioned her in my letter.'

More rustling papers.

'It was Astrid Nilsson, and we can't find anyone with that name. Laura had no social media, and do you know how many Astrid Nilsson's are on Facebook?' asked Audrey.

'Did she not use her credit card?' asked Orla, thinking there had to be a way of finding her.

'No, she used a PayPal account linked to an Irish bank account. She has about three hundred grand in it. All in her maiden name with her mam and dad's address,'

Orla knew there was no crime in saving money, but that sounded like escape money. They chatted for a bit longer, and before hanging up, Orla quickly asked if Audrey had spoken to Louise, Laura's older sister.

'Yeah, Lou said Lars was a pig - they

hated him, and although Laura had an amazing life in Sweden, she was miserable as sin and wanted to come home. She also said they'd never spent a second with Laura in twenty years without Lars in the background. He was always the perfect gentleman, but Laura was never herself.'

Orla thought it sounded like a prison sentence.

'I hate that my family had to go through that.'

By the time they said goodbye, Orla had paid the taxi and sat in her mother's kitchen with a cup of tea. She took out a notepad to mind-map her thoughts while Audrey's conversation was fresh in her head. In the middle of the page, she wrote Laura's name. In little circles around it, she wrote Lars, Astrid, Laura's solicitor, the apartment, her parents, the videos, and the nail in the coffin. As she studied them, she wondered how they were connected. Did Laura discover something that got her killed? She glanced at the circle with *nail in coffin*, her eyes lingering for a few minutes. What could it be? Was it the reason

Laura was dead?

Laura
Where was the phone? I had it after meeting Marcus - I knew that much. Did my killer take it? Even though finding the phone was less important – Lars's beatings had become somewhat irrelevant now I was dead - I was determined to get him for the trafficking girls and for someone to find those bodies. I remembered where the USB stick was – safely tucked away in a make bag, in mam's house that no one would ever think to look in – shit.

24 ~ LARS

The sound of Lars's phone ringing snapped him out of his mood. An Irish number flashed on his screen, and his stomach flipped as he answered.

'Mr Karlsson - Sergeant O'Brien. Could I ask you a few more questions about Laura?' asked the voice at the end of the line.

'Of course,' said Lars, and listened as the same questions he'd answered in Dublin were repeated. *Why did Laura stay in an apartment? Why say her mother was in hospital?* Then, Sergeant O'Brien surprised him with what she said next.

'We spoke to Laura's parents - they said Laura wanted to leave you. Is there any truth in that, sir?' she asked, and years of political training immediately kicked into place.

'Laura and I had a silly little argument, sergeant. She tends to get overly emotional, but we had no plans to separate,' said Lars, sounding relaxed and confident.

'Ah, right, so – well, we also spoke to Laura's solicitor, Marcus Ryan - I believe you met him when you were in Dublin.' Before he could respond, Audrey continued. 'Anyway, he was Laura's solicitor and saw her on Monday before her murder. He said Laura was leaving you and that she had videos of your domestic abuse. Do you have any comment?' she asked again, rattling him this time.

What the fuck? Lars wanted to hang up but took a deep breath.

'Ridiculous,' he said.

'So, they're lying?' asked Audrey.

'Listen to me very carefully, detective. I loved my wife very much, and she loved me. She was a little fragile at times, slightly paranoid too and had been under the care of many psychiatrists over the years,' said Lars, thinking about Laura and her therapists – he could use it to his advantage. 'We were very happy and had no plans to separate.'

'Well, one last thing before you go,' said the sergeant as he braced himself. 'We have a reliable source who informed us about an altercation in a Dublin nightclub in

2000. Apparently, you assaulted Laura quite violently, and there was a hostage situation. We have no record of the incident, but I wondered if you would comment?'

What - the - fuck?

'Surely you don't believe everything you hear, detective,' said Lars, smooth as silk but with slightly sweating palms. 'I'm a public figure. People have been trying to destroy my reputation for years - their stories always turn out to be lies.'

How the fuck had that surfaced? Had Laura spoken to someone? *She wouldn't dare.* With nothing else to be said, Lars asked for progress on locating Laura's killer.

'We're doing all we can, Mr Karlsson - when we find him, you'll be the first to know,' said Audrey.

The call ended, and Lars immediately rang Erik. No answer - he left a message. Who the fuck was their reliable source? Lars had no association with his life in Ireland. In Sweden, he was considered a devoted husband - a respectable businessman and the future fucking Prime Minister of the country. Everything else had been carefully erased, and it had taken years to achieve. Coerced help from a police commissioner who liked underage girls. A recommendation from a minister with a perversion for pain during sex and a few other favours had allowed a poor boy from a small village in northern Sweden into the elite world of politics.

When his party won the upcoming election, Lars would be confirmed as Deputy Prime Minister. After that, it was Prime Minister, the job he wanted - his prize, and he'd do anything to get it. Laura should have been by his side - that was his dream.

Even though it pained him, Lars had already decided to let Laura's funeral take place in Dublin. If he tried to bring her to Sweden, it might seem insensitive, and he knew that old bitch Mona would kick up. She'd looked at him with disgust at the station when he identified Laura's body. She hated him, and so did Mick. As always, he'd been polite and said how sorry he was - reassuring them that the guards would find Laura's killer. They didn't outright walk away from him, but they wanted to.

As he drank his whiskey, he thought about the first time he saw Laura, the day his world stopped and his life changed forever. Walking down Baggot Street one sunny afternoon, he noticed a bright blue dress approaching him. The girl wearing it had an incredible body with long red hair that bounced as she walked, and all he could do was stare. Green eyes lit with mischief when she smiled at him - he was lost.

It took six months before she'd go out with him, and when she did, he vowed never to let her go. At the time, he owned a construction company that built houses for the Irish government and a security company that provided bouncers to upmarket nightclubs. A side-line of supplying cocaine to the club's wealthy clientele proved very lucrative. He had money, a great apartment, and a fabulous lifestyle. Laura had loved it, and they had a brilliant time until that little slip-up in Lily's nightclub - a cocaine-fuelled mess that meant he nearly lost her. For weeks he begged and pleaded for her to come back - having to fight against her friends, filling her head with crap every step of the way.

Once again, Lars's phone interrupted his thoughts - Erik. Lars told him about the conversation with the Irish cop and asked him to check it out.

'There were no witnesses that night,' said Lars.

'Except for her friends - you said they were untouchable,' said Erik.

Only because Laura had begged him not to touch them - it was her one condition, and he would have done anything to get her back.

'Fuck, I forgot about them - it was so long ago,' said Lars, who knew Laura hadn't seen them since he moved her to Sweden - he'd made sure of that. 'Find out what happened to them. I can't even remember their names. One was Maggie, I think.'

Lars hung up and turned on the TV. The Swedish news channels were running stories about Laura - saying she was a victim of a violent robbery and that their minister, Lars Karlsson, was devastated by the death of his wife. Lars hadn't made an official statement - he'd do so the next day but for now - the robbery idea suited him. Later, while getting ready for bed, Erik rang.

'Impressive,' said Lars, knowing he would only call if he had information.

'Not really - they were easy to find. One's a cop - one a famous author - one owns a bookshop in Dublin - and the other a pub in Cork,' said Erik.

Well, well, well, they actually made something of their lives.

'Who's the author?' asked Lars, more than curious - he didn't know those women well but had spent a few evenings with them back in the day.

'Orla Reed - six books published,' said Erik.

'What about the cop?' asked Lars, surprised any of those women would be allowed to join the police.

'Audrey O'Brien - dyke, and working Laura's case,' said Erik, then added, 'she's their source because she was there that night.'

'Which means I'm a suspect in Laura's murder,' said Lars. 'Keep a close eye on the investigation - I want to know every detail. In the meantime, send me any information you have on those women,' he demanded before hanging up again.

Lars thought back to the night in question – a hostage situation! He almost laughed - those girls were invited to stay longer than they wanted to. He smiled as he decided to play dumb in future calls with Sergeant O'Brien. He'd pretend he didn't know exactly who she was or that she suspected him of murdering his wife. Suddenly aroused, the thought of going to bed alone no longer appealed to him. He picked up his phone, toying with the idea for a few minutes. Did he really want her tonight? He thought about it and decided he did. She answered after the first ring.

'Mr Karlsson – to what do I owe the pleasure?' she asked in a sultry voice.

'Be here in ten minutes,' said Lars.

'I need twenty to get ready,' said Olga, trying to sound sexy, but if she knew what was coming - she'd have said no.

'Dress like a slut,' said Lars as she purred, 'and wear the red wig.'

He hung up and walked into the kitchen to open a bottle of wine, his cock already hard in anticipation of what he was going to do to Olga's fat arse.

25 ~ ORLA

If Orla had to describe Marcus Ryan's office, she would have said it was very fecking messy. Files scattered on the floor - discarded cups of coffee here and there - a Dan Brown novel face down on his desk and an old, half-eaten bacon sandwich beside it.

Marcus was handsome - mid-forties with pale blue eyes and floppy blonde hair. As if to match his office – he looked like he'd slept in his crumpled suit that strained to keep his muscular shoulders inside - *definitely a rugby player.* A brown leather school bag lay open on the floor, stuffed with more files and suggesting he took his work home at night. No wedding band - Orla couldn't help looking while wondering if he specialised in domestic abuse because he was subjected to it as a child.

'Can you tell me exactly what Laura said?' asked Orla, grateful for the appointment at such short notice.

Marcus agreed to fit her in because he was a fan of her books and equally keen to discover what happened to Laura.

'Yeah, I will, but first – can we talk about the husband,' he said.

Ohh, yes, please, thought Orla, curious as to what his domestic abuse radar picked up while noticing how white his teeth were.

'What the fuck is his story? He basically threatened me - said he'd drag me through court if I made an attempt to attack his reputation, and that was before he even asked about his wife,' said Marcus, puffing on a vape.

'Such a prince. You can see why I married him!'

That didn't surprise Orla - however, the Lars she knew was more likely to drag him through a back alley and beat the shit out of him rather than a court, but she didn't mention that.

'Sounds like the Lars of old,' she said.

'He wanted the evidence he thought Laura gave me, and I told him the same thing I told the guards - she gave me nothing. I saw videos of him boxing the shite out of her, and in one of them, he kicked her in the stomach while she was lying on the floor - I'm not saying what he did in the other one - disgusting pig.'

'Did you tell the guards?' asked Orla, wondering why they didn't follow it up, or maybe they did - she needed to talk to Audrey.

'Yeah, but things like that can be faked - without the original videos, it's hearsay. I told Laura to get other stuff - conversations that might be considered threatening and showed her how to use the microphone on her phone. She was supposed to send the videos, but obviously, she didn't,' he said with a hint of regret.

'Was she trying to blackmail him?' asked Orla.

'I wouldn't go as far as blackmail, more like her get-out-of-jail card. She wanted to threaten his rep to get away from him. She said he wouldn't let her go, but he had eyes on the PM job in Sweden – a bit of domestic abuse scandal would wreck that for him,' said Marcus.

'I still might wreck it for him – if I can get Orla to hear me.'

'Why didn't she give you the videos, and how could she have them on her phone if he checked it?' asked Orla, assuming Laura told Marcus everything.

'I don't know - she might have had second thoughts about throwing him under a bus. It happens in domestic abuse cases, and she had two phones. He didn't know about one – she'd been hiding it for months.'

Of course, she did - that made sense. So, their feisty Laura was still in there after all - hidden beneath the brokenness. Orla's heart hurt thinking of how frightened she must have been.

'Where was that phone? Audrey said, my bag, phone, etc, were missing – were both phones gone?'

'Where's the other phone?' asked Orla, feeling confused.

Marcus didn't know, so Orla tried to think what she'd do in Laura's situation. After a few minutes, the answer came - *hide it*.

'Yes, I hid it - I remembered that – but where?'

'What time did Laura leave here that day?' she asked.

Marcus, who'd been watching her closely – coughed, then checked his diary.

'She was here for an hour - probably just after eleven,' he said.

Assuming she walked, it would have taken about half an hour to get back to the apartment. The coroner said she was murdered around noon. Did that mean the phone was there? Surely, if it was, the guards would have found it. If Lars murdered Laura or paid someone to do it – he'd have it, so why show up here looking for it?

'Orla is so convinced Lars killed me - I'm beginning to believe it myself.'

'She also asked about sex trafficking laws –I think she had information about certain high-up people,' said Marcus.

Orla didn't say she already knew this for fear of getting Audrey into trouble.

'Laura wrote to me and three others the day before her murder and mentioned a nail in

Lars's coffin – do you think that was it?'

'I don't know, but she was nervous - I got the impression she was involved in something dangerous,' said Marcus, then paused as if trying to remember something, 'she said she needed to talk to her sister, and they'd email me the videos and the information together.'

Orla's ears perked up – Louise was her next port of call.

'Did you tell the guards?' she asked.

'Told them she asked about sex trafficking but just remembered about the sister. I have a feeling her sister knows a bit more than we do,' said Marcus.

Orla thanked Marcus for his time, and as he walked her to his office door without thought or reason, she leaned up and kissed his cheek - an awkward pause followed.

'Eh, sorry, I don't know why I did that, you just seem familiar,' she said, mortified.

He blushed furiously, and Orla practically ran out the door - horrified at her behaviour. She rang Audrey first, but when there was no answer, she rang the Quinns.

Laura

Louise knew about the trafficking and the bodies, but she didn't know where the girls were, and I forgot to tell her about the USB stick in my make-up bag. I kicked myself for not telling her everything when we spoke on Sunday. My paranoia made me stupid, and because of that, Lars could get away with everything.

26 ~ AUDREY

Audrey O Brien loved being a guard - she was dedicated and hardworking but compared to Orla - she felt practically lazy. Like a dog with a big, fat, juicy bone when uncovering the truth, Orla simply wouldn't let it go. Her tenacity was infectious, and her attention to detail impeccable - no wonder her books were bestsellers.

Sneaking out of Dave's office, she wandered over to the evidence board in the open plan office at Kevin Street Garda Station and, as she had a thousand times already, studied the pictures of the crime scene.

Laura, lying on a slab in the morgue - a deep gash in her neck, sloppy and jagged, and suggesting a frenzied attack. Audrey simply couldn't imagine Lars being so violent towards her, and surely, it would have been less messy if he had paid a professional. Laura's face was battered, her wrists bruised, and her arm broken - she'd fought for her life. Audrey tried to consider different scenarios, but it was impossible with no fingerprints - no fibres and not even a random hair.

Her eyes moved to the picture of Lars, handsome and evil - a deadly combination. They knew from Laura's letters that Laura wanted to leave him. Lars beat her throughout their marriage – maybe he went too far and accidentally killed her, but how? Closing her eyes, she allowed her mind to wander through the scene, the evidence, the blood, the coffee, the letters. As she had in Orla's letter, Laura mentioned evidence that could ruin Lars when she wrote to Audrey. Marcus said Laura asked about sex trafficking laws, but everyone on the team agreed Lars Karlsson and sex trafficking didn't fit. One possibility Audrey considered was that Lars discovered Laura was up to something and instructed Erik to kill her - but it seemed farfetched. Surely, he'd just destroy the videos and whatever evidence Laura had. As much as Audrey despised Lars - she was sure he loved Laura in his own sick way.

'A wife beater is not necessarily a murderer,' said Dave when Audrey told him about the nightclub incident all those years ago. 'Anyway, he's a fucking government minister - we can't go throwing around accusations without proof - he'll have us all fired. Even if he boxed ten bells of shite out of her day and night, we can't do anything about it because she didn't report it here or in Sweden.'

He was right, but Audrey couldn't shake the feeling that Lars had something to do with Laura's death - the main reason she wasn't interfering in Orla's quest for the truth. Her eyes moved to the other pictures on the board - an untouched cup of coffee - a smashed one. Did Laura make coffee and drop it, then make another one? That seemed unlikely, and suggested coffee for two. Laura knew her attacker – Audrey was sure of it and wondered if Lars drank coffee.

Dave walked into the room while she stared at the board.

'Got five?' he asked.

Audrey nodded and followed him into his office.

'I'm under pressure to arrest someone or make a statement. Every junkie and known thief in Dublin had been questioned this week, and no one is saying a word. On top of that, her body is being released for burial in two days. Someone rang the husband and parents this morning.'

'If this was a random killing, surely someone would know something,' said Audrey desperately.

Dave agreed that was usually the case - they'd get a whiff of something as criminals tended to brag - but not about this.

Within hours of finding Laura, local parks, rubbish bins, and tips were searched. According to her mam, Laura was wearing her wedding rings, a gold watch and a diamond cross around her neck - all were missing. They hoped the jewellery might turn up on the black market, but nothing so far.

'Does this mean the investigation is over?' asked Audrey.

'No, but we're hitting brick walls everywhere we turn,' said Dave. 'The Swedish PM apparently wants it all wrapped up - they have a general election over there soon, and Lars is a prominent part of their campaign blah blah, some bullshit like that.'

'What about Lars?' asked Audrey. 'Can we go over that one more time?'

Even though Dave thought it was a waste of time, he agreed.

'Tell me again about that night,' he sighed as he sat down.

Audrey went through what happened in Lily's club - what the solicitor said about abuse and trafficking - Laura's letters - her parent's comments. Dave already knew it all, but Audrey hoped something would jump out at them.

'Okay, Audrey - let's say for a minute that Lars is a sex trafficker and an animal who regularly beat the shite out of his wife. She came home to divorce him or blackmail him - whatever. He found out and either followed her to Dublin and killed her or had someone else do it. Where's the evidence?'

'We have none,' she sighed.

'What if Laura was making it up?' he asked.

'She wouldn't do that,' said Audrey.

'How do you know? When was the last time you saw her?' asked Dave.

'Twenty years ago,' she sighed, accepting

his point - she no longer knew Laura.

'Anyway, he's a public person, for fuck's sake. There's photos of him at a conference in Belgium when Laura was killed and no record of him flying into Dublin, which leaves the option of a sloppy fucking hitman. Please tell me where to start with that?'

Dave wasn't trying to be a prick - he cared about finding Laura's killer, and his logic made perfect sense, but it pissed Audrey off.

'It just seems so unfair,' she said, thinking about an unsolved stamp on Laura's case file.

Just after five, having spent the afternoon scouring through evidence and finding nothing, Audrey went home. Nina had the night off, a rare occurrence, and Audrey was thrilled.

'I'll pick up some wine,' she said when they spoke.

The thought of a home-cooked meal instead of a garage sandwich for dinner was divine.

'I've already got wine - just get yourself home,' said Nina.

What an angel. Audrey loved her as

much as when they'd first met. At the time, Audrey was shy about being gay. Her friends knew about it, but she'd never had a girlfriend - just a few snogs at the gay bar in town. Orla and Laura were the only ones to go with her. The idea of being chatted up by a woman was too much for Maggie and Niamh.

'Ah no, I can't - I'd be scarlet - what would I say?' said Niamh when Orla tried to convince her to go.

'Will you stop the lights - they don't fancy every woman they see. It's the same as a boy-girl connection - there needs to be chemistry,' said Orla, then added, 'anyway, full of yourself, aren't you?'

'Well, I'm not going,' huffed Niamh, making them laugh.

Orla loved it - she'd talk to the girls and get their perspective on being young and gay in Catholic Ireland. If Audrey remembered correctly, Orla wrote an article on it.

Nina was sitting in the UCD library when Audrey first saw her. It was two weeks before Christmas - Nina's books were piled high on the table as she furiously wrote in a notebook. Audrey's first thought had been Christ - I'd love to be that focused. Then she noticed long black hair and dark glowing skin. When Nina looked up, and Audrey clocked the red-rimmed reading glasses that framed dark brown eyes, she was a goner.

Audrey, on the other hand, was desperately hungover - her short blond hair resembled a bird's nest, her ripped jeans and t-shirt looked like she'd slept in them, and she might not have showered that day. Nina smiled and feeling mortified, Audrey quickly looked away. When she looked again, Nina was still watching and nodded to the spare seat beside her.

'You look like you've had a heavy night,' said Nina when Audrey sat down.

'Is it that obvious?' asked Audrey, laughing.

'Here, this might help,' said Nina, taking a flask from a rucksack and pouring Audrey a cup of coffee. She then rooted around and produced the most amazing chocolate brownie Audrey had ever tasted. 'Homemade,' said Nina, noticing the look of pleasure on Audrey's face.

'Thanks, it's just what I needed,' said

Audrey.

At the time, Audrey was studying criminal psychology, and although she enjoyed studying, she also lived university life to the fullest, drinking and partying. Nina was an A-star student, studying medicine and didn't drink alcohol. She was super intelligent, devoted to her profession, kind-hearted, and easy to be around. It was love at first sight for Audrey.

When Audrey walked into her house twenty minutes later, her mouth watered. On top of everything else, Nina could cook like a champion - Audrey hit the jackpot as she was known to assassinate food rather than cook it. Over dinner, Audrey filled her in on the case, and Nina listened in disbelief.

'Lars has to have something to do with it. What other explanation is there?' she asked.

Audrey agreed but explained the lack of evidence and Orla's private investigation.

'I love that the girls are back in your life. I can't believe it's been twenty years,' said Nina.

'I know, and it's like we just saw each other last week. So natural, but we were always more like sisters than friends,' said Audrey.

'Why don't you invite them over for dinner? I'd love to see them,' suggested Nina, and Audrey liked that idea.

While eating, they discussed what happened in the nightclub all those years before. Nina knew the whole story, but they'd never had a reason to discuss it.

'Why not make a complaint or is it too late?' asked Nina.

'I thought about it, but what good would it do? Why didn't we do it then, and what would it prove? Lars and Laura married and lived in a different country for twenty years. He became a government minister, and there hasn't been a whisper of domestic abuse. Beating the crap out of us and holding us hostage doesn't fit the bill,' said Audrey.

Nina saw her point and agreed, but what she said next was so unexpected that it took Audrey a few minutes to understand what she meant.

'What about the girls? Whatever happened to them?' she asked casually.

'What girls?' asked Audrey, confused.

'The young girls from the nightclub. The ones being sexually assaulted and raped,' said

Nina.

Audrey stared at her girlfriend with her fork suspended halfway between her plate and mouth. What had happened to the girls being sexually assaulted and raped? She hadn't given those kids a single thought since that night.

27 ~ ORLA

'Come in quickly - you'll catch your death of cold,' said Mrs Quinn as she opened the door to Orla.

The promised snow still hadn't arrived, but it was freezing outside. As a rule, Ireland was unprepared for snow, but Orla loved it and hoped it would fall soon. The Quinn's small living room felt warm and cosy with a fire blazing in the hearth. Orla handed a box of cakes to Mr Quinn - who went to make the tea.

'Sit down, love, what can I do for you?' asked Mrs Quinn as Orla warmed her hands.

'Me poor da - always the chief tea maker in the house.'

Orla asked how they were - probably a stupid question, considering their youngest child had been murdered.

'We're okay. We'll feel better when we

can bury her, and at least she's back in Ireland, where she wanted to be.' Her voice wobbled, and Orla's heart broke as she asked if there was more news from the guards. 'They think it might be a robbery. Apparently, there's lads in town who like the drugs. They might have robbed Laura and, God help us, killed her at the same time,' said Mrs Quinn, wiping her tears as she spoke. 'They're letting us have her body on Wednesday – she'll be in the chapel of rest on Saturday night, and her funeral is next Monday.'

'Has Lars said anything about the funeral?' asked Orla with a lump in her throat.

'Oh Jesus, I won't speak to that man - I just can't face him. He told Mick to go ahead and make the arrangements and said he'd pay for it. We don't want his money - we'll bury our own daughter, but he insisted, so we'll give it to a children's charity in Laura's name.'

'She'd like that,' said Orla.

'Ah, that's nice, mam.'

Mr Quinn came into the room carrying a tray of tea, and with no easy way around it,

Orla got to the real reason for her visit.

'I was wondering if you'd tell me what you think happened? As in, what your gut is telling you?'

They looked at each other, and for a second, Orla thought she'd blown it until Mr Quinn started talking, and he didn't stop.

'Orla, love - I keep asking myself the same question, and it's this. What sort of man hurts his wife? You've no idea how hard it's been for us, knowing our daughter was married to that monster. Lars is an animal, and although he gave Laura everything, material things, I mean, and far more than her sister ever had - she was dying a bit more every time we saw her. She didn't say he hurt her, but we knew he did.'

Orla sighed. Laura had always been good at hiding abuse. She remembered how they'd suspected it twenty years earlier, but Laura so fiercely denied it that they began second-guessing themselves.

'She was probably trying to protect you from it,' said Orla, and he nodded.

'Sure, if we tried to talk about it, she'd insist there was nothing wrong, but she was a shadow of her old self and terrified of Lars.

It breaks my heart to say it, but at least she's at peace and away from him,' he said as tears quietly rolled down his cheeks, settling in his bushy white beard.

'God love him. "I'm sorry, da," I whispered as I hugged him.'

Mrs Quinn openly sobbed, and Orla felt angry. The thought of Lars getting away with years of abuse and possibly murder made her blood boil.

'Do you think he had anything to do with her death?' asked Orla. 'Ignore what the guards say and tell me what you think.'

Once again, they looked at each other, but Mrs Quinn spoke this time.

'If I'm honest, Orla, I think he did. There's something not right. – Laura came home with evidence to get away from Lars, and now she's dead.'

'Oh, Jesus – why can't I remember if my husband killed me?'

'Can you tell me about her life in Sweden?

Her friends?' asked Orla and Mrs Quinn looked sad.

'Laura knew people in Sweden, but she didn't have any real friends, not that we knew of anyway,' she said, and Orla nearly wept.

'What about Astrid Nilsson? Know her?' she asked.

They didn't, but Mrs Quinn offered some valuable information.

'Laura spent most of her time at the lake house - Lars was there sometimes, and in Stockholm for work.' She showed Orla pictures of a beautiful lake house in Uppsala. 'Laura did charity work at a local hospital there - Astrid might be someone from work,' she said.

At least that narrowed things down. Orla felt like she had something to go on - a possible second phone and a hospital in Uppsala, but they didn't know which one.

'Would you mind if I spoke to Louise?' asked Orla.

'Not at all – Louise knows a bit more about what Laura was doing – they talked on the phone when Laura was here on Sunday,' said Mrs Quinn.

'Grand so – I'll ring her later,' said Orla.

When she left the Quinn's house, Orla immediately texted Lou and asked if they could meet, then googled hospitals in Uppsala and found three of them - *which one did you work at, Laura?*

'The university one, love.'

Forming a plan, Orla needed her friends on board - four heads were better than one, and there was work to be done. She wanted to find Astrid Nilsson - Orla felt like she was part of this. She created a WhatsApp group called Laura's Angels and messaged the girls.

Orla: *Hey. I've been investigating Laura's life. There are things I'd like to talk to you about. Audrey, I know you have to be careful, but I'm doing this with the blessing of Laura's parents. I need to talk to some of Laura's friends. Anyone up for a couple of days in Sweden?*

She pressed send and got two immediate responses.

Niamh: *Yep, I'm defo in. Just let me know the details asap.*

Audrey: *Have you lost your fucking mind?*

Expecting that from Audrey, Orla had

her response ready.

Orla: *You said it yourself there's no evidence. We owe it to Laura to at least try to find some – Smirk emoji.*

She wouldn't say no to that.

Audrey: *Fuck's sake, never change, still as nosey as ever - Bored face.*

Orla liked to think of it as curious over nosey.

Orla: *That mean you're coming? Smiley face.*

Audrey: *Yeah, and you're an annoying bitch – middle finger.*

That was two down. It took half an hour for Maggie to respond, and she was as blunt as always.

Maggie: *Don't think there's any point. If he killed her, he'll get away with it. People like him get away with stuff like this, but I'll come. Just let me know the details so I can get cover for the shop.*

Orla breathed a sigh of relief - they were all on board.

Orla: *I'll be in touch, but just left Laura's parent's house. Funeral next Monday. Thinking Wednesday to Friday of same week? I'll check it out and let you know.*

She googled Uppsala, delighted to discover the airport was relatively close. The flights were available, as were the hotel rooms, and an hour later, she sent another group text.

Orla: *Next Wednesday morning @9am, two nights, back Friday morning. Work?*

Three thumbs up, she booked it. Now, all they needed was to get through the funeral, and the thought of seeing Lars again after all these years made Orla want to gag.

Laura

I was nervous about seeing Lars at my funeral. Had he really killed me, as everyone suspected? Had I spent six months wasting my time trying to gather evidence against him? The phone was gone - no one knew where the girls were buried, and the USB was in a make-up bag that no one would think to look in.

28 ~ AUDREY

Audrey's mind was in turmoil.

'I don't know what happened to those girls,' she said. 'In fact, I'd be surprised if they were even eighteen. They were definitely out of their depth with those men.' She remembered she and Orla thought they were high on cocaine. 'When all hell broke loose, Erik and the other men took them from the room. We assumed they got a taxi home because the men returned without them.' Nina didn't look convinced, and suddenly, neither was Audrey. 'Thinking about it, that doesn't seem likely, does it?'

'Well, they'd just been sexually assaulted - had taken cocaine and witnessed the attack on you lot. What if one or all of them sobered up and went to the guards? They could have cried rape or reported what happened. Those men held you at gunpoint and took your phones to stop you from doing that. Would they let three young girls go home and just hope they didn't open their mouths? From the sounds of it, they weren't the kind of men to take chances,' said Nina to Audrey's shocked face.

Audrey's mind flashed back. Who were the girls? Did they say anything? How long had the men been gone for?

'What do you think might have happened?' asked Audrey.

'I don't know, and I've never thought about it until now, but why would four men, probably in their mid-thirties, have three very young girls at a private party - filling them with alcohol and drugs?'

Audrey thought about it for a minute or two.

'To have sex with them,' she said, but even to herself, that sounded weak.

'Really? Men like that with their money and position. They had the pick of the crop - you know what it was like back then. What would they want with three kids? Were they just showing them a nice time? What might have happened if you five hadn't walked in?'

The phrase sex trafficking jumped into

Audrey's mind, but she dismissed it – no, that was too farfetched.

'If they didn't go home, where did they go? The member's bar was empty, but the nightclub downstairs was packed. Erik and the others came back not ten minutes later - maybe the girls went dancing,' said Audrey, clutching at straws.

'Doesn't sound like they were in any state to do that - you said they were freaking out. Surely, they'd just want to go home,' said Nina, making perfect sense as always.

'What if something happened to them? We all assumed they went home - now I'm not so sure,' said Audrey.

'Can you check at work? Is there a missing persons list or something?' asked Nina.

There was, and Audrey had access to it, but twenty years was a long time - talk about a needle in a haystack. Anyway, she couldn't remember three girls ever going missing. That would have been big news in Dublin, and she would have seen it.

At her desk the next morning, Audrey told herself she was being dramatic. Those girls went home, probably kicking themselves for being so stupid and hopefully learning a lesson about not snorting cocaine with Swedish military men twice their age, but she couldn't shake the feeling that might not have been the case. If Lars was as evil as Audrey believed him to be, it stood to reason that his mates were as well. Brushing it aside, she spent the rest of the morning combing through Laura's case, desperate to find a break - she got nowhere and at lunchtime, Dave asked if she fancied a pint.

'Whelan's?' she asked, knowing that's where he usually went.

He nodded - she said she'd follow him, and when he was gone, she logged back into the missing person database, searching for girls missing since early 2000. She'd been browsing it throughout the day, but so far, nothing had surfaced. Hundreds of girls were missing, and even though Audrey wouldn't recognise the girls from the nightclub if they stood in front of her, she searched for connections, a group of friends or family members.

Just as she was about to give up and join Dave in the pub, three girls from Greek Street flats flashed across her screen. Missing since early 2000, they were two cousins and their friend who went out for a night in town and were never seen again. The file said they'd likely moved to England, but that seemed ridiculous and outdated. Early 2000 wasn't the early 19th century when people moved abroad and were never seen again. Quickly downloading the file, Audrey joined Dave, deciding not to tell him for now. She wanted to investigate it further, and she had to be careful. Being accused of witch-hunting Lars because his wife was her friend was the last thing she needed.

'It'll be interesting to see how the husband acts tomorrow night at the funeral,' said Dave while drinking his pint.

They'd already decided to talk to Lars again and see if they could shake anything out of him - Audrey didn't think they'd get anywhere.

'He has a perfect poker face - doesn't give anything away,' she said, remembering how Lars had smoothed over that whole nightclub incident as if it was a slight mishap.

'Hmmm, we'll see,' said Dave, looking thoughtful and drinking the rest of his pint in silence.

When Audrey arrived home that night, Nina was working, and leftovers were waiting in the fridge - *thanks, babe*. After eating, she poured a glass of wine and opened the missing girl's file. As she read, her blood ran cold – it could be them. The lack of case notes shocked her – the case looked like it had barely been investigated. *Please don't be the girls from the nightclub,* she begged while texting Orla and asking her to meet the next day.

Orla: *Yep, sure thing. See you at about ten?*

Audrey was waiting at Bewley's Café when Orla arrived with Patsy.

'We're shopping for mam - she needs a pair of black trousers for the mass tonight,' said Orla, explaining her mother's presence.

Audrey hugged Mrs Reed, then got straight to the point, trying to gauge Orla's memory of that night. She was eager to see if Orla came to the same conclusion as Nina.

'The night of the hostage situation, remember it?' she asked.

'Why was Audrey asking about that?'

'Of course, I remember it - what are you up to?' asked Orla, already knowing this was going somewhere - they'd always been very in tune with each other.

'What do you remember?' asked Audrey.

Recalling the night in her mind, Orla took a minute.

'We walked into the club - Lars had a girl pinned to the table – Erik was screwing one. Lars punched Laura - Erik threw you against a wall, walloped Niamh in the head, then held us at gunpoint.'

'Summed it up perfectly.'

'Who was there?' she asked and could almost see the cogs turning in Orla's head.

'Us five, Lars, Erik and two other men who were with the young girls...' she paused as if thinking about it, then asked, '...what am I missing?'

It hadn't clicked, so Audrey prompted - maybe she and Nina were overacting, and Orla would tell her no such thing had happened - those girls were perfectly fine.

'Who left first?' she asked.

'What was going on? Had Audrey worked out what happened to the girls?'

'We did,' said Orla, but the look on Audrey's face said that wasn't the case.

Then the penny dropped.

'The young girls left with Erik and the other two men. Why are you asking me about this?' Orla asked suspiciously.

'The young girls,' said Audrey finally, 'what do you remember about them?'

'Oh my God – she knows. Audrey knows something happened to them that night.'

'Three of them, one having sex, one almost having it and one sitting at a table looking terrified. When everything kicked off, they were a mess, crying and screaming. Erik and the other two men took them from the room. You and Niamh were on the floor...' she paused again, trying to recall the details, '... Laura was still out cold, and Maggie and I were in shock. I didn't pay much attention but felt relieved they were gone. Erik and the other two came back a few minutes later. Why are you asking about them, Audrey?'

Audrey explained how Nina had asked about them - which led to her finding three girls - two cousins and their friend - all missing and presumed dead while watching the blood drain from Orla's face.

'I couldn't believe it, "Yes, it's them - they didn't go home that night – they were murdered." I was shouting at them.'

'Fuck off - are you telling me it's the same girls?' she asked.

'Stop cursing, Orla,' interrupted Patsy, and Orla rolled her eyes.

'I don't know, but I'm determined to find out,' said Audrey.

'Mother of God, what kind of people did you get involved with?' asked Patsy.

'The worst kind, Mrs Reed.'

Orla took out her notepad.

'The worst kind, ma,' she repeated and

looked around - *who said that?* She turned to Audrey. 'Right, tell me everything.'

'Woohoo, she heard me – I fucking knew she would – eventually.'

Audrey gave Orla the details and explained there were lots of missing girls from that time.

'So, this could be a complete coincidence?' asked Orla, then added. 'They were only kids if I remember rightly.'

'The girls missing were seventeen,' said Audrey to Orla's horrified expression.

'Christ, those girls were about that age. What's the likelihood they just disappeared off to England?'

They both agreed that was very unlikely.

'If it was them, surely they'd be of no interest to Lars,' said Orla, looking hopeful until Audrey made Nina's point.

'Well, they'd just witnessed an assault, were high on drugs, and I don't think the sex was consensual. Would those men just let them walk away? The same men who held us at gunpoint in case we called the guards.'

Orla stared at Audrey as she had at Nina, neither of them ever giving a thought to those poor girls or what happened to them after that night.

'Jesus fucking Christ,' said Orla, writing in her notebook.

'Orla,' said Patsy, blessing herself, but Orla ignored her.

'I never thought of it that way. I just thought they'd scored for the night with a few rich men, got pissed and high and went home,' said Orla to Patsy's disapproving tut.

'Yeah, but as Nina said, what if they'd sobered up and cried rape? There was cocaine in that club, and they were underage. They could have brought a lot of trouble to Lars,' said Audrey.

'Christ, I hope they're not the same girls,' said Orla.

'So do I love, but if those girls are not dead - where have they been for twenty years?'

29 ~ ORLA

Orla and Patsy moseyed through the shops, and even though Orla's heart wasn't in it, they found a nice pair of trousers in Arnotts for Patsy.

'They're lovely, and you'll get loads of wear out of them,' said Orla when Patsy came out of the dressing room.

'They'll do,' said Patsy, then asked, 'do we need anything else?'

Orla shook her head - she wasn't in the mood. They had a quick sandwich in the Arnotts café, then got the bus home.

'I can't stop thinking about those girls,' said Patsy quietly as they sat on the tram. 'This whole thing is getting darker by the second. What if they're dead? What if Lars murdered them? If he murdered them, he could have easily murdered Laura,' she whispered.

'You might be right, Mrs Reed – I just can't

remember.'

Orla tried not to laugh at her mother's dramatics but couldn't. After that night, Orla never thought about those girls again and felt a sharp pang of guilt.

'We don't know if they're the same girls, ma - hold fire,' she said, trying to reassure herself more than her mother.

'I have a feeling they are,' said Patsy and unfortunately, Orla had the same feeling.

They relayed the whole story to Orla's dad when they got home.

'Good God, that's terrible business,' said Joe, folding his newspaper. 'What sort of man did she marry?

'A monster.'

'A monster, da,' said Orla.

'It happened again - I'm finally getting somewhere.'

She went upstairs, opened her laptop, and, with a heavy heart, Google searched for the missing girls who were easy to find. Two cousins and their friend - missing on the same day. Why hadn't she seen this back then? She had no memory of it, and even if she had, would she have made the connection? *What to do? What to do? What to do?* She thought about it for a few minutes, then checked her email to see a file sent by Audrey with a note saying the families still lived at the same addresses. The case was now considered cold, with no plans to re-open it.

'This was unbelievable – they had to find them.'

Orla looked at her watch - just after two - she had time. Picking up her phone, she rang one of the numbers on the file and asked to speak to the missing girl's parents. After a short conversation, Orla was invited to a flat in Greek Street by one of their mothers.
'By any chance, are you free now?' asked Orla, before adding, 'I could be in half an hour.'
Maureen said yes, and Orla jumped into action.
'Back in a tik, mam,' she said, running out the door to a waiting taxi.

'What about the mass?' called Patsy.

'It's not until five, I'll be back in an hour, and we'll go together,' said Orla, jumping into the back seat of the cab.

'Where to, love?' asked the driver.

She gave him the address and opened Audrey's email version of the file, immediately noticing the lack of details. Having read many case files over the years, Orla had never seen one so sparse. She wondered if Audrey had missed something and rang her.

'I thought the same thing,' said Audrey.

'It looks like it was barely investigated,' said Orla, then asked, 'do you want to meet me in at the flats? I'm in a taxi now.'

'Better go alone – the fewer people who know about a possible link between these two cases, the better,' said Audrey.

At the flats, Orla was greeted by three women who looked to be in their late fifties. One had greying hair, and the other two had raging red hair that didn't look like it came from a bottle. They all wore a tired look of grief and, at first, were suspicious of Orla until she explained her interest in another case and said it might be connected to their girls.

'Gillian, Aisling and Sinead were seventeen when they went missing - it still doesn't seem real,' said Aisling's mam, Maureen. 'You'd think we'd be able to move on after twenty years, but not a day goes by that I don't wonder where my daughter is.'

The other two women nodded in agreement.

'My husband is a prick – those poor kids.'

'Back then, the guards said they might have gone to London. I wondered what your thoughts were?' asked Orla, thinking it was a complete brush-off.

'That didn't happen in a million years,' they all said simultaneously, then Gillian's mam, Mags, explained.

'The girls would never have gone to London without telling us. Sure, why would they? If they wanted to go, we'd have let them. My sister Nelly had been living there for years - they had a place to stay. It never made any sense, and when we told the guards that, they still did nothing. The strangest thing is that there wasn't a trace of them - no one saw them.

Three young girls just disappeared into thin air.'

Orla asked if they remembered what the girls were wearing that night - not that she could, but she hoped something might jog a memory.

'I remember every detail of the last time I saw my child - better than that, I have a photo,' said Olive, Sinead's mam.

She reached into her bag for a framed photo of the girls. Olive was Maureen's sister and looked more like her twin. Orla thought how tragic it was that both of them had lost a daughter.

'I took this before they went out,' she explained.

'Even looking at the photo – I didn't remember them.'

Three gorgeous girls, smiling at the camera and looking excited. Orla didn't recognise them but asked if she could snap it with her phone, thinking she'd show it to the others after Laura's mass. Hopefully, one of them recognised them.

'What do you think happened?' asked Orla.

'They were in the wrong place at the wrong time – the poor loves.'

'God, I've asked myself that question a million times,' said Maureen. 'All I know is that the girls were excited - they were nearly eighteen, so we didn't mind them going dancing on a Friday night. They'd been whispering about it all week and asked for new clothes. Someone had invited them to a fancy nightclub in town - a bit older and foreign, I think.'

Orla's heart stopped.

'Erik – scumbag.'

'Don't suppose you know his name or where he was from?' she asked, hoping and dreading at the same time that she'd say Sweden.

Maureen shook her head.

'If only I'd asked, but we didn't know anything like this would happen,' she said sadly.

The description of someone older and foreign - Orla thought of Erik. She didn't know if the other two men were Swedish, but she suspected they were. Had they invited those underage girls to the club? The smartphone hadn't existed then, but mobiles did, and even though she wasn't sure it made a difference, she asked if any of the girls had a phone.

'No, the last we ever saw of them was when they walked out of the flats, waving at us,' said Olive with tears in her eyes.

Maureen made some tea, and they asked about Orla's interest in the case. Orla hesitated - did she tell the truth? Deciding they deserved it - she asked if they could keep it to themselves and gave them an outline of Laura's case.

'Have you seen it on the news?' she asked, and they all nodded.

'I feel so sorry for her family,' said Maureen, 'but what's she got to do with our girls?'

Orla took a deep breath - she'd committed now, and there was no going back.

'Well,' she began, 'the guards think Laura's murder is robbery-related, but I think they're wrong. I think your girls are somehow connected and...' she paused, '...I might have met them on the night they disappeared.'

All three women gasped as Orla told the tale of a night twenty years earlier. She left out the rape, sexual assault and the drug taking, thinking they didn't need to know about that, at least until they were sure it was their girls. Then, she explained how it only came to light recently.

'Imagine finding that out after all these years.'

'There were five of us that night, including Laura, but we haven't spoken to each other in over twenty years. Audrey's a detective working on Laura's murder case and contacted us. She remembered three girls from the nightclub that night and wondered what happened to them. It was random, but she checked the missing person files and found your girls. We're not sure if they're the same girls - that's what I'm trying to find out,' said Orla.

'If it was them, what do you think happened?' asked Maureen.

Deciding to still go with the truth,

Orla said she didn't know but explained how dangerous the men were. As she looked at these women, all quietly crying, she wondered what was worse, finding out your daughter might have been murdered or never knowing what happened to her. Neither seemed appealing. They exchanged numbers, and Orla promised to keep them up to date. They hugged goodbye - Orla grabbed a taxi and rang Audrey again.

'They're devastated, and the original case is dodgy,' said Orla.

'I know,' said Audrey. 'I've searched old data to see if anything was missed. Listen, I'm passing your ma's house in ten minutes, will I pop in?' asked Audrey.

'Yeah, see you there,' said Orla.

As she sat in the back of the taxi, Orla contemplated that awful night so many years before. A table full of champagne and a tray full of cocaine. If those girls were the same ones from the flats, they were only seventeen. It was probably their first time drinking champagne and taking drugs - talk about being out of their depth. While lost in her thoughts, her phone rang and thinking it was Audrey again, Orla answered distractedly, realising too late that it was James - someone she didn't want to speak to.

'Orla,' said James, sounding relieved - *for fuck's sake, what did he want?*

'What do you want, James?' asked Orla wearily.

He'd been leaving messages all week, but Orla ignored them. Quite frankly, she didn't want to talk to him.

'I didn't think you'd answer,' said James, irritating her further.

'Well, I did, so what do you want?' asked Orla, rather abruptly.

He was flustered, but she was past caring.

'I want to come to the house and talk to you in person,' said James.

What the fuck? Talk about what? Orla said no and told him she was unavailable and in Ireland.

'Just say what you want to say now,' she added, still irritated.

He couldn't have picked a worse time to call - her mind was racing with thoughts of the girls - her love life seemed inconsequential.

'I'm sorry,' he whispered, and for a

second, Orla was mute. *He's sorry.*

'Sorry for what?' she asked, but before he could answer, she continued. 'Sorry for cheating on me - for abandoning me? Sorry for leaving me to move into our dream home without you? Sorry for betraying me - for lying? Sorry for destroying what I thought was forever with you? What are you sorry for, James? That's quite a list,' she said, furious now - how fucking dare he be sorry.

'Go, Orla. If I'd spoken to Lars like that, he'd have killed me.'

'I'm sorry for it all,' he said, 'I made the biggest mistake of my life and realised it immediately. I've spent the last eighteen months trying to find the courage to call you.'

Orla couldn't believe he knew this eighteen months ago. She'd have given anything to hear it then, but now it was too late.

'Okay, well, that's grand then,' she said, sounding like a bitch, but unable to help herself. 'James is sorry - everything is well in the world. Is that all you wanted?'

'Love it – You tell him, girl.

'I deserve that, Orla, and so much more, but please let me explain. I want to talk to you face to face,' he whispered, and her heart hardened.

What the fuck was this guy on?

'It's too late, James - stop texting me. I've met someone else, and I'm happy, so the answer is no,' said Orla, thinking that felt good.

'Please, just let me explain,' whispered James.

'Look, I'll let you know when I'm back in the UK, and we can have a coffee,' said Orla, slightly curious about what he wanted to say.

He'd caused so much pain, and even though she was so over him and happy with Neil, maybe she'd listen to his explanation. Call it closure or finality - whatever it is, she decided to hear him out.

'I'll call you in a couple of weeks to see where you are,' he suggested.

'Don't bother, I'll call you when I'm home - let's leave it at that, James,' said Orla and hung up.

'I was in awe of her.'

When the taxi pulled up at her ma's house, the driver, who'd heard the whole conversation, told her not to bother with the likes of that fella, and Orla laughed. Audrey was waiting in the kitchen, eager to find out what happened to those kids. Patsy made the tea, and they looked over the file together.

'Right, what we know so far is…basically nothing,' said Audrey, pulling out sheets of old, worn paper. 'According to these notes, the girls left the flats at half nine on Friday night and were never seen again. There was no sighting of them in bars - no taxi men remembered picking them up - no one saw them on the bus. According to one of their mothers, they were going to a nightclub in town, so how did they get there? Walk? Surely someone would have noticed if that was the case?'

Orla couldn't help but think if Lars was involved, he probably sent a car - he was big into splashing the cash back then.

'Lars always sent Erik to pick me up.'

'And I checked the dates,' she continued, 'they went missing the same night we were in that club.'

So, it had to be them - there was no doubt in Orla's mind.

'Should we have made sure they were okay, Audrey?' she asked, feeling guilty.

'Don't go there, Orla - we don't know if it was them, and anyway, in most cases, those girls would have gone home and woke up the next day with a massive hangover and a few regrets,' said Audrey.

Orla agreed, then remembered the photo on her phone.

'This is a picture of them from that night - why is it not in the file?' she asked.

Audrey shrugged her shoulders while looking at the picture.

'I don't know, but it should be,' she said, studying it.

'Ring any bells?' asked Orla.

'No, I just can't remember - wish I could,' said Audrey.

'I didn't even recall seeing them that night.'

'Why is there no mention of a foreign guy either? Maureen said they met a foreign, older guy, but there's nothing about him in the file,' said Orla.

'I don't know, but there's something off about this. Lars had men working for him in a few nightclubs back then - mainly Swedish. Those girls were going to a nightclub with an older, foreign guy. It shouldn't have been hard to put two and two together,' said Audrey.

Orla agreed while looking at the photo again.

'What happened to you girls? Where are you?' she whispered.

'Murdered and buried in a church garden.'

When Audrey eventually left, Orla dashed upstairs to get ready for Laura's mass. She climbed into the shower feeling a little heartbroken. The idea that Laura might have been killed by Lars was bad enough, but those poor kids - were they dead as well? It seemed like the only explanation.

Laura

Those women deserved to have their daughters back and give them a proper burial. How could Lars be so cruel? How many more had been killed? What happened to the girls chained to the walls? I had to reach Orla tonight – she had to help me.

30 ~ MAGGIE

When Maggie O'Malley first read Orla's books, she was blown away by her talent. At the time, she'd been desperate to contact her, congratulate her, and tell her how proud she was of her, but the past prevented her from picking up the phone. There was just too much water under the bridge. Then Laura was murdered, Audrey was on the phone, and suddenly Orla and Niamh were back in her life, and it was like they never left. *God, was that only two weeks ago?*

When she first heard about what had happened to Laura, Maggie immediately suspected Lars. Even after all these years, she'd never forgotten that night. It wasn't just the punch in the face or the terrifying aftermath – it was how natural those men dealt with that level of violence, and in the months after, trying to convince Laura to leave Lars was excruciating. Maggie was severely stressed -

angry at Laura and sick of talking about Lars. Everything became weird when Laura began cancelling their plans – her friends became distant, the phone calls stopped, and she started to panic - praying it would sort itself out, but it never did.

When their friendship fell apart, so did Maggie. She didn't know how to function without her best friends and had a breakdown. Depression and anxiety prevented her from working, and on top of that, a delayed reaction to what happened in the nightclub was diagnosed with PTSD a year later. For another two years, she could barely get out of bed - couldn't be in public spaces and never socialised. She didn't eat, lost a ton of weight, and hardly saw her family, who were desperately worried about her. Her best friends were gone, and her life hit rock bottom.

Eventually, with the help of her therapist, a godsend called Rose Callaghan, Maggie learned to process the trauma and continued with her life. She started a new job and, within months, met Artie O'Malley, who was writing a book about his life. Maggie was assigned to help him, and their attraction was instant.

Artie had PTSD from events in his childhood, and there was an immediate connection between them. Their relationship was a slow burner for about a year until Artie asked Maggie to move in with him, and she said yes. They married in Gretna Green a year later and eventually had two sons. It took time for Maggie to adjust to Artie's wealth. Although he'd inherited family money, it had come at a terrible price – the loss of everyone. His success as a classical music conductor took him around the world with many different orchestras, and they lived on a leafy suburban road in Ballsbridge in a four-story townhouse that could easily be mistaken for a small hotel.

When the boys started school, Artie financed Maggie's bookstore on Wicklow Street, and she'd been there ever since. Books had always been her thing. She loved everything about them, and owning a bookshop in the centre of Dublin was brilliant. It was her pride and joy - she sold coffee, cakes, Irish mementoes, and rows of excellent books. Books & Brew was its name - she had a team of five students from Trinity College, so the shop attracted a fun university crowd.

While at work, Maggie received Orla's email - smiled and said yes to going to Sweden. She liked being part of their investigation team – even though the circumstances were tragic, the old bond they'd always shared had been reignited. Maybe they'd be the ones to crack the case and bring that bastard to justice. Orla's relentlessness amazed her – if there was proof to be found in Sweden, she'd find it. After responding to Orla's email, Maggie closed the shop and jumped a taxi home. Laura's mass was the next day, and she felt nervous about it. What would it be like to see Lars again after twenty years? To say goodbye to Laura and see her family so broken?

She arrived home to find Artie watching TV in the lounge.

'Hi, love - are the boys here?' Maggie called, heading straight to the kitchen for a glass of wine. 'Want one?' she asked when Artie joined her.

'Don't ask stupid questions, darling,' said Artie with his glass already in his hand. 'The boys are where they always are - in their pits.'

Maggie poured the wine, which they

took into the lounge, and she delivered the news.

'Why do you have to go?' asked Artie.

'I don't have to do anything but want to go. Audrey said there's no evidence - the guards are stuck, but Orla has a bee in her bonnet. It's next week, after Laura's funeral,' said Maggie.

Artie wasn't happy, but he understood Maggie's desire to go. They discussed the ins and outs of it until the boys came barrelling into the room, looking for food.

'Where's the Chinese?' asked David, immediately picking up the remote control to turn off the crap he thought his parents watched - the news. Artie took it off him and turned the TV off.

'Let's go into the kitchen,' he said, standing up and leading his family out of the room.

'Where's the Chinese,' asked Shay, echoing his brother.

'Relax, it's on the way. Christ, you'd think you two were starving.' cried Maggie.

'We are starving - we haven't eaten in at least three hours,' said David, rubbing his stomach in mock pain. Twenty minutes later, when the takeaway arrived, they sat at the kitchen table and caught up on each other's news.

Artie had taken time off from touring with the Orchestra to write another book. The boys loved having him home, and so did Maggie. It meant she could work without feeling guilty for not attending rugby matches or being home for the boys after school. David and Shay had the usual teenage stuff, such as school, rugby, friends, etc. David's girlfriend, Iris, joined them after dinner. She was staying over and supposedly sleeping in the spare room, but Maggie heard David sneaking her into his room when he thought they were all asleep. They were both nearly eighteen, so she didn't mind.

Shay, her fifteen-year-old son, was more reserved. He didn't miss a trick and either had his head buried in a book or played sport – there was no in-between. Rugby, football, running, cricket, horse racing - there wasn't a sport Shay didn't like. He was Artie's sidekick, and together, they could watch sports channels twenty-four hours a day and never get bored. David wasn't quite as sports-mad, but he wasn't far off it - Maggie had no choice but to like it. Over dinner, she told them about her upcoming trip to Sweden.

'What if Lars finds out you're there and throws you into prison?' asked Shay with a worried expression on his handsome face.

He'd inherited his mother's bluntness, so Maggie gently explained they weren't doing anything illegal or dangerous.

'We're just going to see if we can talk to Laura's friend, and anyway, if he somehow finds out we're there, we're going to say it's a pilgrimage to Laura.'

'Lars won't fall for that crap,' said David, biting into a chicken satay skewer.

Maggie looked at him, but David shook his shoulders and licked his fingers.

'You know he won't, mam - don't pretend he will,' he said.

She didn't blame them for worrying. She'd kept them up to date on Laura's case. Right or wrong, they had a policy of telling the truth in their house. Artie's childhood was a web of secrets and lies, and because she was the youngest of six kids, Maggie had spent her whole life trying to figure out what her sisters and brothers were whispering about. She sometimes thought that was why she felt so lonely growing up and swore her kids would never feel the same way.

'Look, you all know where I'm going, and anyway, Audrey is a guard, and we'll be careful. Hopefully, Astrid will help us find Laura's murderer, and it's only for two days,' Maggie said, trying to reassure them.

They weren't happy but agreed it was the right thing to do.

'Just be careful, mam. I don't know what I'd do if anything happened to you,' said Shay, hugging her and causing her heart to melt.

She spent the rest of the night answering emails, then went downstairs to say goodnight to the boys watching the match. David was determined Iris liked sports, and Iris was so doe-eyed in love that she happily went along with it. When Artie came to bed, he made her promise again to be careful.

'Just watch yourself. Lars probably won't even know you're there, but by the sounds of it, he has a bunch of thugs working for him, and none of this...' he waved his hand around the bedroom '...works without you. Something happening to you is not an option.'

Maggie felt blessed - even after all these years, they still had a great relationship. She kissed him and promised to be super careful.

'It's only for two nights, but I hope we find Astrid,' she said.

'I hope so too - maybe you'll get some answers,' said Artie.

'We need some,' said Maggie, climbing into bed.

Artie was all over her in a second - their sex life had always been exceptional, and just before she fell asleep, she turned to her husband.

'We just need to talk to Astrid and anyone else who might know something. Orla is determined to piece together whatever Laura was doing before she died,' said Maggie, yawning. 'I'm sure it will all be fine – I mean – four women asking about a friend - what could possibly go wrong?'

As the words passed her lips, Maggie prayed she hadn't jinxed them.

31 ~ ORLA

On the evening of Laura's mass, held at St Francis Street Church, the skies opened, and like a biblical storm – the rains came. It had been two weeks since her brutal murder, and the whole country was still in shock. Even though Laura hadn't lived in Ireland for years, the church was packed with mourners. Some who knew her personally - her family, friends and so on – others, paying their respects to a woman so tragically cut down in her prime and then there was the sanctimonious - holier-than-thou, zealots, only interested in attending a mass given by the Archbishop of Dublin - who'd jumped in on the act. Orla could spot them a mile off.

As she walked up the aisle, Orla noticed Lars sitting in a pew with his parents and was struck by how unlike them he was. She wondered if he was adopted, like Damien in the film The Omen and felt sorry for them - they didn't look like the kind of people who knew their son was inherently evil.

'The minute I clapped eyes on the bastard – the flashbacks began.'

A few other official-looking types sat behind them - government colleagues perhaps, and of course, Erik beside another shady-looking bloke. Was he one of the men from the nightclub? Orla couldn't remember and felt frustrated.

'Sven, and yes, he was there that night.'

On the other side of the aisle were Laura's parents, her sister Lou and her husband, and their two boys. Behind them was extended family, aunts, uncles, cousins, neighbours, school friends Orla hadn't seen in decades and Laura's work colleagues from years before. Mrs Quinn insisted Orla and the others join them at the front, but Orla tried to dissuade her.

'Ah no, we're grand Mrs Quinn, we'll stay at the back,' she said.

'You will not - Laura would want you here,' insisted Mrs Quinn, 'I'm not having it -

tell her, Mick,' she turned to her husband.

Orla knew if Mick was involved, she was serious and agreed to sit down. While they waited for the service to begin, Orla watched Lars - in his mid-fifties, aged like fine wine, distinguished, elegant, and reeking of money in his fine-cut suit. In twenty years, he'd become even more attractive - how was it possible? *Probably sold his soul to the devil.* His eyes were closed as he faced the altar - giving the impression of praying.

'Making coffee, singing in the kitchen, seeing Lars on the other side of the island - cool as a cucumber - something about that seemed familiar when Audrey said it.'

'Do you think he's praying?' whispered Niamh, watching him as closely as Orla.

'If he is, it's probably for forgiveness,' said Orla, thinking he played the role of grieving husband very well.

'In the name of the father…'

The archbishop began, and the mass started. Orla listened as he paid tribute to Laura and asked God to help her family. When he mentioned her devoted husband, it took everything Orla had not to guffaw loudly. She did an eye roll, but no one saw it except God, and he wouldn't mind because he knew the truth. The archbishop thanked the guards for all their hard work in ensuring Laura's killer was found, then asked the whole country to pray for her ascension into heaven. Yeah, whatever, father.

Orla looked around the church, remembering her school days when she was forced to sit in this church, bored out of her mind and counting everything in sight. How many paintings were on the walls, how many squares in the pattern on the ceiling, or how she and Laura would pretend to need the toilet to have a nosey in the sacristy and get away from the nuns for five minutes. It made being here for her funeral even harder to stomach.

'The punch in the face - washing my hands - the knife block - blood on his shirt – strangling me – stabbing him – begging for my life – My husband had murdered me.'

Sobs from Lars's direction caught Orla's

attention, and his mother was crying, which seemed genuine. Lars was stone cold - expressionless, and Orla couldn't take her eyes off him.

'I flew at him, "you bastard." I tried to scratch his eyes, but my hand passed through his face.'

From the corner of her eye, Orla noticed Erik watching her, watching Lars, but she ignored him – asshole.

'I noticed him too. "Watch the fucker, Orla, he's a savage bastard," I whispered.'

'I know,' whispered Orla, then looked around - *hang on…what?*

Orla looked at the girls, wondering if one of them said something, but their eyes were on the priest. Sensing her stare, Maggie turned.

'You, okay?' she silently mouthed - Orla nodded, but she wasn't.

Someone had just told her Erik was a savage bastard, and it sounded like Laura.

'Fucking finally – I was pissed off now. My husband had murdered me. Oh my God - years of putting up with his shit, and he killed me in the

end.'

Shaking her head, Orla pushed the thought away, telling herself she needed a good night's sleep because she was hearing things. Laura probably said that years ago, and the memory had popped into her head because somehow, she knew Erik was more than a savage bastard - he was a psychotic lunatic. After the service, Lars's parents hugged Laura's parents. His mother seemed genuinely upset, but Lars stood in the background, not saying a word to anyone.

'Fucking prick. How dare he be at my funeral after.'

A few people shook his hand, but everyone soon left except Niamh, Maggie, Audrey and Orla, who sat silently beside Laura in her beautiful coffin. Niamh sobbed, and even Maggie who wasn't one for emotional displays - shed a tear. Orla thought about everything that had happened that day - her mind reeling from it.

'I tried to move my coffin to let them know I was

there - one of the wreaths fell to the ground, but they didn't notice.'

An hour later, as they walked up the road to the Liberty Belle Pub, Orla's mind was on the missing girls. Where did they start? How did they connect them to Lars? How did they prove any of it? They got a drink at the bar - found a table, and Orla told Niamh and Maggie about the girls. She explained about meeting their mothers that afternoon and handed over her phone with the photo on it.

'We don't know if it's the same girls from the nightclub, but it's likely as these girls went missing on the same night,' said Orla, surprised when Maggie snatched her phone for a closer look.

'I screamed in my frustration, "It's them." The light flickered.'

'It's definitely them,' said Maggie, sounding confident.

'How do you know?' asked Orla, surprised.

'I'd never been so scared in my life, and honestly thought they'd kill us or at least kick the shit out of us that night. I wanted to remember their faces, so I studied all of them. I particularly remember the girl in orange hot pants because I wanted them and an arse like hers,' said Maggie, pointing to the picture.

Sure enough, one of the girls was wearing orange hot pants - Orla thought it was a mini skirt until she looked closely.

'What about the other men there? Would you recognise them if you saw them?' asked Audrey, and once again, Maggie surprised them with her immediate answer.

'Yeah, one of them was sitting with that dog Erik in the church tonight.'

'Robert did the world a favour and died a few years ago.'

Suddenly overcome with a torrent of emotions, Orla felt lightheaded. Those poor kids, it was them - what had they gotten themselves into? Erik and the other two only left the room for ten minutes - surely, they couldn't commit three murders in that time.

'They could, and they did.'

'We need to know more about Erik - we don't even know his last name,' said Maggie to no one in particular.

'Olsson. It's Eric Olsson.

'I can find that out,' said Audrey. 'He'll be associated with Lars - I just need to dig around a bit.'

'Erik Olsson,' said Orla as all heads turned to her.

'How do you know that?' asked Niamh.

Orla didn't know. She just knew his name was Eric Olsson, and she was freaking the fuck out.

'I must have heard Laura saying it years ago,' said Orla, deciding to work out what was happening before sharing it with her friends. That was the second time she'd heard Laura's voice.

'She's actually hearing me! Halleluiah.'

'Should we call the guards?' asked Niamh, but Audrey shook her head.

'Not yet – this needs to stay lowkey for now. Who knows what will happen if I reopen the investigation and Lars gets wind of it? We need to find out if he has anything to do with Laura's murder first before trying to pin this on him as well.'

'Lars wouldn't think twice about killing them all.'

They quietly finished their drinks before heading into town for dinner.

'Let's have a cocktail in The Westbury,' suggested Niamh as they walked past.

They followed as she led them up the beautiful staircase, with its dimmed lights, opulent furniture, and a pianist playing soft music in the lounge.

'God, I've missed this place - I haven't been in years,' said Orla.

'Ray and I come here every time we're in Dublin - we love it,' said Niamh.

When the waiter hugged her and asked after Ray, Orla knew she wasn't exaggerating. As they sat down, they didn't notice the group of Swedes in the corner.

'Don't look now,' whispered Audrey, 'but Lars and his gang are in the corner,' she said - her eyes moving to the far side of the room.

'You are joking - I don't want to be anywhere near them,' said Maggie, picking up her bag to leave.

'Just act normal,' said Audrey, squeezing Maggie's hand.

Niamh didn't give a shit, and quite frankly, neither did Orla. Lars didn't know they suspected him of killing his wife and three young girls. They decided to ignore him and succeeded until a waiter turned up with four mojitos, ahead of the drinks they'd already ordered, saying they were compliments of Mr Karlsson. Orla couldn't work out if Lars was deliberately cruel or just had bad taste.

'Both.'

Mojitos were Laura's absolute favourite cocktail, and he knew that. Did they drink them or turn them away? Orla turned to see Lars and Erik watching them.

'Thank you,' she said to the waiter, taking the drink, then turned to the girls. 'Let's just drink them - we don't want the prick to think he's bothering us.'

She hoped that was the end, but as soon

as the waiter walked away, Lars stood up and walked towards them, closely followed by Erik. Fuck!

Laura
I whooshed through him - hoping to give him at least a chill, but nothing happened. It didn't matter – Orla could hear me, and we were going to take this fucker to the ground. Images of my murder bombarded me. I had begged this bastard for my life - pleaded with him as he pushed that knife into my neck. At least I remembered where the phone was, and it might have recorded the whole thing - we needed to get it.

32 ~ ORLA

'Ladies,' said Lars, nodding at each of them.

'Fuck off, prick.'

'Lars,' said Audrey - the only one to reply.
'Ah, Sergeant O'Brien, how nice to meet you in person,' said Lars.

So, he knew precisely who Audrey was - they should have known, but at least he'd shown his hand - a little bit, anyway.

'We're sorry for your loss - we hadn't seen Laura in years, but we're devastated she died. I hope the guards find whoever did it,' said Niamh.

'Thank you, I have every confidence in,' he hesitated, 'your detective friend here,' he nodded towards Audrey with a smirk.

The cut of him thought Orla, and, at that moment, she was positive Lars killed

Laura. She wanted to slap his face but instead remained calm, hoping he'd piss off.

'Laura had all your books - she read them a lot,' said Lars, surprising Orla. 'I always wondered at her fascination with them and only recently found out you were the author. It makes perfect sense now.'

'That's nice to hear. I wish I'd known that when she was alive,' said Orla sadly.

'The books, Orla.'

He didn't bat an eyelid, and Orla suddenly remembered Laura's words - 'if anything happens to me, I want you to have the books.' Why did Laura want Orla to have her books, and how ironic that Lars had reminded her?

'What will you do with her things? Can I have the books? I'd like to have something of hers,' said Orla, surprising herself and him with her candour.

'Yes, Orla! You need to get the books.'

He hesitated, then shrugged.

'Laura's personal items are being sent to her family – the books can be included,' he said. 'Everything else is going to the hospital charity where Laura worked.'

'She'd like that,' said Orla, thinking maybe there was one decent bone in his body.

'There wasn't.'

'What hospital is it?' she asked, and when he looked surprised by her question, she quickly added, 'we'd like to contribute something in her name as well.'

'The University Hospital in Uppsala, Laura worked on the children's ward there.'

Of course, she did – the angel. Orla thanked him but didn't say anything else. He didn't know he'd just saved her the hassle of trying to find that information.

Maggie didn't look at either of the men - she drank her mojito in silence and completely ignored them. Erik asked Niamh how life was in Cork and if she enjoyed running the pub. Niamh didn't answer, but the message was clear- *we know where you live.* Orla wanted to tell them to grow up - that they weren't in a fucking gangster film, but she kept her mouth shut.

'I wished she'd said that. I'd loved to have seen his face.'

An awkward silence followed, and no one said anything. Lars got the message and left, but only after saying he looked forward to seeing them all on Monday.

'I believe the funeral reception is at the Shelbourne, something I know Laura would like,' he said, and Orla vowed to see this prick in prison.

'Oh my God, what an asshole.'

She wanted to scream at him that Laura wouldn't like that at all – Laura would like to be alive and free – having a drink with friends like a normal person. Instead, she told him to have a nice evening. Their original drinks arrived - they drank them in silence, paid the bill and left.

'Laura would have liked her wake being at the Shelbourne. Did you hear that fucker? I can't work out if he's stupid or just evil,' said Orla, fuming as they sat down for dinner in an Italian restaurant Maggie had recommended.

'I wasted my life on the bastard.'

'Both,' said Maggie, then added, 'I think he killed her – he's so arrogant, I can't stand him.'

'I agree,' said Audrey, 'he's also dangerous and powerful. If he did kill her, there's not a hint of remorse. It's almost as if he wants us to know he was involved - his arrogance makes him think he's untouchable.'

'He genuinely believes that.'

The waiter arrived, and they ordered a bottle of wine.

'This place is gorgeous, and the food,' said Niamh, her eyes wide as she took a picture of the menu, 'I have to show it to Ray.'

'A friend of Artie owns it,' said Maggie as an older man arrived at their table.

'Ciao Maggie,' he said, kissing her hand.

'Ciao Alberto, these are my friends,' she

said, waving at the table.

Alberto was happy to meet them and insisted they try the specials.

'Compliments of the house,' he said as he walked away.

'It's nice having friends in high places,' said Niamh, nudging Maggie with her elbow.

While they waited for their food, Orla's mind ran a marathon. She wanted answers, so she put it to the girls.

'Okay, let's say Lars killed Laura - how was he in two places at the same time? No offence, Audrey, but how thoroughly did you investigate him being at that conference? Could you have missed something?'

Audrey took a notepad from her rucksack and flicked through the pages.

'He was there from Saturday afternoon till Monday evening. That said, it was a huge conference, and he was sitting in a dark auditorium. He gave a speech on Sunday morning, and there are photos of him throughout the weekend. I suppose we could pinpoint their exact time, but he physically checked out of his hotel in Brussels at five o'clock on Monday,' said Audrey.

'So technically, he could have said he was in the auditorium with hundreds of people, flown to Dublin on Monday morning, killed Laura, and then flown back in time to check out,' said Niamh, making a very valid point, and something Orla had already considered.

'Logistically, yes, but we checked the airport, and there's no record of him arriving in

Dublin until Tuesday morning,' said Audrey.

Niamh wasn't giving up that easily, and what she said next floored them all.

'What about a helicopter or a private plane? He's a diplomat, isn't he? Surely, he doesn't fly Ryanair like the rest of us,' she said, as Orla thought – fuck the fucking fuck off – that was how the fucker got here. 'It's easy for people like him to do stuff like that,' Niamh continued, unaware she'd just blown up the room with something so obvious they'd all missed it.

'Of course, I hadn't thought of it either, but Lars always used private planes.'

Audrey looked at Orla. A fucking private plane! Why didn't they think of that?

'There's a private airfield near Lucan that Artie uses quite a bit,' said Maggie, surprising everyone again.

'Your husband owns a private plane?' asked Orla, stunned, but Maggie just shrugged.

'He uses one when touring, but that airfield is the most popular one for Dublin,' she said.

Maggie and Orla were definitely revisiting that conversation, but they needed to concentrate on Lars. That fucker had flown into Dublin on the morning of Laura's murder - slipped in like the snake he was, killed her and slipped out again before her body was even cold.

'Prick-face, Erik, was likely with him.'

Over dinner, they agreed Audrey would dig up information on Erik. Orla would check out Maggie's private airfield and others close to Dublin. Maggie would contact the hotel in Brussels to see if there was anything out of the ordinary. They weren't exactly Charlie's Angels - they were Laura's.

'Absolute angels, and I loved them for it.'

The next morning, over coffee and the Sunday papers, Orla updated her parents.

'Sometimes you don't see what's right in front of you,' said Patsy while making Orla a rasher sandwich.

'Thanks, ma,' said Orla, popping a couple of paracetamols before tucking into mouth-watering bacon on thick white bread, spread with Irish butter.

'Just be careful, Orla, that man sounds a few sandwiches short of a picnic,' said her dad, with a worried expression.

Orla thought he sounded more like a sick, twisted psychopath but didn't mention that to her already worried parents.

'That's definitely more accurate, love.'

'And for what it's worth, I think you should leave it to the guards,' he added.

'We need more information, da – we're

not saying anything until we have proof of his involvement,' said Orla.

'I don't like it. Lars sounds dangerous - just mind yourself,' he said, going back to reading his paper.

With her new private detective partner, aka her mam, Orla began ringing remote airfields, but they didn't get far - the information was unavailable as Orla had expected. By lunchtime, she couldn't put it off any longer and mentioned her trip to Sweden.

'Oh, Jesus, he's going to kill you next. What in the name of God are you going there for?' cried Patsy, so shocked that Orla almost laughed.

Her da looked up from his paper.

'You need to be very careful,' he said, calm but worried.

'I know, da and we will be, but we have to find Astrid,' explained Orla, 'she might be able to help us, and the four of us are going.'

A phone call from Breda, inviting them for Sunday lunch, provided a distraction, and Orla was grateful. Later that day, Orla walked the dog with her sister and filled her in on the latest. Breda asked why Orla was so sure Lars had killed Laura.

'You just won't accept any other outcome, will you?' she asked.

'I know from the bottom of my heart that he killed her. You should have seen him last night, acting like he was getting one over on us - I wanted to slap him. Then there's Laura's letters, the fact that she wanted to leave him - the domestic abuse - her solicitor said he saw videos of Lars beating the crap out of her, and Laura asked him about sex trafficking laws. She wrote about a nail in Lars's coffin in her letter – it has to be that. Laura found out something important, and he killed her for it - what else could it be?'

'Poor Laura - he sounds like an absolute bastard,' said Breda.

They walked a bit further, both lost in their thoughts.

'Okay, say you prove he was in Dublin and not at the conference on the day she was killed - will that be enough? Will it prove he killed her? He's a government minister, isn't he? Doesn't that give him diplomatic immunity or something like that?'

Orla wasn't sure diplomatic immunity

stretched to murder.

'He'll use it if he can. Prick.'

'That's why we need to go to Sweden,' explained Orla. 'We need to find Astrid. I'm supposed to talk to her - I can feel it.'

'Well, I think you're doing the right thing, just be careful. You're in Lars's territory, and I wouldn't be surprised if he finds out you're there,' said Breda.

Orla had a horrible feeling she might be right.

Laura
Astrid would tell them what she knew, but they needed to talk to Hilda. I had to make sure Orla knew that. Seeing Lars again had significantly drained me - even dead, he still affected me. Why had I stayed with him for so long? From my current perspective, I realised my life was supposed to be about cherishing moments of happiness, and I'd wasted years living in fear with Lars.

33 ~ ORLA

The storm continued on the morning of Laura's funeral, and Orla woke up early feeling strange - Laura was in her dreams again and it felt very realistic. She switched on the small bedside lamp and tried to talk herself through the past two days. *Okay, you heard Laura's voice on Saturday in the church, and you knew Erik's surname in the bar.* She didn't know how any of it was possible. *Now, you're having vivid dreams about Laura trying to tell you something, and… you thought about Laura non-stop on the day she was murdered.*

'Are you here?' whispered Orla, and the lamp flickered every so slightly.

'I was getting good at this. "Yes, I'm here."'

'No fucking way,' said Orla, her eyes moving to the bedside lamp.
She jumped out of bed – ready to run for

her life until her mobile rang and distracted her – it was Laura's sister, Louise.

'Sorry I haven't answered your text - it's all been a bit much with the funeral, but mam said you're trying to help,' Louise paused, then asked. 'Can we grab a few minutes to talk later?'

'Yeah – we'll find somewhere quiet at the wake?' suggested Orla.

'Grand, so. Well, talk then,' said Louise.

Orla jumped into the shower, praying there were no ghosts lurking about and wondered what Louise would make of everything that had happened. While getting dressed, she noticed the lamp flickering again - was this a supernatural experience or a dodgy lightbulb? She'd always believed death wasn't the end, but this was too much.

'If you're here, Laura - I'm freaked out, but open to it,' murmured Orla as she went downstairs - there was no light on to flicker.

'With Orla's help, I might finally get the bastard.'

The main service was at Francis Street again, with a private cremation in Mount Jerome, followed by soup and sandwiches at the Shelbourne. Orla arrived at the church and sat in her reserved seat with the family.

Laura's dad delivered the eulogy and talked about his daughter - always up to something and with a vibrancy for life that thrilled him. He didn't mention Lars or her life in Sweden – he just tried to describe the pain of losing Laura - something he said he'd never get over. As he spoke, there wasn't a dry eye in the church – except for the psycho Swedes - they were stone cold.

'I hated that my family had to go through this.'

When Lars walked towards the altar, Orla held her breath. What would he say? She looked at her friends, then listened open-mouthed as he described his angel, Laura.

'She was the light of my life, and I will miss her beyond words.'

'Fucking liar.'

'The people of Sweden loved her, welcomed her with open arms and are deeply saddened by her death. I want to thank the

Guards for their continued hard work in trying to find whoever did this. I know they will find Laura's killer, and justice will be done.'

'You're damn right it will,' whispered Orla to Audrey.

'Fucking A to that.'

He thanked everyone for coming to honour Laura and walked back to his seat. When Orla stood and walked towards the altar - she noticed Lars looking at Erik. *Worried dickhead?*

'Shitting himself love.'

Looking at the congregation, Orla felt love for Laura radiating through the church. Flowers practically hid her coffin - people paying their respects and sickened by the unnecessary tragedy of her death. Orla cleared her throat and began.

'Laura was a breath of fresh air. When we were young - she'd walk into a room, a bar, a nightclub, whatever it was, and everyone would notice her. The rest of us became invisible, which was annoying.'

That got a few laughs in between the tears.

'It wasn't because she was beautiful - it was her energy. Laura captivated everyone she met, and her passion for life left people in awe of her - I know I was.'

Orla deliberately didn't look at Lars - this was for Laura.

'She was compassionate and kind – couldn't pass a homeless person without buying them a cup of tea and a sandwich. Then she'd cry at the unfairness of people having no home.'

Mrs Quinn nodded while wiping her eyes, and Orla continued with a huge lump at the back of her throat.

'Her fights against injustice were legendary. If there was a protest march anywhere in Dublin, Laura was front and centre, not caring what it was for - just fighting. Although I hadn't seen her in years, something I'll regret for a long time, I know she was loved. Maybe she was too good for this life and had to leave early - I like to think that's the case. The person who murdered her robbed the world of an angel because, as her husband said - Laura was an angel - walking amongst ordinary people like us, and we didn't even know it.' She let that sink in. 'We'll never forget you, Laura,' Orla lowered her voice to a whisper. 'I promise - justice will be yours in the end.'

Lars watched as she returned to her seat - Orla could feel his eyes burning a hole in her back.

'Ah, that was lovely, thanks, love.'

After the final blessing, Laura's coffin was carried out of the church with Lars leading the pallbearers. At the crematorium, Orla watched her go through the curtains for cremation as The Quinns silently sobbed. Lars stood with Erik by his side, and Orla was thankful they had no children - imagine having just him as a parent. An hour later, when they arrived at the wake, the restaurant was packed with mourners, so they went straight to the bar.

'Jesus, I thought you were going to call him out when you mentioned the angel bit,' said Niamh, laughing.

'I wanted to, but I don't want him to think we suspect anything until we get back from Sweden.'

They all agreed that was for the best.

'It's definitely for the best.'

'Talk of the devil, and he's sure to appear,' said Audrey, nodding to the door as Lars, Erik and Sven walked through.

'Do you want a drink?' asked Orla as Lars approached the bar.

'Thank you, no,' he said.

Orla and her friends moved to a nearby table, away from the Swedes, and Audrey filled them in on the latest.

'Sven Lundin and Erik Olsson run the biggest security firm in Sweden. They provide security for politicians, bands, celebrities, and so on. They have no criminal record, and there's nothing to link them to Lars - only the fact that Erik is a friend who provides security if and when Lars needs it. It's all above board.'

'We got nowhere with the private airports,' said Orla, 'but I'll give them another call tomorrow.'

Maggie spoke to the hotel receptionist in Brussels but got nowhere either.

'They won't give out any information on their guests, especially famous ones,' she explained.

Lars's parents joined him, as did the other Swedish people in his group, but they kept to their side of the room. An hour later, when Orla came out of the toilet, Lars was leaning against the wall - waiting for her. He looked like a film star in a perfectly cut black suit - the collar of his white shirt was open, and a black tie hung around his neck. *God, he's gorgeous.*

'And rotten to the core - I hated him. "You took my life," I screamed and pulled at his hair - he didn't even blink.

'Lars,' said Orla, wondering what the fuck he wanted.

She didn't want him to suspect her of suspecting him, but she was okay with him knowing she didn't like him.

'He made me sick.'

He sighed and looked at her for a few seconds without saying anything, then spoke in a very low voice.

'Thank you for what you said about Laura – she was all of those things,' he said, then hesitated before adding, 'we were happy... Laura was happy.'

Why was he telling her this?

'No, we weren't. You were happy owning me.'

'She had a good life with me, and we were happy,' he said again.

Orla stared at him. Did he actually believe that?

'I had a shit life and I hated it.'

'What happened all those years ago was a one-off, and I'm sorry you fell out over it. I realise how hard losing your friendship was for Laura.'

'You fucking liar. You knew that all along.'

Oh my God, he was trying to cover his tracks. Orla wanted to tell him he was a lying piece of shit, and Laura had written to them, telling them exactly how her life had been with him, but she kept quiet and just nodded.

'Laura's personal things are being shipped to her parents tomorrow - the books you asked for will be there. I think she'd like you having them.'

Orla was dumbstruck. Was he trying to be nice?

'Thank you. I think she'd like that too,' said Orla.

He didn't say anything else - he just turned and joined his family, leaving Orla gobsmacked.

Very soon, the mourners, eating lunch in the restaurant, came to the bar, and the Quinns took over. Orla met Maggie's husband, Artie, and her gorgeous sons, David and Shay – causing her to miss her boys. Nina was there, as was Niamh's clan - her husband Ray, her five gorgeous girls and her mam. *Laura would have loved this,* thought Orla, feeling sad.

'I did love it.'

There she was again, Orla shook her head, and soon, Lars said goodbye to the Quinn's. His parents kissed Laura's goodbye and said they'd stay in touch.

'They won't,' whispered Orla to Niamh.

She was sure they didn't know what kind of man their son was, but they'd be blind not to notice something was wrong. Before he left, Lars turned to nod at Orla - she nodded back, and then he was gone.

'Eh...What was that?' asked Maggie, a look of disbelief on her face.

'I have no idea,' said Orla, who'd told them what had happened outside the toilet - they were furious. 'Maybe he thinks we're besties because he's sending my books.'

They laughed, and with the Swedes gone, the family relaxed, and the party started. Louise and Orla had a quick chat but agreed to speak properly the next day. There was singing and dancing to be done - a celebration of Laura's life - Irish style. When Orla climbed into bed later that night, she fell into a deep sleep.

Laura was there again - this time, she could hear her loudly and clearly. *The coffee machine, love – find the coffee machine.*

Laura
If the phone had recorded my murder, Lars was fucked. Sending the books to Orla was poetic justice. I couldn't wait for her to figure out what was inside them and to see Lars's face when he realised he'd contributed to his own downfall.

34 ~ ORLA

Orla agreed to meet Louise for a dog walk around Marley Park the next day.

'Thanks for coming. Ever since Laura died, I feel paranoid and don't know who to trust,' said Louise as they walked. 'Mam explained what you were doing, and I was relieved,' she continued. 'Laura was always so guarded when we spoke – afraid someone was listening, and I used to think she was over the top, until now.'

'Why - what's going on? Has Lars said something? Did you see Laura before she died?' asked Orla.

'No, he hasn't said anything - but he has people everywhere, and he rang me ma. Can you believe that? Asked if Laura had left anything in the house,' explained Louise, and Orla wondered what he was looking for. 'Me ma said no. Laura left a few things in her old room, but nothing worth mentioning, and I didn't see Laura before she died – I wish I had.' Tears poured from her eyes. 'We spoke the day before, and she told me some of what was happening.'

'I should have told her everything.'

'She wrote to me on the same day – said Lars still abused her and that she had evidence to get away from him,' said Orla.

'Abused her? He fucking killed her - especially in the last year. Laura had more broken bones than anyone I've ever known, and she was never allowed to go to a hospital,' said Louise. 'It breaks my heart, but at least she's away from that bastard now.'

'Lou, I think Lars killed Laura - I just need to prove it,' said Orla.

'Orla, I know Lars killed her, and I want to help you,' said Louise.

'Right then, tell me what you know, and let's see if we can work out what happened in that apartment,' said Orla.

'I only have an outline - Laura was supposed to tell me everything when I saw her, but that fucker got to her - I'm positive of it,' said Louise, then added. 'It started six months ago when Laura accidentally overheard a conversation about three girls murdered in a nightclub in Dublin. That finally spurred her on to leave him, and she thought wrecking his career might be her way out, so she recorded him hitting her. Then, a few months later – she accidentally discovered he was sex trafficking girls and blackmailing people. Laura was shitting herself, but with the videos of his abuse and proof of him trafficking girls, she came to Dublin to finally get away from him. When we spoke, Laura swore Lars didn't know - if he did, she'd never have been allowed to leave Sweden.'

'Holy shit, we know who the girls are,' said Orla. 'They were murdered – Oh my God, Lou – we've been trying to find out what happened to them.'

'Laura knew where they were,' said Louise.

'Where who were?' asked Orla, confused – she just said they were murdered.

'Their bodies, I mean,' Louise clarified. 'She wrote it down somewhere and was going to tell me when we met.'

'Jesus,' said Orla, horrified but pushing

it aside, she pressed on. 'We know about the domestic abuse videos from her letter, but her phone is gone...' Orla trailed off, then asked. 'What could the sex-trafficking proof be - where is it?'

'I don't know,' said Lou.

'In my makeup bag.'

'If Lars killed Laura, he'd have the videos, and he doesn't because he turned up at her solicitors looking for them, and now, you're saying he rang your mam looking for something.' Trying to work it out in her head, Orla asked, 'how did he know about them? In her letter, written on Sunday, Laura said he didn't know – she told you on Sunday he didn't know, which means he found out after she flew to Dublin,' said Orla.

'He's a sly bastard - probably had her followed,' said Louise.

'We're off to Sweden tomorrow,' said Orla. 'We want to talk to Laura's friend Astrid, I'll tell you what she says.'

'You're going to Sweden?' asked Louise, seeming shocked, and Orla nodded.

'We need to – I can't let the prick get away with killing her, Lou,' said Orla.

'Oh my God – thank you so much,' said Louise, suddenly pulling Orla into a tight hug. 'You're our first bit of hope since Laura died,' she sobbed.

They spent the next hour talking about Laura, then said goodbye with the promise of staying in touch. Orla drove straight to the flats to speak to the families of the missing girls, then to Maggie's shop. Maggie was the most logical person in their group, and even though she hardly believed it herself, Orla wanted to put the idea of Laura being a ghost to her before telling anyone else.

'Hello there,' said Maggie when Orla walked into the shop. 'Why are you not at home packing?' she asked.

Orla didn't answer - she just booked around Maggie's beautiful shop in wonder.

'What's going on? Has something happened?' asked Maggie, alarmed, but before she could say another word, Orla hugged her tightly.

Maggie was confused until she remembered the window display dedicated to

Orla's books. There were posters, cardboard cut-outs, and a wooden bookcase built from what looked like Orla's books that housed her novels.

'Oh my God, Maggie - it's fabulous,' said Orla, then added with a smirk, 'so, my books are not your thing?'

'I loved them - you write exquisitely, as I always knew you would,' said Maggie, then asked, 'why are you here?'

They sat on a sofa beside a large square paned window that looked out to the street.

'I went to the flats,' said Orla. 'It was awful. Told the women it was definitely their girls in the nightclub. I said we still didn't know what happened – but Laura told Lou they were murdered in the nightclub that night. I didn't tell them – I just couldn't. Instead, I asked for more time before they went to the guards and insisted on them reopening the case.'

'Super detective. No stone is left unturned.'

'They were murdered that night?' asked Maggie, and Orla nodded. 'I wonder if it was before or after we left the club?'

'I don't know, but I remember the men whispering when they came back into the room – Lars was furious about something, and they had guns,' said Orla with a deep sigh.

'Jesus, Christ - this is getting more insane by the second,' said Maggie.

'Laura knew where the bodies were, Maggie. She told Lou the girls were buried and wrote down where,' said Orla to Maggie's shocked face. 'Lou doesn't know anything about the trafficking, just that Laura had proof.'

It seemed nothing would stop Laura from getting justice, not even her own death. Orla was in awe of her. She turned to Maggie and took her hands.

'Maggie - do you believe in ghosts?'

Maggie laughed and looked confused.

'This was going to be fun.'

'You know - messages from the other side,' Orla clarified.

'You mean from dead people?' asked Maggie.

'Yeah,' said Orla and when the look on Maggie's face said no, Orla quickly added. 'Just hear me out, okay, and keep an open mind.'

'Fasten your seatbelt, Maggie, you're in for a ride!'

'Hang on – anyone could walk in, and I have a feeling this is going to be deep,' said Maggie. She jumped up and closed the shop, then made coffee. 'I put the *'closed for staff training'* sign on the door - Tuesdays are usually quiet anyway,' she called from behind a huge coffee machine, then asked. 'Do you want carrot cake – it's delicious?

'Yes, please,' said Orla and when they had coffee and cake in their hand - they sat back down.

'Okay - I'm ready – tell me everything,' said Maggie.

'It started on the day of Laura's murder. I hadn't thought about Laura in years, but on that day, I couldn't stop thinking about her. As in, she was on my mind every second of the day – I thought I was going mad. Then Audrey rang and said she'd been murdered, and I was like - what the fuck? Why had I been thinking about Laura - all day, on the day she died?'

'When you say on your mind – in what

way?' asked Maggie.

'I desperately wanted a cup of that coffee.'

'Just old memories, nice memories, how crazy she'd been - the things she got up to,' said Orla, and Maggie smiled, remembering them as well. 'I didn't fathom Lars was still on the scene - I just thought about Laura before she met him. When Audrey said she'd been murdered? Christ on a bike, I nearly died myself.'

'Yeah, that's a bit odd, alright. What else?' asked Maggie, intrigued.

'This is going to sound weird, but on the night of Laura's mass, Laura kinda spoke to me – twice, I think. I was watching Lars and noticed Erik watching me - watching him. Someone told me to be careful because Erik was a savage bastard, and it sounded like Laura. At first, I thought one of you had said it, but you were all listening to the priest. Laura was the only person I knew to use the term savage when describing someone she didn't like.'

'I remember you looked funny at the mass - I thought you were going to burst into tears,' said Maggie, then asked. 'What else did she say? You said she spoke twice?' asked Maggie.

'Erik's name. How the fuck did I know his name was Olsson? I'd never spoken to Laura about him in my life - why would I? His name came out of nowhere.'

Maggie agreed there was definitely something going on.

'Niamh would be all over this - she's mad about angel cards and crystals - this is right up her street,' said Maggie.

'I know - that's why I wanted to talk to you first. You're the opposite, and I wanted to make sure I'm not losing my mind,' said Orla.

'I don't think you are, but it's a bit out there. Anything else happen?' asked Maggie.

'Just one more thing, and this is super weird,' said Orla. 'I've been dreaming about Laura – she's been trying to tell me something, but the dreams have been scattered - I haven't been able to make head nor tail of them until last night.'

'Jesus, what happened last night?' asked Maggie, barely able to contain herself.

'For the first time - the dream was crystal clear. We were in Bewley's Café, and Laura told me to find the coffee machine. I have no idea what that means.'

'At last – "yes Orla," - I flickered a dim lamp in the corner.'

'Okay, and I'm still not on board with it, but let's say Laura is communicating with you,' said Maggie. 'Why would she want you to find a coffee machine? It's a bit random, isn't it?'

Orla looked around - did the lamp flicker?

'There were two cups of coffee at the murder scene - that's the only connection I can think of,' said Orla.

The lamp flickered again.

'Oh yeah,' said Maggie, then added. 'Maybe Laura is sticking around until Lars is in prison, or what if she can't rest in peace until…' Maggie thought about it. 'I don't know – the girl's bodies are found or something like that. Jesus, this is all very "Ghost" - I'm expecting Patrick Swayze to walk in any second now.'

Just then, a book on the bookshelf displaying Orla's books fell to the floor.

'Well - that's progress – I almost blew on my fingers.'

Maggie looked at Orla and nervously laughed.
'I think Laura is trying to help us,' said Orla, looking around the room.

'Something was finally going my way.'

'If that was you, Laura, do that again,' whispered Orla, her nervousness causing her to laugh.
Another book moved but didn't fall - it was enough as both women screamed.
'I don't believe this,' said Maggie. 'If Laura is stuck somewhere between life and death - we have to help her,' she added, looking alarmed.
'I don't think Laura is stuck anywhere – I think Laura has unfinished business and that makes me even more determined to find something to tie all of this to Lars,' said Orla.

Laura
Making contact drained my energy, but at least

MS S B FARRELL

I was getting somewhere. For the first time since I died, I had hope. Maybe the girl's bodies would be found, and maybe that bastard would rot in prison for what he did to me and countless others.

35 ~ ORLA

Ryanair flight 274 from Dublin to Stockholm was on time, and four Irishwomen were ready for action.

'Five Irishwomen.'

Having arrived at the airport just before seven and while eating breakfast, Orla relayed her conversation with Louise from the day before.

'Fuck – so, they were murdered that night,' said Audrey, 'and she asked Marcus about sex trafficking because she had proof of something.'

Orla nodded.

'If Laura had proof - Lars had a motive,' said Maggie.

Looking at her friends, Orla realised the time had come to tell them everything. She took a deep breath and dove straight into the deep end. From whispers and dreams to the books falling from shelves - Audrey's toast stopped halfway to her mouth, and Niamh's face was a picture.

'Eh, are you serious?' asked Audrey.

Orla understood her scepticism - she felt it herself and responded with one word.

'Deadly.'

Maggie explained how she'd witnessed the book phenomenon.

'Sure, look - no one is more shocked than me,' said Maggie, 'but I saw it with my own eyes.'

'And the Erik details are particularly odd, aren't they?' Orla interjected.

'Not even death will stop that woman,' said Niamh, laughing. 'Is she here now?' she asked.

'I don't know, but lights usually flicker when she's around,' said Orla.

'Too many lights in the airport – not happening.'

'Hi Laura,' said Niamh, waving. When she noticed Audrey's astonished face, she asked, 'What? Laura's obviously here to avenge her death, like Patrick Swasey in Ghost.'

'Hi Niamh. I'm here.'

'I said the exact same thing,' said Maggie.

Orla couldn't help but laugh.

'Look, I love the idea of Laura being here, but we need to go over a few things before we enter enemy territory,' she said.

She turned to Audrey and asked about the coffee cups.

'Fine, but we're definitely going back to Laura being a ghost,' said Niamh.

Audrey described the scene again.

'Two coffee cups - one untouched and one smashed to bits on the floor.'

'Let's just agree for a minute that Laura gave me a message. Why is she talking about coffee?' asked Orla, then thought - *maybe it was poisoned.*

She asked Audrey about forensic testing, but Audrey just rolled her eyes.

'Yes, we tested it, and it was just coffee, black coffee, strong coffee, but just coffee,' she said.

'Why two cups?' asked Orla.

'Initially, we thought both cups were hers, but I don't think that was the case. She had breakfast at her mam's house. Mrs Quinn said she was in a mad rush because the taxi was late – would she stop to make coffee while getting changed? She left Wicklow Street just after eleven - it takes half an hour to get to Grand Canal, whether walking or sitting in traffic. The coroner said her murder happened at about noon.' The women hung on to every word Audrey said. 'That would mean she'd have made two cups of coffee for herself in fifteen minutes. Didn't drink one and smashed the other - I think it happened in the struggle.'

That made more sense to Orla, but Laura said coffee machine.

'Is there a coffee machine in the apartment?' she asked.

'Yeah,' said Audrey, 'but there was nothing in it.'

Then what did Laura mean?

'So, basically, she was drinking coffee with whoever killed her,' Niamh surmised confidently.

'It seems so, but of course, no fingerprints, DNA, nothing. Whoever owned that second cup of coffee didn't touch it or anything else in that apartment.'

'What about the second phone?' asked Orla, realising she'd forgotten to mention it. 'Marcus said Laura had a second phone with videos of Lars kicking the shit out of her. I'm guessing you didn't find it?'

'We didn't find any phone,' said Audrey, then added,' the killer obviously has it.'

'Then why would he show up at Marcus's office looking for it? If he had the phone, he wouldn't have gone anywhere near him,' said Orla.

'That's if Lars definitely killed her,' replied Audrey, and Orla rolled her eyes.

'I think we can safely assume he did.'

'Okay, but what will the videos prove? Lars is a wifebeater?' asked Audrey, then added. 'We already knew that.'

'A wifebeater who maybe went too far and killed said wife,' said Orla, wondering where it was.

When they boarded the plane, even though it was early, they had a glass of Prosecco.

'Time doesn't exist when you're in the

air,' said Niamh, waving her small bottle, and two and a half hours later, they landed safely at Stockholm Arlanda Airport.

Audrey drove the rented car - the rest agreeing it was too stressful. Driving on the wrong side of the road was bad enough, but - in the snow? No thanks. When they checked into their hotel in Uppsala, it was just after three.

'Meet in half an hour?' suggested Orla as they went to their rooms to freshen up.

The Grand Hotel was a charming boutique hotel. Orla's room overlooked the river and was bright and airy with an old-world elegance. It was like being away for a girl's weekend, except for the tragic circumstances. While touching up her make-up, she paused to look at her reflection. Stress and weariness stared back at her - what if they didn't find Astrid? What if they bumped into Lars? Audrey rang his office the day before on the pretence of updating him, but really to check if he was in Stockholm - he was, and they were disappointed. They'd hoped he was in America or China – somewhere far from Sweden.

While walking through the streets of Uppsala, enjoying the Scandinavian atmosphere, incredible architecture, and fresh, crisp air, Orla suspected Laura loved the city - it was beautiful, and Laura had always loved beautiful things.

'Orla was right - I did love it here.'

When they passed the university hospital, they stopped.
'Why don't we just go in?' asked Maggie. 'Let's see if Astrid is working and talk to her. What are we waiting for?'
Orla was eager to find Astrid but had a feeling she wasn't there.
'Another message from Laura?' asked Audrey, and Orla smiled.

'Nothing to do with me. I wanted them to go in.'

'No. I think it's better to go tomorrow morning - then we'll drive to Laura's house – I have a feeling she wants us to go there."

'I was high-fiving her.'

Even though it was snowing, they

walked around the city – did some shopping and stopped for a glass of wine and an early dinner in a Swedish restaurant. After breakfast the next morning, they walked to the university hospital to find Astrid. The receptionist directed them towards the lifts and the third-floor children's ward.

'Laura always loved kids,' said Maggie sadly.

'I'm not surprised she worked with them,' said Niamh.

'How did things go so wrong for her?' asked Audrey.

They looked at each other and said the same thing.

'Lars.'

Laura
There was no doubt about it - my life would have been very different if I hadn't met him. Still, it was what it was, and we had work to do. Seeing my friends in Sweden was weird. I just hoped they found Astrid and spoke to Hilda. It felt like we were getting somewhere.

36 ~ ORLA

As they walked down the corridor to the children's ward, a nurse approached them, and by the look of recognition on her face, Orla knew it was Astrid. She shuffled them into one of the empty private rooms.

'What are you doing here? Laura talked about you so much that I feel like I know you,' said Astrid, breaking Orla's heart - poor Laura. With tears in her eyes, she looked at each of them. 'Laura was worried Lars would find out what she was doing - now she's dead.'

'What was she doing?' asked Audrey.

'Leaving him,' said Astrid. 'He found out and killed her, ya?'

'We think so, but we need proof - that's why we're here,' said Orla.

Astrid gave them directions to a nearby coffee shop.

'Go, quickly. I'll take a break and meet you there soon.' She practically pushed them out of the room. 'We think one of the nurses watched Laura and told Lars. You ladies being here is news for him. Go,' she said again.

'Another poor cow under Lars's spell.'

They found the small minimalist coffee shop full of doctors and nurses, obviously needing their caffeine fix - Orla ordered four black coffees.
'She thinks Lars killed Laura as well,' said Niamh.
'Another one confirming what we know,' said Maggie.
Astrid arrived half an hour later.
'Sorry - it's never easy to escape the ward,' she said.
'Want a coffee,' asked Audrey.
Astrid nodded as Audrey ordered more coffee for everyone. Similar in age, she was tall, blond and beautiful, with ice-blue eyes. When their coffees arrived, and in broken English – Astrid told them about Laura's life.
'Laura was so unhappy – she hated her husband. Volunteering at the hospital and her home made her smile. Lars was mostly

in Stockholm, but when he returned at the weekend...' she hesitated, then sighed '...he beat her. On Monday, Laura had new bruises - so many of them,' she said, shaking her head sadly, 'but if she tried to leave, he'd kill her.'

'And that's exactly what he did.'

'Did she try to in the past?' asked Audrey.
'Yes – many times and the result,' Astrid shook her head. 'She bought a phone to record his beatings – to use against him. Lars will be Deputy Prime Minister when his party wins election. Laura thought this was her chance to escape - he would not risk this position.'

'I should have just poisoned him.'

'Why go to Dublin to see a solicitor instead of one in this country?' asked Audrey.
'She was afraid of husband's position. He is powerful man - he pay people or threaten their business. She thought better help was available in Ireland,' said Astrid, and Orla agreed it would have been if she'd survived.

'Astrid didn't know he was blackmailing everyone.'

'Is there anything else you can tell us?' asked Orla.

'There is something terrible, and if Lars finds out I know this - he will kill me,' said Astrid.

'They already knew, but Astrid would fill in the blanks.'

'Is it about the girls in Dublin?' asked Orla, then explained what Laura's sister had told them.

'Yes, Laura overheard a conversation between Lars and Erik. They were drunk - Laura was in bed trying to sleep, but the beating had been terrible, and she was in pain.'

'Poor Laura,' whispered Niamh.

'Laura learned to move in silence - be invisible like a ghost and snuck to kitchen for pain medicine. When she passed Lars's office, she heard them talking about girls who'd cost them money.'

'It seemed a lifetime ago when I heard those two bastards talking.'

'Erik said they were lucky and congratulated each other for killing them.' Astrid stopped as if trying to recall what Laura had said. 'Hitting Laura saved them from prison, and girls shot in the head to stop you hearing screams.'

'Those bastards shot them,' said Orla, closing her eyes.

'Laura was ready to leave,' continued Astrid, 'and Lars asked where they were buried. Erik said somewhere in Dublin - I do not know this information - Laura wrote down where Lars won't find.'

Orla thought about the books - that must be what Laura meant in her letter. Then she remembered the young girls, looking like deer caught in headlights and thought of the photo and how happy and excited they'd been earlier that night at the prospect of going out in Dublin. If Lars and his gang hadn't murdered them, they would have trafficked them. It seemed insane that something like that happened in Dublin. Astrid returned to work when they finished their coffee, and Audrey drove them to Laura's house.

'Was it our fault?' whispered Niamh as they arrived.

No one answered, but Orla realised the girls were dead when the men came back into the room that night - she felt lucky to be alive.

Laura's house was nestled in woods and looked down to a huge lake. The colossal glass and wood structure somehow fit in, and as they walked towards it, they noticed an old woman going through the gate.

'I hugged Hilda. "I should have listened to you," I whispered into her ear.'

'Excuse me,' said Orla, walking towards her. 'Do you speak English? We're friends of Laura's and were wondering if you could help us?'

For the second time that day, recognition dawned on the face of someone they'd never met before.

'You're her friends from Ireland - I'm Hilda - I help Laura with house,' said Hilda in more broken English. She pointed to a small path that led into the woods. 'Please,' she indicated they follow her as she walked, stopping a good distance from the house.

When Hilda began to softly cry, Orla looked at Audrey. What the fuck was going on?

'I told her it was dangerous - I knew he would find out,' said Hilda, shaking her head and wiping her eyes.

'What was dangerous?' asked Audrey, then added. 'Laura wrote to us before she died - said she had evidence of Lars's abuse and other crimes. We think he killed her,' said Audrey.

'Oh yes, Mr Karlsson killed Laura – I have no doubt,' said Hilda. 'Laura worked so hard and was afraid, but she got information. Mr Karlsson and Mr Erik sell girls for sex.

'How did she get the information?' asked Audrey.

'Secret room in garage,' said Hilda, 'Laura saw Erik go in one day while in her car. He didn't see her. I show you. Garage has no camera. 'You go to garage - I open.' she said.

She walked back down the path, pointed to where the garages were and disappeared inside the house. Five minutes later, one of the garage doors opened and Hilda hurried them inside.

'This is Lars's big secret,' she said, walking towards a shelved wall and pressing on a hammer. With a click, a shelf slid open to reveal a door. Hilda keyed in a six-digit code. 'Laura found by accident and spent many hours copying,' Hilda didn't elaborate on what Laura was copying - she just said, 'Laura teach me to access - in case she is locked inside.'

'Holy shit, what the fuck is down there?' asked Niamh, taking Maggie's arm.

A flight of stairs led to what could only be described as a surveillance room. A wall of TV screens showed different parts of the house, but Orla's attention was drawn to one room with two beds and chains hanging from the wall. Another room had a large crate and more chains - both were empty.

'I don't think these rooms are in this house,' said Orla. 'This is what Laura found, the sex trafficking,' her eyes moved to the desk, empty except for a dust mark revealing something large had been removed.

'Erik and Sven came two days ago and take computer. They don't mind old Hilda –

they think I don't see - but I see,' said Hilda.

Laura had been copying what? More videos? It seemed like the only explanation.

'We need to get out of here,' said Orla.

'Yes – This is my last day – I go to live with my son in Norway,' said Hilda.

'Go now, Hilda and don't go home alone. No camera in the garage, but there are cameras outside the house. Lars might know you let us in,' said Audrey.

Hilda looked scared but nodded.

'I go to my sister's house before Norway,' she said.

When they said goodbye, Orla got Hilda's phone number and promised to update her on any developments – Hilda cried as she waved goodbye.

Laura
On the day of my murder, I told Lars I knew what he was doing - I don't think he realised I meant this, but he wasn't one to take risks. He must have gotten Erik to move everything, just in case.

37 ~ ORLA

As Audrey drove away from Laura's house, Orla felt relieved. On the way back to Uppsala, they stopped at a Swedish bar and ordered drinks.

'So, Laura accidentally found out about the girl's murder and accidentally found the room in the garage,' said Niamh.

'There were chains on the walls,' said Audrey, then added. 'I think that's the nail in his coffin Laura wrote about. The only reason cameras are in those rooms is to record whoever uses them – which ties in with blackmail. Laura would have used a USB stick to copy the files.'

'So, we need to find a phone with videos of Lars beating her, the location of the girl's bodies that she wrote down somewhere, and now a USB stick,' said Orla, looking at each of them before adding, 'and all three are somewhere in Dublin.'

'Yes, they are – clever bitch.'

As they drank their wine, Orla's phone beeped.

Hilda: *Mr Karlsson tried to ring, but I did not answer.*

'My heart. Lovely Hilda - always protecting me.'

Orla showed the text message to her friends.

'Shit – he knows we're here,' said Niamh.

'Probably know where we're staying,' said Audrey.

'Likely to turn up,' said Maggie.

'If he does, we stick to the story - on a pilgrimage to Laura,' said Audrey. 'It's a public space, he can't do anything.'

Orla wanted to go home - she didn't want to spend another night in Sweden. They finished their drinks and drove back to town - their misery turning to terror when they passed their hotel on the way to the underground car park and a large, black SUV pulled up. The doors opened, and Lars, Erik and Sven stepped out.

In the carpark – they pulled themselves together.

'I don't think I can go in,' said Niamh, nervously laughing.

'We have to,' said Audrey. 'Lars knows we're here - we have to behave as if nothing is wrong, or he'll suspect something, and we need to get back to Dublin and find that proof.'

She was right, but everyone was petrified.

'I don't want to see Lars again - I want to go home,' pleaded Maggie.

'I know you're scared, Maggie, so am I, but Lars has no way of knowing we suspect him of anything - let's keep this about Laura,' said Audrey, trying to reassure her. 'When we see them, act like we don't know they're there,' she instructed as they took the lift to the lobby.

'Jesus Christ, I'm going to have a fecking heart attack,' said Niamh, blessing herself.

Orla could hear her heart thumping as they walked across the lobby and into the hotel bar and were greeted by three angry Swedes.

'Hello Lars,' said Orla, feigning surprise. 'What are you doing here?' she asked.

'I would ask the same question of you,'

said Lars, with Erik and Sven flanking him.

'We came to visit the hospital where Laura worked - we're having a ball in Laura's memory to raise money for her charity,' said Orla, smooth as silk. 'It's in May, would you like to come?' she asked, that idea popping into her head.

'Nice one, Orla.'

'Why were you at my home?' he asked, ignoring her question.

Orla smiled warmly, trying to disarm him.

'I guess you could say it's a pilgrimage to Laura. As well as raising money, we wanted to see some of her before truly saying goodbye,' she said, cringing at how unbelievable that sounded. Then, quickly changing the subject, she asked if they wanted a drink.

'He knows Hilda let them into the garage. Audrey was right – there are cameras outside the house.'

'What were you doing in my home,' asked Lars again and this time Audrey stepped in.

'As Orla said, we wanted to see where

Laura lived. We met Hilda, but she had to go to the doctor, so we didn't go inside.'

'Except for the garage,' said Erik, watching her closely.

'To shelter from the rain for five minutes,' lied Audrey, keeping eye contact.

'Lars wouldn't react – he knew he was watched by everyone in the room.'

There was a standoff. The three men stared at them as if trying to figure something out. Orla was glad of the packed bar, and trying to remain calm, she ordered four glasses of white wine and a bottle of sparkling water.

'Anything for you?' She turned to Lars.

Lars asked for a black coffee - Erik whiskey, and Sven shook his head. The barman got the drinks, and as they stood in awkward silence, Audrey and Orla looked at each other, thinking the same thing - black coffee like the untouched cup in Laura's apartment. The drinks arrived, and trying to defuse the situation, Orla asked about the restaurant they had booked for dinner that night.

'It's an Italian called Il Forno. Do you

know it?' she asked.

Lars didn't answer, but by then, some of the hotel guests had approached him - shaking his hand and engaging him in conversation. Seeing how much of a celebrity he was in this country was strange. Orla was thankful for the distraction and chatted with her friends until Maggie said she was going.

'I have a headache,' she said, leaving before anyone could respond.

Soon after, Lars asked if they wanted another drink, and that was their cue.

'No, thank you,' said Orla, 'we need to get ready for dinner.'

As they walked towards the lift, Orla could feel three sets of eyes burning a hole in her back.

'Jesus, why did you tell him where we're going for dinner?' asked Niamh when the lift doors closed.

'I was trying to be easy breezy, but he didn't buy a word of it,' admitted Orla, pressing the third-floor button.

'He thinks we're up to something,' said Audrey.

'The girls needed to get back to Ireland.'

Orla returned to her room, quickly showered, and checked her email. She was surprised to find one from her mam, whom she didn't know had an email address, and realised why when she opened it.

To: *Orla Reed*
From: *Patsy Reed*
Subject: *Flight Information.*

I just set up this email address today. I can't believe how easy it was. Anyway, I managed to get some information about a flight into Dublin when Laura - God rest her - was killed. I'll tell you when you get home.

Stay safe, and I'll see you tomorrow.

Love mam.

Smiling, Orla realised her mam was playing the role of detective very well. She quickly replied, closed her laptop, and dressed when a loud knock on her door startled her. Looking through the peephole, Orla nearly died when she saw Erik standing outside.

Laura

Erik wouldn't think twice about killing my friends, and he could make them disappear. I'd feel much happier when they were back in Dublin.

38 ~ ORLA

Orla texted Audrey and asked her to come to her room immediately.

'Use the phone, Orla. Pick up the bloody phone.'

Noticing an old hotel phone on the wall by the door, Orla quickly dialled reception, and when they answered, she opened the door.

'Oh, hello,' she said to Erik's surprised face, 'I'm just ordering a taxi,' she mouthed and continued her conversation on the phone. 'Yes, thank you - four people at seven-thirty. I have to go - Mr Karlsson's assistant just arrived.'

She hung up as Erik pushed his way into her room, slamming the door behind him. Eh... excuse me.

'What the fuck are you up to, and don't give me some bullshit story about a fucking homage to Laura,' he sneered.

'I scratched at his face - hating him more than

ever.'

'I don't know what you're talking about, Erik. We're here to see some of Laura's life,' she said, then feeling brave, added, 'why else would we be here?

The look on his face was murderous, and Orla was sure he wanted to throttle her. She felt scared until someone banged at the door, and even though Erik had his back to it, she kept her nerve, walked past him, and opened it.

'Eh, am I disturbing something?' asked Audrey, looking past Orla to Erik. 'Do you two want to be alone?'

Orla almost laughed, either from nervous energy or the look of disgust on Erik's face.

'Lol'

'Erik is just leaving, and I need five minutes to finish getting ready. Come in,' she said as Audrey entered the room.

Erik looked at them with the same hatred in his eyes as Lars.

'I know you're up to something, and I'm fucking watching you,' he said, then walked out, slamming the door…again.

Orla sat on the bed, shaking like a leaf.

'Jesus, this is getting too much,' she said with legs that felt like jelly.

Audrey poured a stiff drink from the minibar.

'I need one of them myself.'

'They don't buy the cock and bull story about a pilgrimage to Laura,' said Orla.

'That's because it's completely unbelievable,' said Audrey before adding. 'Look, let's get everything packed into the car tonight - just keep travel clothes for tomorrow. We'll check out after dinner - just in case we have to flee in the night.'

'What the fuck do you mean?' asked Orla.

'Better to be safe than sorry,' said Audrey.

Audrey left to tell the others, and Orla packed. They met at the lift twenty minutes later, packed the car, and went to the bar to wait for their taxi. The Swedes were gone.

'I'm not hungry,' said Niamh when they arrived at the restaurant. 'We're in a strange country, being followed by murderers and sex traffickers.'

'Nothing will happen,' said Audrey, trying to reassure them.

'What if they come to our rooms tonight? They might shoot us in the head,' said Maggie, causing them to pause - would they go that far?

'Fuck,' said Niamh, looking to Audrey for guidance.

'That's why I wanted us to be ready to leave,' said Audrey as dinner arrived. 'Don't look now, but they're across the road,' she added.

'They need to get out of Sweden!'

'Sweet mother of God, they're going to kill us all,' whispered Niamh, her voice laced with panic.

An hour later, having barely touched their meal, they took another taxi back to the hotel, checked out and explained their early flight. While having a quick nightcap, Audrey made a decision.

'I think we should go now - get in the car and head to the airport. Erik is trying to intimidate us, and although I don't think he'd come to our rooms, let's not give him a chance. It means a long night in the airport, but I'd prefer that to a restless one here,' said Audrey.

The others agreed, quickly went to their rooms, grabbed whatever was still there, and met in the underground car park. They were reasonably sure Erik didn't know about their hired car, but even so, as they passed the hotel entrance, three of them ducked.

'Was he there?' asked Maggie in a muffled voice.

'Yeah, both sitting in the car - they didn't notice me,' said Audrey.

They arrived at the airport just after midnight and drank tea while feeling safer on the other side of passport control. Orla texted Astrid and Hilda to tell them what happened. She got an immediate response from both of them.

Astrid: *Good luck. I really hope you find what you need to put Lars in prison.*

Hilda: *Please finish what Laura started.*

'Why would Lars be trafficking girls if he's a member of parliament?' asked Audrey, who'd been thoughtful since arriving at the airport. 'I mean, why risk it?'

'Maybe being a member of parliament is where the blackmail comes into it,' said Orla.

'God, she was a clever bitch.'

'Yeah, maybe, and what did he do when he lived in Dublin? I remember the security thing for nightclubs but was he in construction?' asked Audrey.

'Why? What are you thinking?' asked Niamh.

'I'm trying to figure out where someone might bury three bodies. It wouldn't have been easy,' said Audrey.

'Maybe they took them to the Dublin mountains and buried them there,' suggested Maggie, and Orla thought they'd never find them if that was the case.

'I don't think so,' said Audrey and because she was the guard, they listened with interest to her theory. 'They were off their heads on cocaine and booze. Would they risk a long drive to the Dublin mountains with three dead bodies and a few shovels in the boot? What if the guards stopped them? I'm more inclined to think they buried them close to where they killed them.'

'They could have thrown them in the river, Liffey,' Niamh quickly interjected, but Audrey shook her head.

'If they had, they'd have found those bodies by now, and Astrid said Lars asked Erik where he buried them,' she reminded them.

'Oh yeah, he did,' said Orla, feeling hopeful. Maybe they'd find them after all.

Landing at Dublin airport later that morning, Orla was never happier to be home. She took a taxi to her ma's house, feeling absolutely exhausted.

'What in God's name happened? You look like you've been dragged through a hedge backwards,' said Patsy, taking Orla's bag to start the washing.

'Ah, thanks, ma,' said Orla, smiling, (*always lovely to hear*). 'I need to shower - put the kettle on, and I'll tell you everything.'

Even though she was exhausted, Orla knew if she went to bed, she'd disrupt her sleep pattern, and anyway, her mam was dying to know. After a long shower, she put on some loungewear, returned downstairs and told her parents the whole story.

'Jesus, Mary and holy St Joseph. Selling girls for sex, what's next?' asked Patsy.

'I know, it's awful,' sighed Orla.

She explained how they were trying to figure out where the girls were buried but, feeling overloaded, decided to sit with her da and watch TV for a while. Her ma joined them, and together they watched a film. However, halfway through it, Patsy jumped up.

'Oh Jesus, I forgot to tell you about the flight,' she said, going into the kitchen for her phone. She proceeded to show Orla photos of an airport control room. 'It's the one Maggie suggested in Lucan,' said Patsy to Orla's stunned face.

'First of all, how did you get in there?' asked Orla, positive they didn't just let people walk around taking pictures, 'and secondly, what am I looking at?'

Patsy explained how she told them it was a lifelong hobby, that she collected flight logs and had been doing it for forty years.

'They thought I was a harmless old woman, so they showed me around and let me see how everything works. They paid no mind when I took a few photos.'

A few? There were photos of flight log screens, the control centre, people chatting in a meeting room, and a vending machine. There was even one of her in the cockpit of a plane. Her ma was turning into Inspector fecking Clouseau.

'Ah, here it is, this is the one I wanted you to see,' said Patsy, turning the phone to Orla. 'A flight from Brussels landed at ten on the morning of Laura's murder. It left at one that afternoon. Look at the names.'

Orla did, and her heart stopped when she saw the first piece of solid evidence they'd found. Two names - *L Karlsson. E Olsson.*

Laura
Sneaky bastard. When I spoke to Lars in my mam's house, I should have known he wouldn't let it go. I tried to convince myself I was safe with him in Brussels, but I wasn't. The evidence was mounting - I just prayed it all came together and that the fucker went to prison.

39 ~ ORLA

All thoughts of being tired went straight out of Orla's mind when she saw the photo on her mother's phone. Oh my God, Lars was in Dublin when Laura was murdered, and they had proof.

'Ma, you're an absolute star,' she said, hugging her delighted mam.

'Mrs Reed, you're a legend.'

'Ah, sure, I was only doing what anyone else would do,' said Patsy in an attempt at modesty but loving the attention. 'Does this mean we can have him arrested?' she asked.

'I'm not sure,' said Orla, loving her use of the word, we, 'but he lied to the guards - that has to mean something,' she said.

Noticing the look of disappointment on her mam's face, Orla decided to go the whole hog and tell her about Laura's messages. She led her into the kitchen and closed the door.

'Da won't want to hear this, and before I start, I want you to keep an open mind,' said Orla to Patsy's bemused face – then, she began at the beginning and told the whole story.

'Jesus, Mary and holy St Joseph,' said Patsy, blessing herself. 'Are you telling me Laura is talking to you from heaven? Oh, sweet mother of God.'

Orla didn't know if it was from heaven per se, but it was definitely from somewhere.

'I think she's trying to help us get Lars,' said Orla.

'Is she here now?' asked Patsy, and Orla couldn't help but laugh.

'I'm here, Mrs Reed.'

'I don't know. Maybe,' said Orla. 'I just get a feeling she's close, and I know things I shouldn't, like Erik's name and so on.'

'My God, I never thought I'd live to see the day. Poor Laura, you'll have to put that man in prison so she can rest in peace.'

'I hope so, Mrs Reed.'

The next day, after a very early night and twelve hours of uninterrupted sleep, Orla took the bus to Whelan's Pub on Wexford Street. Having spoken to Audrey the night before, they agreed to meet for a quick lunch after her shift. Orla hadn't said anything about the photo - she wanted to see Audrey's face when she did.

'How are you feeling?' asked Orla, thinking the night shift must have been tough.

'I'm worn out - I didn't sleep much yesterday, how about you?'

'Grand, a bit shaken from the Sweden dash, but alright. How was work?' asked Orla.

'Dave nearly lost his mind when I told him we went to Sweden,' said Audrey, rolling her eyes.

'Did you tell him everything?' asked Orla.

'No, just what Astrid said about the girls. He remembered them but was working on a different case then,' said Audrey. 'Dave is up for arresting Lars. He thinks he did it as well, but we need proof. Lars has too many connections.'

Orla's moment had arrived - she took her phone from her pocket.

'You ready for proof?' she asked, holding

the phone to her chest.

'What are you on about?' asked Audrey, looking suspicious.

'Is this enough?' she asked, showing the picture to Audrey.

'What am I looking at?' asked Audrey, studying the picture while Orla filled her in on what happened while they were in Sweden.

'Me ma basically conned the staff at a private airfield to let her see the flight log - they didn't bat an eyelid,' said Orla.

'Jesus, she needs to be careful. Lars could have someone working for him there, like at the hospital and everywhere else,' said Audrey, shaking her head.

Orla didn't think anyone would mind an old woman's curiosity but made a mental note to retire her mother as chief inspector. Audrey looked at the photo again - studying it closer this time.

'Is this real,' she asked, and Orla nodded. 'So, he was here when Laura died.'

'It seems so - snuck in on his private jet and out again before Laura's body was cold.'

His callousness made her sick. How could a man do that to his own wife?

'Jesus, this changes everything,' said Audrey. 'I need to talk to Dave and see what he thinks. Can I call you tomorrow' she asked, putting on her coat.

'Yes, go,' said Orla, excited about her reaction.

They parted ways, Audrey home to bed and Orla to meet the mothers of the murdered girls. She didn't know if Lars had people working for him in Dublin and suggested a café on Moore Street, deliberately choosing it because the street market was packed with people selling everything from food to garden tools. If anyone was watching, it might make it harder for them to see. The women sat at a small table in the corner with a cup of tea ready for Orla. She drank it gratefully and got straight to the point, telling them what happened in Sweden. Even though it pained her to do so, she explained Laura overheard a conversation that confirmed their girls had died that night.

'I'm sorry to give you such dreadful news,' said Orla as the women quietly sobbed.

She told them how Laura had written down where Erik buried the girls and how they didn't have the information yet.

'Will we ever find them?' asked Olive, wiping her tears with a napkin.

'Audrey is looking into Lars's other businesses from back then - she has a theory about him burying their bodies nearby. I wish there was a different outcome, but I thought you'd want to know,' said Orla.

All three nodded, and Orla realised telling them was the right thing to do.

'I think we've always known they died that night- there was no other explanation for it,' said Maureen. 'They wouldn't have just run off as the guards tried to make us believe. In an odd way, it makes me feel better knowing it was over quickly and they were together.'

Grief had worn these women out, making Orla even more determined to find their girls. They should be able to bury their children and at least have a grave to visit. After a few minutes, they ordered more tea and asked about Laura's case.

'Well, as you know, we found Astrid in Sweden, which was good, but we also bumped into Lars and Erik,' said Orla to three audible gasps.

She explained what happened in the hotel and what Astrid said about the beatings but didn't mention the trafficking - it was too dangerous to involve them. She told them about Lars being on a flight to Dublin the same morning of Laura's murder, explained how he might have people in Dublin watching and asked them to be on their guard.

'If he gets a whiff of us looking into the murder of your girls, it will be all over. I honestly think he'd have us killed,' said Orla.

'He'd definitely have them killed.'

The woman agreed to be vigilant, and with a promise to see each other soon, Orla left and walked toward The Ha'penny Bridge. With her collar pulled up and her scarf tight around her neck, she smiled as, finally, the snow fell. Crossing the bridge, she walked through the small alley leading to Temple Bar when suddenly, two men appeared before her. Orla tried to calm her beating heart – she'd always been terrified of being mugged and ignored them until one of them – the fat one with a gnarly red face, pushed her against the wall. She smashed her head against the hard concrete and cried out.

'Take my bag - there's not much in it,' she said.

Her hands shook as she held out her handbag, but he wasn't interested. Instead, he flipped open a knife and, in a gravelly voice, said.

'I have a message for you.'

Laura
This was Erik. He'd stop at nothing to protect Lars, and he must be worried. Orla needed to run because these men would stab her with that knife. I tried to knock it from his hand – he looked around, feeling the tug. I wanted to scare the be-Jesus out of him.

40 ~ ORLA

Blood trickled down Orla's face from where she hit the wall.

'Someone's not very happy with ye, Orla,' sang the stranger in her ear.

Orla froze - he knew her name, and it wasn't a random mugging. *Erik.* She wanted to retch from the stink of the man's rancid breath. When his meaty hand pulled her hair and his knife pressed against her ribs – she stayed perfectly still.

'Run, Orla.'

Laura's voice was loud and clear. *I can't,* thought Orla.

'What do you want?' she asked, terrified.

'Come on, hurry up, Macker,' said the man behind him. He was younger and not as hardened as Orla's aggressor. 'There's pigs everywhere around here,' he continued, looking up and down the lane.

'Macker. Is that your name?' asked Orla, deciding to take charge of this situation, even though she was petrified. 'Whatever Mr Karlsson wants you to tell me, can you get on with it - I need to be somewhere,' she added, impressed at how confident she sounded while her insides churned.

Macker inched his knife up her chest towards her throat.

'Listen here - ye fucking bitch. You need te,' he trailed off as a group of office workers walked towards them, laughing and chatting.

Orla seized the opportunity and pushed against Macker, who had to back away to let the group pass.

'Call the guards,' cried Orla, causing the group to stop and look around. Some of them took out their phones.

'Bitch,' said Macker, then quickly turned and walked away - leaving Orla alone with the group.

'Are you okay?' someone asked, but Orla ran back to the quays and hailed a passing taxi.

'He knew my fucking name,' said Orla, having immediately rang Audrey.

'My husband was worried.'

'Sounds like Lars is worried,' said Audrey, 'do you want to report it?'

Orla said no, she just wanted to get home and forget the whole thing. On Sunday morning, the whole of Ireland woke to a blanket of white. The heaviest snowfall they'd seen in years and three weeks later than promised.

'Let's walk through the park before mass,' said Orla, eager to get outside.

'Okay, but I need to put me boots on - it's lovely to look at, but it's cold,' said Patsy.

They enjoyed the unspoilt beauty of the snow. The park was a fairy tale, with snow wreathing bare hedges and ice glistening the path. The iron gates surrounding it were frozen, and the trees were heavy with snow. The crisp, clean and freshness would be shattered when the kids woke up.

'The schools will be closed tomorrow for sure, and the roads will be chaos,' said Patsy as they walked.

Audrey laughed, thinking how typically

Irish it was to see the problem in everything. She felt the stillness and beauty were worth the hassle, and after mass, they walked through the park again, this time to the sound of kids laughing and screaming. Arriving home and after warming herself in front of the roaring fire, Orla rang her boys. Having been attacked the day before, she needed to connect with her sons, and she wanted to talk to Neil. She was delighted Con was out of the jungle and in Sydney - at least she could speak to him there.

'Such a good mama.'

'Erik sounds like a psycho, ma. Seriously, you lot are not Charlie's bloody Angels,' said Con and Orla laughed.

'Believe me, Con - we know that. You should have seen us running through that airport in Sweden - terrified for our lives,' she said.

Neil was supportive but worried.

'I'll try to get over, even if it's just for one night next week,' he said.

'Yes, please,' said Orla, realising how much she missed him.

When they said goodbye, she took her laptop upstairs and worked. Orla needed to go home at some point, get some writing done, and see her dog. Dorothy was a sweetheart and completely understood her predicament, but Orla was growing impatient - she didn't like missing deadlines.

'You have to see it through,' said Dorothy when they spoke later that day.

Orla told her all the news, the flight log - the sex trafficking - how Lars had killed those girls and hid their bodies.

'This is unbelievable - it could be your next book,' said Dorothy and Orla had already thought of that. Maybe one day she'd write it as a tribute to Laura, but first, Lars had to be locked up, hopefully for good.

'I'd love it if she wrote a book about my murder.'

On Monday morning, Orla sat in the kitchen, drinking tea and waiting for Audrey to arrive. Audrey wanted to see the flight log in person, and after a long journey through slush-filled roads and lots of traffic, they arrived at the small private airport. A glass building with a plush reception area - you could see private jets parked on a snow-ploughed runway outside.

'Nice to have money,' said Audrey. 'Not one flight will get in or out of Dublin airport today.'

She flashed her badge and asked to speak to someone regarding flight information, and within minutes, a petite woman - probably in her sixties, walked towards them.

'How can I help you, ladies?' she asked, smiling and guiding them to a seated area.

Audrey asked about the flight information but didn't mention Laura's case. Irene said it was against company policy to share such information until Audrey explained it related to a possible murder case.

'I was holding my breath, even though I didn't have one.'

'I can get a search warrant, but I'd appreciate it if you'd help me out and save me the trouble,' said Audrey.

'Oh, well now - that's something different. Let me see what I can do,' said Irene.

'I'll be back in a tick.'

She left Audrey and Orla sitting in reception.

'If we prove he was here, it blows this case open,' said Audrey.

Orla was about to reply but quickly dropped to the floor.

'Fuck ! Duck,' she said, and Audrey immediately dropped down beside her.

Irene returned to see them on the floor between the two sofas.

'Eh... Are you two okay?' she asked warily, glancing around to see what might have caused them to act like two lunatics, but by then, the coast was clear.

Rather than explain, Orla slowly stood up and asked how she got on.

'What the fuck?' mouthed Audrey behind Irene's back, but Orla shook her head.

Irene handed over the flight data for the day in question, but there was no record of Lars's flight.

'Could someone change it?' asked Orla, wondering if anyone on the planet didn't work for Lars.

'Technically, that's not supposed to

happen, but I guess anyone with access to the system could change it,' said Irene.

'Who would have access to the system?' asked Orla, completely deflated.

'Everyone who works in the control room,' said Irene, then realising something was wrong, asked if they were looking for something particular.

Audrey said no.

'Whoever deleted that flight information works for Lars,' she said as they returned to her car. 'I don't want him to know we're looking for it, but it might be too late.'

'Jesus, that guy is everywhere,' said Orla.

Audrey turned to her.

'Well?' she asked.

'Well, what?' asked Orla.

'Was there a reason we hit the floor, or was that just for fun?'

'Oh shit, yes,' said Orla, preoccupied with the missing flight log. 'Erik and Sven walked through arrivals on their phones - they didn't see us.'

'That explains your attack yesterday. Lars sent them,' said Audrey.

'What the fuck do we do now?' asked

Orla.

'I honestly don't know,' said Audrey. 'We have no proof of the trafficking - we don't know where the girls are buried, and now our first piece of solid evidence has disappeared in a puff of smoke.' She sighed, then added. 'Erik will know where we live, so be on your guard. Niamh is off the radar in Cork, but I'll ring her. Can you call Maggie?' she asked.

'Yeah,' said Orla, but knowing Maggie would likely freak out, Orla decided to tell her in person.

'How did you get on?' asked Patsy, who was waiting at the gate when she pulled up. When Orla explained what happened, she was aghast. 'How can that be? Surely my photo will help.'

Orla hoped so and sent the picture to Audrey, then told her mam about seeing Erik.

'He's a dangerous man - just keep your eye out,' said Orla.

'Right,' said Patsy, looking worried.

'I don't think even Lars would stoop that low, but...'

Half an hour later, wrapped up in coats, scarves, and anything else that offered warmth, Orla and Patsy went back out into the snow. A treacherous bus ride brought them into town, and when they arrived at Books & Brew, it was empty except for Maggie. Maggie's stylish bookshop had old wooden floors – large black squared paned windows - dark walls complimenting very high ceilings, and a mezzanine level of old books accessed by a spiral staircase. It was to die for.

'Will you have a cup of tea, or how about a nice cappuccino, Mrs Reed?' asked Maggie.

'Call me Patsy - you're not little girls anymore,' said Patsy with a wave, then explained she didn't like foreign drinks - Orla tried not to laugh.

'Why don't you try it,' suggested Maggie, cutting into a huge Victoria sponge cake and offering her a slice. 'I was going to close the shop but thought I'd use the time to catch up on paperwork,' she explained.

They sat on sofas near the window with their cappuccinos and cake. Orla noticed a look of pride on her mam's face when she saw the window dedicated to her books. Orla relayed the past twenty-four hours to Maggie, from Lars's name on the flight log - the flight disappearing - her attack in the alley and seeing Erik and Sven at the airport.

'You didn't say you were attacked,' said Patsy.

'Are you okay?' asked Maggie.

'I know. Sorry, ma. I didn't want to worry you, and I'm grand. Scare tactics from the Swedes,' said Orla.

'What happens about the flight log now?' asked Maggie.

'I don't know. Audrey has the photo – she's talking to Dave as we speak,' explained Orla.

'God – does it feel like we're getting closer to something?' asked Maggie.

Orla didn't know. To prove Lars killed Laura, so many parts needed to fit together. The abuse - where was the phone? The murders - where were the bodies? The trafficking - where was the proof? It felt more like a case of one step forward and two back.

Laura

They were closer than they knew. I was sure it would come together because why else would I be here? Erik and Sven being in Dublin was a joke. God, I hated them – so fucking high and mighty. I hoped and prayed they were all thrown into prison for good.

41 ~ LARS

Some mornings, while half asleep, Lars would reach for his wife only to realise she was dead. Other times, during a meeting or even sitting in his office, he'd think about her - look forward to seeing her, then remember she was gone forever. He missed her beautiful face, dazzling smile and gorgeous body, but most of all – he missed her feistiness. Laura was a redhead through and through, and even though her defiance had maddened him, he loved her for it. Never before had a woman made his blood boil the way Laura did - the countless women he'd slept with over the years were incomparable.

Being in Dublin for Laura's funeral had troubled him. Her friends were up to something - he was sure of it, but what? And why the fuck did he talk to the author? What possessed him to tell her Laura was happy - even though he knew she wasn't? He even brought up the nightclub incident and was kicking himself for it. Keeping Laura away from them for twenty years had been one of his better ideas.

On the morning of her death, Lars had been so angry that it took longer than usual to snap out of his red haze, and when he did, Laura was lying on the floor, dead. Her skin was whiter than he'd ever seen, and her eyes thankfully closed. Sorrow had knocked him off his feet - the realisation of what had happened annihilated him as he stumbled away from her body. His own injury didn't register until he glanced down and noticed his blood-soaked shirt and immediately rang Erik.

'Come now, I need you,' said Lars and Erik was there in less than five minutes.

'What the fuck happened?' he asked, taking in the bloodbath in the kitchen.

'She stabbed me,' said Lars, 'then I lost it,' he waved his hand at Laura's dead body.

'Fuck,' said Erik ripping off his sweater and tearing it into large strips that he tied around Lars's torso. 'Any higher and you'd have been in trouble,' he said, then he took a thin plastic sheet from his backpack and laid it on the floor behind them.

Lars stepped onto it while Erik started cleaning.

'You touch anything?' he asked over his shoulder, pointing to the coffee cup on the counter. 'The knife?'

'I was wearing gloves, but she used that knife to stab me,' said Lars, pointing to the knife sticking out of Laura's neck. 'Take it with us.'

Erik nodded and tried to dislodge the knife, but it wouldn't budge. After a few more tugs, it still didn't move - so deeply wedged was it into Laura's neck.

'Fuck, just leave it,' said Lars. 'We need to go.'

'Want me to take her jewellery and bag? Make the cops think it's a robbery?' asked Erik as he stood over Laura's body.

'Yeah,' said Lars, looking away – the sight of his wife's dead body had a strange effect on him – had he really just killed her?

Erik put Laura's valuables into his rucksack and rolled up the plastic as they backed out of the apartment. Then, the two men casually walked to the hired car parked around the corner and drove to the airport.

'What the fuck happened?' asked Erik again.

'I fucked up. I didn't mean to kill her, but she went fucking crazy,' said Lars.

'How?' asked Erik, 'what did she do?'

Lars shook his head, still trying to work it out.

'She hated me and was going to ruin me. She knew what I was up to with kids in Sweden - then she fucking attacked me with a knife.'

'What do you need me to do?' asked Erik.

'Just get me back to Brussels for now,' said Lars, realising he'd just killed the woman he didn't know how to live without. 'Get our doctor to the hotel,' he sighed as the car entered the private airfield, and they boarded the waiting plane. Erik handed Lars a large tumbler of whiskey.

'Take off in twenty minutes,' he said,

Lars drank it in one, immediately waving for another, then another and after a short, boozy flight, they landed in Brussels and were back in the hotel room by four.

'You're lucky, all internal organs intact,' said the doctor as he stitched up Lars.

When he was gone, Lars took a long shower, changed his clothes and checked out of the hotel. He returned to the airport, this time for a commercial flight to Stockholm, and when an Irish number appeared on his phone, he took a deep breath and answered. Upon hearing the news of his wife being found murdered, Lars acted shocked and told the detective he'd fly to Dublin the following day. The fact that he was about to board a flight to Sweden gave him time to think.

That was two weeks ago, and the investigation was going just how he wanted it...nowhere. The guards in Dublin were scratching their heads, and he was confident it would stay that way. Lars found playing the part of grieving husband tiresome. Laura was gone - he wanted to get on with his life, but the people of Sweden expected him to mourn. When the election was over and his new role as deputy PM was confirmed, it would mean even more time in the spotlight. Laura was supposed to be by his side - that was his dream, and she'd fucked it up.

Since her death, Lars had spent one weekend at the lake house, combing through

Laura's things and finding nothing. After Laura's funeral, he instructed Hilda to pack Laura's personal things and send them to Ireland, only agreeing to do so because Laura's mother had asked. He'd have preferred to burn everything but needed to play the part.

A few days after Laura's funeral, while sitting in his office, deep in thought, Erik walked through the door.

'Guess who was at your house this morning?' he said, handing Lars an iPad that showed Laura's Irish friends standing outside his garage. 'Hilda let them in - silly old cunt, and they visited the hospital before that – Freja rang and said four women were talking to Astrid.'

'What the fuck are they doing in Sweden, and why are they in my garage?' asked Lars – his stomach dropping.

Erik shook his shoulders.

'I don't know yet, but I'm going to Uppsala to find out. Coming?' he asked.

'Yes,' said Lars, following Erik out of the office.

As they sped along the motorway, he watched video footage of the women arriving at the hospital.

'I accessed their hotel and flight details. Arrived yesterday and leave tomorrow morning - staying at The Royal,' said Erik.

Lars handed the iPad back to Erik and stared out the window. Why were those women in Sweden? What the fuck was going on? There was a lot at stake right now – it was a crucial time in his career, and these bitches stirring things up was the last thing he needed. Arriving at the hotel, Lars was met by the usual fuss that came with people seeing a government minister. He shook a few hands while Erik asked about the women. The concierge said they'd been out all day – *at his house, it seemed.* They waited in the bar and were about to order a drink when the women walked in, seeming unconcerned about seeing Lars, Erik and Sven there.

When the writer said they were on a pilgrimage to Laura, Lars knew they were lying.

'What do you think?' Lars asked Erik when the women left the bar.

They had found a quiet table in the corner.

'I don't buy the pilgrimage crap,' said

Erik.

'Me either - have we missed something?' asked Lars.

He thought about the nightclub twenty years earlier. It was too long ago for any comeback. Laura's reference to what Lars was doing to kids in Sweden slightly concerned him, but as discussed with Erik – she didn't know anything about his business. One sure thing about Laura was that she couldn't hide her emotions - Lars could read her like a book. On top of that, she had no laptop or email address – he'd made sure of it, and she'd been alone in The Shelbourne Hotel the day before she died. He supposed the Irishwomen could have spoken to Laura's solicitor – the cop would know about the alleged videos, but that was hearsay.

'I don't need this bullshit right now. Go and see if you can get answers from the author. Be discreet, but let her know you're serious. I'll wait here,' said Lars, trying to keep his rage at bay.

When Erik returned ten minutes later and told him what happened, he nearly lost his mind.

'Keep watching them - I've called another car,' he said as he left.

In his apartment in Stockholm, Lars poured a large drink. There was nothing to place him in Ireland at the time of Laura's death, was there? His thoughts went to the private plane - expensive because of the guaranteed privacy, but if the guards got a whiff of it, the airline would have no choice but to share flight information, he texted Erik.

Lars: *Make sure my name is off that flight to Dublin.*

Erik: *On it.*

That was all he needed to say, and Lars knew it was done.

Lars: *Try to get the author on her own again and get the truth out of her. I want to know why they are here - do whatever you need to make sure she tells you.*

Erik gave him a thumbs up, and once again, Lars knew it was already done. When he walked into his kitchen the next morning and found Erik making coffee, he was expecting to hear the whole thing was finished.

'They disappeared before I could speak to them. Had dinner and went straight back to the hotel. We waited, thinking they'd have a drink, and when I went in, they were gone.'

'What the fuck?' asked Lars. 'No one knew I'd kill Laura because I didn't realise it myself. Did she tell those women about her life with me?

'She wouldn't dare. You know her shame stopped her – you've relied on that for years,' said Erik.

'Could she have somehow found out about the business? Is that why those women were in my garage? Is that what Laura meant about the kids in Sweden?' asked Lars.

'No, how could she? Anyway, everything is shut down until this all blows over,' said Erik. 'The surveillance room has been operating from your house for fifteen years - Laura didn't know about it - she would have called the police, and if that had happened, we'd be the first to know.'

Erik was right - he knew his wife - she would have reacted.

'Find out what's happening with Laura's case in Dublin - I want to know everything,' said Lars.

Erik rang his contact in the Irish police

and relayed the information to Lars.

'There's no evidence. Her mother told them about the jewellery - they hoped it would turn up on the black market, but it's in your office safe,' said Erik.

'What about the lawyer - anything from him and the flight into Dublin taken care of?' asked Lars, thinking he needed to get rid of the jewellery, but for some reason, feeling unable to.

'Yes. That cost you two hundred thousand Krona, but my guy in the airport deleted the flight log on both ends, and there's nothing from the solicitor. The guards interviewed him at the start - he saw videos of domestic abuse, but he doesn't have them,' said Erik.

Something niggled at the back of Lars's mind - how did Laura make videos when he regularly checked her phone.

'Did she have another phone?' he asked.

'I thought of that,' said Erik, always one step ahead of him. 'Even if she did and it turns up with videos, we'll say they're fake - someone trying to attack your reputation. Anyway, if there was another phone, the police would have it, and they don't.'

Lars didn't believe Laura had another phone, but the solicitor saw videos, and they weren't on the phone he'd taken from her that day.

'Get someone in Dublin to have a word with those women - start with the writer,' said Lars. 'Then go and keep an eye on what's happening.'

He left Erik in the kitchen and went to work. His first email of the day was from Laura's dad.

Lars

Thank you for Laura's things. It means the world to her mother to have them.

Mick

So, the shipment had arrived in Dublin. He emailed back, saying he hoped they got comfort from them, still trying to look like he cared. The rest of her shit was going to the hospital charity. Laura loved those kids and spent as much time with them as possible. He thought about when they wanted their own family and how Laura found out she couldn't have kids but didn't seem too bothered.

'It is what it is, Lars - maybe we are not

supposed to be parents,' she'd said.

He remembered her words because he'd been so surprised by them. In the early days, all she talked about was having kids.

'We can adopt if you want?' Lars had said.

He didn't want to adopt and had no problem not having kids, but if she wanted them, he'd have gone along with it.

'No, I'm happy with it being just you and me,' she sighed sweetly and kissed him.

Pushing those thoughts aside, Lars got to work, and a few minutes later, Olga strutted into his office, looking excited.

'The Prime Minister has invited you to lunch on Sunday - can you go?' she asked with a knowing smile.

God, that woman irritated him. She was the first to go when he got his new job.

'Of course. Tell him I'd be honoured,' said Lars, thinking this was it, this was what he'd been waiting for.

His party had won the general election, and the role of the Deputy Prime Minister was his.

42 ~ ORLA

On Tuesday morning, Audrey arranged a video call for the group - she spoke to Dave and wanted to update everyone. Niamh was running late, so the others chatted until Niamh finally logged on, looking flustered.

'Sorry girls, the snow down here is making the school run a nightmare,' she explained while peeling off layers of clothing. 'Well, what's happening?'

All eyes went to Audrey, who put them out of their misery and told them what Dave had said.

'I didn't mention the security room in Laura's house and what we think she was up to. I just told him what Astrid said about the beatings and the bodies – and that Louise had said the same thing to Orla. He doesn't know where to start trying to find them, and if we asked Lars about it without any proof, he'd laugh in our face. Dave also thinks Lars is paying someone at the station.'

'My God. Is there anyone Lars is not paying?' asked Niamh, sipping from a large white mug with the words Peggy Flynn's written on it.

'What about the flight log?' asked Orla.

'Again – he won't question Lars without proof. His lawyer would ridicule your mam's photo and say it's photoshopped, and then we'd look like a bunch of incompetent pricks. As far as the girls are concerned, unless we find their bodies – the information we have is useless,' said Audrey.

'Orla will find them - I know she will. "The books, Orla."'

'Well, let's hope Laura gives Orla some kind of message. If you're listening, love,' called Niamh.

'I was trying – but the connection was a bit hit and miss.'

'What about Erik being in Dublin? What's that fucker doing in Ireland?' she asked.

'Obviously, Lars sent him, but why? Ray thinks he might as well have raised a flag saying *I'm guilty* by sending him here.'

'Sven is with him - I don't know why they're here but don't go anywhere alone for now,' said Audrey.

'I'm staying well out of his way,' said Orla, thinking Erik would do anything to protect Lars, including killing for him.

Audrey mentioned a property Lars had owned while living in Dublin.

'It's an old house on Cork Street. I'm not saying it's where the bodies are, but Cork Street is not far from Grafton Street, and a large, private back garden might make a nice burial site,' she said.

The thought of those poor girls buried in someone's back garden for twenty years was shocking, but they all agreed it was worth checking it out.

'I'm going to Laura's parent's house after this,' announced Orla. 'Lars sent the books Laura wanted me to have.'

'Well, if any of you fancy a trip, you're welcome to West Cork. There are rooms at the pub - we only rent them in the summer, so they're free now,' said Niamh.

'I'll come, Niamh.'

Orla loved Kinsale and would love a relaxing weekend there, but not yet - they still had too much to do. They agreed Audrey and Orla would go to Cork Street the following day, and when Orla hung up, her ma was there in a flash.

'Well?' asked Patsy.

She'd been listening to every word, but Orla didn't mind. Her ma was one hundred per cent committed to this, and right now, they needed all the help they could get.

'The investigation is going nowhere. Lars is far too clever,' sighed Orla. 'Even the guards are walking on eggshells around him.'

She asked her mam to put on the kettle.

'I'll be back in ten - just popping to the Quinns to get my books.'

When she knocked on the door, Mr Quinn opened it and smiled.

'Ah, Orla. Come in, come in, what are you doing out in this weather?' he asked.

Orla smiled back and hugged him,

thinking she was constantly being told off by Laura's parents for being out in the cold.

'I'm here for the books and to see how you are,' said Orla.

Mrs Quinn came into the hall wearing a Hermes scarf over a beautiful pale blue cashmere jumper.

'Ah Ma, you look gorgeous - I love that colour on you.'

'Do you like it?' she asked, looking down at herself, 'Laura's things are far too nice for an old woman like me. I feel silly, but wearing them makes me feel close to her,' she sighed. 'There are boxes upstairs - Louise already took some home, but there's so much of it. Why don't you and the girls take a few things? It seems an awful shame to waste it.'

'What a great idea, mam - the girls would have a field day.'

'I'm sure they'd love that,' said Orla sadly - then she asked how they both were.

They wore the same look of grief as the

women from the flats, and Orla silently raged at Lars- how dare he destroy so many lives.

'We're getting by,' said Mr Quinn as he put a tray of tea and biscuits on the table. 'The days after the funeral were the worst - the sense of finality. She's gone, and there's nothing else but to remember her.'

'I wrapped my arms around my da.'

Mrs Quinn wept as she told Orla about scattering Laura's ashes.

'We're going to Blessington Lakes in a few weeks. I'll let you know. Laura loved it there, and I think she'd prefer that,' she said, nodding toward the fireplace, 'than being stuck in an urn up there.'

It was a beautiful urn, but Orla agreed Laura would want to be free. Even though she was nervous about telling them what they'd found out in Sweden, they decided the day before that the Quinns had a right to know.

'We went to Sweden last week,' said Orla, watching them react as her parents did.

'In the name of God, why did you do that?' asked Mrs Quinn.

She looked from Orla to Mick as if he knew the answer, but he just shrugged.

'We wanted to talk to Laura's friend Astrid. Do you remember me asking you about her?' They both nodded. 'It's the name Laura used to book the apartment, and I didn't tell you this, but Laura wrote letters to us before she died. She sent them from the Shelbourne Hotel on Sunday afternoon before she came here.'

Orla didn't know what possessed Laura to write those letters, but she was glad she did. The tears welled up in Mrs Quinn's eyes.

'What did she say?' she asked.

'She said she missed us and was sorry for picking Lars, that sort of thing. She also said Astrid was a good friend, so we went to Sweden to talk to her. As you already know, Laura wanted to leave Lars - the evidence she had was video proof of his domestic abuse. She thought threatening his career might be her ticket to freedom, and she also had information about a crime he committed years ago - our trip to Sweden confirmed that,' explained Orla.

The Quinns listened with bated breath as Orla described what had happened to the girls so many years before, including how they'd met them in the nightclub, what Lars did to Laura, and how Niamh and Audrey got assaulted.

'Jesus, that's awful - that man really is a monster,' cried Mrs Quinn. The worst kind of monster: beautiful, charming and deadly. 'So, the abuse was happening even then? Is that why you all fell out?' she asked.

'There was more to it than that, but that was the start of it. I'll tell you the whole story one day, hopefully when Lars is behind bars,' said Orla, then continued the story of what happened in Uppsala, leaving out the sex trafficking until they had more information about that. 'We bumped into Lars and Erik at the hotel. They wanted to know why we were there and weren't happy to see us. Erik threatened us, so we left ten hours early for our flight.'

'How have you achieved so much?' asked Mr Quinn, shaking his head.

Orla didn't think they had, but she was glad of their approval. She told them about her mother going solo to the airport and finding Lars's name on the flight log - how it had since disappeared and how Erik and Sven were now in Dublin.

'Lars was here when she died?' asked Mrs Quinn, and Orla nodded. 'Oh, Orla, you've no idea what that means to us. We might not have Laura anymore, but if he goes to jail,' she trailed off, and her husband continued.

'It will give us justice for our girl,' he said sadly.

Orla didn't want to give them false hope and prayed this all worked out. The only thing left was to tell them about Laura's messages - she wasn't sure if telling them was cruel or kind.

'I wanted them to know. "Tell them, Orla."'

'Okay, but it's your funeral,' muttered Orla, not surprised by the blatant push from Laura.

'The lines are open today – loud and clear.'

'There's something else,' Orla hesitated. 'Now, I don't want to upset you, but I think you need to know,' she continued. The Quinns looked nervously at each other, but Orla kept talking. 'Laura has been kind of helping us along the way.'

They looked confused, so Orla quickly told them the story, leaving nothing out. Mrs Quinn instantly believed her, but Mick wasn't quite there. Orla knew it didn't matter - if it gave his wife peace, he was on board.

'I wasn't sure if telling was right, but Laura said I should,' said Orla.

Mrs Quinn openly sobbed, and Orla's heart broke for her. Old people crying had always been too much for her to bear.

'Oh Jesus, this means the world to us, Orla,' she said. 'The thought of her not existing anymore was tearing us apart.' She wiped her eyes with shaking hands and asked. 'Can she hear me?'

'Yes, mam – I can hear you.'

Orla nodded her head – Laura's message was clear in her head.

'Can I talk to her?' she asked with hope, despair and anguish in her voice that nearly finished Orla.

She choked out a yes and, wanting to give her some privacy, asked to use the bathroom.

'Just say what you want to say. For some reason, Laura is attached to me. I can't explain it, but I know she can hear you,' said Orla before leaving them alone.

'Ah ma, stop, I was sobbing.'

When Orla returned to the lounge a few minutes later, she smiled.

' "Tell her I'm okay, Orla - it's better here, and I'll see them again." '

Orla passed on the message, and even the disbelieving Mr Quinn was moved - wiping his eyes as he put his arm around his wife.

'Oh, thank God. Oh, Jesus, Mick, she's okay - she's okay,' said Mrs Quinn, sobbing as she hugged her husband.

Orla was a wreck. They had another cup of tea, and Mick gave Orla the package containing Laura's books.

'Can we tell Louise what's happening?' asked Mrs Quinn as Orla left.

'Yes, of course, just no one else for now,' she said and hugged them goodbye.

Orla walked back to her car, deep in thought about poor Mr and Mrs Quinn, when a chill ran down her spine - someone was watching her. She slowly looked around and saw a black Range Rover parked a few cars down...Erik.

Laura

Seeing my parents in pain was hard to take, but hopefully, Orla had given them some peace. We were communicating well today, which was good. Maybe we'd finally nail these fuckers. When I saw Erik standing across the road from my parent's house, I wanted to kill him.

43 ~ NIAMH

Niamh arrived home from her trip to Sweden exhausted and emotionally battered. The terror of fleeing in the night and the grim truth about Laura's life had taken its toll, and although the flight was on time, a three-hour train delay from Dublin to Cork almost finished her off. Thirty-six hours and no sleep, she crawled through the front door.

'Mammy, you're finally here,' were the first words to greet her. 'Where have you been? I've been waiting for you.'

Maisie, her seven-year-old shadow, was sitting on the stairs, and Niamh wasn't one bit surprised.

'Hello baby girl, did you miss me?' she asked, wrapping the little girl in her arms and breathing in her familiar scent.

'I really missed you, mammy. Don't go away again, okay,' instructed Maisie.

Niamh kissed her and said she'd try not

to as they walked down the hallway together. She was dying for a cup of tea, but where was everyone? The house was quiet, and Niamh's house was never quiet.

'Surprise, welcome home, mam,' everyone shouted when she opened the kitchen door.

The gang were waiting - her other four daughters, her mam and her husband Ray, all standing around the kitchen table with a cake that said, *Welcome Home.* They hugged and kissed - you'd think she'd been away for a month rather than two days, but her heart melted.

'What's Sweden like?' asked Rosie, the curious twin, fascinated with travel and determined to go to university abroad – she was working hard at school to make it happen, and Niamh loved her drive.

'Gorgeous, spotless and very different from here,' said Niamh, dishing out Swedish chocolate and other bits and pieces she picked up at the airport. They all got makeup except for Maisie, who got a cuddly white teddy bear with a Swedish flag on his belly.

'Did you take loads of pictures?' asked

Rachel, her hand already out waiting for her mother's phone.

Two things about having five daughters that Niamh got used to as they grew up. One - she had absolutely no privacy, and two - she didn't actually own anything. From a hairdryer to a pair of knickers, makeup to shampoo, anything she bought for herself was considered theirs, collectively. She handed over her phone and sat down for tea and cake.

'How did it go?' whispered Ray, who'd been worried sick since she left on Wednesday.

'I'll tell you later,' mouthed Niamh, then nodded at her mam, who was included in that. 'What's the plan for the pub tonight?' she asked, thinking she certainly wasn't working and hoping Ray wasn't either.

'It's all sorted. The lads are there - we all have the night off. Your ma cooked a stew – it'll be ready in an hour or so,' said Ray.

Niamh's ma's stew was famous in Cork - everyone in Kinsale talked about it, and there were times when they couldn't keep up with its demand.

'Fabulous! Thanks, Ma. A bit of home cooking is just what I need. The food in Sweden is very different - I wouldn't want to be there too long,' said Niamh, describing some of the local dishes and knowing her mam would feel the same way.

They laughed at their Irishness, and soon, the girls were over their mother being home and disappeared in different directions. Ray put a film on for Maisie, who finally left Niamh's side to watch it. As the only non-teenager in the house, she was usually left to her own devices, but Ray's choice of film had caught the attention of everyone and when Niamh popped her head around the door ten minutes later, her five girls were snuggled up on different sofas, under blankets and watching Frozen. Her heart swelled - she couldn't deny it was hard work dealing with teenage hormones flying around the house, but they were happy, and Niamh loved their life in Cork.

The farmhouse was on the same land as the pub but far enough away so they didn't feel like they lived at work. A couple of golf carts took them back and forth between the pub and house, and last Christmas, Niamh bought Ray a quad bike that he loved. As well as five kids, they had three dogs, four cats, and a couple of chubby pigs running around. It was chaos at the best of times, but it was great.

While in the shower, Niamh tried to process the last few weeks. Hearing from Audrey out of the blue and the terrible news about Laura - having her best friends back in her life and running around Sweden being chased by madmen - she couldn't wrap her head around it. She thought back twenty years and how it all came out of the blue for her. Yeah, they were furious with Laura and fed up with the Lars drama, but to stop being friends? She never thought it would come to that and wanted to call the girls every day for about two years, but something stopped her.

Then she met Ray, and it was love at first sight. The big, booming chef at the restaurant where she worked - he was the jolly type with a bushy beard and crazy hair. Nothing seemed to get him down, and she was drawn to him like a moth to a flame. Within six months, they were living together. The twins came along a year after that, and they finally got married when Maisie was born, thinking they all should at least have the same surname.

Dressed in clean pyjamas and trying to fight waves of exhaustion, Niamh walked into her bedroom to find Ray sprawled on the bed.

'Any chance of a ride?' he asked, wiggling his eyebrows.

Niamh laughed - even after all these years, he still made her laugh every day.

'A chance would be a fine thing,' said Niamh as Maisie barrelled through the door with a hilarious look of shock on her face, having realised her mammy wasn't in the kitchen.

'Mammy, ye didn't tell me ye were coming upstairs,' said Maisie in a cross-tone.

Ray shook his head in a, *how dare you, mammy* kind of way and laughed. He knew Maisie was stuck to Niamh like glue and found it funny.

'Sorry baby, I just had a shower. Let's get you some dinner,' said Niamh, taking her daughter's hand and leading her back downstairs.

Ray paused the film, and everyone sat at the kitchen table for nanny's stew. Rosie and Rachel had a party but decided not to go. The snow had started in Cork and was coming down thick.

'I can't be bothered to get home in this,' said Rosie and Rachel agreed.

Although they lived near the village, it was still a hike, and mostly Ray or Niamh would pick them up after a night out, but they were having a glass of red tonight, so it was a walk or a taxi for the girls. A village in West Cork wasn't exactly hot on the Uber list, so they stayed home. When they finished eating, the kids returned to the lounge. Ray shut the kitchen door, got a nice bottle of red from the expensive stash, and poured each of them a glass.

'Right, talk. We're dying to know what happened,' he said.

He knew the gist of it, but he wanted details, so Niamh described the city, the hospital, what Astrid had said, the visit to the lake house and the secret room with chains on the wall.

'We were terrified - it was all getting out of hand. Then Lars, Erik and Sven were waiting at the hotel,' said Niamh. 'Fucks sake, I thought we were goners, but Orla was a champ and told them we were having a charity ball for Laura and wanted to see the hospital.' She burst out laughing at the memory. 'They didn't believe a word of it, but Orla was so quick, then,' she took a large gulp of wine before continuing, 'Erik turned up in Orla's room, threatened her and said he didn't buy the cock and bull story about a pilgrimage to Laura. They followed us to dinner, so we legged it back to the hotel, got our stuff and spent the night in the airport.'

When she looked up, her husband and mother's mouths were open. Then they all fell around the place laughing, obviously shocked because none of it was funny.

'Jaysus, that's some story,' said Ray, shaking with laughter.

'I don't think I've ever heard anything like it,' said her mam, screaming, 'I don't know why I'm laughing because he sounds like the devil himself.'

Well, you haven't heard the best of it,' said Niamh, who'd been saving that till last. 'Are you two ready for this?' Her mam and Ray nodded, and Niamh told them the story of Laura communicating with Orla.

'Holy mother of perpetual help,' said Marie, blessing herself.

Ray looked sceptical, but Niamh was prepared.

'Sure, listen - no one is more surprised than Orla. She doesn't believe in that sort of thing, but Laura is moving books around and giving her messages. We wouldn't have gone anywhere near Laura's gaff if Orla hadn't insisted Laura wanted us to go. Then, we met Hilda, who showed us the sex rooms with the chains on the walls and told us Laura was copying what we can only assume were videos of people having sex. We think Laura hid them on a USB stick in Dublin.'

'Fucking hell, this is mental,' said Ray. 'So, do you have any proof?' he asked.

'We know about it, but we don't know about it – if you know what I mean,' sighed Niamh.

'Well, your one in Sweden who told you about the abuse would be ripped to bits by a good defence lawyer,' said Ray. That's if she even testified and can you convict someone of murder if you have no body?' he asked.

'I don't think so,' said Niamh.

'The sex dungeon in her gaff is likely gone by now. Lars is no fool - if he killed Laura because she found out what he was doing - there won't be a trace of it,' he said, shaking his head, and although disappointed by his summation, Niamh knew he was right.

44 ~ ORLA

Orla opened the car door, threw the bag of books onto the passenger seat, and turned to meet Erik as he strode towards her. Terrified but also heartsick and pissed off – she decided not to be intimidated by him. Who the fuck did he think he was?

'Why are you following me, Erik?' she asked, sounding slightly braver than she felt. Erik didn't respond - instead, he watched her as if trying to work her out - the silence adding to her discomfort, but she shook it off. 'Well?' she asked again.

'I want to know why the fuck you were in Sweden,' he snarled like a vicious dog. 'What were you looking for and don't give me that bullshit story about seeing Laura's fucking house.'

'We weren't looking for anything,' said Orla, holding her ground.

She sensed something different about

him. Like a tiger in a cage, he was ready to blow - danger permeated the air around him. Orla took a step back.

'He was more dangerous than anyone I knew. "Get the fuck away from her, you bastard."'

'Listen to me - you cunt. I don't know what you and your friends are up to, but whatever it is, you better fucking stop, or I will make sure you do.' Orla turned to open her car door, but Erik grabbed the back of her hair and pulled her against his chest. 'I wish I'd used those guns that night and fucking killed the lot of you,' he whispered in her ear.

Stunned, she was about to scream blue murder until she noticed Mr Quinn standing on the path.

'Come here, Orla, love,' he said, holding his arm out for her to go to him. He turned to Erik. 'What are you doing here, Erik?' he asked.

Surprised to see him, Erik backed off but didn't answer - instead, he spat at Orla's feet.

'When I find out what you're up to, you'll wish you were never fucking born,' he snarled, then walked back to his car.

'What an absolute animal. I hated him.'

'You okay, love?' asked Mr Quinn.

'I'm fine,' Orla definitely wasn't fine, but she didn't want to worry him, 'but as you can see, something's up for Lars to have sent him,' she said, nodding in Erik's direction.

He tried to entice her into the house for a cup of tea, but Orla refused.

'Thank you, but I'll just head home,' she said, opening the door of her car.

'Mind yourself, love, and let us know what's happening,' he said, watching as she drove off.

When Orla arrived home, her legs turned to jelly, and she collapsed onto the sofa.

'Ah, Jesus - what's happening? Put the kettle on, Joe,' called Patsy in a complete flap.

Orla explained what Erik had said to her terrified parents.

'The man is a psycho,' she continued while sipping hot tea.

'Put a drop of brandy in that, Joe,' said Patsy.

Joe obliged, poured a grand slug of his

best brandy into Orla's cup, and Patsy picked up the phone.

Half an hour later, Audrey arrived with Dave. Orla was happy to finally meet him and surprised at how handsome he was - *Audrey didn't mention that.* With black curly hair and green eyes, Orla was conscious of her scruffy old tracksuit bottoms as she explained what happened. They all knew Erik was dangerous, but to have it so blatantly pushed in her face was terrifying. She was a writer, not a guard and wasn't trained for that kind of thing.

'Did he actually assault you, as in, did he touch you in any way?' asked Dave, and Orla thought for a minute.

'He pulled my hair, said he wished he'd used his gun to kill us all, and he called me a cunt,' said Orla as her mam gasped. 'I mean, I'm not exactly shy about cursing, but that's just rude. He also said he'd make me stop whatever I was doing, and I'd be sorry I was born. Does that count as assault?'

'Technically, yeah. We can have a chat if you like,' said Dave.

'I'll leave it for now,' said Orla, thinking about the attack in the lane a few days earlier.

They were treading on dangerous ground, but until they had more evidence, she didn't want to poke a sleeping bear. Pissing off Erik was the last thing they needed.

Audrey asked if she was still up for Cork Street the next day.

'Absolutely, we've come this far - we can't stop now,' said Orla, sounding braver than she felt.

'I can't remember the house in Cork Street – the girls are not there.'

When they were gone, Orla opened the books. Well-worn and indicating that Laura read them a lot, Orla's heart melted as she held her breath while mentally preparing to crack the case wide open. A note or a map, perhaps? She was surprised to find the first book empty, but undeterred, she flicked through the second one – surely it would be here. Opening the third book, she felt frustrated, and when the fourth was empty, she was pissed off. When the fifth and sixth books proved unfruitful, Orla flicked through them again. She held them up, shook them and even checked the spine of the books to see if any notes had been hidden inside them – like in the olden days. All six books were empty, and she was devastated. What the fuck, Laura?

Laura
My strength was waning today. 'Look again, Orla,' I tried, but she didn't hear me. When we rested, we'd connect, and at least she had the books – they were out of Lars's possession, and he had no idea of what he'd just done – I laughed out loud.

45 ~ NIAMH

Niamh woke to the usual chaos that came with a farmhouse full of girls on Saturday morning. The four older ones had sports - hockey, football, and horse riding, and Maisie had ballet. The twins usually rode their bikes to hockey, but this morning, they were being picked up because of the snow.

'I thought training might have been called off,' said Niamh when they walked into the kitchen in full kit.

'Why? Sure, it's only a bit of snow,' said Rosie, having none of it.

The horse riding was indoors. Sinead was thrilled, but the pitches were frozen, so Shona's football match was cancelled.

'You can help me do a few jobs in the pub,' said Ray, preparing to leave. 'I'll even give you a few euros for your trouble.'

Shona hesitated, then dashed upstairs to get dressed, thinking about the money. Five minutes later, she was on the back of her dad's quad as they drove to the pub. Sinead was already gone, as the riding centre was on the farm next door. She walked across the field and jumped the fence. That left Niamh, her mother and Maisie.

'Right, so dancing it is,' said Niamh, hanging up the phone.

She'd called to make sure it was still on - it was, so they dropped Maisie off, had a coffee and did some shopping. When they got home later that afternoon, the snow was lashing down, and the girls were showered, fed, watching TV or in their rooms. Niamh asked the twins to mind Maisie while she and her mam slowly drove one of the golf carts down to the pub.

Their traditional country pub was at least two hundred years old. The previous owner had let it go to rack and ruin, but Niamh and Ray restored it to its former glory, keeping its original charm. It was called Peggy Flynn's, after the wife of its first owner - they sold excellent ale, great wine and fantastic food. People came from around the world to visit Kinsale - their tourist trade was huge, and Ray was a brilliant landlord and a fantastic chef – their local trade was even bigger. Although he didn't cook anymore, Ray only allowed the best into his kitchen and thoroughly tested everything on the menu.

'Ah, there you are. What are you doing here?' he asked when Niamh and her mam walked into the packed pub.

He was behind the bar, the fires were lit, and the rugby was on.

'Ah, that's why it's so busy,' said Niamh, turning to her mam and nodding at the TV. Ireland was playing England in the Six Nations in Dublin, where the snow hadn't started yet. 'I thought you might want to head home for a rest. Mam and I will work for a few hours,' said Niamh.

Ray didn't hesitate as he pulled himself a pint.

'Lovely, but I'll go home after the match,' he said, planting a smacker on Niamh's lips and practically skipping to the other side of the bar, where he pulled up a chair and sat down to watch the rugby in peace.

Niamh and her mam worked till closing – it wasn't late as most people went home after the match because the snow was lashing - Niamh closed the doors at about eight.

'I don't think anyone's coming out in this,' she said, locking up, and her mam agreed.

They had a nice glass of red by the fire and were getting ready to leave when Ray arrived.

'You don't want to go out in a golf cart in this weather - I brought the car,' he said, double-checking everything was locked.

Niamh and her mam looked at each other, thinking the same thing. *Swoon. He was the absolute best.*

Sunday was a whiteout - they didn't even open the pub, and on Monday morning, much to the girl's disappointment - school was open.

'What? Sure, it's only a bit of snow,' said Niamh, echoing Rachel's words from Saturday.

It didn't go down well, and after the usual mad dash, everyone was finally out the door. Ray and Marie were in the pub, setting up, and Niamh sat in her kitchen, supposedly doing the accounts but thinking about Laura and the whole Lars drama. The lies, abuse and constant denial that had affected them all so much - she didn't think they'd need twenty years and Laura's murder to get over it. Sighing, she got back to work and, after lunch, collected her mam from the pub for the weekly shop.

'Sorry, mam, it's the pub and the house today,' said Niamh as they pulled into Musgraves car park, but her mam didn't mind.

Over the past few months, Marie had been spending more time in Cork. She loved it, but she also loved her home in Dublin – she had great neighbours and friends and was reluctant to sell up and move down once and for all.

'Not yet,' she'd tell the kids when they'd badger her to stay.

'Please, nanny,' they'd beg, but she held out, and Niamh didn't blame her - she had peace and quiet in Dublin.

'What'll happen now?' asked Marie as they pushed their trolleys down the long aisle.

'I don't know. It was three weeks yesterday since Laura died – I can't believe it, and there's not a speck of evidence,' said Niamh, still unable to believe how much had happened since that horrible phone call. 'I think Orla is determined to 'take down Lars' for want of a better phrase, and Audrey's just doing her job. Maggie and I are more like bystanders.'

As she said this, her phone rang.

'Long time no speak,' said Niamh, laughing before realising Audrey would only ring if something was wrong. 'What's happened?' she asked, stopping the trolley and listening as Audrey told her about Mrs Reed and the flight log.

'Sure, that's brilliant news, is it not?' she asked.

Finally, they had something to pin on him.

'Well, technically, it is,' said Audrey, 'but let me tell you the rest of it first.'

When Niamh hung up, her mam held out her hand.

'Don't say a word, let's get back, and you can tell us both at the same time,' she said.

They dashed through the aisles, finished the shopping in record time, put everything away, and went straight to the pub, where they were now.

'So, someone deleted the flight log, and two of Lars's rottweilers are looking for you in Dublin,' said Ray, as pragmatic as ever.

'Yeah, but Mrs Reed took a picture of it,'

said Niamh.

Surely, that was enough to at least question Lars. Niamh was worried about Orla and Maggie in Dublin and texted to see if they were okay. Five minutes later, she received a selfie from Orla in Maggie's coffee shop. They hadn't seen Erik so far but were being extra careful. Niamh showed the picture to Ray and her mother, who looked at each other - Ray took a deep breath.

'Jesus - this is mental,' he said, 'If Laura is a ghost, I hope to God she tells Orla where those bodies are, if not – it sounds like it's all dead in the water.

46 ~ ORLA

'Should we just knock?' asked Orla.

She and Audrey stood opposite a yellow brick, Victorian-style terrace house on Cork Street. It was one of five on a single block and very stylish, with a black door and windows. Like the lone survivor of ruthless developers, the block of houses stood alone - an ugly university accommodation on one side and a giant Lidl on the other. Opposite was an old folk's hospital where Orla used to do Irish dances for the patients as a child.

'Yeah, it seems like the only thing we can do,' said Audrey, walking towards it.

A woman similar in age answered when Audrey rang the bell. At first, she looked suspicious, probably thinking they'd been casing out the joint, but visibly relaxed when Audrey flashed her badge. As it turned out, Vivienne worked for the guards in the HR department and was happy to help.

'My wife and I bought it from an old couple - they moved to Carlow. I don't know who owned it before that,' said Vivienne.

'It's not actually the house we're interested in - it's the garden,' said Audrey.

'Go ahead,' said Vivienne, opening the back door. 'Do either of you want a cup of tea?'

They both said yes, Vivienne went into the kitchen, and they stepped out into a large, overgrown garden.

'God, I do remember this house - Lars sold it soon after we met.'

Long and wide, with eight-foot walls on either side that were hidden by mature trees - the house was terraced, but the garden was private, and they both agreed - a decent spot to bury a body or three.

'It's possible,' said Audrey, returning to the house.

Inside, Vivienne described the state of the garden when they first bought it.

'We've tidied it up - but haven't had time to landscape it yet. Are you looking for something in particular?'

Audrey said she didn't know yet - they finished their tea, thanked Vivienne, and went straight to Maggie's shop, their new favourite place.

'I suppose the girls could be buried there, but do we dig up a whole back garden just because Lars owned that house when they went missing?' asked Audrey, pacing the floor.

'And because we know Erik and the other two definitely killed them,' said Maggie from the sofa where she and Orla sat drinking coffee and watching Audrey tear her hair out.

'Yeah, but does anyone really bury three bodies in their back garden? Lars is not stupid, and my theory is a pile of crap,' said Audrey, flopping onto the sofa beside them.

After a bit more discussion and coffee, Audrey returned to work, and Orla took a taxi home - no more walking until this was over, to find Patsy reading one of the books Lars had sent.

'Well,' she asked, her eyes demanding an update.

Orla described what was once Lars's back garden in Cork Street and Audrey's idea about digging it up. Patsy agreed it was a long shot but thought it was worth checking.

'I'm not sure Audrey will get approval for it, ma, and we can't exactly turn up with a few shovels and ask if we can start digging,' said Orla.

'That would be odd, alright,' said Patsy, returning to her book.

Orla spent the afternoon working, and even though the idea of Lars getting away with murder infuriated her, she couldn't stay in Dublin forever and prayed they got a break in the case sometime soon.

'If you're listening, Laura - now would be a good time to help,' she pleaded.

'I was already on it – my skills were sharp today.'

A few hours later, when Laura answered her directly, Orla was amazed.

'She just needed to believe.'

While in the kitchen making dinner, her mam joined her for a glass of wine.
'I'd forgotten how good this book is,' said Patsy, putting the book on the table and picking up

the wine, 'but the notes are confusing. Were they added to a later edition?'

'What notes? What are you talking about?' asked Orla.

Patsy picked up the book and flicked through the pages, pointing to various handwritten words added to the text. They looked exactly the same as the printed text - you wouldn't notice unless you knew they weren't part of the book.

'How many of these did you find?' asked Orla, astonished.

Her mother was at least a hundred pages in by now.

'Quite a few - some are just one word, others two or three together, but they don't make any sense and are practically invisible, so I might have missed some,' said Patsy.

No fucking way - Orla started laughing.

'You are something else, Laura,' she whispered, shaking her head.

'I knew she'd figure it out.'

Patsy looked around the room in awe - dinner was abandoned, and Orla collected the rest of the books from a bookshelf in the lounge. She laid them on the table and immediately rang Maggie.

'Can you come to my mam's house right now? I think you'll want to see this, honey,' said Orla.

Audrey was finishing work when Orla called and promised to stop by on her way home. An hour later, when they both arrived, Orla explained what had happened.

'The bodies,' said Audrey, flicking through one of the books.

'Yep,' said Orla.

She handed them a book each, instructing them to write down any extra words they found. There were no notes, just random words, mainly at the end of some paragraphs. As her mam had been reading the third book, Orla gave the first one to Audrey, the second to Maggie, and scoured through the third one herself. Soon, bowls of vodka pasta were placed in front of them to eat while they worked.

'This is delicious, Patsy - what's in the sauce?' asked Audrey.

'I didn't make it - Orla did. I can't cook

anything fancy like this,' said Patsy. 'I'm not sure Joe will like it, but sure, we'll soon find out,' she said, taking a tray into the lounge for her husband.

'What's that? I'm not eating this rubbish,' said Joe from the other room.

'Just try it - Orla said it's nice, and there's vodka in it,' said Patsy.

'Vodka in the dinner? In the name of God, what's the world coming to,' said Joe with astonishment as Orla and her friends laughed in the kitchen.

'It's not just vodka, there's garlic, chilli, tomato and cream,' said Orla.

The work was painstakingly slow, but they kept at it and at about ten, they called it a night.

'Let's wait until we have all the words before trying to make sense of it,' said Audrey, and as she's officially in charge of the investigation, they agreed.

Maggie kept Niamh in the loop, who, at one point, insisted on being Facetimed to see what was going on. When they left, Orla looked over what they'd done before going to bed. If they didn't get Lars for Laura's murder, finding the girls might be enough to lock him up and throw away the key – she said a silent prayer as she fell into a deep sleep. She woke up the next morning, raring to go.

'Boo,' said Niamh from behind the door when Orla walked into the kitchen.

'Jesus,' said Orla, jumping out of her skin.

'She's been here for an hour but wanted to do that so much - she wouldn't let me get you,' said Patsy, laughing.

'Ahh, Niamh is here too. These girls were the best.'

'What are you doing here? How are you here?' asked Orla.

'I was tossing and turning all night - my mind going a million miles an hour. Ray asked why I didn't just drive to Dublin, so I did. We got on the road at five - mam needed to go home and check her gaff, so I dropped her off and came straight here,' said Niamh.

Orla still hadn't told Niamh that her husband shared a name with her dog. When she said things like *Ray said*, it made her smile. Maggie and Audrey arrived, and Niamh pulled the same stunt on them. There was laughing and hugging, and then they got straight to work. Patsy supplied tea while enjoying a full house, as everyone made a fuss of her. After all, she was a hero of the hour and basking in her glory - Orla might never have looked at those books again. Niamh reviewed what they'd done the night before and found a few missed words.

'Christ, she was being super careful, wasn't she,' she said with a magnifying glass held to one of the books. When the others stopped to look, she shrugged. 'I use it to see the tiny writing on receipts when I do the books for the pub. It makes life so much easier.'

'I can't help thinking Laura was like the character in Sleeping with The Enemy,' said Maggie, 'her house was fabulous, but she was like a prisoner. To go to such lengths to get a message out and not be allowed a laptop is barbaric.'

'Yeah, and in the end, she shot that fucker dead. Wouldn't it be brilliant if Laura brought that bastard to his knees,' said Niamh, whooping as the others laughed.

'I liked Niamh's way of thinking.'

At lunchtime, Patsy made sandwiches, and six sheets of paper lay on the kitchen table. Orla's mam and dad were there, Niamh's mam Marie had joined them, as had Laura's parents and her sister Louise.

'You need to tell me the whole story about Laura being a ghost,' said Lou when she first arrived.

'I will, but let's get this over first,' said Orla.

They all stood around the table – the tension in the room palpable.

'Jesus fucking Christ,' whispered Audrey as she read.

'Oh my God.'

She apologised to the oldies for cursing, took a deep breath and began reading aloud.

'This is a statement of a conversation I, Laura Karlsson, overheard on July 15th, 2020, between Lars Karlson, Sweden's first minister for foreign affairs and his employee Erik Olsson.

They laughed while describing how they murdered three girls, missing in Dublin since

March 2000. Gillian Ryan, Aisling O'Keeffe and Sinead Quinn. Erik said they were being sold to a sex trafficker called Nikoli, but after the unexpected arrival of myself, Audrey O'Brien, Orla Reed, Maggie Roach and Niamh Moore at a private party in Lily's nightclub, the girls became a problem and were killed. Erik Olsson, Sven Lundin and Robert Berg, who died in 2010, murdered the girls in cold blood on the same night. Erik described how each of them shot a girl in the head and buried them in the garden of an old church on St Andrew Street.

I hid this information because I'm the victim of violent domestic abuse and wanted every detail of the conversation recorded. I'm recovering from the worst beating of my life and am trying to escape from my husband. If anything happens to me - look in his direction. I hope the girls are found and their families find peace.

There was a stunned silence. Orla's eyes went to the Quinns, who looked shell-shocked.

'My poor girl and those poor children,' said Mrs Quinn.

'I was hugging her.'

'What now?' asked Orla, turning to Audrey.

'I need to talk to Dave,' Audrey announced to the room. 'If the girls are where Laura said - we can arrest Erik and Sven for murder. And...Laura said to look in Lars's direction if anything happened to her - that's at least worth a chat.'

A sigh of relief echoed through the kitchen as everyone rallied around the Quinns - even if only to offer a smidgen of support, Orla knew it meant the world to them.

Laura
If nothing else, the girls would finally be buried properly. My poor parents – I hated them knowing how badly that fucker beat me, but I guess it didn't matter anymore. At least they knew I was still around...for now.

47 ~ AUDREY

Audrey arranged to meet Dave at the Banker Pub on Trinity Street and drove into town in awe of Laura's cleverness and courage.

'What the fuck?' asked Dave when she showed him the encrypted message.

He knew Laura had overheard a conversation – he knew the bodies were potentially buried in Dublin, but Audrey was positive he never dreamed anything would come of it.

'The message was spread throughout six books Orla wrote, but Laura owned,' she said to Dave's confused face.

'How did Orla get books that belonged to Laura?' he asked.

Audrey couldn't help the huge smile on her face.

'That's the best bit. Lars sent them to Laura's parents for Orla,' she said, laughing at the irony of it.

'The night before Laura's funeral, we met Lars in The Westbury, and he mentioned that Laura loved Orla's books. Laura had already said in her letter to Orla that she wanted her to have the books if anything happened to her. Orla asked Lars if she could have them for a keepsake, and he said yes. What Laura did is like a work of art. The words looked like they were part of the book – the same print but handwritten - very fucking clever,' she explained.

'Where are the books now?' asked Dave.

'I left them with Orla until I spoke to you,' said Orla.

He re-read the message.

'Are you trying to tell me those girls have been buried under our noses for twenty years?' he asked, shaking his head in disbelief.

'Well, we'll have to dig them up first and see if they're there, but basically, yeah,' said Audrey.

They sat silently for a few minutes, Dave thinking - Audrey waiting.

'There's definitely someone at the station working for Lars,' said Dave, and although Audrey knew he suspected it, she asked why he was so sure. 'Files being tampered with - important forensic evidence contaminated - something's not right. I don't want Lars to get wind of this until we confirm if that church garden is a grave, but I don't see how we can hide it.'

Audrey didn't care if Lars found out - she just wanted to find the girls.

'We need to arrest that fucker. Laura said if anything happened to her - look in his direction. Something did happen, and he was in Dublin when it did,' said Audrey, flashing the flight log photo.

Dave finished his pint in silence, then blew out a breath.

'I suppose now is as good a time as any to let the cat out of the bag - I'm going back to the station. Coming?'

'Yep,' said Audrey, draining her glass and following him out the door.

Audrey stood beside Dave when he dropped the bomb.

'If these girls are where Laura said they are, this case has blown open,' said Dave, pausing to let that sink in. 'Laura said if anything happened to her, her husband would likely be our man.' He held up the photo of the flight log as an excited murmur rippled through the room - this was big news, and it was about to get bigger. 'This flight log, from a private airfield in Lucan, is from the day of Laura Karlsson's murder. A flight landed at ten in the morning with Lars Karlsson and Erik Olsson on board - it left at one the same afternoon. These details have since been deleted, and we need to know why.'

The room erupted - every guard wanted to know what was going on. Where was Lars Karlsson? Why hadn't they been told about this? Did he kill his wife? Dave hushed them all and explained how Audrey had been quietly investigating, and the whole room turned to look at her.

'This man is a member of parliament in Sweden and very powerful - we needed to be careful,' said Dave.

He'd been worried about keeping it a secret, but his boss was delighted. Audrey immediately eliminated him from her mental assessment of her colleagues. *Who was the snitch?*

'Well, let's dig them up,' said Colin,

practically beaming, 'this is excellent work.'

Audrey looked at Dave, thinking the same thing - they'd better be there.

The following morning, a forensic team arrived at St Andrew's Street church to find a small but mature garden on each side of the building. Audrey thought it incredible that three bodies may have lain undetected for two decades. White tents were erected on the grounds, and bright yellow tape with the words' crime scene' stuck to the iron gates. The lashing rain seemed morbidly appropriate as the digging began - the team treading carefully in case it was a grave. A crowd soon gathered – this was a drama for a Friday morning in Dublin's city centre. Dave and Audrey stood waiting for news while drinking cups of lukewarm tea.

As the hours ticked by, Audrey felt increasingly nervous. What if Erik heard Laura that night? What if he'd moved the girl's bodies? What if, what if, what if. Scenario after scenario tormented her until, at last, they got the news - the bodies were there, and Audrey sighed with relief. Soon, the whole street was cordoned off as word spread like wildfire, and the press arrived. Orla and the others were huddled together under a big blue umbrella with the words Books & Brew in florescent yellow emblazed across it. Audrey delivered the news, and they jumped around, laughing, crying and hugging each other.

'Fucking well done, Laura,' said Niamh, sobbing.

They couldn't believe it. Twenty years later, they'd actually found them.

'I'm going to see the parents - will you come, Orla?' asked Audrey, then added. 'They'll appreciate you being there, and it won't be long before this is being reported by,' she nodded to the RTE News van.

Arriving at the flats, all three women waited with their husbands and other family members. The news was on in the background, and Audrey explained that it was their girls.

'The bodies will go for forensic testing, but I think it's safe to say it's them,' she said sadly before adding, 'I'm very sorry for your loss.'

'Thank you so much and thank you to Laura. That poor woman lost her life and still made sure we found our girls - we can never thank her enough,' cried Maureen.

'The least I could do. I'm just glad they found them.'

'At least they've been on the consecrated ground the whole time,' said Olive. 'That makes me feel better. I was so worried about them being buried somewhere without a prayer or a flower.'

The rest of the family nodded in agreement, some crying and others laughing. A bottle of prosecco was opened, a celebration under the most tragic circumstances and noticing the look of bewilderment on Audrey's face, Olive explained.

'We've always known they were dead – they'd never have left home like that,' she said. 'This is a celebration for us- we have them back, and we can bury them on our terms.'

Orla had a glass of prosecco, *no excuse needed*, but Audrey stuck to the tea.

'We'll re-open the case and interview Lars, Erik and Sven. There will be an autopsy, but because of the length of time,' Audrey trailed off. 'As you already know, the news channels are reporting it,' she nodded to the television in the background, 'so don't be surprised if they knock on your door.

'What will we say?' asked Maureen.

'This happened to your girls - say what you want - it's entirely up to you,' said Audrey.

These women and their families had suffered enough and should be allowed to tell their stories in whatever way they wanted to. They soon said goodbye, everyone thanking Orla again for everything she'd done. They thanked Audrey as well, but Orla was their star. Audrey was just happy they finally had some closure.

When they returned to Maggie's shop, Niamh practically knocked them off their feet.

'You are not going to believe who was sitting in a car across from the church,' she said, jumping up and down.

'Let me guess, Erik and Sven,' said Audrey, thinking the cat was definitely out of the bag.

'No, drum roll, please,' said Niamh, imitating the drums, before adding, 'I mean, yeah, those two were there, but so was Lars.'

48 ~ ERIK

When Erik saw the security footage from Lars's house, showing Laura's friends lurking outside his garages, he nearly lost his mind. What the fuck were those women doing in Sweden? Sighing, he walked down the hall to Lars's office - knowing he had to tell him, even though he didn't want to - even though this might tip him over the edge. Erik had never seen Lars so broken and distracted. He'd made a mistake in killing Laura, and his timing couldn't have been worse. Politics had always been Lars's endgame, and now the Laura situation could destroy everything.

Back in Dublin, when Lars rang to say he'd killed her, Erik was delighted and nearly high-fived him. He hated the bitch, and hated Lars's obsession with her. Erik would have preferred to get rid of the body that day, but with no time or equipment - a clean-up was their only option. He made sure there was no trace of Lars in that apartment, that was the best he could do. Since then, Lars had slumped into a depression - drinking more, his moods were darker than Erik had ever seen them. When he walked into his office and found Lars staring into space, Erik wanted to shout at him to snap the fuck out of it.

'You need to see this,' said Erik, handing Lars the iPad.

'What the fuck are they doing at my house?' asked Lars, with a stunned expression.

As they sped towards Uppsala, Erik explained how they'd already been to the hospital, but Lars looked out the window, seeming defeated. Lars had always been more than a boss to Erik - the only person to ever give a fuck about him, and he would do anything to protect him. When they'd met, Erik had been a skinny eighteen-year-old kid who'd been bounced from one foster home to the next. He didn't know his parents, only that his mother was a junkie who'd overdosed and died. He'd have died, too, if the neighbours in the shitty flat in Malmo hadn't heard a baby crying nonstop for two days and called the police. That was the beginning of his foster life, and Erik couldn't remember one foster family ever being kind to him. As soon as he turned eighteen, he joined the army and met Lars.

They went through their training together, became Marines and were stationed all over the world until one day - out of the blue, Lars announced he was moving to Ireland and Erik went with him. They worked on building sites during the day and provided security to nightclubs in Dublin at night. They had money, access to whatever drugs they wanted, and so many women, it was a joke. Life was great until Lars met Laura, and everything changed.

At first, Erik thought she was just another fling, but Lars's obsession grew to the point of madness. That fateful night when she walked into the nightclub had been a disaster, but ultimately, it saved their skin. Erik had been fuming - he'd worked hard to entice Lars out for a night - insisting he test the goods because his reputation was on the line. Lars finally agreed and was enjoying himself for the first time in months until Laura and her mates turned up, and everything went to shit.

When she broke up with him the next day, Lars lost his mind, and even though Erik tried to convince him she wasn't worth it, Lars went after her with such determination that Erik knew nothing would stop him. When he got her back, he would never let her go again, and even though there had been other women over the years, Laura had an unbreakable hold on him.

Shaking himself from his thoughts, Erik walked into the hotel lobby where the women were staying, watching as Lars dealt with the usual crap that came with being a government minister. About fifteen minutes later, the women walked in, entirely at ease about seeing them.

'They're up to something,' said Lars when they left the bar.

Erik agreed, but when he tried to talk to Orla, she was clever and made sure the hotel staff knew he was in her room, *fucking bitch*. Then they hightailed it in the middle of the night back to Ireland. When Lars told him to go to Dublin, Erik was relieved - this was more like it, but his run-in with Orla caused Lars to go nuclear.

'Don't you lay a fucking finger on them - do you understand me?' Lars screamed down the phone. 'This is a different situation - just watch and tell me what's happening.'

The next day, when he reported that two of them had gone to Lars's old house on Cork Street, Lars was silent for so long that Erik thought he'd hung up.

'Why go there, Erik? What are they looking for?' he asked, sounding nervous.

Erik didn't know, but he was nervous as well. His contact at the station assured him nothing had changed, but his gut told him it had. The day after that, all four women were at the writer's house, then Laura's parents arrived while Erik was on the phone with Lars.

'Let me go in – I'll break the door down and find out what they're up to,' said Erik.

'Don't you fucking move - do not do a thing,' said Lars.

Just then, someone left the house.

'It's the cop - she's on her own - what will I do?' asked Erik.

'Follow her. I'm coming to Dublin tonight,' said Lars.

'I don't think that's a good...'

Erik trailed off when Lars hung up. He followed Audrey into town, where she met another detective, the one investigating Laura's disappearance, and the penny dropped. She was reporting to him - their own little private investigation. No wonder his guy at the station said nothing had changed - he didn't know. An hour later, Erik received a text message that made his blood run cold.

Larry: *Digging up the church in Andrew Street tomorrow. Think three bodies might be there. O'Brien has been investigating Lars on the quiet for the past few weeks. She found them.*

49 ~ AUDREY

'Lars won't stick around now that the bodies have been found,' said Orla.

'Probably tearing his hair out wondering how it happened,' laughed Niamh.

'Hope it drives him mad,' said Maggie.

'I'd love to see his face.'

'I've got to go – I'll see you all later,' said Audrey.

Nina was cooking dinner for them all that night.

'I cannot wait - I've missed Nina's cooking so much,' said Niamh with a sigh.

Audrey remembered Niamh being Nina's biggest fan – she'd loved her cooking almost as much as Audrey. She said goodbye to her friends and arrived at the station to find Dave pacing in his office, looking furious.

'Guess who's in Dublin,' said Audrey.

'I know, I saw him when I left the site,' said Dave, 'guess what else happened? Marcus Ryan was attacked - someone tore his office apart - I'm just back from talking to him at James's hospital.'

'Jesus. Is he okay?' asked Audrey.

'Fine - a bit bruised and battered,' said Dave.

'Let me guess, Erik?' asked Audrey, sure he was responsible.

'Marcus didn't know, but likely. He said there were two of them - they wore balaclavas, didn't say a word, just searched his office and beat the crap out of him. Come on - I'm heading over there now,' said Dave, grabbing his vape and walking out the door.

When they got to Marcus's office, it looked like wild animals had run through it. Two forensic guards searched for fingerprints, but Audrey knew they wouldn't find any.

'Any files missing?' asked Dave, but the guards didn't know yet.

'Lars's first thought must have been Laura's solicitor. Can we arrest him now, please?' asked Audrey.

'Arrest him for what?' asked Dave. 'We

don't know if he has anything to do with this. It could be completely random.' Dave was a fantastic detective, but he didn't get carried away - Audrey would learn from him. 'We'll question him, but you know how that will go. He won't bat an eyelid and deny everything.'

'What about the girls - the message from Laura?' asked Audrey.

'Finding the girls is great, but let's be honest - there'll be no evidence on their bodies after twenty years. Laura said they were shot in the head – where's the gun? Everything is circumstantial, based on the statement of a dead woman,' said Dave.

'A statement that led to the discovery of those bodies twenty years later. A statement that said her husband would be responsible if anything happened to her. Surely that's worth something,' said Audrey, unable to keep the frustration out of her voice.

'What if Laura made it up?' asked Dave to Audrey's confused face.

'Made what up?' she asked. 'Why would Laura make something like that up?'

'What if she knew where the bodies were all along and wanted to frame her husband?'

asked Dave. Audrey was mortified, but before she could leap to Laura's defence, he continued. 'I'm not saying she did - I'm just saying what a good defence lawyer would argue. You can see how this looks. Lars is a respectable businessman, a member of parliament, and an ex-military man with no police record. According to her medical records, Laura was under the care of shrinks for years,' he said.

'Lars is a dangerous psychopath who regularly beat the shit out of his wife, obviously went too far and killed her. I know we don't have the flight record, but the photo shows he was here,' she pleaded.

'Inadmissible, and even if Lars boxed ten bells of shite out of Laura on a daily basis, it's irrelevant because there's no proof. Not a hint of domestic violence - no reports - no arrests - just you four and your one in Sweden saying so.'

'He can't be allowed to get away with this,' said Audrey, feeling defeated, 'it's not fucking fair.

'Listen, Audrey, I want to arrest him as much as you do, but this is out of my hands. I'm going back to the office to have a chat with

Colin. Go home - I'll text you and let you know what's happening,' said Dave.

Later that evening, when her friends arrived, Audrey smiled - her best friends were in her house for the first time, and it felt weird. They immediately fell into how it had always been, as if dinner parties had been a weekly occurrence for the past twenty years. The chat was constant, the wine flowed, and the smell of garlic and rosemary was mouth-watering. Although they missed Laura, there was an air of celebration about deciphering her message and finding the girls. Audrey didn't tell them what Dave said until it was time for them to leave.

'How can that be? Surely, they'll be arrested and charged?' asked Niamh, almost apoplectic.

'We'll question him and the others - I'm just not sure if there's enough evidence to charge them, and on top of that, his position in Government makes it complicated,' said Audrey.

Just then, a loud knock on the front door startled them. It was already eleven.

'It might be the Uber,' called Nina as

Audrey walked down the hallway.

Maggie ordered it five minutes earlier, but Uber drivers didn't knock, did they?

'Shit, don't answer the door.'

Audrey's senses kicked in as she reached for the latch. Another knock, louder this time, brought everyone into the small hallway.

'Who is it?' asked Nina nervously.

'I think it's Lars,' mouthed Audrey and watched as, one by one, their faces dropped. 'I'll let him in. Nina, go next door to Lorraine's house and call Dave.'

Nina nodded, picked up her phone and quietly left through the back patio door. The others returned to the kitchen, and Audrey opened the door to Erik, who pushed his way past. Lars and Sven followed.

'Don't say a fucking word - I want to talk to you, then I'll leave,' growled Lars, barging his way into Audrey's tiny kitchen.

'Eh, excuse me, if you don't get out of this house, I'm calling the guards,' called Audrey after him, then added. 'Oh wait, I am a guard. Get out now.'

He ignored her - she shut the door and followed the three men into her kitchen. Erik scooped up all four phones from the kitchen table and handed them to Sven.

'Does this seem strangely familiar? Erik taking our phones,' mocked Niamh, putting her finger to her lip as if trying to recall something, 'oh yeah, when Lars knocked Laura out, now she's been murdered. Deja Vu, anyone?'

Erik moved towards her threateningly, but Lars held his hand up and looked at each of them.

'I want to know who you spoke to in Sweden,' he said, his words slow and deliberate.

Audrey was over his bullshit, but she played along.

'We spoke to a lot of people in Sweden, Lars. Can you be more specific?' she asked.

He didn't answer. Audrey watched him closely, realising he was backed into a corner. Even if they didn't arrest him for the girl's murder, which she hoped would happen - his connection to it could ruin his career – can a government minister be a murder suspect? She didn't think so.

'I hope they fire his arse.'

'Why did you come here, Lars?' asked Orla, breaking the tension.

Audrey's kitchen was packed, the women on one side of the table, Sven and Erik on the other, standing close to Lars. Erik watched Lars closely - Audrey suspected it was his first time seeing his boss so unsure.

'It gave me a small sense of satisfaction seeing him so unsure.'

'Who did you talk to in Sweden?' Lars asked again, sounding desperate and feeling concerned for Astrid - Audrey tried to throw him off the scent.

'We spoke to some of the nurses at the hospital, who all thought Laura was wonderful. Two old men at reception said they missed her, and Hilda let us shelter from the rain at your house - that was it,' she said.

There was nothing more to say - Lars seemed confused, and Audrey almost felt sorry for him. He stood still for a few more minutes, not saying a word, then nodded at Erik.

'Give them back their phones,' he said and walked out.

Sven threw them on the table, *rude* and, along with Erik, followed Lars out the front door. The relief in the room was audible. What the hell had just happened?

'He's worried, but there's something else. Is it regret?' asked Orla.

'I thought so too - he's shaken. I almost felt sorry for him,' said Audrey.

'Don't feel sorry for him, love - think of Laura,' said Maggie.

'I said almost,' said Audrey, winking at her.

'He knows he's fucked when this gets out.'

'Well, my nerves are gone - Jesus, I'm not able for this,' said Niamh, laughing nervously and taking a large gulp of wine while Maggie put the kettle on. 'That was intense, but I think you're right, Orla, he seemed confused,' she added.

Just then, Nina walked through the kitchen door, followed by Dave.

'Where are they?' asked Dave, then added, 'I can bring them in.'

The women jumped around the kitchen at this bit of news.

'Hold your horses. I'm not arresting them - just asking them to come to the station,' said Dave.

At least, that was something.

'Finding those girl's bodies is proof Laura was telling the truth when she wrote that note,' said Orla, and Dave agreed but explained further what Audrey had already told them.

'Why would Laura make up something like that?' asked Maggie, gobsmacked.

'Great, I'll be described as a mad bitch while my husband gets away with murder.'

'You all know she wouldn't. You know Lars was beating her. You know how dangerous he is but look at it from the point of view of a jury. They'll know none of that, and Lars's defence lawyer will paint a very different picture. On top of that, it's political. If he wasn't a member of parliament, he'd have been arrested by now. That's the only reason everyone is so cautious,' said Dave.

Red tape and bureaucracy might be why Lars Karlsson got away with killing his wife and three innocent girls. When everyone left, Nina tried to reassure Audrey.

'You'll get him, love, I'm sure of it,' she said as they lay in bed.

'I keep going over the details in my head, and I'm getting nowhere. We seem to take one step forward and two steps back where Lars Karlsson is concerned,' said Audrey, feeling utterly deflated.

'Keep going, love - something will happen, and it will happen soon,' said Nina.

Audrey hoped she was right. She'd been desperate to prove Lars was involved in the girl's murder. If they couldn't get him for Laura's death, at least they'd get him for that. Now, she wasn't sure that would be the case.

50 ~ ERIK

Only four people in the world knew about those bodies. Robert was dead, and Lars and Sven hadn't said anything, so how did they find them? When Erik picked up Lars from the airport a few hours later and told him the news, Lars was silent as the colour drained from his face. Erik tried to persuade him to return to Sweden immediately, but Lars refused, and the following day, they watched events unfolding at the church.

Erik thought back to that night so many years before. They weren't the first girls to be sold. Lars had a contact in Belarus, and sex trafficking was a lucrative business. They'd sweeten the deal for the girls - show them a great night - top dollar with champagne and cocaine. Get them a little drunk - a bit high and break them in. The girls would have a fantastic night in Dublin - probably the best night of their lives, then wake up in the hull of a ship bound for Eastern Europe the next day. Lars would get a nice pay-out, and the girls would start a new life in the sex industry – it was a win for everyone.

Those women interrupting the party meant the merchandise had to be destroyed. They might have pulled off the deal and discussed options until one of the girls tried to run. When Robert put a hole in her head, Sven and Erik were forced to do the same. The church garden was the perfect place to bury them. Erik had passed it many times, thinking how secluded it was for such a busy street. Each of them had carried a girl there in the middle of the night, buried them under the trees and planted flowers to make it look like the gardener had been. That was twenty years ago - now they were being dug up, and Erik had no idea how.

'This has something to do with Laura – we need to see the lawyer,' said Lars. 'Don't touch him – just bring Laura's file to me.'

Lars waited in the car while Erik and Sven confronted Marcus Ryan. He tried to fight them and got a bit mouthy, so Erik knocked him out. Sven searched his office and found

Laura's file, but there was no mention of the bodies.

'What the fuck,' roared Lars in a rage. 'How the fuck did they know?'

'We need to go home now,' said Erik, wanting them out of Ireland, but Lars insisted on speaking to Laura's friends. 'Why? It's a waste of time. You need to get the fuck out of here. If the cops come for you, it will be harder in Sweden,' he pleaded.

'I want to know how they found those bodies,' insisted Lars.

Erik knew there was no point arguing. Lars would do what he wanted, so they drove to the guard's house that evening. Sven had been following her and said all four women were there.

'Having a little fucking party, are they?' asked Erik, wanting to kill someone.

When they got into the house, Lars started acting strange - asking questions - not asking them - he looked shaken and confused. The cop watched him closely - she knew something was different, and when they left, it was too late for a flight to Sweden, so they checked into a hotel.

'They can't prove anything - there's nothing to tie you to any of this,' said Erik, drinking whiskey with Lars and Sven in their hotel room. When his phone rang, Erik put Larry on speaker, and they listened to him explain how Laura was somehow involved in finding the girls. Erik looked at Lars.

'How if she's dead?' he asked.

'Something to do with books – there was a message in them,' said Larry and Lars closed his eyes. 'Also, there's a flight log - Lucan airport, the day Laura died - your name and Karlsson's on a flight from Brussels. It was deleted from their system, but someone got a photo before that happened,' Larry continued. Erik froze, but things were about to get worse. 'Laura said in the message that if anything happened to her, Lars was involved. They know he's in Dublin and want to talk to him - you as well. I can't be involved anymore, so don't call me again,' he said and hung up.

There was complete silence in the room.

'The fucking books,' said Lars, shaking his head again and asking. 'Did we check them?'

Erik nodded - they'd gone through

Laura's things with a fine toothcomb the weekend after her murder.

'Obviously not well enough,' said Erik.

'The cop was getting help from the other three - they've been investigating me the whole time. That's why they were in Sweden - sneaky little bitches,' said Lars, then added, 'I'm the prime suspect in Laura's case - how did she get those cunts involved and where are those fucking videos?'

Lars downed his drink in one, and Erik re-filled his glass - glad to see him angry. This was better than staring into space. Fucking Laura - constantly fucking things up. Their flight to Stockholm was at noon the next day. They were getting the fuck out of Dublin, but first, Erik wanted to check Laura's apartment one more time. If the cops suspected Lars - videos of him kicking the shit out of Laura wouldn't help him. If there was a phone with videos on it - maybe Laura hid it. The next morning, he drove to Grand Canal and told Lars he'd see him at the airport.

'Where are you going?' asked Lars.

'Just want to check one thing before we go,' said Erik.

When he pulled up to Laura's building, Erik was surprised to see the cop and Orla at the entrance. He hung back and called Lars, but it went to voicemail. Ten minutes later, he tried again, and the same thing happened. Checking his watch, Erik decided enough was enough - he was going to confront those bitches - beat the shit out of them if he had to, but he would find out what the fuck was going on. However, as he stepped out of his car, his phone pinged with a text from Lars.

Lars: *Being questioned by cops. Looking for you - Get out of Ireland. NOW.*

Erik didn't hesitate and drove out of the city. An hour later as he drove to Northern Ireland, Lars rang him.

'I don't have much time,' he said, then quickly told him what had happened.

When they hung up, Erik knew exactly what to do. He arrived in Belfast, ditched the car - got a ferry to the UK and flew from Manchester to Gothenburg.

Returning to his apartment in Stockholm, he packed a bag - got an extra passport, another phone, and a new laptop. Then he met Olga, who gave him Lars's laptop.

After that, he drove to the lake house, where he cleaned up the security feeds, and then he went to a cabin Lars owned in Gotland, where Sven was waiting.

51 ~ ORLA

When Audrey asked Orla to meet her at the apartment where Laura was murdered, Orla didn't want to go, but at the same time - she did. Maybe they missed something - her curious mind couldn't help but wonder.

'When is it being released back to the owner?' she asked as they wandered around the gorgeous apartment. 'He must be losing a fortune in rent.' Audrey raised an eyebrow. 'What? I'd hate it if it were my business.'

'Tomorrow,' said Audrey, 'that's why I wanted to come today - one last look.'

Even though it was a beautiful apartment, it felt eerie.

'Think anyone will rent it in the future?' asked Orla, wondering who'd stay where a murder had been committed.

'I'm guessing the landlord won't advertise the fact,' said Audrey, opening and closing kitchen presses.

'I can't believe they're here.' "The coffee machine, Orla."'

Audrey pointed to where Laura's body had lain and described the scene.

'There was coffee and blood everywhere. It's obviously had a good hoover and a specialist clean since then, and what was left of Laura's things are at the station,' she said.

Orla checked the coffee machine, wondering if her dream about Laura had meant anything, but it was empty and clean. They went into the bedroom to find the bed stripped and a lonely wire hanger hanging on the rail in a large walk-in wardrobe.

'What are you looking for?' asked Orla, thinking the place was spotless.

'Nothing in particular. I just wanted to see it one last time,' said Audrey.

They wandered back into the kitchen where Laura had lost her life.

'It's strange being where she took her last breath - don't you think?' asked Orla, feeling more uncomfortable by the second. 'She mentioned a coffee machine in my dream

- I told you that, didn't I? Audrey nodded. 'Anyway, there's nothing in it,' said Orla, pointing at the built-in coffee machine.

'The whole place was searched – if there was anything to be found – they would have found it,' said Audrey, then sighed. 'I'll never get seeing Laura's body lying on that floor out of my head,' said Audrey.

After a few minutes, they got ready to leave.

'They can't leave. "The coffee machine, Orla."'

Audrey opened the apartment door, but Orla thought about the coffee machine again - why was it on her mind? She'd already checked it, but she hesitated - wondering if this feeling meant something in her new world of the supernatural...Laura?

'Yes.'

'Hang on, Audrey,' said Orla,' walking back into the kitchen and standing before the coffee machine again.

'What's going on,' asked Audrey,

standing beside her.

'I have a weird feeling about this coffee machine,' said Orla.

Audrey shook her head in confusion.

'What do ye mean?' she asked.

'Something's tugging at my mind,' said Orla.

'Oh my God, Orla...Yes.'

She lifted the lid again and looked inside again. - empty. What was she expecting? She tried to look behind it, but it was part of the unit and wouldn't budge.

'Why did Laura say coffee machine in my dream?' she asked,' but Audrey just shook her shoulders.

Orla's eyes moved to a tiny gap at its base. She took her phone from her pocket, switched on the torch and shone it into the gap.

'There's something in there,' said Orla.'

Audrey bent for a better look.

'Shit - there is,' she said.

Orla got a knife from the drawer and slid it into the gap - it didn't reach. Remembering the coat hanger - she ran to the bedroom and grabbed it. Very slowly and with a fair bit of manoeuvring, a black phone slid from beneath the coffee machine.

'Holy shit,' said Audrey, astonished.

'Laura's been trying to tell me about this from the start,' said Orla.

'My heart swelled with love for these women.'

'Let's get out of here. The others are at Maggie's shop. We'll take it there, charge it and look at the videos together. Then I'll take it to the station. Dave was bringing The Swedes in for questioning this morning.'

The two women walked back to Audrey's car in a daze - unable to believe they'd found Laura's phone. Even though Orla dreaded watching what was on it – it might be what they needed to get Lars. Had Audrey not suggested going there one last time - it might never have been found.

52 ~ LARS

Lars sat, drinking coffee in the lobby of his hotel - feeling somewhat light-hearted. The flight to Sweden was at noon - he was leaving Ireland and never returning. Being in Dublin had cured him of his grief - he felt free of Laura for the first time since meeting her – the spell had broken, and he was ready to move on. When Larry revealed what her friends were doing, Lars talked to his lawyer, who confirmed their evidence was weak. There was nothing to connect him to those bodies. The flight log was inconvenient, but Tom assured him a photo was inadmissible.

His mind wandered to the young Russian girl in his stable. Red hair and green eyes - she reminded him of his wife but was even more beautiful and young. He'd already decided to keep her and instructed Erik to hold her back from the next shipment to Eastern Europe. Maybe it was time to have a couple of kids – he was warming to the idea of a family.

Sven was on the other side of the lobby, watching everything. Lars checked his watch - it was time to go. However, as he rose from his chair, several cops entered the building - the detective from Laura's case leading the way. With a subtle shake of Lars's head, Sven disappeared down a corridor.

'Mr Karlsson – good morning, how are ye? Can we have a little chat?' asked the detective, and Lars sat back down. 'Ah not here – you'd be more comfortable down the station,' said Dave.

Lars stayed seated – he didn't have to go - his diplomatic immunity meant he could say no, but it would look like he had something to hide.

'Certainly,' said Lars, 'as long as it's quick.'

He followed the detective out the door and into the waiting car while texting Olga to clear his schedule for the afternoon. Worst case, he'd have to catch a later flight. Then he texted Erik and instructed him to leave Ireland. If there was more to this - Lars's immunity would help him, but Erik and Sven didn't have any. Arriving at the station, the cops tried to take his phone, but Lars shook his head - that was one step too far. Dave led him into a small interrogation room with a table against the wall and a chair on either side.

'Will you have a cup of tea?' asked Dave, and Lars shook his head – fucking Irish and their tea.

'Can we get this over with - I have an appointment in parliament this afternoon,' said Lars.

'Certainly – just grabbing a cup for meself,' said Dave, leaving Lars to sit alone for half an hour. 'Sorry about that - just needed to check a few things,' said Dave when he eventually came back. 'Are ye sure you don't want one of these?' he asked, holding up two plastic cups.

'Thanks, no,' said Lars, shaking his head and trying not to roll his eyes.

'Right, so, well, I suppose we better get started,' said Dave, looking at some paperwork in front of him. 'Nikoli Antonava...Know him?' asked Dave.

Lars was surprised and somewhat confused. Why the fuck was he asking about

Nikoli. Yes, Lars knew him very fucking well - he shook his head.

'Never heard of him,' said Lars.

'Right, well, he was arrested in Ireland in March 2000, blah blah,' said Dave, scanning the pages in front of him. 'Did five years before being extradited to Belarus,' he continued reading, 'sex trafficking minors and two counts of rape.'

'What's that got to do with me?' asked Lars.

'Your deceased wife - sorry for your loss, by the way,' said Dave, 'left a note saying you were supposed to sell three girls to him twenty years ago, but things got messy, and they got a bullet to the head instead,' Dave raised his fingers to imitate shooting himself. 'The girls in question were missing since then, but your wife told us where they were, so we dug them up yesterday.'

'I have no idea what you're talking about, detective. How could my deceased wife send a note?' asked Lars.

'I'll get to that in a minute, but the girls were last seen with you and your mates in a nightclub here in Dublin. It was some night by the sounds of it - champagne, cocaine and an orgy thrown in for good measure. Your wife, or your girlfriend at the time, and her friends turned up and apparently ruined the party. She was knocked to the other side of the room for it, and her friends were threatened and held hostage. Ring any bells?' asked Dave.

'None,' said Lars, cool as a cucumber.

Dave put Laura's books on the table.

'Recognise these? asked Dave, but before Lars could say a word, he continued. 'You sent them to Orla Reed, unaware that your wife had left a message in them.' Lars already knew this, but he didn't react. 'One of my colleagues recently visited Sweden, I believe you met her,' said Dave, 'anyway, she was told an interesting story. Want to hear it?'

'I think you're going to tell me, anyway,' said Lars.

'Correct,' said Dave, then began the tale. 'So apparently, about six or maybe eight months ago – after giving your missus a good hiding, you got drunk with your mate Erik. Your wife woke up needing painkillers and overheard you talking about good ole Nikoli and how the girls were supposed to be sold to him, but you murdered them instead.'

Sneaky little Laura. Lars remembered the night - hearing something and checking to see if Laura was asleep. He looked at Dave without any emotion.

'Completely made up. My wife was delusional, detective - and under the care of many psychiatrists over the years - she often made up stories,' said Lars.

'Well, delusional or not – she helped us find the bodies,' said Dave.

'I'm happy for you, but maybe Laura killed them and decided to frame me - you'd have to ask her,' said Lars, pausing, then added, 'but of course, you can't.' Dave watched him closely – Lars could tell he wasn't expecting that. 'If that's all, I'd like to leave now,' said Lars.

'Not quite,' said Dave. 'there's a bit more to it.' He took a photo from his file and laid it on the table. 'Your name was on a private flight into Dublin on the morning of Laura's murder - any comment?' asked Dave.

Once again, Lars was ready.

'Impossible,' he said, 'I was at a conference in Brussels on the day my wife died. 'A mistake, obviously. May I see the flight log?'

asked Lars, holding his hand out.

'That seems to have disappeared from the system - we only have the photo,' said Dave, pointing to the table.

'The photo,' laughed Lars and didn't comment further. 'If that's all detective,' he said.

Dave rose to his feet.

'Just need to check one more thing with the boss,' said Dave, picking up the dirty cup. 'If you don't mind - I'll be back in a tik,' he called over his shoulder as he left the room.

Lars almost laughed at the ridiculousness of the situation – they had absolutely nothing – idiots, wasting his time. He took out his phone to answer some emails, thinking he might make his noon plane after all.

53 ~ ORLA

On the way to Books and Brew, Orla rang Louise, who she'd been in regular contact with - Louise was keen to be involved in their private investigation. Orla explained what had happened and asked her to meet them at the shop. When they arrived, the sign on the door said - *closed for staff training* and Maggie had a charger ready and waiting. Louise arrived a few minutes later - Audrey plugged in the phone, and the five women sat on sofas by the window, watching it and willing it back to life.

'How in God's name did you find it?' asked Louise.

'Laura,' said Orla.

'Should have known with my sister - not even death would stop her,' she said sadly.

'She's been trying to tell me about this from the start,' said Orla.

'They had the phone - now let's see if it recorded

anything.'

After a few minutes, a ping alerted them that the phone was back to life.

'I'm nervous about seeing what's on it,' said Maggie, handing out mugs of coffee.

Orla felt the same way, but they needed to know. With no security lock, Audrey searched the videos and found four.

'You girls ready for this?' she asked.

They weren't, but they all nodded. Audrey pressed play, and they watched in horror as Lars beat Laura to a pulp. She cried, screamed, and begged him to stop - he called her a bitch and a slut as he battered her. Then as Marcus had described - he kicked her in the stomach as she lay on the floor and pissed on her. His viciousness took their breath away.

'I'm sorry you had to see that,' said Orla to Louise.

'Always knew it was bad - just not that bad,' said Louise with tears in her eyes.

Two other videos showed Laura in a mirror, recording bruising around her stomach and legs. Niamh sobbed - Maggie was quiet - Orla felt sick, and Audrey was angry.

'I need to take this to the station - Dave has Lars there. He's denied all knowledge of the girl's bodies - said Laura was talking nonsense, and there isn't enough to charge him - this might help in some way,' said Audrey.

As she walked to her car, something niggled the back of Orla's mind. There had to be more to this, or why would dead Laura go to the trouble of contacting her when she should be off enjoying eternal paradise? She watched Audrey cross the road and suddenly remembered her conversation with Marcus Ryan. He'd said something about showing Laura how to record voice messages.

'Bloody well done, luv.'

'Audrey,' called Orla, dashing after her. 'Come back for a minute - I need to check one more thing,' she said.

Audrey followed her back into the shop, where Orla plugged in the phone again and checked the voice memos. There was one - recorded on the day of Laura's murder. She turned on the speaker, pressed play and watched the shock register on the faces of her friends when Laura spoke.

'Why did you follow me, Lars?' said Laura.

There was a scuffle and the sound of something smashing - the coffee, then Lars's voice.

'What the fuck are you up to, Laura?' he asked. 'Why are you in this apartment? Who are you here with, a lover?'

Orla closed her eyes. It was him. Even though she knew it - hearing his voice was devastating. Beautiful Laura - betrayed by the person supposed to love and protect her the most.

'Probably inevitable.'

'I haven't got a lover, Lars,' said Laura.

'Do you think I don't know every fucking move you make,' said Lars and went on about what she'd been doing for the past two days. 'You were in Wicklow Street this morning. I don't know why, but I'll find out,' he continued.

'Marcus,' said Audrey.

A few minutes of silence passed, then sounding calm - much to the surprise of them all, Laura asked Lars to let go of her hair and told him to fuck off before letting rip at him about their marriage being over and him being a filthy wife-beater – then more silence.

Orla thought the message had ended until Lars asked Laura if she thought she could blackmail him and started laughing while calling her a stupid bitch. When Laura spoke again, she was less calm.

'I also know what you did in that nightclub. I have proof, and I'll get the girls to make statements,' she said.

Did she tell him about the conversation she'd overheard? Orla's mind was frantic, but Lars brushed off her comment, saying his lawyers would deal with anyone who tried to attack his reputation.

'Ha! You think I give a fuck about your reputation,' said Laura. 'I know what you did to those kids. What you're still doing to kids in Sweden. How could you? You make me fucking sick.'

He said she didn't know what she was talking about, called her a tramp and said they were going home. There was the sound of a thump, then a crash – more silence, then water running. Orla couldn't work out what was happening until Laura spoke again. She called Lars a piece of shit, told him she hated him, and she was never going back to Sweden. Lars said what the fuck and told Laura to put the knife down.

There was a struggle, and they assumed Laura hit the floor. The sound of thumping was something Orla would never forget.

'You fucking slut,' said Lars - thump. 'I own you' - thump. 'I'm going to make sure you never forget that' - thump.

More banging and crashing - a muffled scream - Lars saying fuck - it was excruciation, but nothing could have prepared them for what was about to happen. Laura asked Lars to stop, and Orla looked at her friends and knew they were thinking the same thing - this was the beginning of the end for Laura.

'Stop? You think you can threaten me with a fucking knife? You think I'd let you away with that,' said Lars as Laura begged him to stop again and said she couldn't breathe.

There was another scuffle – Lars said what the fuck again called Laura a bitch and a cunt – he sounded almost deranged. Another scream from Laura – a struggle and finally Laura begging him to stop.

'Lars, please stop, I'm sorry,' she said. 'Lars, stop please,' she begged. 'I don't want to die. It's me, Laura - please stop, Lars,' she begged again. 'Please, Lars,' she screamed, and Orla couldn't bear it.

Then, there was a prolonged silence, and no one moved. Had they really just heard that?

'Jesus Christ, she asked him to stop. Why didn't he stop?' cried Niamh.

'Fucking bastard,' said Louise, sobbing.

A few minutes later, the message started again. Lars on the phone, then Erik. A conversation between them played out as if they were talking about football scores - not a scrap of emotion. Erik tried to get the knife out of Laura's neck - Lars told him to leave it - Erik asked if he should take Laura's jewellery - Lars said yes - the rustle of plastic - a door closing, and they were gone.

'Should have known Erik was there. Scumbag.'

'Oh my God,' said Louise, hyperventilating.

Orla wasn't surprised by her reaction – they were all in shock.

'Try to breathe,' said Maggie, hugging her.

Louise fell into her arms and sobbed. Orla hugged Niamh, and Audrey stared into space. After a few minutes, they pulled themselves together.

'Right, what happens now?' asked Niamh, wiping her eyes with her sleeve – she was pissed off.

'Station – let's go. We all need to be there when Lars hears this,' said Audrey.

They quickly cleaned themselves up and jumped into Audrey's car, and like a bat out of hell, she drove through the streets of Dublin.

'He's one fucking smooth dude,' said Dave as he walked toward Orla and her friends. He hadn't seen them and continued talking to his colleague. 'I have no choice - I have to let him go.'

He looked up when Audrey called his name.

'Got a minute?' she asked as Dave looked at the women, recognised Louise and nodded at her suspiciously.

'Yeah - walk this way,' he said, nodding towards his office.

When they were inside, Audrey asked how it was going with Lars.

'It isn't - he denied all knowledge - claimed his wife was trying to pin the murders on him and knows the flight log is wafer-thin. I'm just about to let him go.'

Audrey put Laura's phone on his desk.

'This might help,' she said and pressed play.

Once again, they watched Lars beat the shit out of Laura and listened to her being murdered.

'How?' asked Dave when it was finished.

'The phone was in the apartment,' said Audrey. 'Laura hid it under the coffee machine. Orla came with me this morning and found it - then she remembered Marcus saying he showed Laura how to use the voice record app.'

Dave looked at Orla, who shook her shoulders. They'd agreed to keep Laura's supernatural involvement to themselves.

'Jaysus Christ,' said Dave, 'she was some woman, wasn't she? 'She made sure those kids were found - now you're telling me - she recorded her own murder.'

Everyone in the room sighed. Yeah, she was some woman, alright. Beautiful and brilliant, Laura had made sure she didn't die in vain – it was bittersweet.

Laura
My friends were absolute stars - I was so happy they'd found the phone. Now let's see what that fucker makes of it. I was dying to see his face – could he talk his way out of this one? I bloody well hoped not.

54 ~ LARS

When the detective returned, Lars rose from his seat.

'If you don't mind – I have a noon flight,' said Lars.

Dave looked at the clock - it was almost eleven.

'Of course, just one more thing before you go,' said Dave, taking Laura's phone from his pocket and placing it on the table.

Lars looked at it – his mind quickly assessing the situation. So, he'd been right - Laura had another phone, and he knew what was on it. Recalling Laura's words, *videos of you beating the shit out of me* – Dave's next question confirmed his suspicion.

'Ever hit your wife?' he asked.

Lars studied the detective and, for the first time in his life, felt unprepared.

'No comment,' said Lars.

'Well, let's say, for the sake of it, you did.

How violent would you get? Punch her? Kick her while she's lying on the floor - cause her to throw up? Piss on her?'

Lars didn't respond - instead, his mind frantically tried to figure out what Laura had recorded. How did she do it without him noticing? His anger threatened to consume him. When the detective pressed play and turned the phone towards him, he watched for a reaction. Lars was stone cold - he knew what was coming, and although outwardly calm, he was seething inside - how fucking dare she record their private disagreements. She was lucky to be dead, or he would have killed her for this.

'Are you charging me with domestic abuse, detective?' asked Lars, thinking he needed to get out of there and find out what else his wife was doing. 'Because if you are, can you get on with it so I can call my lawyer,' said Lars.

'Ah, sure - domestic abuse is only the start of your problems, Lars,' said Dave, 'but I'd say you'll need your lawyer when you hear this.'

Dave fiddled with the phone until Laura's

voice filled the room, and Lars paled. He listened as the events of that morning so many weeks before unfolded, wondering how the fuck his wife had fucked him. When it got to the part of her begging for her life, he flinched and, afterwards, while discussing her murder with Erik, Lars had to admit - it sounded callous. Neither of the men spoke, but Lars's expression asked how?

'Laura hid it under a coffee machine in her apartment and recorded you killing her,' said Dave, answering Lars's unasked question.

Lars almost smiled - his feisty little rocket had fought hard. He knew the detective couldn't arrest him without a waiver of immunity, and Dave knew it, too. Any evidence would be deemed useless if his rights were violated.

'I'd like some privacy to speak to my lawyer,' said Lars, and with no other option, Dave led him into another room where he dialled Erik's number.

'I don't have much time. Laura hid a phone in the apartment. Recorded everything – they're going to charge me with murder, and they're after you. Clean up everything - Laura had been busy in the months before she died – find out what else she found. I caught her using my laptop at work a few months ago. I thought nothing at the time, but she acted strange. Get it from Olga,' said Lars.

'Can you walk out of there? Just leave now,' said Erik.

'I'm going to - but if you don't hear from me in the next two hours, call Tom and get him here. The cops have been stalling and scrambling behind the scenes. I underestimated the bitch - she's royally fucked me. I'm leaving now, but it might be too late.'

Lars hung up as Dave entered the room again - this time with another man.

'Mr Karlsson, my name is Hans Aberg – from the Swedish embassy,' said Hans, shaking Lars's hand, then turning back to Dave.

'Mr Karlsson has nothing more to say - I need to see the waiver of immunity I assume you have - authorising you to question a diplomat from another country?'

'Mr Karlsson is here of his own free will and is free to leave at any time,' said Dave as Lars realised, he'd been played. 'But... we'll happily make things official for ye – if you wait here, I'll get that waiver,' said Dave, leaving the room again.

Hans turned to Lars.

'Your situation is dire. The government contacted the embassy - they have no choice but to grant a waiver to the police. The evidence against you is too much, but if your detective friend doesn't bring it to me,' Hans looked at his watch, 'in the next five minutes - we will go straight to the embassy and get you out of this country immediately.'

55 ~ ORLA

Orla, her friends, and Louise watched with bated breath as Lars was questioned. They huddled together around a small TV screen in a different part of the building. Orla's eyes didn't leave Lars's face as he listened to the voice recording of him murdering his wife. She was unable to detect a scrap of emotion. She was so shocked when the Swedish lawyer turned up and played the diplomatic immunity card that she couldn't watch.

'Please tell me, we have a waiver,' said Louise, horrified.

'You can only apply for one with sufficient evidence - that came with the phone,' said Audrey, then added, 'the boss is on the phone now, but the Swedes are trying to delay.'

'Jesus Christ, he can't be allowed to walk out of here,' said Orla.

'I almost laughed - my husband, the murdering

politician, might walk away.'

Lars had shown no mercy when Laura begged for her life - he snuffed her out, and Orla wanted him to rot in prison for years, but instead, he could walk out the front door at any minute.

'If he gets back to Sweden - it will complicate things,' said Audrey.

She left the room as the others waited - drinking tea and hoping for a miracle.

'Why delay the waiver?' asked Maggie.

'Who knows,' said Orla, then added, 'maybe they'd rather deal with their dirty washing in private.'

'Whatever the case, I think we can agree - his career is over,' said Niamh.

'Something, at least.'

'It's not enough. The bastard murdered Laura and those kids – we haven't even scratched the surface of the trafficking stuff,' said Orla, then added. 'Laura knew something - she downloaded something, and we need to find whatever it was because the more Lars Karlsson is charged with – the longer he stays in prison.'

'My thoughts exactly.'

Orla was sure she'd scream if Lars walked out the door. When Audrey returned, she nodded towards the TV screen, and everyone turned to watch. Hans had stood up, and Lars put his coat on - they were leaving, and there was nothing anyone could do to stop them.
'They still haven't got it – we can't stop him,' said Audrey.
'No,' said Louise. 'He can't get away with it.'
Devastation spread through the room as the women watched Lars walk out. They followed Audrey down a corridor to an open-plan reception area to see Lars, led by his lawyer, walking towards them. When he noticed them, he nodded, and Orla was positive there was a hint of a smile on his face.

'Bastard.'

Suddenly, Dave came barrelling out of a room. He noticed Lars standing by the lift, quickly composed himself, and approached him. Orla couldn't breathe – was that a sheet of paper in his hand?

'Please, please, please,' she whispered.

The women couldn't hear what Dave said to Lars - but Lars turned and, together with Hans, followed Dave back into an interrogation room. Orla and the others practically fell over each other, trying to get back to the TV screen. When they did, they saw Dave officially charging Lars with the murder of his wife. No one heard their cheer when he was handcuffed and escorted to a holding cell.

'Oh my God, they got him.'

'You watching this, Laura,' Orla whispered.

'You bet I was.'

'The boss is on the phone with the Swedish PM. I think it's safe to say Lars is fired.

Imagine when this gets out in Sweden - people won't believe it,' said Audrey.

Laughing, crying and hugging - the women soon left the station and went straight to Wheelan's pub. Lars had been charged with Laura's murder, and whatever happened now - he was going to jail.

'Love you girls.'

Audrey raised her glass.

'As hard as it was listening to that recording, I'm glad Laura made it. I wish she didn't die, but at least she had the last laugh. If you're listening, Laura -bloody well done. Proud of ye,' she said.

'Laura,' said her friends simultaneously.

'Cheers.'

'I'd love to know what's going through his mind right now - he must be kicking himself for underestimating Laura,' said Maggie, raising her glass again.

'I wonder if she'll stick around now that he's been arrested,' said Orla. 'I hope so - I'll miss her if she goes.'

'My sister won't miss that bastard's day in court,' said Louise, and the others laughed.

'I didn't know if I was going upstairs or staying.'

After a few drinks, the five visited the Quinns, and Audrey broke the news. Lars had been charged with Laura's murder - the waiver of immunity being granted at the last minute, and he was going to jail. Mr and Mrs Quinn cried, tears of sadness and joy mixed together.

'We never want to hear that recording,' said Mrs Quinn.

Orla looked at Louise, who nodded. Both of them thinking that was for the best. How would anyone get over listening to their own daughter being so brutally murdered?

'I hoped Lars rotted in prison for what he'd put them through.'

Orla asked Audrey if there was any news on Erik. Apparently, Lars had called him from the station and warned him off.

'I'd say he's long gone. There's a warrant

out for his arrest - here and in Sweden, so we might get lucky, but I have a feeling if Erik doesn't want to be found, we won't find him,' said Audrey.

'What about Sven?' asked Orla.

'Same - he's gone as well,' said Audrey.

'They'd never find those two fuckers.'

They spent a few hours with the Quinns, drinking wine and reminiscing about Laura. When Orla got home, she felt emotional - Laura's life had been turned upside down when she met Lars. A chance meeting that ruined her and her family's lives forever. Even though the Quinns would never get over losing Laura, hopefully, Lars being in prison would ease their pain. She wondered if Laura would float off to oblivion now, but when the light flickered, Orla knew that wasn't the case.

'It seemed I was still here.'

When she finally fell asleep, Laura wrapped her in a hug and thanked her.

'You all mean the world to me – I don't

know what will happen now, but I feel really peaceful,' said dream Laura.

Looking at her friend, Orla realised she was no longer broken by Lars - she was finally free of him and for a few seconds, Orla felt her peace.

Laura
Lars being arrested for my murder was the best moment of my death so far. We got the fucker, and no matter what happened now, he was ruined. It made me want to dance, and I did while wondering if I'd float off to heaven.

56 ~ ORLA

The world woke to the news that a member of the Swedish Parliament had been arrested in Dublin for the murder of his wife and his involvement in the disappearance and murder of three young girls twenty years earlier. It was broadcast on news channels worldwide, and people were shocked - especially in Sweden.

'The people he was blackmailing are probably shitting themselves.'

'Lars's house and office were raided by the police this morning - the jewellery Laura was wearing on the morning of her murder was found in his office safe,' said Audrey.

'Wonder what Olga thought of that – her precious Lars.'

'Why the fuck did he hang onto it?' asked Orla, unable to believe he was that stupid.

'I don't know, sentimental reasons,' mused Audrey. 'Or maybe he believed he was untouchable. Either is fine with me.'

'Defo the latter.'

'Let's see him get out of that one,' said Niamh, high-fiving Audrey.

They were in Maggie's shop, discussing what had happened.

'I still can't believe Laura turned on the voice recorder while Lars was there. How did he not clock that?' asked Niamh, in awe of Laura's courage.

'I don't think she realised she'd be recording her murder. Probably just another beating to use against him,' said Audrey.

'If I'd known, I would have gotten out of there like a bat out of hell.'

It was a hard pill to swallow - being so desperate to get away from your husband that you had to take a beating to use as evidence.

'I couldn't have done it,' said Niamh. 'I'd have crumbled to the ground or ran.'

'Yeah, but you weren't conditioned to it -

that was Laura's normal,' said Orla. 'I wish she had run. She might have been alive today, but thanks to her, the girls were found, and three families have peace, speaking of which.'

'It was amazing what became normal for me.'

They turned to the large TV screen on the wall, and Orla turned up the volume. Maureen was being interviewed on morning TV – she talked about how it felt to finally find their girls.

'Orla Reed helped us so much, and we're so grateful to her,' said Maureen.

Niamh gave a mock round of applause, and Orla bowed.

'She was very kind, and so was Sergeant O'Brien. Not like the guards twenty years ago. They tried convincing us our girls ran to England when we knew they hadn't. That poor woman being murdered led to our girls being found. We're so sorry for her family but thankful for what she did.'

The reporter asked what happened next.

'We wait until the police finish with the forensics, then we give our girls the burial they deserve.'

Orla couldn't imagine what those families had gone through for twenty years. The pain Lars and Erik inflicted on so many lives was unbelievable. She couldn't work out who was worse, Lars or Erik and suspected Erik. As Laura had said, there was something savage about him.

'Definitely Erik. At least, Lars hated himself for who he was. Erik didn't.'

'Any news on Erik and Sven?' she asked. 'I can't imagine they'll be handing themselves in.'

'Nothing yet - vanished, both of them. We're collaborating with the Swedish police to find them. I'm going to Stockholm next week for a meeting,' said Audrey.

'They need to be stopped,' said Niamh, then asked. 'Anything on the trafficking?'

'No, but we're taking the allegation seriously - it will be investigated. The security room at the lake house was tampered with. There was no sign of chains on walls or anything else, but it's on the table to be discussed in Stockholm next week,' said Audrey, then added. 'Lars's defence is already underway. As expected, he was fired from Parliament.'

'Woohoo. That will kill him.'

'Yay,' said Niamh.

'The Swedish government is trying to distance themselves from him. Personally, I think it will take years of PR for them to recover - a member of Parliament being a murderer is bad enough, but he'd already been offered the job as deputy Prime Minister - it's excruciating.' said Audrey.

'They're probably scratching their heads wondering how they missed it,' said Maggie.

'They didn't miss it – he was blackmailing them.'

'Dave thinks he'll plead guilty to manslaughter, and he has a good case. The recording proves he killed Laura, but he's claiming she attacked him with a knife first, and he has PTSD from being in the army – it's all very messy,' said Audrey.

'It was a brutal and vicious murder.

Laura begged for her life and begged for him to stop,' said Orla incredulously.

'He blacks out if provoked by violence - apparently, that's a thing, and it happened when Laura pulled the knife,' said Audrey, shocking everyone in the room. 'And as far as the bodies are concerned - he denied it all, and there's no way to prove otherwise.'

Orla had suspected it might be tricky to pin that on him. Erik more or less admitted it was him and the other two men who shot those girls.

'How long will he go to prison for?' asked Maggie.

'Hard to say. The level of violence was shocking - the maximum sentence for manslaughter is around ten years,' said Audrey.

That meant he'd be out in five with good behaviour. Five years didn't seem long enough for the amount of pain he'd caused, and it didn't seem fair to Laura.

'His life being in tatters was enough for me.'

'That's shit,' said Orla.
'It's disappointing, but bear in mind

what this has done to him. Lars's career in government is over - he's ruined. He's been remanded in custody and sitting in Mountjoy Prison as we speak. His solicitor is trying to get him out, but that won't happen. On top of that - his reputation is in the gutter - his finances are being investigated, and his past is being dug up by journalists all over Sweden,' said Audrey, smiling.

'I'd love to know what's going through his mind.'

Orla felt slightly better but would have preferred a life sentence without the possibility of parole.

'When are the girls being released for burial?' she asked.

'I'm not sure, but there's not much evidence. They all had a bullet hole in their head - from different guns. It seemed Erik was telling the truth about that,' said Audrey.

'Imagine shooting three beautiful young girls like that. Young and innocent, out for a night in town and shot in the head. It's unreal, something you'd see in a film,' said Maggie.

They finished their coffee, and Audrey

returned to work. The others went to The Quinn's house to raid Laura's boxes.

'I can't believe Audrey didn't want to come,' said Niamh, shaking her head in disbelief.

'Fashion is not high on Audrey's list of important stuff, you know that,' said Orla.

'That's just weird. Laura was always a fashion queen – this is like shopping in Brown Thomas's for free,' she squealed. Maggie and Orla laughed as Niamh rummaged through boxes. 'Laugh all you want, but remember, I have five girls - fashion is life in my house,' she said, digging in.

'My kind of house.'

Orla picked a couple of scarves - a tweed jacket, and she couldn't resist a gorgeous Chanel handbag. She chose two sweaters for Audrey and a leather rucksack. Niamh went crazy, but Mrs Quinn encouraged it.

'Take it - otherwise, it will end up in a charity shop,' she said.

Niamh filled a box full of clothes, handbags and shoes for herself and her girls.

Maggie took a small evening bag and a pair of Jimmy Choo's. It felt nice to own something that had belonged to Laura.

'I loved the idea of Niamh's girls wearing my things.'

'God bless you all for getting him locked up - Laura can finally rest in peace,' said Mrs Quinn as they left.

She hugged them at the front door and promised to see them soon.

Laura
I knew Lars had a good case, and I did try to kill him, but it didn't matter – he was ruined, and he'd hate that. Underneath it all, he was a country boy who needed to be accepted by society, and now he was disgraced. If he spent a few years in prison, it would be a bonus.

57 ~ ORLA

'Jesus, your house is gorgeous,' said Niamh, her eyes wide as Maggie led them into the biggest hallway Orla had ever seen in a house.

In the centre of a gallery landing hung a fabulous chandelier, and beneath it was a large round table holding three giant vases filled to the brim with fresh flowers. Orla handed over a measly bunch of daises from Marks & Spencer's, feeling self-conscious, and her twelve-euro bottle of wine, feeling ridiculous.

'Thanks, Orla,' said Maggie, leading them further into the house.

In the kitchen, people were cooking and laying the table - you'd think there was a wedding instead of dinner for four. They followed Maggie through to an Orangery, where champagne was served.

'This is a bit posh, isn't it?' whispered Audrey, her eyes wide.

Orla nodded, thinking exactly the same thing. Maggie's boys, David and Shay, came to say hello.

'The boys are not staying - Artie is taking them to the cinema,' said Maggie.

'I hope they're not leaving on our account,' said Orla, and Maggie laughed.

'You're damn right they are. Don't worry, they've already been fed - they're not missing out.'

'It's okay, Orla, we don't mind being kicked out for the night. We've wanted to see this film for ages,' said Artie, walking into the room and kissing them all.

When they left, the girls sat down for a perfect evening of reminiscing about Laura, laughing, crying, and celebrating her life while wishing she was with them.

'It was lovely.'

'Imagine being strong enough to stick around to make sure your murder was solved – her spirit is pure vengeance – I love it,' said Niamh.

'Lol - thanks, chick.'

'Vengeance and justice – she wanted to save everyone,' said Orla. 'Such a shame she had to die.'

'Being dead wasn't that bad.'

'If Laura found proof of the trafficking - the Swedish police will find it. We've done our part - it's up to them now. Thanks to our little investigation team - Lars is in Mountjoy,' said Audrey.

'I'm delighted we had a small part to play in it,' said Orla, then added, 'but I think it's best left to the professionals from now on – I'm not sure my nerves could take much more of dealing with those mad Swedes.'

They laughed - never in a million years could they imagine what was about to happen with those mad Swedes. The next morning, after a tearful goodbye with her mam, who'd gotten used to her being around, Orla drove to the ferry terminal, stopping at the flats for an update. A bottle of wine and a bunch of white roses waited for her.

'Thank you for everything you did. Knowing what happened to the girls - even though it was terrible, is better than not knowing,' said Maureen, handing over the gifts.

Orla hugged them and promised to see them soon, then she drove to the North Wall and boarded the ferry. When she arrived home, Ray and Neil were waiting. Neil took her bags and handed her a glass of wine.

'Welcome home, darling,' he said as he kissed her.

Her cottage seemed quiet after the craziness of Dublin. Orla drank her wine while reflecting on all that had happened. Only a few weeks earlier, her friends were all but a distant memory. Then Laura died, and they were catapulted back together as if they'd never been apart. When her phone pinged, she smiled. Their WhatsApp group would remain Laura's Angels as a tribute to her.

Audrey: *You two home?*

Her friend was checking in, and it felt nice. Niamh gave a thumbs up, Orla did the same, and Maggie did too.

Laura

My four brilliant best friends. We'd wasted so much time, and I was glad they'd re-established their bond. I was still here, and I didn't know why, but I had a feeling it was because we had unfinished business.

EPILOGUE 1 ~ ERIK

Even though it was May, the snow continued to fall as Erik sat on the old front porch of the cabin. Like most mornings, he drank coffee and wondered how Laura and her friends got one over on them. Lars was sitting in an Irish prison, and he was being hunted by the Swedish and Irish police for the murders of© those girls twenty years earlier.

Until he'd discussed it with Lars that fateful night - they'd committed the perfect crime - a secret that should have gone to their graves. In one drunken moment, it was destroyed. He should have known Laura might be lurking in the shadows – she snuck around that house like a fucking ghost.

Sven walked out of the cabin and pulled him from his thoughts. They'd spent every minute since Lars's arrest making sure the trafficking – drugs - money laundering, and girls who'd met the same fate as the ones in

Dublin were untraceable. Their biggest source of income was trafficking, and that had to be protected. Erik worked hard to make sure it was secure.

'We need to move the next shipment soon. Where's the one Lars wanted?' asked Erik.

'Denmark,' said Sven.

'Keep her there - no work - get her doing something else and make sure she's clean,' said Erik.

Lars's trial was coming up, and Tom was working on getting him a deal. He might not have the politics anymore, but Erik was making sure it was business as usual for Lars when he got out. He was certain he'd get away with Laura's murder.

'How solid is your contact in Stockholm?' asked Erik as they got ready to leave.

'She'll keep us up to date on everything,' said Sven.

They left the cabin with a plan. Sven was going to Stockholm to deal with business there. Erik was crossing the border to Finland, where Lars had trusted business associates.

'One more thing,' said Erik as they walked to their cars. 'Get every piece of information you can on those Irishwomen - this is not finished,' said Erik.

Sven nodded his head, hating them as much as Erik. They'd pay for what they'd done.

EPILOGUE 2 ~ LOU

In the five months since Laura's death, Louise had spent most of her time crying. Chasing after Lars had distracted her from her grief, but when he was arrested, and the dust had settled - she grieved for her sister. Lars's trial was coming up, and the whole family was nervous. Her mam and dad couldn't speak about it without crying – what would happen if he got off? Louise didn't want to think about that.

She sat on Laura's old bed as she often did when she visited her parents. The guards had dropped off Laura's things, and Louise had searched through them but found no evidence of trafficking.

As she sniffed one of Laura's scarves - the smell of her perfume fading, she thought back to when Laura first met Lars and how in love she'd been. Louise had liked him to begin with, and their parents were thrilled. A wealthy, handsome businessman had fallen in love with their girl. It wasn't until the day before their wedding that Louise realised something was wrong. The reception was held at the Shelbourne Hotel, and Louise stayed in the penthouse with Laura the night before. When Laura came out of the shower, she noticed bruising on the tops of her legs.

'Are they fingerprints?' asked Louise, but Laura quickly brushed her off.

'No,' she said, covering herself and rolling her eyes. 'You know how clumsy I am. Left the kitchen press open and walked into it.'

Louise let it go, but she was suspicious and paid more attention. At the wedding reception, her suspicion was confirmed. As any bride would, Laura happily chatted to everyone and danced with a few uncles. Louise noticed how Lars watched her every move. When he pulled Laura away from their guests and into a side room, Louise followed and watched through a crack in the door. She was shocked to see her new brother-in-law furious with his new wife - his face inches from hers as he lay into her. When they returned to the reception, Laura stayed by Lars's side for the rest of the night, and Louise's stomach dropped. Over the years, she tried to convince Laura to leave him, but Laura denied everything – Louise never knew why.

Signing, she picked up Laura's make-up bag and opened it – not surprised to find everything inside new and expensive.

'Always had the good stuff,' whispered Louise, opening a Chanel lipstick.

Could she use her sister's make-up? She knew Laura would want her too. The blood-red lipstick shined, and as Louise spread it across her lips, she realised it wasn't lipstick at all – it was plastic. She stared at it, then pulled off the red tip to reveal a USB stick.

'Holy fucking shit, little sister – you clever bitch,' she whispered and picked up her phone to ring Orla.

THE END

Printed in Great Britain
by Amazon